I0614658

He couldn't give information he didn't have, but he knew they would never believe him, so all he could do was stall…

"What do you want?"

"I want to know where you've hidden the computer virus."

"None of your business," Tommy grunted, glaring at his hawk-nosed captor. "You tell that little whiny twerp Jacob to go screw himself."

Someone behind him slipped a plastic bag over his head, and Tommy began thrashing about and rocking in his chair in an effort to free himself. The oxygen in the bag was quickly depleted, and Tommy began struggling to breath. He tried and failed to bite into the plastic over his face to create a hole to allow air to flow into the bag. Small black dots darted across his vision as he felt himself about to, once again, black out. The bag was removed, and Tommy's chest heaved as he took lungs full of air to re-oxygenate his blood.

"You kill me, and you'll never find the virus, asshole," Tommy yelled at Ralf, spittle flying from his mouth.

"The plastic bag is just the first in my arsenal of tricks, Mr. Luck. But I find it to be very effective. Sort of like a dry version of water boarding," Ralf's soft voice said calmly. "It has a way of wearing a person down for my follow-on performance."

Once a sought after structural engineer and manager of complex construction sites across the country, Tommy Luck is now nothing more than an unemployed drunk. His lifestyle is simple—drink himself into a stupor each night and run each morning to minimize the effects of the daily hangovers. Having spent all the money he earned delivering a package to Bangkok the year before, Tommy is now short on cash and willing to do just about anything to rectify his current financial woes. Receiving a one sentence note and post office box key with a promise of a large payoff, Tommy once again finds himself entangled in a complex web of murder and deceit. Implicated in a murder of a CIA agent, Tommy works to uncover the truth. He finds that no one seems to be who they say, and the only thing he is able to control, as he peels back the layers of betrayal surrounding his situation, is his relentless schedule of drinking and running.

KUDOS for *Tommy's Troubles*

In *Tommy's Troubles* by Patrick Ashtre, Tommy Luck is again in trouble with the NSA. The computer virus that Tommy delivered to Bangkok the year before for the NSA Inspector General is back on the market again, and everyone seems to think Tommy has it. But he doesn't. Not that telling that to the thugs trying to steal it does him any good. Kidnapped, beaten, tortured, and framed for murder, Tommy decides it is time to fight back. But who can he trust? The man he suspects of being behind his troubles is supposed to be dead, and no one else is who they seem to be. As Tommy searches for the truth, he discovers that, once again, he is just a pawn in someone else's deadly game. Well written, fast paced, and filled with twists and turns that will surprise and intrigue you, this one will keep you turning pages from beginning to end. ~ *Taylor Jones, The Review Team of Taylor Jones & Regan Murphy*

Tommy's Troubles by Patrick Ashtre is the second book in his Tommy Luck series. A former structural engineer, and now an unemployed drunk, Tommy Luck will do just about anything for money. Just about. He does have lines he won't cross. The year before he took a job for the NSA delivering a package to Bangkok and nearly got himself killed in the process. Now the computer virus that was in the package he delivered is up for sale, or at least a copy of it is. Since Tommy was the last person to have possession of the virus before it was handed off to the buyer, everyone assumes that Tommy made a copy and is now trying to sell it. Tommy knows nothing about the virus until he gets an envelope with $10,000 in it. Desperate for money, Tommy keeps it, even though he knows it will come back to bite him in the ass later. And sure enough, the money has barely been received before Tommy is suspected in the murder of a CIA agent, and thugs of various sorts are trashing his house, kidnapping him, and beating and torturing him for information that he doesn't have. On top of that, beautiful women are throwing themselves at him. Even though he's a drunk, Tommy's no fool. He knows things are not right, and he is determined to get to the bottom of it before he ends up in jail—or, worse, dead. With an exceptionally likeable and clever main character, a solid plot filled with intrigue and suspense, and lots of fast-paced action, *Tommy's Troubles* will keep you glued to your seat, turning pages all the way through. ~ *Regan Murphy, The Review Team of Taylor Jones & Regan Murphy*

Note from the Author

This book is a continuation of *Tommy Luck*, the story of a delivery to Bangkok that begins to establish much of the main character's persona. *Tommy's Troubles* is a standalone story, but it is my recommendation that you read the two books in order. The linkages between the stories are numerous, and many of the first book's mysteries and surprises are revealed in the second.

TOMMY'S TROUBLES

PATRICK ASHTRE

A Black Opal Books Publication

GENRE: MYSTERY/THRILLER/INTERNATIONAL CRIME THRILLER

TOMMY'S TROUBLES

Cover Design by Jackson Cover Designs

Print ISBN: 978-1-626948-47-1

First Publication: JANUARY 2018

Published by Black Opal Books **http://www.blackopalbooks.com**

To Amelia, Benjamin, and Alison

CHAPTER 1

East Falls Church, Arlington, Virginia, April 24, 2016:

The light was beginning to fade along Washington Boulevard as Danny drove his white Chevrolet Impala into the Westover shopping area. Tall ornate green lampposts began coming on in random order, illuminating the darkening streets in a yellowish hue. A spattering of car and truck headlights added to the glow, fighting off the growing gloominess. It was an unusually cool April evening by Arlington standards. A fine mist of rain fell, moistening the streets and sidewalks, the warm pavement turning the dampness into a low rising fog. People dressed in an assortment of pricy brightly colored windbreakers and sweaters wandered amongst the buildings holding the few businesses that populated the shopping area. As he made a right turn into the Seven-Eleven parking lot, a green Christmas tree shape air-freshener hanging from the rearview mirror bounced when the tires glided over the slightly elevated entry. Pulling the car into a space next to a large brown trash dumpster, Danny turned the ignition off and leaned back in the Impala's driver seat, letting out a long sigh.

"Another long night," he muttered to no one but himself, thinking about the proposition of the surveillance job before him.

Stepping out of the car and locking its doors with the small black electronic device attached to his key ring elicited a loud chirp that echoed across the otherwise silent parking lot. Walking toward Washington Boulevard, he decided to buy a cup of coffee at the Seven-Eleven even though he knew there was a boutique shop just across the street. He had always preferred Seven-Eleven's regular blend to those of Starbucks or the other high-end coffee vendors. It was not as bitter as the other brands. An overweight woman with greasy black hair, dressed in dirty pink tights and an oversized black sweater, sitting on a short brick retaining wall next to the store's entrance, begged for his spare change. Stopping next to the woman, Danny reached into his pocket and pulled out just under a dollar in dimes, nickels, and pennies, saving the quarters for himself. A sour smell wafted the air around the woman, and Danny wondered where she was living. Maybe one of the many pedestrian underpasses along Interstate 66, not two blocks from Westover. Her pleading eyes gleamed with delight at his generosity as the coins tumbled into her outstretched hand.

Opening the red-and-green-striped convenience store doors, he was met with a warm draft that smelled of brewing coffee and fresh donuts. A young Middle-Eastern woman in a red and black Seven-Eleven shirt, that looked more like a bowling outfit than that of a convenience store uniform, greeted him with a wave and smile. To Danny, she looked Pakistani. They seemed to manage all the Seven-Elevens in North Arlington. Immediately realizing that his assessment of her nationality was prejudice, he tried to imagine her from some other country—and failed.

He returned the clerk's greeting with a smiling nod, making his way to the rear of the store and the brewing pots, the source of the pleasant aroma of simmering coffee. He poured the hot black liquid into a tall paper cup he had pulled from the dispenser. It burned his hand through the container's thin walls when he picked it up.

Carrying the hot coffee in his right hand, he walked back to the front of the store and stepped up next to the newspaper rack where a slender middle-aged man with wavy brown hair, wearing faded blue jeans and a Hawaiian shirt under a dark blue button-up sweater, was perusing a copy of the *Washington Post*. The odd sense of fashion would have made the man seem homeless, if not for the cleanliness of his attire. Smelling of alcohol, the man wobbled slightly, surprising Danny. A drunk in this upper-middle-class neighborhood was an unusual sight. Maybe he was homeless, after all.

He reached out for a *Post* with his left hand. Its center pages fell on the floor as he pulled it from the rack. With the newspaper's contents spilled out between the two men, the drunken man hesitantly stooped down and helped him pick up the scattered paper.

"Thanks," Danny said, looking into the man's deep blue eyes.

Without making eye contact or uttering a word, the drunken man halfheartedly attempted to straighten the paper before handing Danny the portion he was holding.

Paying the bowling outfit-clad Middle-Eastern woman for his merchandise, once again failing to imagine her from any country other than Pakistan, Danny walked out of the Seven-Eleven and past the greasy-haired female beggar. Crossing Washington Boulevard, he wandered down the opposite sidewalk, passing the boutique coffee shop he had seen on previous visits and then a dry cleaner.

Walking across a long narrow parking lot, crowded with cars, standing between the boulevard and a short strip mall of green gable-roof trimmed businesses, Danny began looking for his co-worker.

He saw Devin, sitting in a sandwich shop with large windows facing out onto Washington Boulevard and the post office across the street. Still holding the steaming cup of coffee, with the *Washington Post* wedged under his arm, Danny entered the café, passing the hostess while silently pointing to his partner when asked if he wanted a table. He maneuvered between several small tables and a long wooden bar, teeming with patrons, the smell of fresh bread and grilled chicken now competing with the aroma of the coffee in his hand. Sitting down across from Devin, Danny set his coffee and *Washington Post* on the table.

"You ready to get out of here?" Danny asked.

Devin's eyes flashed an immediate look of relief. "Yeah, I think the waitress wants to kill me for staying at this table too long."

"I don't blame her. Think of all the business she lost with you hogging up a prime spot for several hours. I think I'll take a seat at one of those outside tables next door," Danny replied, pointing out the window to a wooden deck topped with white plastic tables and colorful umbrellas at one end of the parking lot.

Nodding to the Seven-Eleven cup in Danny's hand, Devin chuckled. "She's probably not too happy you brought in your own cup of coffee. More lost revenue."

"Anybody tampering with our box?"

"No one even came near the damn thing. I'm not sure why there's so much interest in an advertisement offering a previously used computer virus."

"I don't know, but the boss picked up on it right away when the information came in from the National Security Agency as low priority intelligence. The NSA caught it but didn't see too much significance," Danny explained as he sipped at his coffee, steam rising from its rim across his face. "I'm not sure why it got the boss in such a twitter or how he convinced the director to give this so much attention. For us to get authorization to work a domestic issue takes a lot of clout, and we're working a domestic issue."

"I think what the boss said was that it might appear to be a domestic issue, but due to the likelihood that it's the same computer virus the CIA and NSA used against a foreign target last year, it falls under our purview. Thankfully the advertisement for the virus was in the Economist Journal. At least we know that the potential clientele will be well educated." Devin punctuated his comment with a short laugh while waving to the waitress for his bill. "Liberal but well educated."

"Maybe the clientele, but not the seller. Think about it, the seller puts an advertisement into the *Washington Post* about a used computer virus that made its debut in Thailand last year and uses an antiquated code to direct potential buyers to the Economist Journal. In the Economist the seller places the name of a post office and a box number. A child could have followed that trail. That's probably why the NSA marked it as low priority. They realized that the seller has to be an idiot," Danny replied as the scowling waitress, dressed in blue jeans and a yellow T-shirt depicting a sleeping dog with some catchy phrase about canines, showed up carrying Devin's check. "Idiots are rarely dangerous."

"You never know. We know an envelope containing a lot of money was placed in the box two days ago. The seller might have some other way to retrieve his or her mail other than just walking in and opening up the post office box. The seller could surprise you."

"Yeah, and we know the envelope is still there, and

that means another long night for me. And if he gets a hold of that envelope without us noticing, then the seller may be clever, but the boss will be furious."

"It could be a she," Devin commented absently, pulling a black leather wallet from his khaki trousers.

After a brief rundown on what had happened during previous shift, the two men pushed their chairs out from the table, and Devin handed the waitress some cash. Even with a fairly robust tip, the waitress accepted payment without a smile, and the two partners walked out of the restaurant, separating on the sidewalk out front with a simple nod.

Stepping up on a wooden deck belonging to a small Thai restaurant next door to the sandwich shop, Danny found a seat at one of the round plastic tables. Ordering a green curry from the waiter, he began watching the Westover Post Office. With an overhead red and white umbrella shielding him from the misty rain, he opened his *Washington Post* and began reading the sports section, glancing up every few seconds to keep tabs on the post office box.

As the last evidence of the sun dipped below the horizon, the temperature began dropping, and Danny found himself sitting alone, all the other customers seeking warmth inside. Streetlights and a light over the post office illuminated its entrance, and the lights inside brightly displayed the interior, allowing him a good oblique view of the box he was keeping watch through the tall floor-to-ceiling windows.

With his coffee long gone, and a continuous flow of cars moving along the boulevard, Danny waited patiently, reading the newspaper and nibbling at the curry. Not really caring for spicy food, Danny picked at the thick green liquid, pulling out small bits of chicken while trying to avoid the dark red chilies. He pulled a thin napkin from a plastic dispensing box and dappled the edges of his lips in a failed attempt to stifle the spicy heat building up at the corners of his mouth.

Noticing a man sitting in the Thai restaurant behind him, Danny thought he seemed to be paying a significant amount of attention to the activity in the parking lot and Washington Boulevard. With dark bushy hair and beady eyes, dressed in a white shirt, dark green pants, and a matching dark green jacket draped over the back of his chair, the man looked as if he could have been a fashion model for a Chinese Chairman Mao Zedong wardrobe line, except he was missing the little green cap with its red star. Sitting next to the restaurant's large front window, the beady-eyed man had been peering outside for as long as Danny had been at the table. Each time Danny would turn and glance in his direction, the beady-eyed man would shift his attention and act as if he was immersed in eating a plate of food sitting on the table in front of him. While it seemed a bit unusual, Danny didn't give it much thought, as the beady-eyed man could have been simply wondering why a man was sitting by himself on the outside deck on such a cool, damp night. Danny would have wondered the same thing, and he considered moving to a less conspicuous spot.

A short time later Danny saw the blue-eyed drunk, who had helped him pick up his newspaper in the Seven-Eleven, walk up the ramp toward the entrance to the post office. Pulling a small monocular device from the pocket of his brown jacket, Danny peered at the drunken man approaching the entrance and noted in the bright lights over the post office's entrance a thin scar running from the edge of his lip to the corner of his jaw. He hadn't noticed the scar in the Seven-Eleven, attributing his oversight to the angle at which he had seen the drunken man earlier. He immediately discounted the drunken man being involved with his surveillance job, knowing that no seller of such allegedly valuable illicit computer virus would ever hang-out at a Seven-Eleven in the vicinity of his drop site for an extended period before making a pick-up. Not to mention come to the drop site drunk. On the other hand, he and Devin had already joked about how the seller might be an idiot. Maybe he was a drunken idiot?

"It couldn't possibly be this easy," Danny muttered to himself, watching the drunken man move along the rows of silver post office boxes, their little glass windows twinkling against the bright interior lights.

But it was that easy. In the brightly lit post office, the drunken man stepped up to the long bank of postal boxes that Danny had been keeping watch over. Peering through the small monocular device, Danny watched as the drunken man inserted a key and opened up the small door of the postal box. Danny looked on as the drunk withdrew the manila envelope.

Waving down his waiter, Danny asked for his bill before slipping his cell phone from his belt, its thick clip pulling at his waist before finally releasing. Selecting a number from his speed dial list, he made a call.

A low, solemn voice answered, "What've you got?"

"The package just got picked up." Danny tried not to sound excited.

"Anyone we know?"

"No, some drunk with blue eyes and brown wavy hair. Thin, maybe five foot ten or eleven, he's got a scar on his face, edge of his lip to the corner of his jaw. I ran into him in the local Seven-Eleven about an hour ago," Danny said as the waiter showed up with his bill. "He's been hanging around Westover for quite some time."

"Which side of his face is the scar?"

"Right," Danny answered, wondering why that was important.

"That's unusual. Follow him. Let me know where he goes. It shouldn't be too difficult to keep track of a drunk," the somber voice directed before disconnecting the call.

As the drunken man began walking back down the ramp leading from the post office, holding the manila envelope loosely in his right hand, Danny stood up and glanced at his tab, dropping a twenty dollar bill on the table and pocketing the receipt. Remaining on the opposite side of the street with his newspaper tucked under his arm, Danny followed the drunken man as he turned west and began walking along the Washington Boulevard sidewalk. Walking up a hill past the neighborhood library, the Westover shops quickly gave way to colonial homes and tall old growth trees as the rain became slightly more resolute. Overhead streetlights shone through tree limbs, creating a shadowy mosaic pattern on the dark wet sidewalk and the lights from the passing cars scattered in the low fog standing over the street. The night air was cold and wet, and Danny shivered in his dampening clothes. He heard several dogs bark in the distance as he walked along the dark sidewalk, then a cat shrieked close by. Between the drunken man's dark blue sweater mixing into the shadows and the blinding headlights from cars moving along Washington Boulevard, Danny began to have a difficult time keeping his track of his quarry.

With the storm becoming even more intense, Danny picked up his pace and began to worry that he might lose the drunken man. The drunk made a right turn onto North Nottingham Street and disappeared from Danny's view. Having to wait for several cars to pass before jogging across the boulevard, when Danny finally turned onto to

Nottingham Street the drunken man was nowhere in sight.

Danny jogged north along the street, hoping to reestablish contact with the drunk. The cascading rain stung his eyes and soaked his clothes. A strobe-like flash of lightning, followed by a deafening boom, told him the storm would be getting worse. Finally giving up when he could see the lights from cars and trucks, through torrents of rain, moving along Lee Highway several blocks in the distance, Danny stopped, his shoulders drooping in defeat.

"Crap!" he cursed, standing under an enormous oak surrounded by four smaller pine trees.

Absently kicking at the water running down the sidewalk, Danny wiped the rain from his face and pondered what to do next. He knew that his boss would be livid at his failure to keep track of the drunken man and the manila envelope filled with cash.

"I am so screwed."

Startled by another bolt of lightning and thunderous clap, Danny placed his *Washington Post* over the top his head in a feeble attempt to stay dry. With his chin on his chest, he tried to think what his next move should be when a sharp blow struck the back of his head, knocking him to his knees. Arms dangling at his sides and the *Washington Post* now a pile on the sidewalk before him, his vision tunneled, and his ears sang a piercing ring. Wavering on his knees through a blunt-trauma haze, he could smell a mixture of oily grime from the street and fresh pine needles from the trees surrounding the overhead oak. A second blow, as he blindly reached for his nine millimeter Berretta, sent him onto his hands and knees. The weapon fell from its holster and clattered on top of the pile of wet newspaper. Water coursed down the sidewalk and across his extended fingers. In his blurred vision, he could see blood mixing with the fast-moving water as it dripped from his head. Danny was barely hanging onto consciousness. Fumbling beneath himself with his right hand, once again reaching to retrieve the handgun that he knew lay someplace on the sidewalk below, he was met with yet another sharp blow to the side of the head, knocking him to his side. Danny's last recollection was his head viciously striking the sidewalk.

Coming to, he was laying some ten yards from the sidewalk with his back against the oak tree looking up at a hazy outline of a face. Deep in the shadows, small shrubs and plants surrounded him, and he could feel the prickly ends of what felt like a bed of pine needles beneath his hands as the storm continued to rage. A small wooden clapboard house stood dark and silent to one side. Danny imagined it to be red, but it appeared gray in the darkness. Competing with the scent of pine needles and damp earth, he could smell what seemed to be a pungent aftershave. He could see his assailant looking down, dark eyes seeming to be jiggling on a hovering white face. Everything seemed to be in shades of gray.

The figure above him had a dark shirt or jacket on that mixed into the shadows beneath the trees, but in the darkness, Danny couldn't make out the color. His assailant's face seemed as if it were a floating decapitated spirit, only inches above his.

"Who are you?" the hovering face asked hoarsely.

"Just out for a walk," Danny mumbled. Looking up through a haze of semi-consciousness, he shifted his foggy vision from the floating spirit to a dark shadow, whose outline appeared to be a revolver in his assailant's hand, and then back again to the face looming above him. Wet and cold, with a tremendous headache, Danny's normally calm disposition began to waver as he shivered in the darkness. There was something in that shadowy face that terrified him.

"Who do you work for?"

"I'm just out for a walk," Danny said again, rubbing his eyes in an attempt to clear his vision. He could feel water streaming off the end of his nose. Trying to sit up, pressing his palms into the bed of pine needles beneath him, he felt his arms give out. They were weak from fear-stimulated fatigue.

"Bullshit," the face hissed.

Taking a step back, his assailant kicked Danny in the left cheek, slamming his head back into the trunk of the oak tree, muddling his vision yet again. Feeling something oozing from his mouth, Danny absently wiped his face with his left arm.

His assailant jammed the muzzle of the revolver under Danny's nose, growling, "You have one minute to tell me who you are and what agency you work for."

The revolver painfully gouged Danny's nose and felt cold on his skin. On the verge of panic, he began thinking about his wife and young daughter. He wanted to go home and hug them. He wanted to be as far away from this place and this man as possible.

"The Central Intelligence Agency. I work for the CIA," Danny confessed, hoping his assailant understood the implications of harming a federal agent. "My name is Daniel."

The floating face hissed again, "Bullshit. What's the CIA doing working an operation in Virginia?"

"Special permission. We have special permission. What we're working on has international consequences."

"Who do you work for?"

"I told you, the CIA," Danny muttered, pushing himself back against the tree. Pressing his palms into the bed of pine needles, he wanted to push his entire body through the tree trunk to get away from this man. There was something outwardly wicked and immoral in his assailant's eyes and facial expression. Danny had never been as frightened as he was at that moment.

Placing his mouth next to Danny's ear, the suspended face growled, "You don't understand. I want to know who at the CIA you work for? I want a name."

Danny could smell alcohol on the man's breath mixing with the pungent aftershave. Rain pounded at an already saturated ground around the tree. Another bright flash and loud clap seemed to shake more water from the surrounding foliage, creating small pools around his hands pressed into the bed of pine needles. At that moment, Danny caught a glimpse of the face. He saw cold, emotionless eyes and unremorseful expression looking down. Danny suddenly realized that the man standing above him had already decided how the evening was going to play out.

"Sid—my boss's is name is Sid." Danny's voice trembled as he reached out with open palms. Rainwater ran down his fingers and dripped from his outstretched hands. "I work at the Special Investigations Branch. Sid runs the branch."

"Have you already called Sid and told him who you were following?"

"Yes, I gave him a description," Danny whimpered. "I don't know his name."

"Pictures? Did you take any pictures?"

"No, I was just supposed to follow."

Without saying another word, the hovering face stepped away. Danny could hear the distinctive metallic click as the weapon's hammer was pulled back. While he could not clearly see his assailant's face in the shadows, Danny recalled the cold, emotionless eyes and a mouth with a hint of a smile at its edges that he had momentarily seen not one minute earlier.

The floating face pointed the revolver down at Danny. “Wrong answer.”

“Wait! It’s the truth!” Danny pleaded, shielding his face with his hands. “I’m not lying! I work for Sid at the CIA! I called and gave him a description of the man who picked up the envelope. I didn’t take any pictures.”

“I know Sid, and that may be the right answer for me, but that’s still the wrong answer for you.”

The last thing Danny saw was a bright white flash of light. The last thing Danny felt was a lead slug ripping through his outstretched right hand and smashing into the flesh and bone just below his left eye. He never heard the loud crack of the weapon being fired that echoed across the North Arlington neighborhood.

CHAPTER 2

Fort Meade, Maryland, April 26, 2016:

A squat man with silver hair and dark eyebrows, dressed in rumbled khaki pants and a brown tweed jacket, stepped from the elevator on the sixth floor into the small reception area. Wood-paneled walls and a small reception counter with a similar façade that attempted to give the lobby of one of the National Security Agency department head suites an elegant look failed, making it only a step up from the typical government office sterility.

A slender blonde woman, who couldn't have been more than twenty-five years old, wearing a blue dress with a red sash sitting behind the reception counter, greeted him asking, "Can I help you, sir?"

"Looking for Howard Macintyre, the inspector general," the man grunted in his usual solemn voice.

"Just down the hallway, sir," the young receptionist replied in a slightly shrill voice, smiling and pointing down one of three short hallways protruding from the lobby.

Walking down a corridor carpeted in plush navy blue, he passed a large square mirror with black wooden frame hanging on a beige wall. His ruddy complexion and green eyes, bracketing a large bulbous red nose with deep pores, shimmered in the passing reflection. Thinking it strange to have a mirror hanging on the wall of a government office, he imagined it had been a decorative touch by one of the more vain employees who worked at the NSA. Maybe one who needed to see his or her likeness as a way to bolster their self-esteem on an hourly basis? The man detested mirrors, his contrasting silver hair, dark eyebrows, and large red nose gave him an unavoidable clown-like appearance. At the end of the hallway, he arrived at a small foyer with another desk. A middle-aged secretary, her auburn hair spilling over a white silk blouse, flipped through a pile of papers stacked neatly to one corner. A brass plate on the desk identified her as Judy.

Glancing over at a thick wooden door, the man saw a shiny brass plate emblazoned with the inspector general's title. Below that was a smaller brass plaque engraved with the name Howard Macintyre, confirming that he was at the correct office.

Judy looked up from the papers with large dark brown eyes, and the man nodded in the direction of the inspector general's door, asking, "Is the boss in?"

"Yes, sir. You must be the gentleman from the Central Intelligence Agency. The inspector general didn't give me a name, though."

The smell of flowery perfume drifted in the air around the secretary's desk and mixed with the stale cigarette odor emanating from the man's tweed jacket. Looking up, he quickly recognized the fire extinguisher mounted on the ceiling above doubled as a hidden camera.

"Sid," he grunted, looking back down at the secretary and examining her milky white skin. Sid felt an immediate attraction to the secretary's quiet beauty but knew his appearance was anything but appealing. "My name is Sid."

"Just one moment Mr. Sid. I'll see if the inspector general is available," Judy responded, her dark brown eyes sparkling.

"It's just Sid. You can leave out the mister."

"Okay, Sid. Just a moment," the attractive secretary replied before picking up the phone and talking in a muted voice to who Sid presumed to be the inspector general on the other end of the line. Hanging up the phone, she stood. "You can go right in."

As Judy began moving around her desk to open the door, Sid beat her and opened it himself. The heavy door easily swung inward, and Sid stepped into the office.

Hearing the door click shut behind him, Sid stood examining the office. The navy blue carpet continued in from the hallway and reception area and lay across the floor of the inspector general's office. One side of the office was decorated with a wide oak bookcase, bare of any embellishments, and on the other was a long narrow window, reaching from the floor to the ceiling, with views of the NSA compound. Two overstuffed burgundy leather chairs stood in front of a large maple desk. A wide flat screen computer monitor was to one side of the desk, and several department awards adorned the white wall behind. Next to the departmental awards, the wall held four nails surrounded by a slightly brighter paint, indicating to Sid that several long-standing pictures had recently been removed. Two cardboard boxes, one with its top wide open showing a content of files and several pictures stood in one corner, additional proof to Sid that the NSA's Inspector General Office had recently changed hands.

Howard Macintyre, the National Security Agency's Inspector General, sat behind the desk smiling at Sid, his head and shoulders towering above the computer monitor. The room was awash in a powerful pungent smell of aftershave.

The inspector general was a tall, thin man with red curly hair, dressed in an open-collared white shirt and dark blue trousers. His matching dark blue jacket hung on a hanger hooked on the back of the office door. A fair complexion and a liberal dousing of freckles, along with his Gaelic-rooted name, testified to his heritage.

With a wide smile on his face, the inspector general stood as Sid walked across the room and the two men shook hands, before sitting down across the desk from one and other.

Sid noticed that the leather chair he sat in had a slight forward cant. Along with a slick leather cushion, the chair put him in a somewhat problematic situation. He had to hold his feet firmly on the ground in order to not slip out.

"Nice chair," Sid grunted sarcastically.

"A leftover from my predecessor. I never liked those chairs either, but I haven't been in the office long enough to replace them."

"I'd keep them," Sid replied in a perfectly serious voice, shifting in the chair, trying to find a comfortable equilibrium on its slick leather surface. "Nice way to put your visitors at an immediate disadvantage,"

Sid pinned Howard as having hailed from Kansas or Oklahoma, or maybe even Missouri from his Midwestern accent. He wondered if the inspector general had been a farmboy who had made it big at the United States' premier intelligence agency.

Howard laughed. "I think that's why the former inspector general put them there. He wasn't a very imposing man."

"Never met the man face to face," Sid grunted. "You're just moving into the office, but your predecessor has been dead for over six months. Why such the long delay?"

"You know the government. Every move is methodical, slow, and full of bureaucratic red tape. I've been the acting inspector general since his demise, but the final decision took some time." The inspector general then shifted in his chair. "The NSA Director has told me to cooperate with you completely. No secrets."

"That was nice of him. So let's get down to business. You were involved with the investigation into a rogue organization operating inside the NSA last year?"

The inspector general, who wasn't sure whether his guest had poised the statement as a question or a declaration, answered, "I was. We code-named the investigation 'Black Fly.' A small group of disgruntled NSA agents had begun to use agency assets to break into corporate databases and steal secrets. They then would then sell those secrets to the highest bidder, making the delivery in one foreign country or another. The stolen data was always delivered on a flash drive. I started my investigation when an agent came to me, claiming she had been recruited by the organization that was conducting an authorized operation for the NSA. But she thought something was fishy.

"The NSA doesn't operate overseas in the fashion that the organization described to the agent. Turns out the CIA, your people, had uncovered the plot before we got wind of it and teamed up with the former inspector general, hijacking the organization in order to weed out one of the buyers. The inspector general kept his team small because he wasn't sure who within the agency was involved with the criminal organization. Even though I was his deputy at the time, I was not a member of his team. When it was all over, I was told the target of the inspector general's efforts had been the Chinese Government."

"Do you know what merchandise the final delivery passed?" Sid asked, absently looking down and brushing speckle of ash from the lapel of his tweed jacket, presumably from the cigarette he smoked before entering the building.

"Yes, while advertised as corporate secrets outlining some electric car technology or another, the final delivery actually consisted of a computer virus that was capable of downloading all the data from any mainframe on which the program was placed and activated, sending it to one here on the NSA compound. The computer virus would then self-destruct, taking with it all the data from the source mainframe." Then, hesitatingly, the inspector general asked, "Why am I telling you this? If I'm not mistaken, you were among the team working with the former inspector general?"

"Looks like your predecessor's computer virus resurfaced," Sid replied, twisting on the slick leather seat cushion, ignoring the inspector general's question.

"How do you know it's the same virus?"

"Can you tell me who had possession of the virus before, during, and after the delivery?"

Holding up a different long thin freckled finger each time he named off an individual, the inspector general answered, "The NSA employee who developed the virus, of course; the former inspector general, now dead; a man named John Smith, the lead field operative for the rogue organization, also dead; the deliveryman, a Mr. Thomas Bacon Luck; a computer hacker, a talented individual who lives in Northeast Thailand; the client's agent, a Turkish man, dead; the recipient or buyer…who knows how many hands it passed through there before it was downloaded in China?…an NSA agent named Becky, who was my mole during the investigation; and myself.

At least nine individuals had possession in the end. The copy I have is locked away in our classified records vault."

"That seems to be a lot of people who had access," Sid commented, "considering the devastating power of the computer virus."

"The former inspector general didn't have much control over the operation once it had begun. The deliveryman, Tommy Luck, threw several wrenches into the delivery—don't you think?"

"He was merely trying to survive the delivery and get paid," Sid replied, finally giving the inspector general some indication that he had knowledge of the computer virus and the delivery in Thailand. "Tell me about the death of your predecessor, the last inspector general."

"Found dead on a park bench along the National Mall, near the Reflecting Pool."

"How'd he die?"

"A powerful muscle relaxant. A syringe was found in his jacket pocket containing what was left of the drug. The inspector general's were the only fingerprints on the syringe."

"And you think he took his own life?"

"No, but the NSA Director stopped any further investigation into the incident."

"What other evidence did you have to pursue?"

"Trace DNA led us to believe that, along with the inspector general's, there was someone else's hand in his pocket at the time he was injected with the muscle relaxant."

"Whose hand?"

"The trace DNA matched that of Thomas Bacon Luck."

"Why would the director stop further investigation into the former inspector general's death?"

"There was also evidence that the inspector general was complicit in his own death. Looks like my predecessor tried to dispose of Tommy Luck—an act not authorized by the NSA or CIA."

Sid paused for a moment, thinking about the information the inspector general had told him before asking, "Tell me about Luck."

"A talented structural engineer and construction site manager, but now nothing more than an unemployed drunk. He has uncanny survival instincts. He likes to take long runs to alleviate his daily hangovers. He was hired by John Smith to act as the deliveryman but had no idea what he was carrying until the delivery operation was well underway. He did finally deliver the computer virus at the bequest of the former inspector general. He was not a part of the criminal organization."

"You know why he drinks?" Sid asked while examining the departmental awards mounted on the wall, over the shoulder of the inspector general.

"I'm not sure he even knows why he drinks." Howard chuckled. "According to Becky, the NSA agent working with me during the delivery last year, he drinks in order to sleep at night. She claims he's racked up a little too much regret for one lifetime. But personally, I think he uses his past as an excuse to drink. He's just a drunk." The inspector general chuckled again as he leaned back in his adjustable office chair, its hinge giving off a faint squeal. "You worked with him last year. What do you think?"

"Clever, drunk, and unpredictable," Sid grunted, "and, as you pointed out, he has uncanny survival skills."

"That is a great description." The inspector general laughed, the squeal in his office chair singing in unison with his heaving chest. "Clever and unpredictable work well together. Drunk and unpredictable aren't unusual, but the three put together would be like trying to describe how well oil and water mix."

"Yeah, funny," Sid said flatly.

Quickly regaining his composure, the inspector general asked, "Why do you think it's the same computer virus?"

"An advertisement for the computer virus was published in the *Washington Post* several days ago, directing interested parties to the *Economist Journal*. The advertisement offered a computer virus only used once that was unveiled in Thailand. The fact that the virus your former boss put on the market was delivered in Thailand piqued our interest, so we put a stakeout on the post office box that was to act as the drop site between the buyer and seller. It was in Westover, North Arlington. According to the postmaster, it was a box rented by a gentleman named John Smith. Both the *Economist* and *Washington Post* advertisements were paid for with money orders belonging to a John Smith who resides in North Arlington, as well."

"I know Westover. Did you check out John Smith's address?"

"Of course, it was an empty building."

"There are a lot of John Smiths out there," the inspector general commented, a concerned expression momentarily appearing on his face.

"Four days ago an envelope was mailed to the post office box with no return address and no fingerprints. Contained inside was ten thousand dollars in cash. No instructions. Two nights ago one of my agents witnessed some drunk with blue eyes and a scar on his face—not my description, my agent's—take that envelope from the box."

"That's a pretty vague description."

"We both know it fits Luck—not to mention, Luck lives in the Westover area. But there's more. My agent was murdered while following the blue-eyed drunk and Luck's fingerprints were discovered both on a shell casing and a newspaper found at the scene."

The inspector general looked at Sid in disbelief. "So John Smith is still alive, and Tommy Luck is trying to sell the computer virus?"

"John Smith is dead. We know that for certain. Luck is not a dumb man and the way this merchandise has been advertised, the trail to the drop site, and leaving his fingerprints at the murder scene, are far too unprofessional for him. If nothing else, we know Luck is clever and a proactive individual when cornered. On the other hand, he's unemployed, and his bank account is nearly empty. I know he's strapped for cash and desperate. I watched him do some outrageous things last year while he was trying to deliver the flash drive with the virus, and while this doesn't seem to fit his modus operandi, it wouldn't surprise me if it was Luck, and he has something else up his sleeve. Maybe paying for the advertisements and renting the box under the name of John Smith is only the tip of the iceberg."

"So, what can I do?" the inspector general asked while tapping the long gangly fingers of his right hand on the top of his desk.

Sid looked out the window, only seeing the tops of distance oak trees from his vantage point. "Your agent Becky managed to get pretty chummy with Luck last year?"

"Once her cover was blown with the rogue organization, she ended up working with Tommy Luck in order to obtain evidence against John Smith and his crew. As far as I know, their relationship didn't go beyond that."

Turning away from the window, Sid looked directly at the inspector general. “I need her to contact Luck and re-kindle their old friendship, or whatever it was. I want her to find out what Luck is up to.”

CHAPTER 3

Denver, Colorado, December 20, 1983:

The windows of the car had a faint etching of ice beginning to form, creating a medley of translucent art on a night wintry background. A light snow fell across the bright light from a street lamp as eleven-year-old Tommy Luck looked over at his father. Each exhale blew a misty cloud from his nose and mouth. Each inhale brought a refreshing coolness to his throat and lungs.

"Now you sure you'll be okay?" Tommy's father asked looking down at him, the cloud of fog from his breath reaching across the car's interior.

Sitting on the far side of the front bench seat of his father's dark blue Dodge Challenger parked outside a red brick apartment building in Denver, Tommy replied, "I'll be fine dad. You won't be long, will you?"

"Just give me ten or twenty minutes. I'll drive us home when I'm finished. I just need to talk with the lady who lives here," his father responded, pointing up to a brightly lit window on the second floor of the apartment building. Sheer pink curtains hung at each side of the window directly above the building's entrance. His father smiled down at him with deep blue eyes that looked to Tommy as if he were peering into a mirror.

Stepping from the car into the cool night, his father closed the door and looked up at the window above the apartment's entrance. A thin man with close-cropped blond hair, his father wasn't big, maybe five foot seven or eight, but he looked enormous to Tommy. He seemed colossal to Tommy. He was the center of Tommy's universe.

When his father disappeared into the apartment building, Tommy rolled the passenger window down several cranks to let the cool night air blow into the car, carrying with it a scattering of frozen flakes of snow. It felt refreshing as it mingled with the smell of stale cigarette smoke that permeated the interior of the car. Tommy could remember riding in the Challenger over Loveland Pass as he and his father drove to go skiing together the year before. He had nearly vomited in the mixture of hot air blasting from the heater and the cloud of smoke rising from a cigarette clinging to the corner of his father's mouth. Nonetheless, cigarette smoke was a smell Tommy always associated with his father, and it was a smell that he loved.

Looking up through the apartment window, he saw his father embrace a younger woman dressed in a filmy moss-colored nightgown, with a hug and kiss. Tommy watched as his father swept his hand through her long dark hair and smiled his boyish smile. The woman was clearly happy to be in his arms and began unbuttoning his shirt. When he looked down through the window and saw Tommy gazing up, his father grabbed the sheer curtains, pulling them across, turning he and his mistress into pinkish shadowy figures.

The shadows disappeared, and a faint light appeared in an adjacent window with matching sheer curtains. Tommy presumed the light from the brightly light room now shown through an open door into the other.

Trying to alleviate his boredom, Tommy first opened and inspected the contents of the glove compartment. He then ran the tips of his index fingers along the outline of the instruments on the driver's side, as if they were racing one and other.

Noticing a man walking toward the car in the shadows along the sidewalk, Tommy stopped his play and hunkered down, peeking over the dashboard. As the man moved closer, Tommy checked to make sure the doors of the car were locked before slipping down onto the floorboards, not wanting to be seen alone. Looking up, he could see the man's red parka pass by the car's window. Rising up on his knees, Tommy peeked over the edge of the window and watched the man turn up the path leading to the apartment building's entrance. As the man pulled the doors open, disappearing into the building, young Tommy Luck returned to his play.

Several minutes later Tommy heard a scream from above. Looking up, he saw that the adjacent room's lights were now on and two shadowy figures were face to face. One struck the other. The woman appeared, spiriting someone into the main room. Now behind the pink sheer curtains, one of the two shadowy figures raised a hand, and Tommy heard something break, followed by another scream.

The window to the adjacent room flew open, and Tommy could see his father dressed in white boxer shorts, holding his blue polyester pants, white shirt, and brown jacket in his left hand, stumbling over the sill before falling to the ground one-story below, his impact creating a plume of dusty snow. Jumping to his feet, his father raced toward the Dodge, and Tommy unlocked the driver's door. At the driver's side door his father hastily began pulling on his trousers. Clumsily, he put his pants on backward and had to remove them in order to turn them around.

As he was preparing to zip up the front of his pants, the big man came bursting through the apartment building's entrance, shouting at his father. Grabbing at the driver's side door, his father swung it open so hard that it slammed abruptly against the stops.

His father grunted as the door bounced back and struck him in the thigh.

As the big man ran toward the Dodge Challenger, Tommy made sure his door was locked again. Tommy could feel fear welling up within him. He wanted to cry but knew that his father would reprimand him if he did. The big man stopped next to the passenger side of the car, hesitating when he saw Tommy looking up with wide eyes through the ice etched window.

Then looking across the car's interior at his father trying to insert keys into the ignition, the big man's anger once again erupted, and he began pounding the top of the Challenger's roof, screaming something.

Tommy didn't know what the big man was screaming. Tommy was barely holding his emotions in check.

The Dodge Challenger started with a loud rumble, and his father stepped on the gas pedal. The car shot forward on the icy street, weaving left then right, leaving the angry young man standing in the street yelling and waving his arms.

Several blocks down the street, his father looked over at Tommy and, in a perfectly calm voice, said, "Please don't tell your mother what happened."

"I won't," Tommy responded. He knew he wouldn't. He never told his mother anything. Tommy hesitated for a moment before saying, "Dad, what are you going to tell mom about your eye?"

"What about my eye?" his father asked, glancing over at Tommy.

"It's turning purple."

Reaching up and adjusting the rearview mirror so he could see his face, Tommy's father growled, "Oh, for Christ's sake!"

CHAPTER 4

East Falls Church, Arlington, Virginia, April 27, 2016:

Rolling over on his bed, Tommy Luck saw long dark hair budding from under a white quilt and coiling across the pillow next to him. There was the faint scent of a flowery perfume in the air that oddly mixed with his nausea induced from an overindulgence of alcohol the night before, causing him to gag. A golden forearm and hand with pink-polished nails protruded from under the soft white quilt. Turning his head, he looked out over his sage green bedroom and saw a red silk dress lying across the long mahogany dresser standing against the wall. A pair of black lace panties lay on the floor next to the bed, and a matching bra was strewn next to the door. Struggling to remember who was lying next to him, Tommy ran his fingers through his wavy brown hair as his head pounded a silent siren, sounding the alarm for the dissipating whiskey and beer in his system. For a moment, he thought he was with his old girlfriend Lawan, but quickly realized she was back in Thailand. It couldn't be her.

Reaching up, Tommy ran his fingers across a welt under his left eye. He tried to recall the previous evening's events and how he had come to have a shiner on his face. He couldn't. The last thing he remembered was standing next to the bar at a local Irish pub and tossing a shot of tequila into his mouth.

The golden hand reached up and pulled the quilt aside, revealing a beautiful round face with large brown doe eyes that sparkled. A wide smile on her face, the doe-eyed woman reached out and caressed Tommy's cheek.

"*Buenos Dias*, Tommy," a soft and sweet Spanish accented voice said.

"Good morning." Tommy eyed the young woman who couldn't have been more than thirty years old. "You know where I got this?" he asked, pointing to the puffy red cheek on his face.

"You don't remember?" The woman softly giggled. "You were *magnífico*."

"Magnificent?"

"You took two men with very little effort." She giggled again.

"What two men did I take?"

"One was my boyfriend, Jesus. The other was his best friend, Emanuel."

Tommy sighed, putting his hands over his eyes to block out the offensive sunlight pouring through a window next to the bed. "Why did I take on Jesus and Emanuel?"

"They were, how do you say *disgustar*…upset…with you," the woman replied as she threw the quilt aside, revealing a thin naked body with round, voluptuous hips and breasts topped with brown erect nipples.

"And why would Jesus and Emanuel be *disgustar* with me?"

"They saw you touched my *nalgas*."

"What's a nalgas?"

"My bottom," she whispered while rolling over on top of him, her warm, soft skin rubbing across his thighs.

Her moist lips parted with a hint of a smile as she ran

her hands across his chest. Tommy took the woman into his arms and rolled her over onto the mattress, making love with the young Latin beauty, presuming it was at least the second time since they met, even though he could not remember her name. After making love, Tommy pulled the white quilt back over her before stepping out of bed and slipping on his running clothes and shoes. Leaving her naked, sleeping under the covers, he headed out the front door for his morning ritual jog.

Sweating the alcohol out from the previous evening, Tommy ran along one of the many narrow pathways leading from Arlington to Falls Church. It was a cool morning with a heavy dampness in the air, but the sun sprinkling through thick overhead limbs warmed him. He felt like he needed to vomit but held back the urge, hoping another mile or two would vanquish his nausea.

Out of work for nearly a year and a half, other than a short delivery job to Bangkok, Tommy spent his mornings trotting down one path or another that crisscrossed Northern Virginia, listening to music through a set of small earphones attached to his cell phone. Up until eight months ago, he had struggled with memories gathered over a lifetime of mistakes. The endless deceit, death, and destruction he had witnessed had taken a toll. Having spent many years pondering his days as a structural engineer and construction site manager, Tommy was now happy that his thoughts and memories had turned to his childhood. He occasionally would recall a memory from some blunder he had participated in, but, thankfully, those were few and far between. And normally those memories would occur if he hadn't adequately numbed his mind with a large quantity of alcohol before sleeping. Tommy wasn't sure whether he had finally come to terms with his past, but for now, he was happy to reminisce about his childhood. While it had not been perfect, he would never trade those memories for someone else's.

With his wavy brown hair bouncing in cadence with his pace, Tommy contemplated the memory of his father jumping from the apartment window all those years ago. While not obvious to him then, his father had clearly been having sex with the woman Tommy saw through the window before her husband or boyfriend had interrupted the interlude. Tommy had to laugh at the memory of his father falling out of the second-floor window and then trying to simultaneously hold up his trousers and open the door to the old blue Dodge Challenger. He grimaced at the memory of the argument that ensued when he and his father arrived back home. With more than a foundation of a black eye growing on his face from the scuffle with the bigger man, Tommy's father squabbled with his mother over his version of the story. Having passed away several years before, Tommy could not help but miss his father. Even considering his infidelities, Tommy had always known the man had loved him with all his heart. The feeling had been mutual.

Tommy was not a big man. At the age of forty-four and standing just under six foot tall, he was tan and slender from his incessant running. His father had bestowed on him deep blue eyes, high cheekbones, and a boyish smile through genetics, but he had also bequeathed him a love for beautiful women, as well. Having always been capable of attracting a woman with a wink and a smile, Tommy had used his looks and charm on many women. Sadly this habit was partially responsible for his current financial woes.

Having never been able to control his wandering eye, which understandably neither of his former wives had tolerated, Tommy was twice divorced with three children, living on what was left from a short but lucrative career in managing complex construction projects.

Running up to four hours each day, Tommy believed that his daily exercising and nightly drinking were a representation of his ID and Ego. As long as he kept those two components of his life in balance, he was in equilibrium. So each night he drank himself into a stupor and each day he made up for his unhealthy consumption with a long run. Today was no different. Pushing his childhood memories aside, Tommy began contemplating his current financial state, or lack thereof.

While he was the recipient of a monthly allowance credited to nearly twenty years in the construction business, the small portion he received was not nearly enough to support even his austere lifestyle. This financial fact required him to creatively augment his coffers by occasionally doing odd jobs. His latest short-term employment had been to deliver a flash drive to Bangkok, Thailand. He had been told the delivery was strictly legal but had quickly discovered otherwise. And even more surprising to everyone involved was that the flash drive had not included what had been advertised to the clientele bidding on the device. It had contained a powerful computer virus designed by the NSA. He eventually passed on the merchandise and had been well paid, but it had been a difficult delivery that had nearly ended his life on more than one occasion as several despicable people vied for the flash drive.

As he jogged along a trail in a heavily shaded wash, a small creek running along its center, a dog bounded up behind him. Glancing over his shoulder, Tommy looked down at the dog. With blue and gray eyes and a head that looked somewhat wolfish, the black, brown, and white dog had a wiry patch of hair on its back and looked to be a mix of some type. Maybe a Terrier and Coyote, Tommy thought to himself, as the dog trotted along behind him. Pressing forward, Tommy tried to wear the dog down, but with its tongue lapping from the side of its mouth, the blue-and-gray-eyed dog dutifully took up stride on his left side.

Several miles later, Tommy growled, "Go on home."

The dog just looked up with eyes that seemed to be laughing.

As Tommy crossed a wide wooden bridge that spanned a low rocky wash, a thin blonde woman dressed in black spandex leggings and a heavy gray sweatshirt jogged up next to him. Glancing over, Tommy examined the woman. With bright blue eyes, soft white skin, and straight blonde hair that abruptly ended just below her ears bouncing in tune with her stride, she was stunningly beautiful. Tommy calculated that the woman was around thirty-five years old. He also noticed that the woman was not wearing a wedding ring, a check he instinctively performed on every attractive woman he met.

Striding alongside, with the dog trotting between them, the blonde woman turned. "How are you today Mr. Luck?"

"I'm great except for this stray dog that I can't seem to shake," Tommy replied, gesturing down to the dog at his side. "How is it that you know my name, and I don't know yours?"

"A woman must have some mystery about her," the blonde woman teased.

"As long as the mystery isn't scary." Tommy chuckled. "Maybe I just need verification that you're not a stalker."

It immediately dawned on Tommy that he really didn't care whether the woman was a stalker. She was beautiful. In fact, he thought, having a woman as attractive as the one jogging next to him as a stalker might be a welcome addition to his somewhat monotonous life.

Laughing at Tommy's comment, she said, "We attend the same pool at the Knights of Columbus."

"So you're a Catholic?"

"No, like you, I'm just a summer pool member."

"How come I've never seen you there?"

"You weren't looking hard enough."

"I doubt that I would have missed you. Beautiful, no wedding ring, and nice eyes."

"You weren't looking hard enough," the blonde woman said again, before turning down an intersecting trail. Over her shoulder, while striding away, she called out, "See you later, Mr. Luck."

"I didn't get your name," Tommy yelled after the woman.

"Caroline," she replied before disappearing around a bend in the trail.

Two hours into his shortened run, with the dog still trotting along beside him, Tommy slowed his pace to a walk three blocks from his house and unplugged the earphones from his cell. The sun had adequately warmed the neighborhood, and the overhead old growth trees provided a cooling counterbalance. As if on cue, his phone began ringing and vibrating in his hand, the dog looking up with now-curious eyes.

"Tommy here," he answered the call with his traditional greeting, the sweat on his hands making the cell phone slick.

"Hi, Tommy, it's Becky from the NSA," a sweet voice emanated from the cell's tiny speaker.

"Hello, beautiful. I haven't heard from you since we last saw each other in Thailand," he replied while a vision of Becky's petite body, long brunette hair, and sparkling blue eyes formed in his mind.

“What a night that was.” She laughed. “I’m not sure I ever adequately thanked you.”

“What can I do for you? Why the call?” Tommy asked while wiping damp hair back from his forehead with his free hand.

“You think we could get together? I need to talk to you about something going on around here.”

“I’m finished working odd jobs for the NSA. I’d rather rake lawns for a couple of bucks an hour.”

“You’ll want to hear this.”

“No, I won’t.”

Becky was silent for a moment before saying, “You’ve been implicated in a crime. Actually two. You need to hear what I have to say.”

“What crimes? Surely the NSA doesn’t have jurisdiction over public intoxication, or drinking and driving infractions.”

“You need to hear what I have to say face to face. We don’t know who’s listening in on these cells,” Becky said, clearly trying to emphasize the gravity of some situation that Tommy was unaware of.

“Your pals at the NSA.”

“What do you mean?”

“I mean your fellow employees are probably listening,” Tommy clarified. Then with a sigh, he added, “When and where?”

“Let’s meet tomorrow, one o’clock in the afternoon at the Ballston Silver Diner. That should give you time for a short run before our meeting. You know where that is?”

“Of course, I know where it is. I’ll be there,” Tommy said before disconnecting the call.

As he slowly walked the last block, the stray dog patting along beside, his thoughts shifted from his current financial crisis to wondering what Becky could have been talking about. As far as he knew, he had stayed out of trouble since the Thailand delivery. Looking up at his front door, Tommy then began wondering if the Spanish beauty he had left naked in bed would still be there, hoping she would be.

Standing at the base of the steps leading up to the front door, Tommy turned and swung a foot toward the dog. "Get outta here, mutt. I don't need a sidekick." The dog easily dodged his foot and jumped out of the way. "Oh for Christ sake," Tommy muttered, shaking his head as he turned and began striding up the steps.

Walking up to his front door, an uneasy feeling came over Tommy. Over the years he had come to trust his gut instinct, these innermost feelings having saved him more than a few times in the past. He called it his little voice. The feeling was a bit like someone whispering into his ear in a language he didn't understand. The only perceptible element of the little voice was the tone in which it spoke. Tommy could tell whether it was calm, apprehensive, or panicked. As he strode up the steps to his front door, he could tell his little voice was apprehensive.

Tommy never locked his home, thinking the upper-middle-class neighborhood he lived was somewhat impervious to theft, nosy neighbors always scrutinizing the activity outside their windows. Standing on the front stoop with his right hand on the doorknob, he felt something was out of place but couldn't put his finger on what. When the blue-and-gray-eyed dog next to him began a low guttural growl, Tommy tried to kick him, once again attempting to shoo the animal away. Once again, the dog easily leaped away from his swinging foot. After a few minutes of trying to make sense of the little voice's warning, Tommy finally attributed his apprehension to the call from Becky and the mystery of being implicated in some unknown crime.

Opening the door, he peeked into the house. The dog nosed his head past him, peering inside, as well. The house was a mess. Couches overturned, cushions ripped open revealing their fluffy core, and drawers lying on the floor in disarray with their contents strewn everywhere.

“What the heck?” Tommy whispered, taking one step into the house’s small foyer, closing the door in the stray dog’s face.

Absently picking up a heavy iron decorative cross someone had given him as a housewarming gift that was lying on the floor, Tommy looked down the short hallway leading to the rear of the house and kitchen. He saw and heard nothing. Stepping farther into the house, to the edge of the living room, he peeked around the corner. The dog on the front stoop began barking, adding audio confusion to the already puzzling situation.

A powerful blow to the back of his knees folded his legs and knocked him to the floor. Dropping the cross and his cell phone, both bouncing across the parquet floor, Tommy abated his fall with his hands. Stunned, he found himself on his hands and knees with the backs of his legs burning from the wallop he had just taken. A second blow came down hard on his left shoulder, knocking him to his stomach. With the back of his knees and left shoulder screaming in agony, Tommy lay on the floor, trying to find the wherewithal to move.

Two men stepped out of a bedroom behind him, one short with dark hair pulled back into a ponytail wearing khaki pants and a hunter green sports jacket. The other stood well over six feet tall and had short white-blond hair and a thick jaw. The bigger of the two, dressed in neatly pressed blue jeans and light blue shirt, stood over Tommy casually swinging a golf club back and forth as if warming up to drive a ball down a long fairway. From Tommy’s angled view, it looked to be the three wood he kept in the hallway closet. The blue-and-gray-eyed dog continued barking wildly on the other side of the door.

"Your names don't happen to Jesus and Emanuel, do they?" Tommy muttered over the clatter of the dog barking just outside the door, turning his head to better see his assailants but remaining on his stomach.

"Do we look like a Jesus or an Emanuel?" the smaller of the two mocked Tommy in a pitched squeal of a voice.

"I never was much good with that golf club," Tommy said, pushing himself back up onto his hands and knees.

"Welcome home, Mr. Luck," the smaller of the two whined, the pitch of his voice irritatingly high. "We didn't expect you for another hour or two."

"Is there some reason you've chosen to redecorate my house?" Tommy asked, trying to push off the floor to his feet. "Not to mention, it's not nice to hit a man with his own golf club. I manage to abuse myself enough with that thing on the golf course."

A third blow struck the side of his rib cage, knocking him over onto his side. He tumbled into a small table in the entryway knocking picture of his children off the top. The framed picture fell from the table, the glass shattering next to his head as it struck the wooden floor. The barking on the other side of the door intensified.

Grabbing his chest, Tommy growled, "For Christ sake, guys. What the hell do you want?"

"We want nothing. You just happened to come home at an inconvenient time," the small man with the ponytail squealed again.

"Is there any way I can convince you guys to leave? Don't worry about the mess, I'll take care of cleaning up," Tommy responded, looking over at the feet of the smaller man who was wearing shiny brown leather loafers, partially obscured by khaki pant legs that were too long.

"Let's just put this drunk out of his misery and get out of here," the bigger of the two said in a deep booming voice.

"I really got to work on my reputation," Tommy moaned, still holding his side where the last blow had struck.

"We've accomplished what we came for, and the boss doesn't want him dead. Hit him again. A really good one, and then we'll leave," the smaller of the two squealed to his companion.

Out the corner of his eye, Tommy watched the bigger man raise the golf club high above his head, preparing for a long downward swing. As the big man started to swing the club down, pitching his shoulders forward to accelerate the speed of the impromptu weapon, Tommy abruptly rolled into the ankles of the smaller man, knocking his feet out from under him. The smaller man stumbled into the path of the downward swinging club. The bigger of the two's facial expression changed from one of wicked enjoyment to helplessness as the club struck with a terrific crack across the side of his companion's head. Tommy quickly twisted onto his back and then with all his strength, kicked his foot up into the bigger man's crotch. It struck with such force that Tommy could feel the big man's testicles roll across the heel of his running shoe. A high-pitched shriek erupted from the big man's mouth before he fell into the fetal position on the floor, grabbing himself between his legs. The golf club clattered on the floor next to him.

Painfully, Tommy rolled back on his stomach, pushed himself onto his hands and knees, and then onto his feet. His legs, shoulder, and chest howled in pain with each move. Noticing the dog had quit barking, Tommy wondered if the animal somehow sensed the altercation had come to a victorious close.

Stiffly walking down the hallway to the kitchen, he first retrieved a short, clear glass from a cabinet above the sink and then two cubes of ice from the freezer across the room, before pouring three fingers of Jameson's Irish whiskey from a bottle that stood next to the phone.

Tossing his head back and the drink down his throat, he then withdrew a large knife from a kitchen drawer before returning to the two men still lying on the entryway floor.

Picking up his cell phone from the foyer's wooden floor, Tommy called Becky.

"Hey, beautiful, I need some help," he said when she answered the phone.

"What is it, Tommy?"

"I found two guys throwing my place around. I'm not sure what they were looking for or if they found it, but they're currently sprawled out on my entryway floor."

"You don't know what they were looking for?"

"I haven't asked them yet. Nothing here is worth much anyway. My current problem is simply their presence, and I can't help but think that they are somehow mixed up with the allegations you claim are against me, whatever they are."

"You need me to send someone over?"

"That would be nice. They're not going anywhere. One likely has a pretty severe concussion. The other is conscious, but I doubt he will be walking anytime soon. And I've got to go pick my kids up. If I don't, their mother will be pissed and won't let me see them for a month. I'm going to ask these guys a couple of questions, but I doubt I'll get much out of them. Maybe a couple of NSA ID cards might convince those two thugs to talk."

"How will my men get inside the house? Will you leave the front door unlocked?"

"I never lock my door."

"Have you considered that's maybe why you have two men in your house?" Becky commented in a business-like tone.

Rolling his eyes, Tommy answered, "Never dawned on me."

"It'll take me ten or twenty minutes to get someone there."

"Like I said, they're not going anywhere. I see you tomorrow in Ballston—and, thanks."

"Sure, here to help. See you tomorrow and try to stay out of trouble until then."

"You know me. I can find trouble where there is none to be had."

Disconnecting the call, Tommy turned his attention back to the two men, tapping the bigger man with the toe of his running shoe. "Who's your boss, pal?"

"None of your business," the big man whimpered, his booming voice lost to the pain between his legs.

"One more chance before I go to work on you with this knife. Who's your boss?"

The big man rolled his head to the side so he could see Tommy out of the corner of his eye. After a short delay, he replied, "John Smith."

"John Smith is dead."

"A guy named John Smith hired us."

"What were you looking for?" Tommy asked while glancing at his watch.

"Nothing," the big man groaned.

"I'm glad to hear you found what you were looking for. Now, tell me what you were really looking for. Your companion next to you said you had accomplished what you came for. What did you accomplish?"

"We came for the money."

"What money?"

"The money you took from the post office box two nights ago."

"You didn't find it," Tommy replied flatly. "So you didn't accomplish what you came for."

"No," the big man groaned.

Looking at his watch again, Tommy said, "Lucky for you I haven't got time to play twenty questions. A vengeful ex-wife outweighs my curiosity as to why two thugs decided to rearrange my house."

With the larger of the two assailants, his white-blond hair now shining with droplets of sweat clinging to the ends, still in the fetal position, Tommy reached down and sliced off his right earlobe. The big man screamed as the knife cut through soft flesh. Blood flowed freely from the wound across his cheek and chin, before puddling on the floor beneath his head and shoulder. Tommy then turned to the smaller of the two and repeated the procedure. There was no resistance, no screams of agony. The smaller of the two was clearly unconscious.

Turning back to the big man, Tommy leaned down and whispered into his bloody ear, "Just a little reminder of our encounter each time you look into a mirror. Now, I've got some people coming over to help you guys clear out, so you can hold tight. And if you decide you want a second round, I'll be removing more than just an earlobe. You'll be able to audition for a soprano seat with the Baltimore Symphony Orchestra."

Walking back into the kitchen, Tommy dropped the two bloody earlobes in the white porcelain sink before refilling his glass with another three fingers of Irish whiskey, the ice cubes inside a fraction of their former size. He managed to empty the glass in two long swallows. Setting the glass in the sink next to the bloody ear-lobes, he walked to the linen closet, removing a blue and red beach towel, and then to the bedroom, pulling a pair of dark blue swim shorts from the top drawer of his mahogany dresser. As he was preparing to turn and leave the bedroom, he noticed a white sheet of paper scribed with a light flowing script sitting on the top of the dresser that simply read, *Anna*, followed by a phone number.

"Anna," Tommy muttered looking down at the paper, "So that's your name." A thin smile blossomed across his face as he recalled their morning interlude, before turning and walking from the bedroom.

Stepping over the two men, Tommy opened the front door and found the blue-and-gray-eyed dog sitting on the front stoop, looking up with his tongue lapping to one side.

"A lot of help you were. Now, go on home. Get outta here." Another halfhearted swipe with his foot didn't dissuade the dog, who once again simply jumped out of the way.

Walking down to his ancient white Chevy pickup, Tommy climbed in and slammed the heavy door shut, it moaning a high-pitched squeal as it swung. Not latching on the first try, Tommy had to open the door and slam it a second time. As he reached out to insert the keys into the ignition, he heard a racket in the truck's bed behind him, something knocking and scratching across its metal base. Glancing over his shoulder, Tommy saw the dog standing in the bed looking back at him through the cab's rear window.

"Oh for Christ's sake," Tommy muttered to himself as he put the truck into gear.

Five minutes later, Tommy and the dog arrived at his ex-wife's house. His children, Will and Ann, waiting for him on the front lawn in their swimming suits, ran over to the truck's bed and began petting the stray dog.

"Hi, Dad," Will called as he scratched behind the dog's ears. "Where'd you get the dog?"

"Hey, Dad," Ann said as she stroked the dogs back. "Why'd you get a dog?"

"Get in and let's get going, and it's not my dog," Tommy called back to his children. "It's just a stray I can't seem to get rid of."

Will, a tall, lanky fourteen-year-old boy with brown eyes and wavy brown hair, stepped away from the dog and pulled the passenger door open. Sixteen-year-old Ann, petite with green eyes and long straight brunette hair, hesitatingly followed her brother. Jumping up onto the cracked blue vinyl bench seat, Will slid to the center, next to Tommy. Ann climbed in and pulled the heavy metal passenger door shut, its hinges giving off a loud squeal similar to that of the driver's side, but latching on the first try.

"You do anything fun today?" Will asked.

"Just the usual, a long run," Tommy replied smiling down at his two children.

"What are you going to name the dog?" Ann asked.

"I'm not going to name a dog that's not mine."

"How about Captain?" Will chirped.

Ann giggled. "How about Lucky?"

"We're not naming the dog."

Turning his attention to the road, Tommy drove the truck to the nearby Knights of Columbus pool where he hoped to run into Caroline. Thankfully for Tommy, Catholics liked to drink, and the pool had a bar.

CHAPTER 5

Georgetown, Washington, DC, April 27, 2016:

Sitting in a high-backed gilded walnut chair, elaborately carved with ornamental shells and lambrequin motifs, Jacob Livingston, a slender man with neatly combed blond hair and light green eyes, took a deep draw from the long ivory pipe held between his teeth. Shuffling his feet across a beautiful blue and red Persian rug with intricate gold highlights, laying across a highly polished wooden floor, Jacob was deep in thought. He let his eyes wander across a bookcase filled with rare and valuable books that took up the entire wall to his right.

His gaze caught sight of a first edition of *Catcher in the Rye* then a 1937 copy of JRR Tolkien's *The Hobbit*. He briefly glanced over his left shoulder and examined a small Monet painting and even smaller charcoal sketch by Georgia O'Keefe hanging on the wall behind him. He blew a soft cloud from between his thin lips, the bluish smoke moving with the room's currents until slowly dissipating in the tentacles of an elaborate golden chandelier that hung from a high ceiling of crisscrossing dark wood beams.

Jacob, dressed in a red and gold paisley silk robe, then looked out through two long narrow glass paned windows onto the garden at the rear of his Georgetown home pondering the best way to obtain the computer virus of which his previous evening's guest had spoken. Running his thin fingers through his thin blonde hair, his manicured nails effortlessly gliding across his scalp, Jacob considered the power such a computer virus would bestow on its proprietor.

He had known that the one-hundred-year-old brandy was the favorite of his guest and had proven to be a powerful elixir in loosening the government man's lips during their weekly gatherings. Last night's meeting represented why Jacob had spent months nurturing the relationship with the man, acting as if social status did not matter. Learning that a man named Thomas Bacon Luck was allegedly in possession of and in the process of selling the powerful computer virus, Jacob had called his longtime special projects employee, Ralf, immediately after the meeting.

"Simply watch the man for now until I have time to verify the story," Jacob had said to Ralf, adding, "Be careful. Apparently, Mr. Luck is somewhat deceiving. According to my source, he is drunk but clever with good instincts."

Ralf wasn't educated enough to ever to work in the corporate office of Jacob's software firm, a front to his true profession of acquiring sought-after databases. Jacob did trust the man, and his knowledge of the less prosperous side of the life, with some of the more distasteful jobs that arose from time to time. Placing his spent ivory pipe down on a small writing table made of tulip and kingwood with gilt-bronze molding around the lower edge, Jacob's attention turned to a rose bush whose green vines had wrapped across the trim of the two long narrow windows. The rose bush's small green leaves and bright red flowers bordering the windows seemed to endlessly fascinate him. He wasn't sure whether his attraction to the delicate plant was simply because its tolerance to the harsh Washington, DC, winters or whether his interest was purely focused on its thorny beauty. Perhaps both, he thought.

A cell phone sitting next to his now dormant pipe on the writing table began buzzing and vibrating. Picking the cell up, Jacob looked at the caller ID. *Unidentified* flashed on the screen. Unhesitatingly, Jacob pressed the call button before holding it up to his ear.

"Mr. Livingston, I have the information you were looking for," a business-like voice echoed from the cell. Jacob immediately recognized the voice as that of his executive secretary.

"Tell me what you have," Jacob replied in his naturally nasally tone.

"According to my contact with United Airlines, Thomas Bacon Luck, a resident of Arlington did board a flight to Bangkok last summer. He returned some two weeks later. I've also spoken with my contact at the agency. He was able to verify the existence of a file concerning an operation in Thailand during the same time period that was worked in conjunction with the NSA."

"Could your agency contact verify that Thomas Luck was involved in the operation? Or was there any indication that the operation involved a computer virus?"

"My contact's security clearance isn't high enough to view the file. It's classified at the highest level. The only person able to authorize access to the file is the CIA Director, himself."

"Very well. If any more information becomes available, please give me a call."

Jacob disconnected the call and leaned back into the high-backed chair. Holding his cell phone in his right hand, he gently stroked the chair's velvet cushion with his left, looking up at the ceiling. After a few minutes, he turned his attention back to the cell phone, scanning his contacts, before selecting one and pressing the call button.

"Yeah, Mr. Livingston, it's Ralf," a clear voice called through the cell's speaker.

"I know it's you, Ralf," Jacob replied, trying to keep the frustration out of his nasal voice, "I called you." Jacob knew Ralf to be a bright man, but at moments like these that he sometimes wondered if his part-time employee hadn't had a head injury early in life. "What has Mr. Luck been up to?"

"Yeah, well I was watching this Tommy character's house, waiting for him to get back from running, and two guys arrived and ripped the place apart. And then this Tommy character comes home, surprising the two men, and getting the best of them. He left them on his entryway floor."

"So someone else is after whatever Mr. Luck is trying to sell. Must not be his client or they wouldn't have searched his home. Or maybe his client is dissatisfied with the deal. Could the men have been government agents?"

"No way. Those two men weren't professional enough. And another thing, I don't think they were looking for anything. The way they tossed his place looked more like vandalism than a search."

"Now, Ralf, why in the world would someone want to vandalize Mr. Luck's house? It had to be a search."

"Yeah, you're right, boss. It had to be a search."

"Where is Mr. Luck now?"

"Like I said he left the two men on his entryway floor and then drove over and picked up his kids. He's now at some pool in Arlington. It's behind some big mansion-looking building. His kids are swimming, and he's sitting under an awning reading a book and drinking. And he's got a dog lying at his feet. I'm not sure where he got the dog."

"Here's what I want you to do, Ralf," Jacob patiently requested, "Get a couple of your friends together tomorrow and pick Mr. Luck up in the early afternoon. I want to have a chat with him. Pick him up and give me a call, and I'll tell you where to bring him. You understand what I want?"

"Yeah, boss, pick this Tommy character up tomorrow afternoon and call you to find out where to bring him—right?"

"That's right. Remember what you saw today. Mr. Luck seems to be a very resourceful man. Be careful."

"All right, boss, see you tomorrow."

Disconnecting the call, Jacob contemplated what he would say to Tommy Luck the next day. Should he ask to buy the computer virus or simply threaten the man? He wasn't sure. He would need to sleep on that question.

CHAPTER 6

East Falls Church, Arlington, Virginia, April 27, 2016:

Sitting in a white Nissan Altima sedan parked on a street in North Arlington beneath a stand of tall old growth trees with bright green leafs shimmering in the sunlight, Steve had just watched what had occurred at Tommy Luck's house, and he wasn't surprised. He had seen him survive much more lethal situations during their adventure in Thailand the year before. Tommy Luck was either extremely talented or very lucky. Maybe both.

Glancing up into the rearview mirror, Steve looked at his reflection, a pale face and small dark eyes looking back. His whole life he had heard the whispers calling him beady-eyed.

It didn't help matters that he was only five foot tall. With short, skinny arms and legs, and small hands and feet, Steve wished he had a more imposing stature, but genetics had been unkind, leaving him with the worst of his parent's physical traits.

Reaching across to the brown polyester fabric covered seat next to him, he picked up a small black prepaid cell phone and rolled through the short list of contacts before selecting the one he needed.

Punching the call button, he waited for the other end to pick up.

A voice with a distinct Midwestern accent answered the call. "How are things going?"

"He's got more people watching him than you can count," Steve replied grimly.

"Who are the interested parties?"

"Three groups that I've counted so far." Steve scratched the dark bushy hair on his head with his small pale fingers. "Couple of goons. I'm not sure who they work for, but they're not professionals. They searched his place looking for it."

"You sure they were looking for it?"

"What else could it be?"

"You're right," the Midwestern man responded with a hint of concern.

"Didn't go as planned though, Mr. Luck came home early from his run, before they had left."

"Not good news for the goon team."

"You know Mr. Luck. While it looked bad for him at the onset, he managed to get the upper hand in the end. He left them sprawled on the floor just inside his front door."

"That's not surprising. Tommy is resourceful, is he not? Who are the other two interested parties?"

"Some guy in a black BMW was parked up the street watched the whole thing, as well. It was pretty obvious that he wasn't connected with the two goons. And the CIA or local police have set up surveillance in a yellow house next door."

"Did the government agents question the men that Tommy assaulted?"

"No, they followed Mr. Luck when he left," Steve replied. "The Black BMW did as well."

"Maybe they already knew who they are," the Midwestern voice commented.

"Yeah, the government agents have probably wired

the house. They probably took pictures and listened in on what was said. Stepping in would have blown their cover."

"You sure the BMW man isn't a government agent?"

"Government agents don't drive BMWs. Especially ones in need of bodywork."

"Everything seems to be coming together," the Midwestern voice calmly answered. The slightly concerned tone had all but vanished. "But we do need to keep an eye on the other interested parties. I am mildly concerned about the black BMW, and it would be worth our time to find out who the two goons work for."

"Yeah, it's coming together nicely," Steve agreed while watching the neighborhood mailman. Dressed in the post office's summer uniform of gray shorts and light blue shirt, the mailman made his way up to Tommy's mailbox next to the front door. "But I'm not sure the other interested parties are worth worrying about."

"We should worry about them," the man disagreed. "They're the only element to this transaction that could throw our plans off track."

"The deal has been agreed on. I can't see anything getting in the way of the transaction." It was Steve's turn to disagree. "It all seems to be a foregone conclusion at this point."

"Until we have the computer program in our possession nothing is a sure thing."

Shrugging his shoulders, Steve asked, "What do you want me to do?"

The voice at on the other end of the line hesitated for a moment before saying, "I want you to let Tommy see you. Don't let him get near you, just let him see you."

"Why? You know Mr. Luck will recognize me," Steve challenged.

"I'm counting on Tommy recognizing you. I want to get inside his head. He's probably already figured out that the NSA and CIA suspect that he's trying to sell the computer virus. He's just had two men search his house. Knowing Tommy, it won't take him too long to figure out there's a surveillance team next door, and he's probably already noticed the man in the BMW. And it won't be long before the police come to talk to him about the CIA agent murdered several nights ago. Seeing you will add one more concern. I want him to be overwhelmed with what's going on around him, so he's more apt to make a mistake. I want him to feel some pressure."

"You think that'll work? We've seen him under pressure before, and he seemed to do quite well."

"He's made mistakes in the past. We just didn't capitalize on them. This time we will."

"One more thing," Steve commented, "He's gotten himself a dog."

"A dog?"

"Yeah, a dog," Steve replied. "I never thought of him as the dog type."

"Me neither."

Watching a man dressed in khaki shorts and black socks mowing a lawn in front of one of the many 1940 post-war bungalows that filled this neighborhood, Steve disconnected the call. Hearing Lynyrd Skynyrd's "Southern Man" faintly echoing through the Nissan's radio, he turned the volume up and watched over the North Arlington neighborhood, tapping his feet on the car's black rubber floor mat in tune with the music. Running his small pale hand through his dark bushy hair again, he wondered how this transaction would all pan out. His boss had made what was initially a very simple plan to acquire the computer virus into something far more complex, all for the sake of revenge. It was not that Steve didn't think revenge was a good idea. Tommy Luck needed to pay for what he did last year, but, for Steve, the money that the virus would bring in was far more important. A well-financed revenge could come later.

As "Southern Man" came to an end, Steve twisted the keys in the ignition of the Nissan Altima and started the car. Making a U-turn on the narrow neighborhood street, he began driving back to his hotel room, contemplating the best way of honoring his boss's request of letting Tommy Luck see him. Steve knew he would need to be careful when he did so. Luck was a resourceful man who could quickly turn the tables on him.

CHAPTER 7

Twenty miles north of Greeley, Colorado, September 14, 1986:

With the Rocky Mountains reaching up into a cloudless bright blue sky as a backdrop, Tommy gazed at the young girl before him. She was beautiful, with long blonde hair and fair skin with light blue eyes. She had small round breasts that had just begun to sprout. She looked sixteen, but Tommy knew she was his age, only fourteen years old. Dressed in a floral patterned light summer dress that hung loosely on her body, she smiled at Tommy, and he immediately felt himself become aroused.

"Want to go for a walk?" she asked, running small delicate hands through her long blonde hair.

Smiling his boyish smile, Tommy replied, "I'd like that." Of course, he accepted. She was beautiful.

They walked along the edge of a cornfield, tall stalks and bright green husks towering above them. A soft hot breeze blew across their backs, carrying the musty scent of freshly turned earth and ripening sweet corn. Each step created a small brown plume of dust from the dry loose soil at their feet that was whisked away by the light wind. She let her hand brush up against his as they walked and Tommy's heart raced. The two slowly made their way toward a tall faded red barn with white trim at the far end of the field.

When they arrived at the barn, she turned to Tommy and said, "Let's go inside. It's really neat in there."

"Okay," Tommy replied, her soft voice captivating him and leaving him at a complete loss for words.

The large doors groaned as they pulled them open and a blended odor of gasoline and freshly cut hay exploded from the inside. A large green John Deere tractor with a thick yellow strip advertising the manufacturer stood in the center of the barn between high stacks of hay bales. The two walked around the tractor, deep into the barn before coming to a stop just below a loft filled with more hay bales. With a pile of loose hay laying at their feet, and burlap bags full of seed and large tools leaning against the barn's wooden planked walls surrounding them, the teenagers turned and looked at one and other. Tommy reached up and touched her cheek, and the girl responded by pushing her face into his hand with a smile. The young girl reached up and touched his chest, moving her hand down the length of his shirt.

Tommy was ready to explode and gently pushed her right shoulder strap free. The dress fell, hanging awkwardly on the girl's body and revealing a soft white shoulder.

The girl reached down and gently unclasped his belt, then took a step back, shyly dropping her eyes.

"I want to see you," Tommy said innocently, gently raising her face with his right hand.

"I want to see you too," she replied, the innocence in her voice matching his, taking his left hand into her right.

Looking at the ground, Tommy hesitated for a moment before looking up with his boyish smile. "I mean want to see you naked."

"I want to see you naked too," the girl whispered, her light blue eyes flashing with mischief.

As Tommy reached over and began unbuttoning the front of her summer dress, she pulled the top of his pants apart, the thick metal button begrudgingly giving way. She then unzipped the front and pushed them downward. Tommy pulled the girls dress open, and it fell to the ground, landing in the scattered hay that had fallen from the overhead loft.

The two awkwardly explored each other, giggling and laughing. Afterward, the young girl lay next to Tommy on a pile of hay, pulling her dress across her naked body. Tommy pulled his trousers across his. Neither knew what to say. With a tingling sensation in his stomach, Tommy knew he would never forget that day or moment.

After a few minutes of silence, the two sniggered again as they hastily put their clothes back on, before running back to the girl's house, more dust from the dry soil pluming behind them as they ran. The girl ran into a long low brick ranch style house, and Tommy wandered out to a water pump near a faded wooden shed where his father was busy taking samples.

"You ready to go, son?" his father asked, looking over his shoulder with deep blue eyes and a wide grin on his face, making Tommy wonder if he knew what had just happened.

"Yeah, I need to use the bathroom first, though."

"Go knock on their door and ask," his father said as he turned back to the wellhead. "We'll head north from here. I got a job in Nebraska tomorrow. We can spend the night sleeping in the car near Kimball."

Running past his father's green Chevy Caprice, up to the house, Tommy climbed the red brick steps to the front door, running his hand along its cool black iron handrail and knocking lightly on the door. A slender strawberry blonde woman answered the door, directing Tommy toward the bathroom. Looking at the family pictures adorning the walls along a narrow hallway as he strode toward the bathroom, he could hear several girls giggling in one of the back bedrooms. It sounded as if one of the voices was that of the young girl he had just been with.

He hit a switch next to the door as he entered. The light came on, and a noisy fan began whirling in a small window at the rear of the cramped room. With white tiles covering the floor and lower half of the walls, the narrow bathroom had the faint smell of urine. A small shower stall was tucked in the back corner, and the toilet was so close to the entrance that Tommy had to step back to shut the door. As he began to unbuckle his belt, he heard a loud voice booming in the house, but the noisy bathroom fan kept him from comprehending what was being said.

Just as he began to relieve himself the bathroom door burst open, slamming against Tommy and throwing him into the back wall. His urine sprayed across the room as he fell into the wall. A big man, well over six foot tall, with broad shoulders, and dressed in blue jeans and a white western style short-sleeve shirt stood in the doorway with a large kitchen knife in his hand. Tommy stepped away from the wall, looking for a way around the imposing figure of the man.

"We invite your father to work on our well, and you go and take advantage of my little girl? What kind of person are you?" The big man's voice boomed in the bathroom, echoing off the walls.

"I didn't mean…" Tommy started to say as he zipped his pants back up.

"I'm going to cut your john off, you little shit," the man's thunderous voice interrupted.

The big man heaved Tommy into the back wall as he

tried to scamper through the bathroom door. Enormous sunburnt and calloused hands grabbed Tommy's pants. Having never been that frightened, Tommy attempted to push the man's large hands away, but his efforts easily were swatted away. The big man pushed his shoulder into Tommy, forcing him into and up the wall. Pinned half-way up the tiled wall, Tommy began to have difficulty breathing with the pressure applied by the big farmer's weight. Pulling at Tommy's pants, the man jerked them down.

Tommy couldn't breathe, and his heart raced. He grabbed for the bigger man's eyes and then brought his knee up, slamming it into farmer's face. Blood spewed from the big man's nose, forcing him to release Tommy and take a step back to wipe his face.

Suddenly Tommy's father burst through the door, tackling the big farmer from behind. The two men fell on the narrow floor at Tommy's feet, their legs sticking out into the hallway. Tommy watched in horror as his father ripped the seat from the toilet and began pummeling the side of big farmer's head. Blood splattered across the walls and floor. His father didn't stop until the big man's arms limply dropped to his sides.

Tommy quickly pulled up his pants before his father grabbed him by the hand and led him from the bathroom. They passed the young blonde girl and her younger sister standing near the bathroom door, both crying.

Between sobs, the youngest cried, "I'm sorry. I'm sorry. I didn't mean to tell Daddy. I'm sorry."

They walked down the hallway leading to the front door. They passed the slender woman with strawberry blonde hair, holding the door open for them.

The strawberry blonde woman patted his father on the bottom as they passed by. "Get your ass out of here. He's going to be one pissed off farmer when he wakes up."

They walked out to his father's Caprice, its rear window glistening in the setting sun. Climbing into the passenger side of the Caprice, Tommy was immediately taken by the smell of stale cigarette smoke, the odor oddly calming him.

They drove down the dirt road leading from the farm, then down a narrow two-lane paved road, turning North on Interstate 25. The farther away from the farm they drove, the more guilt Tommy felt.

That night, lying in the back seat of his father's car outside Kimball, Tommy looked up at the stars through the Chevrolet's rear window. Unable to sleep, Tommy asked, "Dad, do you ever regret the things you do?"

Lying in the front seat, his father was silent, and Tommy wondered if he hadn't already drifted off to sleep. After nearly a minute of silence his father said, "Tommy, we all make mistakes in life. The little ones are like grains of sand. The big ones are like pebbles. Each time you do something you regret you put either a grain of sand or a pebble in your pocket. The small mistakes, the grains of sand, eventually work their way through the seams of your pocket and are lost. The big ones, the pebbles, stay with you forever. You can always feel the added weight, each time you put your hand in your pocket you can feel them, and when you walk they chaff your leg. They never go away. I have a pocket full of pebbles, and I use them to try to avoid creating more. While I regret each and every one of them, I don't want to ever lose those pebbles. Along with my accomplishments, those pebbles represent who I am. Losing my pebbles would be like losing part of myself."

"I feel guilty about today," Tommy whispered.

"Son, what you did today was a grain of sand."

"I feel like I ruined it for you. Those people will tell

others what happened and you won't get any work around there. I really blew it for you."

"Tommy, it takes two to make what happened today happen. And that girl didn't fall too far from the tree. That girl's mother is one of the horniest women I have ever met. I've slept with that farmer's wife at least a dozen times."

Silent for a moment, Tommy then asked, "What about me?"

"What'd mean?"

"How far from the tree am I?"

A deep laugh erupted from the front seat of the Caprice and Tommy's father said, "Son, based on what happened today, you've got your arms wrapped around the trunk of the tree."

CHAPTER 8

East Falls Church, Arlington, Virginia, April 28, 2016:

Lying in bed in the early morning, with his hands over his eyes to block out the sunlight shining through the window, Tommy was thinking about the grains of sand and pebbles his father had spoken of all those years ago. Having acquired a pocket full of pebbles over his lifetime, he wondered if he would ever learn enough lessons to stop adding more. Between a chaotic career in construction, two divorces, and his daily mistakes, the pebbles and grains of sand seemed to keep coming. His pockets were so full that he felt as if there no room for more, making each step difficult.

With his eyes tightly closed, he took hands from his face and rubbed the sides of his head, muttering, "I really need to get some curtains for that window."

Cracking his eyes open and glancing to his left, he saw thick auburn hair blossoming from under the white quilt and spilling across a white pillow. With the faint smell of pungent perfume wafting the air, Tommy examined a milky white hand and forearm protruding from under the quilt. Small delicate fingers, with nails polished a sparkly green, lightly gripped his left arm.

Turning his attention to the bedroom floor, his eyes followed the line of strewn clothes—his faded jeans, T-shirt, and boxer shorts, then a white blouse and bright green skirt that oddly clashed with the room's sage green walls. Finally, a pair of white lace panties and bra lay next to the bed.

His head throbbing and his mouth feeling as if it was full of dust, Tommy pondered the night before. He had met up with Amber, the petite woman now lying next to him, at a local pub on Washington Boulevard in Clarendon. Having met six nights before, this was their first interlude, and Tommy somehow knew it would not likely be their last. Amber was a successful investment banker whose professional lifestyle had no room for a full-time relationship. Tommy, on the other hand, had sworn off relationships for an entirely different reason.

Amber threw back the quilt, her light green eyes danced and her red lips warped into a wide, crooked smile. Small milky white breasts topped with pink nipples, and smooth bare hips immediately aroused him. Pushing back his nausea induced from too many Irish whiskeys the night before, he reached out and pulled her toward him.

"Want to get lucky again?" Tommy grinned a crooked smile of his own at the beautiful auburn haired woman.

"I need to go to work. Some of us actually have a job," she chortled while tracing her delicate index fingertip down the thin scar on his face.

"A quickie then?"

"You got five minutes to make it worth my while."

Thirty minutes later, stepping from the bedroom, Tommy nearly tripped over the dog, its blue and gray eyes looking up with surprise.

"How the hell did you get in here?" Tommy snapped, swinging a foot at the dog.

The dog once again bounded out of the way of Tommy's halfhearted kick and looked up with sad eyes.

Calling out from the bedroom, Amber asked, "Who are you talking to?"

"This mutt started following me yesterday, and I can't get rid of him. He's like a mixture—between wolf and terrier—he's a mongrel. I have no idea how he got into the house."

Wandering naked from the bedroom, Amber looked down at the dog.

"You probably don't remember going to bed last night. Maybe you don't remember letting him in." Reaching down, she scratched the back of the dog's head. "He's is a mongrel, but he's mostly cattle dog."

"A cattle dog?"

"Yeah, an Australian Cattle dog." She laughed. "They're smart, stubborn, and cautious. A lot like someone else I know."

"I'm not stubborn."

"Yeah, right."

After inspecting the house for open doors, trying to figure out how the stray dog got inside, Tommy wandered into the bathroom. Standing in front of the bathroom mirror brushing his teeth after a cold shower, he could hear Amber in the bedroom talking to someone on her cell phone. Spitting the last of the toothpaste from his mouth, Tommy stepped into the bedroom, pulling an olive drab T-shirt over his head.

"It happened yesterday. That's right, two guys," Amber spoke into her cell, abruptly stopping when Tommy entered the room. Turning and smiling, she ended her call by saying, "I'll give you a ring later."

Walking up to Amber, brushing her auburn hair aside and kissing her on the forehead, Tommy asked, "What happened yesterday?"

"I had two guys came into my office yesterday wanting to invest a bundle into grain futures. It would have been a great investment six months ago, but now the word is out. There's a drought in the Midwest."

A few minutes later, with the dog padding along behind them, they walked down the short hallway to the front door—Amber in her white blouse and bright green skirt with a long black rain jacket draped over her shoulder, Tommy in his running shorts and shoes with a thick gray sweatshirt over his olive drab T-shirt.

Turning at the front door, Tommy kissed her again, this time on the lips.

Looking up at Tommy, she said, "Tommy I really enjoy your company. You want to come over to my place tonight? I have a huge apartment in Rosslyn overlooking the Potomac. It's really a great place."

"You mean it's a clean place," Tommy replied as he opened the door. A fresh cool breeze blew through the open door. "Like I told you, I haven't had time to clean up since those two guys tore this place apart." Looking back over his shoulder, he glanced at the torn cushions with their stuffing strewn on the floor and the papers and magazines lying about. He had planned on cleaning it up, but each time he began something interrupted the task.

Amber's light green eyes flashed. "Maybe you should just hire a maid?"

"Cleaning ladies charge too much. I'll get around to it."

"I doubt it." Amber quietly giggled. "What about tonight at my place?"

"Can I have a rain check? After all, as you've pointed out, I need to clean my house."

Taking Tommy's hand in hers, she said, "I don't think I've ever met anyone quite like you." She kissed him lightly on the cheek before walking down the steps to her black Porsche 911 Carrera convertible parked on the street behind his beat-up white Chevy pickup and drove away.

Running down a quiet street lined with postwar homes surrounded and old growth trees, Tommy began pondering his upcoming meeting with Becky. With the stray dog trotting alongside, he began wondering in what crime he could possibly be a suspect. While there were typically several times a week he had no recollection of evening events due to his over-consumption of alcohol, those nights he was normally too drunk to harm anyone or even leave his house.

Turning into a narrow park, Tommy could hear a pair of shoes padding along the path as someone ran up behind him. Out of the corner of his eye, he could see the stray dog turn his head a take a look at the approaching runner. The dog turned his attention back to the path, seeming to sense no danger, with what looked to Tommy as a smile on its face. Caroline, with her bobbing blonde hair, suddenly appeared next to Tommy, a wide grin on her face.

"Hello, Mr. Luck," she said, greeting Tommy. "How are you today?"

"Are you sure you're not a stalker? If you're going to keep showing up like this, you need to call me Tommy."

"We both like to run, Tommy. We both like to run in the same area. I see you still have your dog."

"It's not my dog. Sadly, I can't seem to shake the mangy mutt. I did learn he's mostly cattle dog."

"They say that cattle dogs are smart and stubborn. I think you ought to keep him. They say dogs reflect their human owner's personalities. Not to mention, that dog has an uncanny resemblance to you."

"You left out cautious—and I'm not stubborn."

Caroline giggled. "That's up for debate."

"With your comprehensive knowledge of my life, perhaps you'd care to tell me something about the two men searching my house yesterday?"

"The two men you left lying in your foyer, each suspiciously missing an earlobe?"

"The two men I left in my foyer," Tommy confirmed. "I left their earlobes in the sink. They could have found them if they wanted."

"I don't know anything about the two men. They weren't professionals, that's for certain."

Jogging along in silence for several minutes, Tommy said, "Caroline, what's going on? I met you yesterday, and you knew my name. Today you show up on a quiet path and know about things that are happening to me—who are you?"

"I'm a professional executive headhunter who likes to run," she responded with a thin smile on her face. "I'm a woman who saw you at the pool and liked what I saw."

"How did you know about the two men I left in my foyer yesterday?"

"As I said before, a woman must keep some mystery about herself," Caroline called over her shoulder, turning down an intersecting street. "I'll see you later, Tommy."

After a three hour run and another shower, Tommy locked the stray dog in the house and walked out to his old white Chevy pickup for the drive into Ballston and his meeting with Becky. Before climbing into the driver's seat, he looked up the street leading toward Lee Highway. Yesterday, he recalled seeing a late model black BMW in need of some body work, and a man dressed in gray slacks and silver-brown sports jacket that seemed to shimmer in the sunlight parked at the end of the street. The same car, parked across the street from its former position, marked it as abnormal. What caught Tommy's eye was that man sitting in the driver's seat wore the same silver-brown sports jacket he had had on the day before. The thought of wearing the same attire two days in a row would be grounds for eviction from this upper-middle-class neighborhood. He was obviously an outsider. Today, two other men were in the BMW with the silver-brown-jacketed man, their shoulders too wide for their seats.

Climbing into the pickup, it took Tommy three attempts to get the raucous driver's door to latch. Hesitating before slipping the key into the ignition, Tommy sat in the front of his pickup and wondered about the black BMW and its odd occupants. He then recalled seeing three men entering his neighbor's yellow house the previous evening. Dressed in dark suits and ties, one of the men had awkwardly glanced in the direction of Tommy's house as they stepped through the front door. Drunk at the time, Tommy thought nothing of the men. Today, however, he remembered that his neighbor was out of town for several weeks and no one should have been in the house. He looked up at his neighbor's yellow house. The windows were dark, and he could see no movement from within.

"What the hell is going on here?" Tommy muttered to himself, as he inserted and turned the key in the ignition. The truck started with a low rumble.

In the process of making a U-turn on the narrow city street to avoid the black BMW and its occupants, the truck's poor turning radius required Tommy to stop and back up several times. Driving away from Lee Highway and the parked BMW, Tommy pulled up to the first stop sign along the street, with the truck idling at the intersection. A brown Nissan sedan slowly drove past in the opposite direction, its driver looking up as if taunting him. Tommy's heart raced, and adrenaline surged through his veins when he saw the driver's face. The small beady-eyed and dark-bushy-haired man peeking out from behind the steering wheel could have been only one person.

Tommy slammed the gear shift into reverse and floored the accelerator. The truck's tires spun, screeched, and smoked as it shot backward. Watching the brown Nissan sedan speed up and race away through his rear-view mirror, he spun the steering wheel to the left, driving the truck into an empty driveway, standing on the brakes. The truck screeched to a halt three inches from a large white garage door. Ramming the shift into drive, Tommy slammed his foot down on the gas pedal again, and the truck sprang forward with more spinning and screeching tires. The old pickup fishtailed as he turned out of the driveway. Its oversized engine accelerated the pickup down the street, flying by cars parked along the curb, as he chased the brown Nissan Sedan. As the truck screamed past, the black BMW abruptly pulled from the curb and began following.

Seeing the Nissan take a right on Lee Highway at the top of the hill, Tommy tried to push the accelerator farther into the floorboard. At the top of the hill, all four of the pickup's tires took flight and Tommy rose off the seat, his head brushing the top of the cab. He spun the steering wheel to the right as the truck impacted the ground with a metal crushing bounce before rising up on its two left tires, skidding into the traffic on Lee Highway.

Cars swerved and honked their horns as the truck staggered into the traffic. Searching through the windshield, Tommy could not see the Nissan sedan or its beady-eyed occupant. Stamping down on the accelerator one more time, Tommy sped down Lee Highway, weaving in and out of its slower moving traffic and shooting through a yellow light at the Harrison Street intersection.

There was no sign of the Nissan sedan. The car had virtually vanished. Tommy cursed his luck under his breath and slowed the truck before turning down George Mason Drive. Five minutes later, Tommy's truck rumbled into Ballston.

CHAPTER 9

Ballston, Arlington, Virginia, April 28, 2016:

A broad silver banner with red and blue lettering marked Tommy's destination some half a block ahead on Washington Boulevard. Wedged between Wilson and Washington Boulevards, the Silver Diner was somewhat difficult to get to while driving eastbound. After a few turns, tracking through the back streets of Ballston, Tommy finally pulled into the parking lot behind the diner.

Walking past several people dressed in casual business attire waiting for the pedestrian walk sign on Washington Boulevard, Tommy found his way to the entrance. An aroma of coffee and freshly baked bread filled the air as he pulled open the polished silver doors of the diner. The heavy doors easily swung outward.

A stout woman with mousy brown hair stood behind a dark wooden podium, dressed in black pants, a white shirt, and a name tag indicating her name was Natasha. Greeting Tommy with a wide toothy smile, the woman asked, "Seating for one?"

"Meeting someone here. Petite, dark hair, blue eyes."

"Yes, sir, just around the corner," Natasha answered while pointing a plump index finger to the far end of the restaurant.

Tommy walked down an aisle between a counter and wooden booths. The long white counter was lined with silver stools topped with hunched over men in a variety of muted manual labor style clothes. The row of wooden booths had shiny black vinyl bench seats and was filled with rotund business attired customers. Making his way through the restaurant, a black and white clad waitress pushed past on his left carrying a wide round tray of entrees high above her head with an aromatic exhaust of fried beef, fresh bread, and melted butter. Then he maneuvered around another similarly clad waitress busy talking with an elderly lady dressed in a purple dress at a booth on his right.

Conversational chatter between the diner's customers filled the air, drowning out the soft, easy rock music playing from hidden overhead speakers. Scanning the crowd as he wandered through the restaurant, he saw nothing unusual. The normal Silver Diner crowd of day laborers, portly middle-aged businessmen and women, and the elderly were locked in conversation with one another behind plates heaped with food.

Turning the corner at the rear of the restaurant, Tommy saw Becky's long dark hair. She was sitting in a wooden booth with her back to him. She glanced over her shoulder as Tommy walked up to the table.

"Hello, beautiful," Tommy said, looking into her bright blue eyes while slipping into the bench across from her. His jeans whispered a chafing moan as he slid onto the long black vinyl seat.

"Tommy," Becky replied, reaching across the table and taking his hands into hers. "You look great. Your scar seems to have healed well."

"A nice reminder of our Thailand adventure."

Mesmerized by her sparkling blue eyes and feel of her

soft hands, he sat silently examining her delicate features. Her soft light brown skin, thick brunette hair, and slender figure had always electrified him. Today was no different. Watching her give him a similar examination, he thought back to their encounter in Thailand. He could still clearly envision the wide bay, rimmed by long white beaches and tall palm trees with Becky standing waist deep in crystal clear water in a green bikini. He wondered how he could have ever deprived himself of such a beautiful woman.

"Sid, the CIA agent who worked Bangkok during the delivery of the flash drive last year, has evidence that you're in possession of and trying to sell the computer virus. He also has evidence implicating you in a murder of a CIA agent."

"What computer virus?" Tommy inquired, even though he knew exactly what she was talking about.

"Don't play stupid with me, Tommy. I'm talking about the computer virus that was on the flash drive that you delivered to the Turk in Thailand last year."

"What kind of evidence?"

"A man fitting your description was seen picking up an envelope that contained a large sum of money from a post office box in Westover. The post office box happened to be the drop site for a computer virus that was advertised in the *Washington Post* and *Economist Journal*. The advertisement claimed it was a computer virus unveiled in Thailand last year."

"I have fairly common features, and there was probably more than one computer virus unveiled in Thailand last year. Is that all they got?"

"Do fairly common features include a scar running from the corner of your mouth to your jaw? Not mention your fingerprints were found on a .38 shell casing and a newspaper at the scene of a CIA agent's murder. The

CIA agent had been following the man who picked up the envelope. And you just had your house ransacked by two unknown men, for unknown reasons."

"I guess your folks didn't get to my house before they departed yesterday?"

"No." Becky sighed. "They were already gone by the time I could get someone there."

"That would have taken a small miracle. Those two guys were definitely out of action. Someone must have given them a hand. What else does Sid have?"

The waitress, her black pants looking as if the top button and zipper were ready to burst open from the pressure exerted by a large round belly, delivered two glasses of ice water to their table. With condensation glistening on the sides, thick cubes of ice jumped as she set the glasses on the table.

"You think they need more than fingerprints at the scene of a murder—"

"Okay, I get the connection," Tommy interrupted, hearing a building frustration in her voice. "I seem to have more than one group of admirers watching me. It would seem that someone has gone to a lot of trouble to set me up."

"Who's been watching you?"

As he began carefully pushing the condensation on the glass downward with his right index finger, creating a pool of water at its base, the overweight waitress reappeared at the end of the table with a pen and notepad in her hand. Tommy and Becky quickly rattling off their orders and with smile and nod, the waitress turned and walked away to deliver their meal requests to the kitchen.

"Who else is watching you?" Becky asked the question again.

"I'm not sure. A couple of thugs were at the end of the

street when I got into my truck to come over here, and there might be a group of guys watching me from my neighbor's house," Tommy replied. "And I got a dog watching me."

"A dog?"

"A dog."

"How can a dog be watching you?"

"This dog started following me yesterday, and I can't seem to get rid of it." Tommy chuckled lightheartedly. "I even found the thing in my house this morning. All the doors and windows were closed, but I found the dog sleeping next to my bedroom door. With all this sudden scrutiny on my activities, I'm beginning to suspect the dog is yet another interested party."

"Maybe you were drunk and don't remember letting him in," Becky teased. "Where's the dog now?" She playfully glanced around the restaurant as if looking for the dog.

"I locked him in my house. I didn't think the Silver Diner management would approve of my canine companion. What can you tell me about our old pal Steve?"

"Steve, John Smith's righthand man? The former inspector general claimed he had been eliminated along with John Smith in Thailand. No one has heard anything from Steve since. That's interesting you would ask. According to the *Washington Post*, *Economist*, and Westover Postmaster, all were paid by a man named John Smith. Why do you ask about Steve?"

Busying himself with pushing the condensation from his glass again, Tommy said, "I thought John Smith was dead?"

"John Smith is dead," Becky said flatly. "That was verified by our Thai counterparts."

"Thais can be bribed."

"Why did you ask about Steve?" Becky asked again.

"I thought I saw him on my way over here."

"Why would Steve be in North Arlington?"

"Why do I, all of a sudden, find myself implicated in a crime I didn't commit?"

After a moment of silence, Becky asked, "The envelope with the cash from the Westover post office box?"

Tommy groaned, before looking up at Becky's sparkling blue eyes. "It was me. A couple of nights ago I received an envelope from a Federal Express deliveryman. Inside was a key and note describing a box number in the Westover Post Office. Also on the note was message simply saying 'payment due to Thomas Luck.' While my instincts told me to avoid the post office box and toss out the key, I had already consumed half a bottle of Jameson Irish whiskey. You know me. I make great decisions while the sun is up but by six in the evening, about the time I get a snoot full, everything goes out the window."

Pausing for a moment remembering that night, Tommy continued, "A current need for cash, a little curiosity, and a lot of inebriation got the best of me. After walking down to the Westover shopping area, and a short delay at the local Seven-Eleven, for reasons that I can't remember, I found myself standing in front of the post office box. Inside the box, I found a single manila envelope. Inside the envelope was ten thousand dollars in crisp one hundred dollar notes. My drunken heart raced as I looked down at the cash. That ten thousand dollars represented another three months near my children in the expensive Arlington neighborhood where I've chosen to reside."

The next morning, with a clearer mind, Tommy had known he had made a mistake. While the money was a godsend in one respect, he knew that he should have listened to his instincts. Now, three days later, Tommy knew that he would pay for the mistake. He knew at some point that he would be called upon to earn the cash, in one way or another.

"The shell casing and newspaper with your fingerprints?"

"Not me. I haven't touched a weapon since Thailand. Although, I used a .38 revolver in Thailand at one point and I read the *Washington Post* daily."

"Why are several groups of people watching you?"

"No idea. Based on what you just told me, I imagine that at least one of the groups is the CIA or FBI waiting for me to make a move with the computer virus and/or further implicate myself in the murder of the CIA agent."

"Why did the two men search your house? Did they tell you why they were there?"

"They said they were looking for the money. I used most of it to pay the back rent and overdue electric bills for the house where I live. What little was left I've hidden in the attic. I didn't want the Internal Revenue Service questioning me about the extra income."

"And you don't have the computer virus?"

"It would seem that a lot of folks think I do and believe I'm trying to sell the damn thing. So many people and so much circumstantial evidence, in fact, that at this point no one would believe me if I denied the accusation. If everyone believes I have the virus, then it must be so."

"Do you have the computer virus?"

"What do you think?"

"Maybe…"

Tommy interrupted her. "My point exactly, you think I have it simply because what's happening around me."

"What will you do?"

"I'm not sure, but a losing proposition is to claim I don't have it."

"So you do have it?"

"I didn't say that," Tommy said, calmly refuting the

accusation. "I just said that at this point no one will believe me if I said otherwise."

"What are you going to do?" Becky asked again.

"I was watching a movie on television recently. I think it was called *The International,* and there were a couple of scenes with some great lines. One was 'when there's no way out, it's best to go in farther,' or something like that. Pretty fitting for my situation, don't you think? I just need to wait till a way out presents itself." Looking across the restaurant and through window at the traffic moving along Wilson Boulevard, Tommy then said, "Another great quote from the movie was 'the difference between fiction and the truth is that fiction has to make sense.'"

The waitress appeared at the table with the food they had ordered. After a twenty minute meal and conversation that focused on catching up with each other, Tommy and Becky arranged to meet in two days at a small restaurant in Westover. Walking out of the diner, they made their way to Becky's car in the parking lot. Standing next to her red Volvo S60 sedan, they turned toward one another, and, as Tommy leaned down to kiss Becky on the cheek, she turned and kissed him on the lips.

Tommy laughed. "Some things never change."

"You've never accepted my advances," Becky replied, as she gently drew her fingers along the thin scar running from the corner of his mouth to his jaw.

"You know the whole goose thing, right? Chase them, and they run. Run, and they chase you. I just never wanted you to run away."

"Eventually, the hen quits chasing," Becky said just loudly enough for him to hear.

"Eventually, the gander quits running."

Tommy kissed Becky again, her lips feeling warm and

soft. As she climbed into her Volvo, he closed the door and smiled down at her, feeling himself become aroused. She shook her head and smiled back at Tommy, as if she knew exactly what he was thinking.

Turning, he began walking toward his truck and noticed the beat-up black BMW parked four spaces down from his white pickup. The three thugs that he had seen before driving to Ballston were standing next to the car. Walking over to his pickup, Tommy ignored the three men and began pulling the keys from his pocket. The tallest of the three, wearing the shimmering silver-brown sports jacket, stepped forward. The tall man, slender with wavy black hair that shined as if it needed washing, had a long hawk like nose. His eyes, soft and kind looking, seemed too large for the width of his face. The two other men, standing several inches shorter than the tall hawked-nosed man, had wide shoulders and thick biceps and thighs. Dressed in white open collar shirts and dark suits with short military style haircuts, to Tommy, they could have been linesmen for a football team protecting their less bulky quarterback. The linesman to the left of the hawk-nosed man had short black hair, dark brown eyes, and a scar over his right eye. The linesman to the right had green eyes, blond hair, and a thick, misshapen jaw, as if it had been broken and not set correctly.

"Hello, gentlemen, what can I do for you?" Tommy asked, turning toward the tall hawked-nosed man who seemed to be in charge.

"Mr. Luck, my name is Ralf," the tall man said, greeting Tommy with an extended hand. "I work for a very powerful gentleman here in Washington, DC."

"Congratulations, Ralf. I'm happy for you. Now, what can I do for you?" Tommy repeated his question without taking Ralf's extended hand.

"Mr. Luck, my boss would like to meet with you."

Ralf's large soft brown eyes looked dejected as he withdrew his long spindly right hand and placed it into his pocket.

"Sure, let me give you my number, and he can call and make an appointment. Unfortunately, I have a pretty busy schedule."

"You don't understand. He wants to meet with you right now," Ralf responded, canting his head to one side and innocently grinning at Tommy.

Looking over toward Becky's car, Tommy saw the petite blue-eyed woman watching the encounter with the obvious thugs. He felt a measure of comfort. At least there would be a witness who could identify these clowns if he were injured or worse.

"Don't tell me, he wants to talk about a computer virus? You don't happen to have two friends, one who will likely be doubled over of the next couple of months and one who is probably still unconscious?"

"You're talking about the two men that you caught in your house yesterday?" Ralf softly laughed, his large brown eyes flashing with humor. "Those pigs? Lord, no. We're professionals."

"Professional what?" Tommy asked. "Professional thugs?"

Without saying a word, the two linesmen stepped up and ushered Tommy into the rear seat of the nearby black BMW. The two enormous figures squeezed in on each side of him, Scar to his left and Jaw to his right. The smell of stale cigarette smoke was overpowering in the tight interior of the small car, and Tommy could not help but think of his father.

Opening the driver's side door, Ralf pulled a cell from the outside pocket of his shimmering jacket and made a call. "Yeah, boss, we got him. Where'd you want us to meet you?" After few nods and a reply of, "Okay, boss, see you in about fifteen minutes," Ralf closed his cell and climbed into the driver's seat before lighting up a cigarette.

With Ralf at the wheel, a smoldering Marlboro Light cigarette dangling from the corner of his mouth, the BMW drove west along Wilson Boulevard, taking a right on the smaller Kirkwood Road. Ralf hadn't bothered to turn the air conditioning on and with the windows rolled up the BMW's interior quickly became hot, smoky, and humid. The smell of the burning cigarette had a suffocating effect, and Tommy had a flashback of riding over Loveland Pass with his father all those years ago. A vision flashed in his mind of smoke rising from a cigarette dangling between his father's lips and the heater blasting hot air into the cramped quarters of the Dodge Challenger as they wound their way to the top along the icy two-lane road. Trying to keep from coughing, Tommy squirmed between the two wide shouldered linesmen, looking out the rear window to see if Becky was trailing them. He didn't spot her red Volvo following.

Kirkwood Road led across Washington Boulevard and then though a residential district filled with ranch and colonial style homes, and tall leafy silver-barked trees before crossing Lee Highway onto Spout Run then under Interstate 66. As the BMW drove down the narrow ravine, the dense foliage and high trees along the steep slopes of Spout Run seemed to briefly cool the small car, and give some repose to the smoke, heat, and humidity trapped inside. Spout Run emptied onto the George Washington Memorial Parkway, and Tommy could see Georgetown across the glistening brown waters of the Potomac River as they approached Roosevelt Island.

"One of you guys smell like a gut wagon," Tommy commented, first looking at Scar then Jaw with a crinkled nose. "Ralf, can we please roll a window down back here?" Scar roughly smashed his elbow into Tommy's chest, silently telling him to be quiet.

The black BMW turned onto the entry ramp for Interstate 66, and they began crossing the Roosevelt Bridge with the tall white box-like Kennedy Center of Performing Arts looming in front of the car on the other side of the Potomac.

CHAPTER 10

Washington, DC, April 28, 2016:

Crossing the Roosevelt Bridge then turning onto the Rock Creek Parkway, Tommy squeezed between Scar and Jaw, once more found himself gliding along the edge of the Potomac, on the other side of the river. Passing under the Roosevelt Bridge, Ralf turned the BMW into the Kennedy Center for Performing Arts. Its expansive white cube-like structure and enormous tall windows facing the Potomac River's brown waters appeared daunting.

Ralf made an immediate left turn into the underground parking below the building, easily passing under thick yellow tubes warning drivers if their cars or trucks were too high for the low-ceilinged garage. Pulling up to a glass enclosed elevator bank, Scar and Jaw roughly pulled Tommy from the BMW.

"Come on guys," Tommy complained as they forcefully pushed him toward the elevator bank.

A security guard wearing black pants and an oversized white shirt, with matching oversized red patches on each shoulder advertising the company currently holding the Kennedy Center's security contract, watched as Scar and Jaw directed Tommy into one of the elevators. The guard seemed oblivious to the pushing and shoving, lazily leaning against a wall watching as if the scene were from his favorite television program.

The four men stepped into the elevator, and Ralf pressed the button for the roof top terrace with a single long gangly finger. The red-carpeted lift's brushed-brass doors swiftly shut, and Tommy could feel the elevator begin its slow climb to the top. Coming to a temporary halt in a foyer off the Hall of Nations, a tall and wide shouldered man with large bulging dull brown eyes dressed in a tailored suit stepped into the elevator. The dull-eyed man clutched a radio in his hand that emitted disjointed static.

With a gold front tooth and short black hair budding from his head, the man stood a good six inches taller than Tommy.

A voice squawked from the dull-eyed man's radio, "P-Two, base. Mr. Jenkins from the Secret Service wants access to that storage room."

"This is my house. Youse tell him this is my house. I don't care if he from the FBI, CIA, or KBD," the man shouted into the radio, sweat glistening from his forehead and his gold front tooth flashing a reflection from the overhead light.

Tommy immediately identified the dull-eyed man as one of the Kennedy Center's security managers. The suit, the radio, the gold tooth, and the loud, demanding shouts clinched it.

"KGB," Tommy said looking at the large dull-eyed man. "It's an acronym that stands for the Committee for State Security."

Scar and Jaws looked at each other, then at Ralf. Ralf shrugged his shoulders.

"Whose you?" the security manager barked at Tommy as an immediate flustered expression crossed his face.

"The correct way to say it is 'who are you,'" Tommy corrected. "My name is Thomas Luck."

"Mr. Luck, please," Ralf chirped in.

"Youse wants me to ban youse from the center? Youse wants that?" the security manager barked even louder at Tommy, his gold tooth blinking between his lips.

"You, not youse. 'You' should never be pluralized. 'Do you want me to ban you,'" Tommy corrected again in a calm tone and with a perfectly straight face. "And want should never be pluralized, either."

"Mr. Luck," Ralf said, stepping between the two men and turning to face Tommy.

Looking over Ralf's shoulder at the large dull-eyed man, Tommy continued, "Said correctly, it should be 'Do you want me to ban you from the center.'"

"That's it!" the security manager yelled, his loud voice echoing in the tight elevator. Placing the radio to his lips, the dull-eyed man bellowed to the unseen face at the other end, "I needs me two security officers to the roof terrace, ASAP."

"You're retired military and never made it too high in the rank structure, right?" Tommy said, still looking over Ralf's shoulder at the dull-eyed man. Sweat glistened from the face of the panting security manager. "I can see a failed military career self-consciousness a mile away, and, brother, you got it."

"Mr. Luck." Ralf's large brown eyes glared at Tommy, his hawk nose pointing down at him. "You need to stop this."

"Youse are outta here!" the security manager screamed as the elevator doors opened to the roof top terrace.

Hearing the man's loud voice booming as the doors opened on the roof top terrace, several elderly blue-haired ladies dressed in knee length floral dresses standing in the elevator foyer took a step back. Shifting to one side of the foyer, the old women began whispering to one and other, while scrutinizing the scene of five men standing in the elevator.

"Maybe an army staff sergeant, right? Didn't have the intellect to go any further, did you? You're probably a GS-fourteen in the civil service now. The military is good at weeding out poor performers. On the other hand, government service would rather promote than actually have to point out someone's failings and worry about follow-on courtroom reprisals."

As the Jaw and Scar began pushing Tommy from the elevator, the security manager yelled, "No ways. Get his ass back in this elevator!"

"You heard him, get me back in the elevator," Tommy told Ralf, who was clearly confused at what was happening.

"Where's my mens?" the security manager shrieked into the radio.

Turning and facing the angry security manager, Ralf said, "He's here at the invitation of Mr. Livingston."

The security manager seemed to take a step back at the news. Sweat was now flowing freely down the dull-eyed man's face, dampening his white collar. "When Mr. Livingston is finished with him, I wants him outta here," the man said in a low trembling voice.

"Want. I want him out of here. Like I told you before, you shouldn't pluralize want," Tommy called over his shoulder as he was forcibly pushed away from the elevator foyer by Scar and Jaw. A low whine erupted behind him, the dull-eyed man's frustration echoing in the elevator. Then looking over to Jaw on the left, his misshapen jaw clenched, Tommy said, "I'd bet a thousand bucks that guy was army and never made it past staff sergeant," while nodding his head.

"I was an army staff sergeant," Jaw replied in a low growl, narrow green eyes glaring back at Tommy.

"Considering that idiot is likely a GS-fourteen, and you're nothing but a common thug, I'd keep that to myself," Tommy calmly commented to Jaw.

Jaw and Scar roughly guided Tommy down the wide, high-ceilinged corridor over a plush red carpet and turned into the Roof Terrace Restaurant. Empty with the exception of an elderly couple at one table and a lone man at another, the restaurant had gold carpet and long matching curtains, with views of the Potomac River and Roosevelt Island. Small round tables with ivory white clothes draped over the top, red napkins, and short chrome chairs cushioned in more gold fabric attempted to give the room an elegant façade. In Tommy's mind, the restaurant seemed like a diner attempting to be a country club.

The thugs delivered Tommy to the far edge of the room, to a table situated between the two tall corner windows, where a thin man with neatly combed blonde hair, pasty skin, and light green eyes sat alone. A bottle of wine carefully tucked in a silver bucket of ice stood to the side of the table. The man, about Tommy's size, dressed in tailored tan pants and a brown sports coat with a red ascot, looked up with a thin smile and gestured to the chair across the table.

Catching up with Tommy and his escorts, Ralf blurted out, "He really pissed the deputy security supervisor off on the way up here, boss. He almost got himself kicked out." Ralf's shimmering silver jacket oddly fitted in with the room's decor.

"Enough, Ralf, go find a table and eat some lunch," the man's nasally voice whined. "Instruct the waitress to put your food on my bill."

"But, boss, the deputy security supervisor really wants to kick him out," Ralf continued, his large soft brown eyes pleading for the man to understand.

"I don't care about the deputy security supervisor. He is a dumb ox. He is nothing. He will do as I say. Now take these two gentlemen with you and move away," the pasty-skinned man demanded, his nasal tone hinting at frustration.

Ralf, followed by Scar and then Jaw, stepped away from the table, moving across the restaurant, taking a seat on the opposite side of the room. Ralf worriedly eyed Tommy and the whiny-voiced man from across the room.

"Please join me, Mr. Luck," the pasty-skinned man said, gesturing again to the seat across the table from him.

Sitting down, Tommy pulled the red napkin from atop the ivory white table cloth, folding it onto his lap. "It's about the virus, right?"

A wide-hipped middle-aged waitress with a bouffant seventies hairstyle, dressed in a gray skirt, a white blouse, and wide black leather shoes in need of shining, stepped up to the table, silently pulling the bottle from the ice bucket and filling Tommy's wine glass with its shimmering light yellow liquid. Tommy couldn't help but notice that her wedding band looked to be cutting off the circulation on her plump ring finger, making it slightly redder than the rest of her pallor. Taking a sip from his glass, Tommy tasted a dry, smooth wine like he had never experienced before. It was fabulous.

"My name is Jacob Livingston," the man whined an introduction, smiling at Tommy from across the table. "Please, let's eat first."

"Look, I'm all for a good meal, not that you could get one around here, but I just ate," Tommy said before taking a large swallow from the wine glass, the residual creating iridescent fingers on its glassy interior. Jacob cringed at the sight of Tommy gulping the wine.

Dapping the corner of his mouth with his red napkin, Jacob replied, “I am sorry to hear that. I had hoped we could enjoy a nice meal before discussing an offer.”

“Now, let’s get down to business so I can get the hell out of here,” Tommy responded curtly.

Jacob shooed away the large-hipped hostess looking to take lunch orders before saying, “Very well. You are in possession of something I desire and would be willing to pay for.”

“It’s about the computer virus,” Tommy calmly repeated, putting his red napkin back on the table top. “What’s it worth to you?”

“What is your current client willing to pay?”

“Five million.”

“Then let’s make it five and a half.”

“Let’s make it ten.”

Softly laughing, Jacob said, “Mr. Luck, let’s be reasonable. Your current client is offering five, and I am offering five and a half. I’m sure you don’t need a math lesson from me to show you that is a sizable increase.”

“Mr. Livingston, my math skills are somewhat limited. In addition to my academic failings, you had your thugs kidnap me from the Silver Diner parking lot. I find you a nasally twerp to whom I have taken an immediate dislike. It’s ten million, or it goes to my other client,” Tommy said, grinning at Jacob from across the table.

“Mr. Luck, I am a very rich and powerful man. You will take the five and a half I have offered, or I will make you regret the day you met me,” Jacob replied just as coolly, his nasal voice lowering an octave. “You will take five and a half, or I will obtain the virus from you for free.”

"I already regret knowing you and nothing is free, Jacob." Looking down at his glass while slowly twirling the wine around inside Tommy asked, "Have you ever heard the phrase 'pigs get fat, and hogs get slaughtered'?"

"No, I can't say that I have," Jacob replied, leaning back in his chair and adjusting his red ascot, waiting for Tommy to explain.

"It is a phrase that really makes no sense. You could say hogs get fat and pigs get slaughtered, and not change the meaning."

"Can you get to your point, Mr. Luck?"

"It's a pig's nature to eat as much as it can, and that same disposition drives them to become fat. That very nature made pigs an attractive meal for humans in terms of economic efficiencies. In fact, humans have eaten so much pork that we have acquired an insatiable appetite for the animals. The odds are that a pig will die under the hand of a butcher and be eaten by a human all because of their instinctive eating habits and the end result of growing fat."

"Is there an end to this drivel?"

Ignoring Jacob's comment, Tommy continued, "In that respect, humans aren't much different than pigs. Just like a pig's natural instinct is to eat and become fat, people have an instinctual need for more power and possessions. Now the drive behind the instinct varies slightly from person to person, but the common denominator is an incessant need for more. Just as the odds are that a pig will be eaten by a human simply due to its instinctive need to bloat itself, the odds are that a person's downfall will occur because they can't avoid the need to acquire more. This instinctual need to acquire more eventually results in people over extending themselves financially or politically or both. In other words, a pig is a hog, and that can't be changed, and people are people, and we can't avoid our shared weakness."

"Is your plan to bore me to the point that I don't want the computer virus?"

"So the pigs instinctively get fat, and humans instinctively overextend themselves one way or another. And those that are more skillful at acquiring power and possessions are at higher risk of being slaughtered first. Think of it this way, each week the farmer will pick the plump hogs from the pen for market and those, that have been successful at raiding the trough and have gotten fat before their peers, are the unlucky ones to be selected. And just as the pigs, the people who are skillful at the trough of power and possessions will become more fragile simply because they will risk more to acquire more. And like the pigs, the people that are more successful at the trough of power and possessions will likely get slaughtered before their peers.

"In the end what the phrase means is that whether you're a pig or a human, we all succumb to our instinctual needs. People and pigs are naturally self-destructive, and it's just a matter of time before we all get slaughtered."

"Is this why you've given up on making anything of yourself? Are you afraid of being enticed by the power money can buy? You didn't want to fall prey to your own instincts?"

Tommy laughed. "No, my instinctual needs are simple. I like to run, and I like to drink—sex is good, too. Not much interests me beyond that. And I'm pretty sure it'll be either my enjoyment of drinking or sex that will be the cause of my demise."

"What are you trying to tell me with your long-winded story?"

Taking another long drink of wine, Tommy emptied

his glass. Jacob's expression mimicked his earlier reaction.

"What I'm trying to tell you is that we all eventually get slaughtered because of our incessant need for more, but it's those people who recklessly and ferociously search out more power and possessions that get slaughtered first." Looking across the table at Jacob, Tommy added, "In other words, if you try to take the computer virus from me, I will make it my personal quest to slaughter you."

Silently glaring at Tommy, Jacob waved Ralf, Scar, and Jaw over to the table. The three men lumbered over, leaving newly delivered meals on white porcelain plates at their table across the room. Scar took a position on Tommy's left and Jaw to the right.

"Yeah, boss? What'd you need?" Ralf asked looking down at Jacob with submissive eyes.

"Call that idiot, the deputy security supervisor," Jacob whined, his nasal voice hitting a higher note from a clear loss of patience with Tommy. "Tell him there's a panhandler at my table that needs to be thrown out into the street."

Smiling across the table at Jacob, Tommy asked, "You wouldn't happen want to loan me some cash for the cab ride back to Ballston, would you? I'm flat-ass broke."

CHAPTER 11

Prince George's County, Maryland, April 28, 2016:

Traffic was light as the red Volvo sped north along the Baltimore-Washington Parkway, a low brown brick wall and tall old growth trees crowded the edge of the highway. Crossing over the Washington, DC, Interstate 495 beltway, Becky drove past a beat up green Toyota Civic while fumbling with her cell phone. Selecting a number from the phones contact list, she made a call.

A low, somber voice answered the call, "Becky, what do you have?"

"Hi, Sid, I finished up my meeting with Tommy about thirty minutes ago."

"What do you think? Does he have it?"

"Definitely. He admitted picking up the envelope with the cash but was illusive about whether he had the computer virus."

"Then why do you think he has it?"

"He wouldn't outright tell me so, but he said enough that I would stake my reputation on it."

"What exactly did he say?"

"He said he received a FedEx package with the key to the post office box and a note inside claiming someone owed him money. But he didn't know who or why. He then went to Westover and picked up the envelope. He also confessed he had been drunk and doesn't remember the entire night. When I asked him if he had the computer virus, he kept talking in riddles. At first, he denied having the computer virus but then he said if everyone believes he has, it then it must be so," Becky answered while swerving around an old light blue Ford F-150 pickup broken down on the side of the road. The brown bricks of the highway's retaining wall rippled by on her right and a yellow Nissan 280Z screamed by on the left. "He said that if there's no way out, then the trick was to go farther in."

Sid was silent for a moment before grumbling, "We should have wired you."

"We talked about that. We both decided that he's too clever and unpredictable. He might have found the wire and had he, it would have blown any chance of me getting close enough to find out who the client is or recovering the computer virus." Becky retorted, "You either trust my instincts or send me back to the NSA."

"You're not a trained field operative. We should have wired you," Sid repeated. "What about Danny's death. What'd he say about that?"

"He said he had nothing to do with his murder, and I believe him. Think about it, if he caught a CIA agent following him, he would know the gig was already up. The real threat is the CIA involvement, not a single CIA agent. Killing a CIA agent would only complicate his situation," Becky said firmly into her cell. "He's much too smart to make a mistake like that. That's not his style."

"We've both seen him take a life before with no remorse. He's strapped for cash—maybe it was a mistake. Maybe he confronted Danny, and things got out of hand. After all, he was drunk."

"Drunk or not, when have you ever seen him let things get out of hand?"

"He has made mistakes when he's drunk. Remember he killed Jainkul's son in Thailand by mistake when he was drunk—Maybe things got out of hand with Danny," Sid repeated. "If it wasn't Luck, then who killed Danny?"

"Maybe someone else was following Tommy. You surveillance team has told you that there is more than one person watching him."

After a moment of silence, Sid grunted, "Okay, let's say someone else was following Luck the night of Danny's death. Why would they kill Danny? How could Danny's death possibly aid in some unknown cause?"

"Acquiring the computer virus is the cause," Becky stated. "Maybe his client killed Danny to put pressure on Tommy for some unknown reason? Or maybe two forces are involved, and one will do anything to stop the transaction? There could be a number of reasons, but I do not believe it was Tommy who pulled the trigger."

"So we need to figure out how a CIA agent's death fits into the sale of a computer virus. As you said, it only complicates the situation for Luck."

"Maybe he planned on disappearing back to Thailand after selling the virus," Becky offered. "Maybe his client is trying to quicken the transaction and figured that the police investigating Tommy for murder would make him want to sell the virus and get out as quick as possible. Or maybe Danny saw the client following Tommy."

"If someone killed him because he saw the client, then that person would have to be concerned that either Danny recognized them or that he could figure out who they were," Sid commented.

"What do you want me to do next?" Becky asked while putting her foot down on the accelerator and surging past a silver Buick LaSabre driven by an old white-haired man. The white-haired man scowled at Becky as she flew past. "I'm supposed to meet with him again in two days."

"Meet with him. Get close. Like you said, we need to find out who the client is. We also need to find out where he's hidden the computer virus. I think it's time I question him about Danny's murder and search his house."

"In an official capacity?"

"In an official capacity."

"One more thing," Becky added, "Tommy says he saw Steve."

"Steve from the Thailand operation?" Sid groaned. "He's dead."

"He says he saw him."

"He's mistaken," Sid replied in a low growl.

"Did we ever get confirmation that he was dead?"

"The former inspector general arranged for his termination," Sid grumbled. "The Thai Royal Police confirmed his death."

"You're right, he was mistaken," Becky commented. "By the way, he got himself a dog."

"A dog?"

"A dog."

"He doesn't seem like the dog type to me," Sid grunted.

Winding through the low green hills north of Washington, DC, Becky disconnected the call and smiled at the passing scenery. She loved the rolling green hills of Maryland. It always brought a smile to her face. Glancing down at her cell again, Becky selected another contact and pressed the call button.

"Howard Macintyre, Inspector General," the NSA Inspector General answered.

"I met with him," Becky told the inspector general.

"Does he have the virus? Was he surprised at the charges?"

"Tommy Luck surprised? You don't know him well enough." Becky laughed. "I could have told him that he had just won fifty million dollars, and he wouldn't act surprised. And, yeah, he's got the virus. He wouldn't tell me directly, but he said enough."

"So what'd he say?"

"He admitted picking up the money from the post office box but initially claimed that he didn't have the computer virus. Then he said that no one will believe that he doesn't have the computer virus so he's going to play along like he has it until he can find a way out," Becky replied, slowing down for a construction project on the turnpike, two lanes merging to one. "But he has it. He was way too calm when I explained the criminal allegations against him."

The inspector general chuckled on the other end of the line, "Yeah, he's got it, all right."

"There's something else. As we left the diner he was picked up by three men," Becky continued.

"Did you follow them?"

"There was no need. One of the three men was Jacob Livingston's man, Ralf," Becky answered.

"Really?"

"Honest," Becky responded.

"Excellent, I'll put a request in for the transcripts of Jacob's cell conversations and locations during the last ninety-six hours. Did Tommy know anything about the death of the CIA man?"

"He claims he had nothing to do with the murder," Becky responded. "And I tend to believe him. He's way too smart for that. Killing a CIA agent would only complicate his situation and hinder a successful sale of the computer virus."

"Then who and why?"

"Maybe there's more than one person vying for the computer virus. Maybe someone is trying to put pressure on him to sell to them, or may be someone is trying to stop the transaction."

"I guess that's up to Sid to figure out who and why concerning the CIA agent's death," the inspector general commented. "It doesn't concern our interests."

"It might end up affecting our interests," Becky replied flatly.

"Maybe. We'll let this play out for a while and see who else shows up to the party. If it becomes a problem, then we'll deal with it. Well, great work, Becky. When do you meet with him again?"

"Two days," Becky replied. "And I almost forgot to tell you."

"What is it?"

"Tommy has got a dog."

"A dog?"

"A dog."

"That's the last thing I'd have expected from Tommy Luck."

CHAPTER 12

East Falls Church, Arlington, Virginia, April 29, 2016:

The morning light shone through the window, giving the normally subdue sage green walls an unusual brightness. Rolling on his side, Tommy examined Anna's golden face peeking out from under the white quilt. Anna had knocked on his door the night before, prior to him having a chance to get too drunk. It was a pleasurable evening, her presence limiting his intake of alcohol. After eating a small dinner in his still search strewn house, the two had retired to the bedroom where they had quickly stripped off their clothes and made love. Afterward, they had talked until the early hours of the morning.

Learning that Anna was the middle child of a family of five from Peru, a graduate from the Le Cordon Bleu Peru Culinary Institute in Lima and currently a graduate student at American University, he had been pleasantly surprised. They had ended their discussion with one more roll under the sheets before she fell asleep in his arms. It had been a wonderful night. But sadly, without his normal dose of intoxicating liquids, Tommy had not slept.

Anna's eyes cracked open, and she smiled at Tommy watching her. Reaching out, she caressed his cheek with one hand and cupped his neck with the other.

"You look *magnifico*, my love," Tommy teased her.

Anna giggled. "You are *magnifico*."

Hearing a knock at his door, Tommy turned his attention away from his beautiful companion, wondering who might be at the calling so early in the morning. "Excuse me, beautiful. Let's see who's at the door."

Climbing from the bed, he stepped over her black panties and bra on the floor and skipped across her blue dress. Slipping on the jeans that he had hastily dropped on the floor the night before, Tommy grabbed a faded red T-shirt from atop the mahogany dresser.

Tripping over the dog lying next to his bedroom door, he cursed. "How the hell did you get in here, again?"

"Who are you talking to?" Anna called from the bedroom.

"Some dumb mutt that keeps getting into the house. I know I closed this house up with the dog outside last night. I wasn't drunk. How in the hell did he get in here?"

"Maybe he let himself in." Tommy could hear Anna softly laugh from the bedroom.

"That wouldn't be surprising," Tommy muttered as he began to make his way to the front door.

Walking down the short hallway to the entryway, the blue-and-gray-eyed dog dutifully followed and took a seat behind Tommy as he cracked the door open. Peering out onto the house's front stoop, he saw Sid and two younger men, with a small group of men and women dressed in a mix of the familiar gray Arlington County Police Department uniforms and others wearing navy blue jackets emblazoned with a bright yellow *FBI* standing close behind. Sid's squat figure, dressed in khaki trousers and a light blue jacket, stood on the stoop looking at Tommy with his customary scowl.

Tommy couldn't help but chuckle at Sid's sharply

contrasting silver hair, dark eye brows, and a large red nose, giving the man a clown-like appearance.

"Hello, Sid. It's been a while," Tommy said, greeting his visitors, pulling the front door open just wide enough to fit his face, "May be not long enough, though."

"Luck, I am here in an official capacity. These gentlemen behind me are Lieutenant Dave Heywood with the Arlington County Police Homicide Department, and Agent Jason Scott is with the FBI," Sid replied, gesturing to two men standing next to him. Both men had matching scowls.

"A lot of different law enforcement agencies on my front lawn can't be good news."

Agent Scott, tall with dark hair and blue eyes, wore pressed blue jeans and camel brown jacket. Lieutenant Heywood, about Sid's height, was slightly pudgy with blond hair and brown eyes, and he wore dark gray slacks and a hunter green jacket. Both eyed Tommy with suspicion.

"The officers behind us are here to search your house," Sid continued, ignoring Tommy's comment.

"Don't tell me, it's about the CIA agent murdered four nights ago down the street? Or is about some computer virus that's been put on the market?"

"You seem to be well informed, Luck," Sid answered, looking down at several documents he was holding in his hand.

"You know me. I like to know what's going on."

"Wouldn't we all? It's about the murder of the CIA agent," Sid grunted, looking up at Tommy with his usual serious facial expression. "Someone killed a federal employee on US soil. That's why Agent Scott is here. Someone was murdered in Arlington Country. That's why Lieutenant Heywood is here."

"And the CIA?" Tommy looked from Sid to the other two men. "Why are you here?"

"I'm here because we believe there's a classified computer virus on the market."

"So it's about both the murder and computer virus."

"They seem to be linked. It's about both," Sid admitted, nodding.

"Come on in." Tommy stepped aside and pulled the door wide open. "I do have a guest in the backroom. Would you mind if I took a few minutes to explain to her what's going on?"

"We'll take care of that," Sid groaned as he stepped past Tommy. "Is that your dog?"

"Not my dog. I figured he worked for you. Another loyal CIA agent keeping track of a notorious international criminal."

Agent Scott and then Lieutenant Heywood silently walked past Tommy into the small house. As Lieutenant Heywood stepped across the threshold, he handed Tommy the search warrant. Four more police officers and two FBI agents followed them into the house. They all stood in the entryway looking around.

"Don't mind the mess. I haven't had time to clean up since the last search."

"Yes, I understand someone broke in and searched your home two days ago," Sid replied as he glanced around the living room still strewn with cushion fabric and magazines.

"I'm not sure it would qualify as a break-in. I never lock my door." Gesturing over to a small round wooden table in the equally small dining area just beyond the living room, Tommy said, "I imagine you have a few questions. We can sit over there if you like."

The three men made their way through the mess to the

round wooden table, their associates began searching the house, and Tommy stepped into the kitchen, pouring himself a glass of whiskey on the rocks. The dog stood at his side peering out into the dining area.

"Would you gentlemen like a drink?" Tommy called out to Sid and the two men.

When none of the men replied, Tommy shrugged his shoulders and walked out to join them carrying his drink in one hand and the bottle of whiskey in the other. Setting the whiskey bottle on the table's wooden surface, Tommy sat down across the table from three grave looking faces. The dog sitting down at his feet looked up and whimpered.

"Tommy, what is going on?" Anna asked as she was being ushered out of the bedroom by a female officer. Her clothes were slightly askew as if she dressed in hast.

"These guys think I'm guilty of some minor infraction of the law that occurred a couple of nights ago," Tommy called out to her slim retreating silhouette before taking a long swallow of whiskey.

"Murder is not a little crime," Lieutenant Heywood commented, just loud enough for Anna to hear.

"Murder?" Anna cried, as the female police officer gently pushed her out the front door.

"Thanks, Heywood," Tommy muttered, "I probably won't be hearing from her again." Leaning back in the wooden chair, its joints giving a faint groan from the change in pressure, and sipping at the Irish whiskey, Tommy said, "Fire away, Sid. I've nothing to hide."

"What do you know about the CIA agent's death?"

"That he was following a gentleman that fit my description and that my fingerprints were found at the scene," Tommy rattled off a summarized description of what Becky had told him the day before.

"You are indeed well informed," Sid said before asking, "And your involvement?"

"Nothing with the murder. I did pick up an envelope from the post office that night but had no idea I was being followed. Actually, I had several drinks before going to the post office and don't really recall the walk home."

"What was in the envelope?" Lieutenant Heywood asked.

"Money."

"For?" Agent Scott inquired, slightly agitated with Tommy's short answer.

"A job," Tommy replied, then adding, "I wasn't sure what job at the time. I'm assuming it has something to do with a computer virus, now."

"You picked up an envelope with ten thousand dollars inside from a post office box for an unknown job," Sid replied, pronouncing it in a way that Tommy couldn't tell whether it was a question or statement. Either way, Sid's voice carried with it the tone of skepticism.

"I guess we're both well informed. You know tampering with mail is a federal offense, don't you?"

"I had the authority," Sid somberly declared. "I can show you the documents if you like."

"No need for the paperwork and yes, I picked up an envelope with ten thousand dollars inside for a job. I wasn't sure whether it was a down payment for an upcoming job or an adjustment from my last job. I'm pretty strapped for cash right now," Tommy confessed, taking another swallow of whiskey. "But I'm sure you're aware of that, as well."

Tapping his index finger on the wooden table top, Agent Scott asked, "How did your fingerprints end up at the scene?"

"No idea. I haven't touched a weapon since I was in

Thailand late last year. I understand my prints were found on a thirty-eight shell casing."

"That's right, a thirty-eight," Sid replied, looking over at Agent Scott as if to see if his confirming Tommy's information had upset his younger colleague. Agent Scott seemed undisturbed with Sid's admission.

"I used a thirty-eight Smith and Wesson revolver for a time in Thailand. Maybe someone got a hold of one of those shell casings and placed it at the crime scene to throw you off?"

"So you're claiming that you've been framed?" Lieutenant Heywood said with the clear sound of disbelief in his voice. "That would imply that someone saved a shell casing from your Thailand exploits to frame you nearly a year later."

"I didn't have anything to do with the CIA agent's death, and my fingerprints were on a shell casing at the crime scene. What else could it be?"

"What about the fingerprints on the newspaper?" Lieutenant Heywood retorted. "The paper was published that day."

"I have no idea." Tommy shrugged his shoulders. "I have a faint memory of reading something at the Seven-Eleven that evening. Maybe it was that paper."

"What are the chances that the agent bought a paper that you had previously read?" Lieutenant Heywood sarcastically replied. "Maybe you don't remember killing the agent?"

"I've killed a few people in my time and remember each and every one of them," Tommy countered the chubby detective.

"Why was your house searched two days ago?" Agent Scott then queried.

"Someone is looking for something," Tommy replied with a bit of sarcasm of his own in his voice.

"What were they looking for?" Agent Scott snapped, clearly irritated with Tommy's answer.

"According to one of the gentlemen, they were looking for the money."

"Do you have the computer virus?" Sid calmly asked, changing the subject.

"Is it against the law?" Tommy queried as he poured himself another Irish whiskey.

"This computer virus is classified and the property of the United States government. In that case, yes," Sid grunted, "So let's try it again, do you have the computer virus?"

Tommy thought about how he should answer Sid's question before saying, "I probably have a few on my computer. Doesn't everyone? As for the computer virus your referring to, the answer is no."

"You're saying that you do not have a copy of the computer virus you delivered to Thailand last year?" Sid asked with frustration now building in his gruff voice, as well.

"I'm saying that I am not currently in possession of that computer virus, and you won't find it in this house," Tommy stated in an even and unemotional tone, knowing that his answer would lead them to believe that he had a copy elsewhere.

Sid, Agent Scott, and Lieutenant Heywood took turns questioning Tommy for the next two hours while the police officers and FBI agents searched his house. Refilling his glass of whiskey four times during the questioning, Tommy began to feel a comfortable numbness build on his brow.

"Sir, we've finished up," one of the FBI agents stepped up to the table, interrupting the interrogation. The other agents and deputies, stood near the entryway with five cardboard boxes filled with Tommy's belongings on the floor next to them.

"Very well," Agent Scott responded. "Wait for us outside. We'll be out in a few minutes."

"What shall I do with this?" the FBI agent asked, placing a stack of twenty crisp one hundred dollar bills packed into a clear plastic bag on the table.

"That's my pocket money," Tommy exclaimed, concerned they would take the money. "I need that."

"Did this money come from the envelope?" Agent Scott asked.

"Yes, but I need it to eat," Tommy replied, hoping they didn't sense his alarm.

Turning to the FBI Agent, Agent Scott said, "We'll take it with us."

Repeating his plea, Tommy said, "I need it to eat."

"It is evidence in a murder investigation," Agent Scott replied.

"Great, you gentlemen nearly finished? I need to go for my morning run soon."

The sound of shuffling cardboard resonated from the foyer as the deputies began picking up the boxes and moved outside. Agent Scott pushed his chair back from the table, signifying he was finished. Sid sat across the table from Tommy, peering at him with a quizzical look on his face.

"You realize that with the shell casing alone, we've got you for murder," Lieutenant Heywood threatened. "Based on the evidence we have right now, you're on your way to the local lockup while we process what's in those boxes. With the shell casing, the newspaper, and fingerprints, we'll easily get a conviction."

"Look, let's drop the drama for a moment," Tommy said flatly, "You think I capped this CIA man a couple of nights ago. Your evidence is fairly straightforward, I was in the vicinity, and he was threatening an important financial deal for me, and you've got my fingerprints on both a shell casing and newspaper left at the scene. You think I made a mistake and accidently left a shell casing at the scene. I also took the time to read the paper to ensure my fingerprints were on a Washington Post left at the scene, as well."

"That's about it," Lieutenant Heywood replied, nodding his plump head.

"How many rounds were fired at the scene?" Tommy asked.

"Just one," Sid mumbled, his facial expression showing that he knew what Tommy's point was about to be.

"Was it a rimmed cartridge?"

"Yes," Sid grumbled. "It was rimmed."

"Tell me why I would take the time to open the cylinder and pluck a single shell casing from a revolver I had just used to kill a CIA agent, leaving it at the scene of the crime?"

"Criminals make dumb mistakes," Lieutenant Heywood answered, with a hint of superiority in his voice. "Especially drunken ones."

"So can cops, and they don't even need to be drunk," Tommy shot back before saying, "The four of us know you won't be taking me in or charging me—not yet, anyway."

Sid and agent Scott sat silently as Lieutenant Heywood stated, "I wouldn't be too sure of that Mr. Luck." Pulling a pair of handcuffs from his belt, the detective laid them on the table.

"Let me rephrase my comment. Sid won't let you take me in or charge me for two reasons. First and foremost, there's still the question of the computer virus and an alleged client. With me behind bars, the trail runs cold, and the CIA man's death is for not. On the other hand, with me running loose there's still a trail to follow. Secondly, he knows I'm not dumb enough to leave that shell casing from a revolver at the scene."

Picking up the handcuffs, Lieutenant Heywood began standing up.

"Drama aside, Luck's right," Sid interrupted. while pushing his chair back from the table, Agent Scott nodding in approval.

"What are you talking about? This man killed someone," Lieutenant Heywood howled while his pudgy face took on a pinkish tinge and stunned expression.

"Sid," Tommy said, looking up at the CIA.

"What is it, Luck?"

"Just for the record, I told the truth about the money, and I had nothing to do with your man's death. You watched me in Thailand and, hopefully, you know that's not my style."

Standing next to the table, looking down at Tommy, Sid said flatly, "As I recall, you killed several people in Thailand and, from what I can remember, it never seemed to bother you. I also recall an incident twenty years ago when a young construction manager stepped into the middle of a store robbery. Two guns and perps dead. Somehow the scene didn't seem right."

Tommy nodded his head. "That was you, the young police officer with the dark bushy eyebrows."

"That was me," Sid acknowledged.

"You stepped out of your way that day to help me."

"Have a nice day, Luck," Sid grumbled. "We will be watching."

After Sid, the FBI agents, and Arlington County Police departed the house, Tommy put his running clothes on and headed out for a long jog. The dog followed him out the door and took up a position on his left side.

CHAPTER 13

San Diego, California, July 12, 1995:

It was a sunny day as Sid walked along the cracked sidewalk just north of downtown San Diego. He felt the sun on his back and the smell the briny waters of the Pacific filled the air. Dressed in his navy blue San Diego Police Department uniform, Sid had left his patrol car several blocks from the waterfront in order to get some fresh air. Striding along Ash Street, Sid thoughts were consumed with a recent interview he'd had for a position with the Central Intelligence Agency, a lifelong personal dream.

In a small local hotel room, while hooked up to a lie detector, Sid had answered each of the interviewers' questions with confidence. One of his finer qualities, Sid knew, was his habit of never telling a half truth or lie. Nor had he ever strayed from what was right to what was wrong. He told those he lived and worked with the untarnished truth, knowing those who did not, inevitably found themselves in a preverbal corner.

Suddenly a woman ran up to him, panting heavily. "Up there!" The woman was clearly panicked as she frantically gestured up the street. "Up there!"

"Calm down," Sid replied in his low baritone voice. Reaching out, he placed a reassuring hand on the woman's shoulder. "What is happening up there?"

"A robbery," the woman squealed. "At the Seven-Eleven—two men!"

Reaching for his radio, Sid asked, "Are they armed?"

"Yes! Yes!" Tears began to fall from the woman's eyes. "They've hurt the clerk!"

"What are they armed with?"

"Guns! Both of them had guns!"

"I want to you stay here around the corner," Sid replied, gesturing to the side of the building they were standing next to. "I or another patrolman be back to question you. Please don't leave. We'll need a statement from you."

Turning, Sid began jogging up the street while relaying the information the woman had told him to the dispatcher monitoring the radio. Seeing the Seven-Eleven less than a block ahead, Sid crossed the street and moved up to the edge of the convenience store, peeking around the corner through the window and into the store. From his oblique vantage point, he could make out a revolver sitting next to the cash register and the silhouette of someone kneeling next to the counter. He knew he should wait for backup, but the woman had said the perpetrators had injured the clerk. He wasn't going to wait. The clerk's wellbeing might depend on his quick action. Pulling his weapon from the holster, Sid quickly moved to the doors and took a deep breath.

"San Diego Police," Sid shouted as he stepped into the convenience store. Pointing his revolver at a young man kneeling over the clerk, Sid saw the body of a man in a black silk jacket lying nearby with a broken jar of pickles at his side. There was also a man wearing a dirty white T-shirt with several gunshot wounds to the face lying next to the young man and clerk. "Put your hands where I can see them."

The young man, with wavy brown hair, slowly stood up and raised his hands. With clear blue eyes, the young man seemed calm as he turned to face Sid. The young man had a crooked smile on his face and a sparkle in his eye that relaxed Sid. The young man came across to Sid as completely harmless.

"Hey, officer, I work down at the construction site on Harbor Drive," the young man began explaining. "I walked in to find these two guys beating the clerk."

Slowly walking down the aisle with his weapon still pointed at the young man, Sid stopped next to the man lying next to the broken pickle jar. In a low, solemn voice, he asked the young man, "What's your name?"

"Tommy."

"Tommy, there are two dead men on the floor who have obviously been shot, and I count only two weapons. How is it you managed to subdue two men?"

Gesturing to the broken jar of pickles, Tommy said, "I threw the pickle jar at the older guy and knocked him out."

Lowering his weapon, Sid replied, "That doesn't explain the three holes in his chest."

"I used his weapon on the younger guy and then shot him when he tried to get up."

"You shot an unarmed man trying to get up?"

"Well." Tommy scratched his head. "Unarmed would be a subjective description."

CHAPTER 14

Langley, Virginia, April 29, 2016:

Watching a steady flow of agents walking to and fro the different buildings within the CIA complex, Sid was sitting in his office looking out the room's long and narrow vertical window, thinking about that day in San Diego when he found a young man standing over the bodies of two criminals in the Seven-Eleven. He could still remember the young man telling him his name, "Tommy." Since meeting him in Bangkok last year, Sid had often wondered if he and Tommy Luck had not crossed paths in that San Diego Seven-Eleven years ago. While there was a resemblance, there was also a twenty year gap.

Something else had occurred that day that had been unusual. Sid had modified the crime scene to protect the young blue-eyed man with the crooked grin. Completely out of character for Sid, a straightforward and bluntly honest man, he had never some much as bent a regulation. But looking at the crime scene, all those years ago, he had known that the long arm of the law would have undoubtedly put the young man in prison for his actions. Sid had never regretted his actions that day, and in some ways, it had taught him a life lesson: laws and regulations have no friends or relatives. In other words, a law or regulation is written to restrain bad behavior, but it would be impossible to articulate each and every detail of what the scribers had intended into the same. While killing the unarmed robber had clearly been a violation of the law, the young man named Tommy had unquestionably saved the clerk's life.

Once backup had arrived, Sid's duties had quickly diminished to that of a witness, and he had never learned the last name of the young man. While he had often thought of obtaining the crime investigation report from the San Diego Police Department, he knew the chances of it having been Tommy Luck were minuscule at best. How could the bright-eyed young man with the crooked smile he met in the convenience store all those years ago have turned into an unemployed drunk?

Sid's office was on the fourth floor of the main building, and, while it wasn't large, it did provide a nice view of the Central Intelligence Agency's main courtyard. A glass partition and door separated his work space from the larger cubical filled Special Operations Department. Its white walls were decorated with the awards that he had earned over the years, as well as several family photos of his wife and three children at various stages, the last showing his squat figure surrounded by three tall and fit adults, his grown children. His gray metal desk, with a white laminate top, had an ivory colored computer monitor and keyboard to one side and a black multi-line landline phone to the other.

A calendar desk mat sat beneath one of his elbows with dog eared edges and various colored scribbling marking nearly every date box. On one corner of the desk sat a thick red and white stripped folder with the words 'Top Secret' emblazoned on the top. A smaller white sticker affixed to the front of the closed folder identified the file as 'Operation Black Fly' in black print.

The adjustable office chair on which Sid sat was anything but comfortable, its black fabric cushion frayed and worn, provided little protection from the chair's hard metal seat. Restful and relaxing would make a good descriptive antonym to the feel of his office, but Sid didn't mind. He rarely found himself in that disposition.

Turning his thoughts to his conversation with Tommy, the unemployed drunk, earlier in the day, Sid pondered Tommy's complicity in the death of his agent, Danny, and the computer virus. Sid aimlessly turned his attention to two equally uncomfortable looking chairs covered in green burlap like fabric sitting across the desk from him. As he sat gazing on the worn chairs, wondering how he could coax Tommy into telling him the truth about the computer virus and the death of his CIA agent, something kept nagging at him. What if everything Tommy had said during the interrogation at his house had been true? What if someone was trying to frame the unemployed drunk?

Sid looked up at the white acoustical ceiling tiles of his office and decided to try another approach. What if he created a spectrum of solutions? A scenario which Thomas Luck telling the truth formed one end of a spectrum and the unemployed drunk as a killer trying to sell a classified computer virus defining the other end. The answer must fall between those two boundaries.

Thumbing through the red stripped folder, Sid found the page that outlined who had had possession of the flash drive that contained the computer virus during the Thailand delivery a year prior. Standing, Sid lumbered over to a large whiteboard fixed to one of the room's walls.

He picked up a red marker and drew a horizontal line across the top of white-board, marking one end "Truth," the other "Lie." Sid knew that whoever was responsible for the murder and whoever was selling the computer virus must have had access to the flash drive. Using a blue marker, with the exception of Tommy's name, Sid vertically scribbled the names of those individuals under the "Truth' end of the horizontal line who had possession of the flash drive at some point. He then wrote Tommy's name under the "Lie" end of the spectrum. Taking a step back, Sid peered at the names and scratched his ruddy chin. If someone other than Thomas Luck killed Danny and if someone other than Thomas Luck was trying to sell the computer virus, the list of suspects under the "Truth" end of the spectrum would be small. Taking a step back up to the "Truth" side of the horizontal line, he began to wipe the names of the dead off the list. When he was finished, there was a list of five names: the NSA software specialist who had developed the virus, the Thai computer hacker, Becky, the inspector general, and the final Chinese recipient.

Rubbing his red bulbous nose, he then considered the requirement of knowledge concerning the Thailand operation. The use of John Smith's name on the post office box, the *Washington Post,* and *Economist Journal* indicated that whoever was behind the sale of the computer virus and Danny's murder had knowledge of what occurred during the Thailand operation the year before. Sid knew very little of the Thai computer hacker, except that he resided in Isaan, or Northeast Thailand, in the small city of Kalasin, and his knowledge of what occurred during the operation was limited to that short period. Sid wiped the Thai computer hacker from the names under the Truth side and rewrote his name closer to the center. Using the same logic, he then wiped the NSA software specialist and the Chinese recipient from the list, repeating his action of rewriting their names closer to the center, under the Thai computer hacker's name. When finished he had two names on the "Truth" side, one on the "Lie" side, and three between the two ends of the spectrum.

Taking a step back from the whiteboard, Sid pondered the list of names at each end of the horizontal line—the NSA Inspector General and Becky under the "Truth" side and Tommy on the "Lie" side. The Inspector General, Becky, and Tommy had possession of the virus and detailed knowledge of what occurred during the operation in Thailand. These three individuals were his prime suspects behind the murder of Danny and sale of the computer virus.

Sid ran his short, thick fingers through his silver hair and examined the names under the truth side. He had a difficult time believing that either Becky or the inspector general was the culprit behind the events unfolding around the sale of the computer virus and Danny's death. What kind of motive would they have? Both seemed to be devoted National Security Agency employees on a fast track to a successful career.

Who could he be leaving off the list? The only other individual that could be orchestrating the events was Luck. It had to be the unemployed drunk who was looking to earn a large payoff. No one else had possession of the virus, the knowledge of the operation, or the motive, but Sid still had lingering doubts.

But then he had another thought. What if the requirements to be a suspect were not mutually exclusive? What if the knowledge of Thailand came from another source? What about two individuals, each holding one of the requirements: knowledge of Thailand and access to the computer virus? Digging through the red and white top secret file, he pulled two sheets of paper from the folder. The first sheet contained the list of individuals who had participated in the operation, the second contained a list of those briefed on the operation during or directly after the operation. Extracting the list of individuals who had detailed knowledge of the Thailand operation but had never had custody of the computer virus, he wrote those names on the whiteboard.

Like his list of those who had had custody of the computer virus, he then wiped the dead off the list. Pausing a moment, reflecting on the list of names he had just written, Sid picked up the red marker and wrote John Smith and Steve's name just below the horizontal line, between those with knowledge of the Thailand operation and those who had custody of the computer virus but no knowledge of the operation.

"If it's not Luck, the culprit could not have set up a better person. He has the knowledge of the Thailand operation, he had access to the computer virus, and he clearly has the most to gain," Sid whispered to himself as he walked back to his desk, sitting down.

It suddenly dawned on him that someone could have reviewed the classified operational report currently sitting on his desk. He had written the report directly after the operation, and it had spelled out in detail what had occurred in Thailand. He had no idea how many CIA and NSA agents had reviewed the report prior to it being stored away in the classified vault at the CIA headquarters. In a moment of frustration, he stood up and walked back the whiteboard, scribbling a large question mark across the horizontal line and names.

He knew that he was still missing something or someone. His thoughts were interrupted by a buzzing sound coming from the black phone on his desk. Turning toward his desk, he picked up the receiver, its short curly cord pulling taut as he held it up to his ear.

"Sid, Special Investigations," he answered the phone with a grunt.

"Hello, Sid, it's Howard Macintyre from the NSA. I have some interesting information for you."

"What is it?"

"We've been keeping an eye on a gentleman named Jacob Livingston for over year. He is an individual who allegedly deals in stolen corporate databases. We've been after him for quite some time but have not had much luck accumulating enough evidence against him to pass it off to the FBI."

"Go ahead," Sid muttered, as he moved around his desk and sat down.

"Well, I just received an update on his activities. Apparently, he met with our mutual friend Tommy Luck yesterday."

"What'd you mean?" Sid asked, leaning forward and reaching for an unopened pack of cigarettes sitting at the far edge of his desk.

"We've had a phone tap on Jacob for quite some time. I periodically request information on the tap, the numbers he calls and receives, and transcripts of the conversations. I did so today. Three days ago Jacob contacted an employee of his and instructed him to keep a watch on Tommy Luck. He made a second call to another employee asking him to check into a duel agency operation last year. He wanted to know if Tommy Luck participated in a July timeframe CIA/NSA operation in Thailand last year. Two days ago that employee called back indicating that there was an operation in Thailand during that time but he could not confirm Tommy Luck's participation."

"He couldn't get that information unless he contacted the director for authorization to access the file," Sid grumbled, looking at the file sitting on his desk. "That file is top secret."

"That's right. Apparently, Jacob Livingston's employee has a contact within the CIA, and that contact could only tell him that a highly classified CIA/NSA operation did occur in Thailand. That same employee was able to confirm that Tommy Luck was in Thailand at the same time as the operation by checking with the airlines. Well, anyway, Jacob Livingston met Tommy Luck yesterday."

"The meeting at the JFK Center," Sid mumbled.

"That's right. How did you know?"

"My men followed him there," Sid added. "They couldn't listen in for fear of giving themselves away. But they did see Luck meet with a gentleman at a restaurant on the top floor, before being escorted out of the building by security. Do you have any information on what was said at their meeting?"

"No, just the transcript of the phone call where Jacob Livingston instructed his employee to pick up Tommy Luck. The next day there was another phone call from his employee to Jacob Livingston indicating that he had picked Tommy Luck up and needed to know where to take him. Jacob Livingston directed his employee to bring Tommy Luck to the Kennedy Center."

"We've been trying to identify the man Luck met with," Sid remarked, now leaning back in his chair, pulling the black multi-line phone closer to the edge of the desk by the tautly stretched cord. "That helps. Do you think Livingston is Luck's client?"

"No. I think Jacob Livingston is just now entering the game. I do think he will try to obtain the computer virus, though. Knowing Jacob Livingston, I believe it's a toss-up whether he will attempt to obtain the virus via financial incentive or physical force. He lacks a strong moral base."

"Send me what you have on Livingston," Sid groaned into the phone.

"I'm preparing to hit the send button as we speak."

Looking back out his window at the activity on the CIA courtyard, Sid hesitatingly asked, "What's the inspector general doing watching a suspected criminal outside the NSA? Your job is to investigate crimes within your agency."

"Things have been slow in the internal investigations department since the Thailand fiasco. The NSA Director asked for my help with Jacob Livingston."

Hanging up the phone, Sid looked up at his whiteboard and mumbled, "There's got to be a team working together. I just need to figure out who's on that team."

Walking back over to the whiteboard one last time, Sid circled the Thai computer hacker's name. What if the computer hacker had made an additional copy? What if the Thailand connection was still in play? He then wrote the name "Lawan" under the "Truth" end of the spectrum.

Stepping over the glass office door, Sid pulled it open and called out, "Devin, get in here."

A man, standing just under six feet tall with short blond hair, jumped from behind one of the cubicles and briskly walked over, stepping into Sid's office.

Sitting back down in his office chair, Sid grunted, "Pack your bags. You're going on a trip."

"Sir?" Devin responded somewhat dumbfounded.

"You're going to Thailand."

"Thailand?"

"Yes Thailand," Sid grunted again.

"What am I doing in Thailand?"

"I want to know the whereabouts and activity of two people," Sid replied while writing on a piece of paper.

"Who are the two people?"

"A Thai computer hacker and a girl named Lawan. They both live in or near the city of Kalasin in Northeast Thailand."

"Who are they?" Devin asked again.

"Luck's former girlfriend and the man who first opened the computer virus during its delivery in Thailand."

CHAPTER 15

East Falls Church, Arlington, Virginia, April 29, 2016:

Sitting at an outdoor table, Anna was drinking a glass of Chardonnay wine while listening to soft music being piped into the small outdoor garden of a Westover deli. A shadow was cast over the entire area from the branches of a wide river elm sprouting from the center of the courtyard, and a short white picket fence separated it from the sidewalk and street. With her arms stretched across the table, its metal top feeling cool and refreshing to her skin, Anna was reading the *Washington Post Entertainment Section* while waiting for a meeting with her current employer. Stepping into the courtyard behind Anna, a white-haired man with gray eyes wearing a tailored black suit silently gestured the waiter for two glasses of wine before moving to the table and sitting down next to her.

"Hello, Anna," the white-haired man greeted the Peruvian beauty with a distinct French accent. "You look splendid today."

Startled at his sudden appearance, she jumped in the chair before replying, "Archibald, you surprised me," her Peruvian accent becoming more pronounced.

Anna had met with the white-haired man on one other occasion and quickly surmised during that first encounter, based on the texture of his skin, that Archibald's hair had prematurely whitened. The man next to her could not have been more than forty years old, but, from a distance, his white hair made him look sixty. Reaching out across the table, Archibald took Anna's hand into his and smiled. His cold, clammy touch sent a tremor down her back. She wasn't sure why the white-haired and gray-eyed man scared her, but he did. There was something sinister about Archibald, and it unnerved her to be with him. To have him touch her was terrifying.

The waiter delivered two fresh glasses of wine with fine sheens of condensation on their sides, and Archibald released Anna's hand. Picking up one of the glasses, a small portion of the yellowish liquid sloshed over the rim, splashing onto his hand. Raising the wine glass above his head into a small band of light that had managed to penetrate the overhead river elm's thick branches, he turned it in the sunlight, before lowering it to his nose. After a long inhale of its aroma, the white haired man took a sip.

His face contorting into a grimace, Archibald said, "These Americans, they know nothing of good wine."

"I think it very nice," Anna responded, quickly regretting her retort and dropping her head in submissiveness.

Ignoring her defiance, Archibald asked, "Does he have it?"

"I think he does. Someone rummaged around his home two days ago," Anna replied, her anxiousness easily heard in her heavy accent. "His place is still a mess. And today, while I was there, the FBI and police department showed up and began searching his house, saying he is a suspect in a death or murder."

"I know of the searches by both the two men and the police, and of the police's suspicions. The police are not our concern. The search by the two men was an interesting addition, though," Archibald replied in a contemplative manner. "What else?"

"He has many people watching him," she answered, her voice trembling slightly, before taking a sip of her wine to calm her nerves.

"So we're not the only ones who believe he has it," the white-haired man stated matter-of-factly, raising the glass of wine to his nose and sniffing again. "Who else beside the police?"

"I counted at least two different groups, the police being one. His house has many microphones. I was able to find three while he was using the bathroom last night."

After taking another sip of wine, Archibald repeated his question, "Do you know who besides the police?"

"No, but I know there is at least one more group—maybe two. And there are two cars along the street that seem suspicious."

"Where did you learn to search for microphones?" Archibald softly laughed.

"I spent time in Venezuela working for the Peruvian government," she responded, slowly beginning to feel more comfortable around the white-haired man. "It was on my resume."

"Obviously an oversight that I missed such important talent. When will you ask Mr. Luck?"

"I think I will wait a day or two. If I approach him too soon, the police will wonder why I have not been frightened away. Maybe I will arrange a meeting someplace public. The police will think I didn't want to meet him in private. They'll think I'm afraid to be alone with a suspected murderer. I don't want them to think of me as anything but an ex-girlfriend."

"Once again, do not worry about the police. It is the others attempting to buy the computer virus that we need to mislead."

"By the way," Anna commented. "He now has a perro."

"Mr. Luck has a dog?"

"Yes."

"And your point would be?"

"Perros always complicate matters."

CHAPTER 16

Boulder, Colorado, September 6, 1988:

His long wavy brown hair was tousled about by wind pouring over the windscreen as sixteen-year-old Tommy Luck drove the racing green Triumph TR-3 down the road, dust and gravel pluming behind the speeding convertible. With its rolling teardrop fenders, wide round headlights, and spinning silver spoke wheels, Tommy pressed further down on the thin chrome plated accelerator and the car shot down the long straight dirt road.

Under a cloudless blue sky, the small sports car topped a low crest, and Tommy felt himself rise out of his seat. The sensation thrilled him. Looking through the sportscar's narrow windscreen, he could see his destination in the distance, a stand of tall trees next to a slow moving greenish river. Depressing the clutch, while manipulating its short chrome stick shift at his side, he felt the Triumph's engine shudder slightly before howling a bit louder, and the car began to slow. Tommy gave another push on the clutch and shift of the gears. The dust and gravel plume began to abate.

Pulling up between a polished brown Jeep Gladiator and a dirty mellow yellow AMC Gremlin with a black racing stripe, the Triumph idled with a low rumble. The nearby river's cool waters and overhead tree's shade delivered a refreshing chill to the otherwise hot day. Sitting in the idling sports car, Tommy scanned a group of approximately twenty teens standing under the trees listening to music blaring from a portable boom box and, talking, and laughing. Turning the Triumph's ignition off—the sports car sputtering several times before chugging to a stop—

Tommy pushed open its small door, stepping onto the grassy turf.

As he approached the crowd of teenage men and women, Tommy called out to his friend Kevin with a wave and smile. Kevin, with freckles and long shaggy white-blond hair, held a thin black hose attached to a beer keg in one hand and returned Tommy's gesture by raising a red plastic cup with his other, beckoning him into the boisterous crowd.

"Where you been, Tommy?" Kevin asked, handing him a red plastic cup of his own, with beer sloshing over the top edge.

"Had to finish some chores around the house." Tommy took a long drink of the cool beer, its froth running from the corners of his mouth.

From behind, a large young man bumped Tommy with his shoulder, knocking the frothy top of beer over the edge of his freshly filled cup onto the ground. Immediately knowing the collision had been intentional, Tommy took a step away. He and the young man had been having a silent dispute over a girl, both competing for her attention at school. His competitor was a member of the varsity football team, tall and bulky. Tommy was a member of the baseball team, lean and trim, without an ounce of fat on his body. Knowing he was at a disadvantage in a physical confrontation, Tommy ignored the larger teenager, hoping he would turn his attention elsewhere.

Another intentional collision, with the same beer spilling effect, and Tommy took another step away from the larger teenager. Kevin looked at Tommy with wide eyes, silently telling him he knew what was going on. Normally having a calm demeanor, Tommy began to feel an unusual anger begin to grow, but inwardly knew that his best course of action would be to simply walk away.

"I think I'm going head down to the river." Tommy smiled at his friend. Glancing to his right, he saw the young girl that had been the source of the conflict looking back at him with a smile on her face. Tommy winked and nodded his chin in the direction of the river. Looking over his shoulder, he saw that larger teenager had seen the silent exchange.

As Tommy began to move from the crowd, the bigger teenager reached out and grabbed his arm, spinning him so they were facing each other. The football player's shoulders eclipsed Tommy's and, with wide arms and thick thighs, he stood a good five inches taller.

"You're a queer, and your father's a drunk," the larger teenager bellowed, spit spewing from his lips and spraying Tommy's face.

It wasn't an audible crack inside Tommy's mind, but a crack nonetheless. Adrenaline surged through his body, and his heart rate increased, sweat immediately breaking out across his forehead. Tommy dropped the red plastic cup, sending a spout-like stream of beer skyward as it struck the ground next to his right foot. Taking a step forward, Tommy threw a tightly closed right fist, reaching up and smashing the big teenager in the nose with a cartilage-snapping and blood-erupting effect. The bigger teenager stumbled back several paces, but Tommy didn't stop. Leaping at the retreating teen, Tommy began to pummeling his face with more blows. The bigger teenager fell backward, dragging them both to the ground. Hitting the grassy turf atop the football player, Tommy could hear the wind knocked from the bigger teenager. Grabbing a fallen branch lying next to them on the ground, Tommy went to work with the makeshift wooden mallet, smashing the sides of the football player's head as if he was sweeping a floor.

Hands began grabbing Tommy, pulling him back. Someone struck him on the side of the head with a fist. Someone pulled the branch from his hand. Tommy squirmed free and re-attacked the now motionless and bloodied football player lying on his back in the grass. More hands pulled him away, again. The hands threw Tommy on his back, and a group of his peers surrounded him. Looking up at the crowd that had formed around him, Tommy's rage began to abate.

Lying on the ground, Tommy looked up at astonished faces peering down. Among the faces were his friend Kevin, sweat rolling down his temples and panting, and the young blonde girl who had been the cause of their conflict, tears streaming down her reddened cheeks. Tommy looked at his bloodied hands, the flesh on his knuckles broken and blistered. Looking over to the larger immobile teenager, he saw two fellow football players trying to revive the unconscious teenager.

Standing on his back porch later that evening, Tommy examined the Flatirons rising from the suburban foothills. White clouds shimmered with gold and yellow bands as the sun began to descend below the tops of the peaks. Still visualizing all the astonished faces looking down at him as he lay on the ground, Tommy pondered the afternoon's events. They had not been faces smiling with surprise at the smaller aggressor's victory, but rather ones of terror. They had been faces wondering who the person they had known as a happy and quiet friend had gone. They were looking at a person who had lost all control and became recklessly violent.

Hearing the long wooden planks of the deck groan as someone stepped up next to him, Tommy looked over at his father's smiling face. Holding a glass of bourbon, his father gently patted Tommy on the shoulder as a cool breeze blew down from the Flatirons, carrying the aroma of pine needles.

"I could have killed that guy today, Dad," Tommy admitted, feeling a faint bit of rage still brewing inside. "And the funny thing about it is that I'd do it again. That guy needed to have his ass kicked."

"Have you ever heard of a man named Edward Whymper?" his father asked.

"No."

"Edward Whymper was a nineteenth century mountain climber who tried eight times to ascend the southern face of Matterhorn, failing at each attempt. He finally succeeded with a party of seven, being the first to do so, but on their descent the most inexperienced climber in the team fell, dragging three others with him. The rope linking them together was broke or cut, saving Whymper and the other remaining two members of the team. Whymper later wrote a book called *Scrambles Amongst the Alps*, where he talked about the experience. In the book, he advocates that each step we make is a reflection of our last. Now, he spoke in terms of climbing mountains, but I think what he wrote holds true in every aspect of our life."

"You mean it's like the grains of sand and pebbles?"

"Not exactly, this is different," his father replied looking at Tommy with his deep blue eyes. "What I mean is that every decision we make has a bearing on our next. You can't make what you did today go away, and it will have some influence on what you do tomorrow."

"I'm not sure I understand."

The shadows cast across the ridgeline from the sun setting on the far side. Pointing to the tallest Flatiron along the crest, his father said, "Let's say you are going to climb to the top of that peak. You go forth and begin climbing up the northern edge. If something happens along the way, you will still be on the northern edge. You can't magically move yourself to the south. Your decisions will have to take into account that you're on the northern side of the Flatirons."

"But I could walk to the southern side."

"Sure but you would still need to traverse the northern side to get to the south."

"Yeah, I get it," Tommy muttered.

"Life is a lot like climbing a mountain. You always have the choice of taking the easy route or more difficult," his father continued. "The easy route will undoubtedly have less risk along the way. The more difficult will have more risk." Hesitating for a moment, his father then asked, "Does that mean you should always take the easy route?"

"No, of course not. The most difficult route is likely more challenging—more fun."

"That's right. It will be more challenging but will also hold more rewards. Life is like that, as well. We always have the ability to choose the easiest route, but some choose the more difficult because they know that it will hold the most rewards, also realizing that it holds more risk of failure. But if you elect to take the more difficult route you can't magically move to the easier route when things get tough."

"So I chose the more difficult route today?"

"Not necessarily," his father replied. "Probably the

most famous of Edward Whymper's quotes is 'Climb if you will, but remember that courage and strength are nought without prudence, and that a momentary negligence may destroy the happiness of a lifetime. Do nothing in haste, look well to each step, and from the beginning, think what may be the end.'"

"What's it mean?"

"That whether you're on the easy route or hard, think about everything you do because even the smallest decision you make will affect the next. Even after a hundred good decisions, one small bad decision could eventually lead to disaster. More importantly, we don't always know which route we're on, the hardest or easiest. You never know what's ahead."

"Are you saying that I made a mistake today," Tommy asked, slightly confused at his father's story.

"No, what I am saying is take care to choose what route you select in life and then take a moment to consider each decision you make. Every decision we make has a consequence that will be reflected in our next."

Looking back over to his father, Tommy responded, "I get it."

Locking eyes with Tommy, his father added, "And there will be times in your life where, much like if Edward Whimper had cut the rope that cast his friends to their death, that none of your options will be good. The choice of decisions will all be bad, and you will be left with selecting the least damaging."

CHAPTER 17

East Falls Church, Arlington, Virginia, April 29, 2016:

Walking back from the grocery store at the top of the hill along Lee Highway, the blue-and-gray eyed dog trotting alongside, Tommy considered his teenage memory of the fight along the river and his father's words of advice. "Take care to choose what route you select in life, and then take a moment to consider each decision you make. Every decision has a consequence," Tommy quietly repeated his father's words, as he had done time and time again throughout his life. Between his childhood experiences, a twenty year stint working construction, and his activity since, Tommy's route in life had been anything but a straight line. And according to his father's words of advice, it had been a path of his choosing. Having had long ago decided that destiny was what had driven his path, Tommy speculated that life might be a combination of destiny and personal choice—a blend of his and his father's version of reality.

If that was true, he wondered if his father had consciously selected a route in life that included being a philanderer. He then wondered if he had selected a life filled with violence, infidelity, and remorse. Had it been conscious decisions or his nature that had brought him to this place and time? Or had it been destiny?

Tommy recalled that later that night, after the cryptic counsel, his father had become so intoxicated on bourbon that he had stumbled down a set of stairs, falling and breaking his wrist. Tommy had set the wrist with the use of a windshield ice scraper and an ACE bandage, his father howling and laughing all at once throughout the procedure. The next morning, his father had gotten out of bed, inspected Tommy's job of setting the broken bone, and then gone to work, never seeing a doctor. With a vision of his father in his mind and a smile on his face, Tommy looked up at tops of the tall trees lining the road and continued walking down the street, his small house beaconing him at the end.

The sky was bright blue with several clouds tracking above the tree tops. With the faint sound of the stray dog padding along the street beside him and two brown plastic Safeway grocery bags swinging in each of his hands in rhythm with his pace, Tommy began to consider the problem of the computer virus. Lieutenant Heywood, the local police department homicide detective, had been right. The police had enough circumstantial evidence and motive to charge him, with a better than even chance of sending him to prison for a very long time. His thoughts then turned to his children. Their mother had called earlier, indicating that they couldn't see him today as they were attending a school function. Even just a one day absence from visiting his two youngest children seemed torturous. He suddenly imagined what type of visitation he would have while serving a long prison sentence. He couldn't let that happen.

Mumbling, "It's time to go on the offense," Tommy decided that it was time to find a way to extract himself from the murder of the CIA man and computer virus.

As he began to mount the narrow concrete steps leading to his front door, carrying the two plastic bags full of groceries, Ralf's black BMW pulled up alongside the curb, its tires screeching across the pavement as it came to a stop. Scar and Jaw leapt from the car, as Ralf's hawk nose and large soft brown eyes peered from the driver's side window.

"Mr. Luck," Scar, the closer of the two, called out.

"What now, another meeting with the whiny asshole? I haven't got the time or inclination to see him today," Tommy calmly responded over his shoulder, the dog growling over his.

Pulling an M1911 Colt .45 automatic handgun from his dark blue coat, Scar said, "No meeting with Mr. Livingston. Today you get to chat with us. One on one."

"More like one on three," Tommy commented, turning to face the two men. "What's the topic?" The dog turned in unison and began growling.

Walking around the hood of the BMW, Jaw pulled a black nine-millimeter Berretta from under a dark green sports coat, grunting, "Come down the steps. You're coming with us." Jaw kicked the dog in the side of the head as it started after him. The dog yelped and ran behind Tommy, whimpering.

"No one kicks that dog but me," Tommy snarled at Jaw.

Pointing the Berretta at the dog, Jaw said, "Maybe I should just shoot the mangy mutt."

Momentarily considering running, Tommy realized that after his long morning run he couldn't outrun a child, much less a bullet. Setting the grocery bags on the steps, he began walking toward Scar and Jaw.

"The topic?" Tommy asked again as Scar grabbed him by the forearm, forcing the Colt into his side and pushing him into the rear seat of the BMW. Jaw kicked the dog again as it tried to follow Tommy. The dog, repeating its earlier yelp, ran back up to the grocery bags on the steps. With the blue-and-gray-eyed dog growling again, Jaw walked back around the car and jumped into the seat next to Tommy, on the opposite side of his companion Scar.

"Mr. Livingston has asked us to convince you to turn over the computer virus," Ralf said from the front seat just before Jaw struck Tommy in the back of the head with pistol grip of his Berretta. Tommy slumped on the seat between the two wide shouldered linesmen, unconscious.

Regaining consciousness sometime later, Tommy found himself sitting in a metal chair in what appeared to be a windowless single-car garage. His wrists had been strapped to the armrests with silver duct tape, and his were ankles similarly bound to the chair's legs. He had a terrific headache and had no idea what time it was. Sitting in a chair in front of him, Ralf smiled when Tommy opened his eyes. Two large ancient wooden doors stood at one end, stained a dark brown, with a bright light shining around its edges. Three light bulbs dangled overhead from electrical wire, dimly illuminating the small space. Spider webs and dust clung to the beams, and the gray concrete floor had numerous paint and oil stains.

"Sorry about that, Mr. Luck, but we were warned not to give you any chance to escape," Ralf's soft voice echoed in the small garage. "You proved yourself clever in the Kennedy Center, nearly getting yourself thrown out before your meeting with Mr. Livingston. And you're quite good at turning the tables in a physical altercation. I was somewhat skeptical of the advice to be careful until I saw you deal with the two men you caught searching your home the other day. Now I am a true believer."

"How long have I been out?" Tommy groggily asked, his head pounding in rhythm with his heart.

"Just under an hour."

"What do you want?"

"I want to know where you've hidden the computer virus."

The smell of gasoline and grime permeated the otherwise empty garage, and Tommy looked up to see the exposed skeletal roof structure above him, like the doors, its beams and trestles stained a dark brown. Standing behind Ralf, in front of the ancient wooden doors, was a 1960s folding game table, supported by thin round aluminum legs and topped with a brown padded surface that was cracked with age. Several items stood atop the table, but from his vantage point Tommy couldn't make out what. Behind him, he heard what sounded like a rustle of plastic.

"None of your business," Tommy grunted, glaring at his hawk-nosed captor. "You tell that little whiny twerp Jacob to go screw himself."

Someone behind him slipped a plastic bag over his head, and Tommy began thrashing about and rocking in his chair in an effort to free himself. The oxygen in the bag was quickly depleted, and Tommy began struggling to breath. He tried and failed to bite into the plastic over his face to create a hole to allow air to flow into the bag. Small black dots darted across his vision as he felt himself about to, once again, black out. The bag was removed, and Tommy's chest heaved as he took lungs full of air to re-oxygenate his blood.

"You kill me, and you'll never find the virus, asshole," Tommy yelled at Ralf, spittle flying from his mouth.

"The plastic bag is just the first in my arsenal of tricks, Mr. Luck. But I find it to be very effective. Sort of like a dry version of water boarding," Ralf's soft voice said calmly. "It has a way of wearing a person down for my follow-on performance."

Over the course of the next thirty minutes, Ralf silently directed his man to don and un-don the plastic bag from Tommy's head. Eventually, Tommy quit struggling when the bag was placed on his head, instinctively fighting for a breath of air then seeing the small black darts in his vision. Just as he was about to pass-out, Ralf would gesture for his man to remove the bag. At one point, Tommy vomited into the bag, the thick acidic yellowish fluid spilling over his chin and down his shirt, forcing them to use a spare.

"Are you ready to talk yet?" Ralf finally asked.

With the vomit beginning to dry on the front of his shirt and weariness in his voice, Tommy replied, "Go fuck yourself. You kill enough brain cells from depriving me oxygen, and I won't be able to tell you where I live."

"You don't need to play John Wayne. We will eventually get the answer," Ralf said softly.

Tommy knew Ralf was right. He had learned long ago, everyone eventually broke. It was just a matter of time. But his dislike for Jacob gave him the fortitude to continue his silence.

"I'll let you think about it for a while, Mr. Luck. You take a break and think about my request. We'll be back in five minutes, and we can talk some more," Ralf said while standing up and walking past Tommy.

Hearing a door behind him open and close, Tommy struggled with the heavy duct tape strapping his wrists to the chair. Failing to dislodge his wrists, he began working his ankles back and forth, slightly loosening the duct tape on the right. Using the negligible freedom he had created on his ankle, Tommy used his right foot to rotate the chair, so it was facing the rear of the garage. A narrow door with four small dirty glass panes at the top stood at the back of the garage where he could see several shadows moving through its semi-transparent surface. The smell of his drying vomit overwhelmed the musty smell of the garage.

Five minutes later, Tommy watched Ralf then Jaw reenter the garage through the door and walk toward him. Jaw had obviously been behind him donning and undonning the plastic bag over his head earlier. Tommy immediately began regretting his comment about army staff sergeants at the Kennedy Center. While Ralf walked past him to his table of tools, Jaw twisted Tommy's chair around to its former position, its metal legs scraping across the dirty concrete floor.

Retrieving a small block of wood from the table top, Ralf handed it to Jaw. Roughly grabbing Tommy from behind and forcing his mouth open, Jaw slipped the block of wood between his front teeth. One side of the block was narrow, the other wide. Jaw then rotated the block so the broad side forced his mouth into a wide open position. Narrow grooves cut into the wood lined up with his front teeth. Tommy attempted to spit the block out, but his teeth were captured in the grooves, prohibiting him from doing so.

"My next trick is quite painful, Mr. Luck," Ralf announced looking back down at the table with all his tools.

Jaw then grabbed Tommy's head, holding it steady between his powerful arms and limiting the movement he could make. Turning away from the game table, Ralf faced Tommy with a small black cordless Dremel Tool in his hand, pressing the small trigger. The machine let out a high-pitched whine as the small drill mounted at its tip spun at high speed. Tommy whimpered at the thought of the pain Ralf was about to inflict.

As he frantically tried to pull his head from Jaw's grasp, sweat broke out across Tommy's temples, freely flowing down his cheeks. He tried to scream, but only a muffled unintelligible mumble came from his mouth with the small block of wood wedging it open and depressing his tongue.

"I really do not like this trick, but it is quite effective," Ralf commented, his large soft eyes inspecting the drill in his hand. "It is so messy that sometimes I wear a smock. Of course, you will need to see a dentist when I'm finished. Are you sure you don't want to tell me where the virus is located? A simple tap with your right hand on the chair's arm rest at any time, and, of course, I'll stop, and we can chat about where you've stored the computer virus."

Letting out another muffled cry, Tommy tried to rock the chair over, but Jaw held him steady from behind. His eyes shooting left then right, Tommy looked for some way out of the pain he was about to endure but saw none.

Slipping the tip of the Dremel tool into Tommy's mouth, Ralf went to work on one of his lower teeth. The grinding sound echoed in his ears, and his entire skull felt as if it was vibrating against the rotating drill bit. A smell burning enamel rose from his mouth and bits of blood and saliva flew from the edges of the block of wood. Then Ralf hit one of Tommy's nerves, fiery piercing pain shot through his body. With tears streaming down his cheeks, and blood and saliva running from his mouth, Tommy let out a long muffled moan, as Ralf pushed the drill bit further into his tooth. Tommy wanted to pass out. He wanted to get away from the pain, but Ralf would expertly pull the drill from his mouth before he could lose consciousness. Biting into the block of wood with all his might, Tommy was only able to splinter the edges.

Thirty minutes of agonizing pain later, Ralf stepped back from Tommy, once again looking down at him with his large soft eyes. Tommy wanted to give him a look of defiance, but with a blood-saliva-and-vomit-stained shirt and tear-soaked cheeks, he knew that the only look he was able to present was that of a beaten man.

"Let's take another break, shall we?" Ralf asked, "You look awful, Mr. Luck. Are you sure you don't want to talk?"

Looking over at Jaw, Ralf directed him to release Tommy's head and remove the block of wood from his mouth. The second Jaw released his grip, Tommy's head fell to his chest. When Jaw removed the block of wood from his mouth, Tommy was so tired that he was unable to talk, choking out blood, several small pieces of teeth, and a few splinters of wood onto his lap. A long thin drool of saliva and blood reached from his lips to his chest, but he didn't have the energy to spit it from his mouth.

Setting the Dremel tool back on the table, Ralf turned. "You have another five minutes to consider my request, Mr. Luck. My next trick is sadly quite crude, but as painful as what you just endured."

Patting Tommy on the shoulder as he walked past, Ralf and Jaw again stepped out the door at the rear of the garage, leaving Tommy to contemplate his situation and immediate future.

What seemed like only seconds later to Tommy, Ralf and Jaw stepped back through the door with dirty window panes and moved a small, sturdy table up next to his right hand. Ralf walked to his table of tools and picked up a large hammer, handing it to Jaw.

"You don't happen to play the piano, do you Mr. Luck?" Ralf asked while sitting back down in his chair.

"Oh, crap." Tommy sighed, immediately knowing what Ralf's next trick was.

Jaw produced a small knife from his pocket and cut the duct tape, freeing Tommy's right hand and arm from the chair's armrest. Laying the knife on the table's edge and picking up the hammer, Jaw grabbed Tommy's right pinkie finger, laying it out on the tabletop. Tommy fought back as Jaw slowly swung the hammer upward, but he was weak from the previous hour of torture. Peering at the hammer high over Jaw's head, Tommy watched as his tormentor arched his back before swinging the hammer down onto the last digit of his right pinkie finger with all his might, the crushing blow hitting with a resounding whack. The pain was searing, burning from the tip of his finger across his hand and then all the way up to his shoulder. Tommy held back a terrific scream, but just barely, as blood spouted from under the finger nail and several holes where the broken bone had penetrated the skin from inside. He sucked in lungs full of air, the coolness igniting the exposed nerves in his teeth, sending a colossal pain from his mouth that met with that from the finger at his right shoulder.

"You fuckers," Tommy yelled in a trembling voice. "I am going to fuck you up when I get out of this chair!"

Jaw held the next finger in place has he drew the hammer up again. Watching Ralf's calm expression, Tommy saw his eyebrows arch just before the hammer struck the second finger. The same searing pain shot up Tommy's arm, this time he couldn't help but let out a low-pitched scream. His eyes watering again, Tommy looked at Ralf. "Tell that little whining shit Jacob that my revenge will be to screw his fingers up as efficiently as you're screwing up mine."

Tommy watched Ralf again as Jaw drew the hammer back up, this time holding the next finger in line on the table. When Ralf arched his eyebrows, Tommy added, "When you wake up," as he shifted the table out from under his hand with his loosened right foot.

The momentum of the hammer missing the table

knocked Jaw off balance. He released the hammer and stumbled forward, falling to his knees. The hammer clattered on the floor next to Tommy's right foot, and he quickly picked it up, his injured fingers screaming in pain when it wrapped about its wooden handle with the rest of his uninjured ones. Tommy, with the hammer now in his right hand, ratcheted it back before directing it down on the top of Jaw's head. The blow hit with a chilling crush that sounded like muffled pottery breaking. His days of pitching for high school and university baseball teams would now pay off. Looking up at Ralf, who was wide-eyed watching events unfold, Tommy quickly cocked his arm back and threw the hammer, striking him dead center of the forehead and knocking the hawk-nosed thug backward, off the chair.

The two bodies lay motionless on the floor. Trembling, Tommy reached across the table and grabbed the small blade Jaw had used to strip the duct tape from around his wrist, cutting the rest of his limbs free. Standing, Tommy stepped over Jaw and moved to the door at the back of the garage. Looking through the dirty panes of glass, he could see Scar sitting on the hood of the BMW, with his back to the garage, smoking a cigarette, its bluish smoke quickly dissipating in a light breeze blowing down the street. Scar was obviously posted out there to insure intruders did not interrupt the conversation taking place inside. Moving over to the large doors at the other end of the garage, Tommy slipped outside, hidden from Scar by the corner of the building.

Finding himself not too far from his house, Tommy cut across a neatly trimmed yard and turned down an intersecting street. A block from the garage. he saw a white Chevy Impala parked along the street with two well-dressed men sitting inside. The stray dog was lying on the grass opposite the sidewalk from the car and began wagging his tail as Tommy approached. Recognizing the two men in the Impala as those staying at his neighbor's house, Tommy walked up to the car and tapped on the window with the knuckles of his undamaged left hand.

Rolling down the window, the man in the driver's seat asked, "What can I do for you, sir?"

"Tell Sid thanks for the help," Tommy growled at the two CIA agents. "I just spent an hour being screwed up by two thugs while you yahoos sat down the block eating donuts."

"I'm not sure what you mean, sir," the well-dressed driver responded.

Giving the men the finger, Tommy began to walk home. The stray dog took up stride behind him. Looking over his shoulder at the dog, Tommy shook his head. "A lot of good you are. The least you could have done was bite Scar on the ankle."

The dog answered with a whimper.

Arriving at his bungalow, Tommy picked up the two bags of groceries he left out front and made his way up the steps to the front door. Entering the house and walking down the short hallway, he dropped the grocery bags on the kitchen counter and went to work splinting his damaged fingers.

After dousing his fingers with peroxide, he found an old wood tongue depressor his children had used to make some art craft and then wide brown strapping tape used for binding boxes. His fingers blazed with pain as he laid the shattered digits over the top of the tongue depressor, sending another tremendous burning sensation from his hand to his shoulder. He then wrapped the depressor and fingers in the heavy brown strapping tape. Slowly the pain ebbed.

Stripping the vomit-stained shirt from his torso, he

threw it into the kitchen trashcan. Tommy then pulled a large pouch of dog food from one of the grocery bags and poured it into a bowl, placing it on the floor. The stray dog immediately began consuming its contents. Opening a cabinet over the sink and extracting a glass, Tommy filled it with two ice cubes from the freezer across the room and then three fingers of Jameson from a bottle on the countertop. He then took a healthy mouthful of the amber fluid. The cool liquid rolled across the holes in his teeth, numbing the throbbing pain in his mouth. With the glass in one hand and the bottle of Jamison in the other, he stepped from the kitchen through the dining area into the living room. Carrying the bottle and his whiskey-filled glass to the cushionless couch, he turned on the television and drank himself into a stupor. He was asleep on the couch by nine o'clock with the blue-and-gray-eyed dog at his feet.

CHAPTER 18

Loveland Pass, Colorado, February 2, 1990:

It was cold and windy, the gusting breeze lifting snow from the ice-crusted ground and blowing it across their scarf-covered faces as the three boys stood atop the cornice. Standing just above eleven thousand feet on Loveland Pass in Colorado, three teenagers looked out over the scene before them. With churning overhead clouds belching pockets of dense snow, the view from the cornice was spectacular.

A long deep valley surrounded by steep slopes covered in wind-ravaged trees and gray granite formations stood before them. The tops of mountains surrounding the valley were bald, bleak, and white. A narrow icy river, bordered by tall evergreen and blue spruce trees, meandered along the valley floor. Turning their attention to the task below them, a steep, narrow chute bracketed by tall scraggly evergreen trees, each teenager examined the seemingly treacherous route off the mountain.

Dressed in an orange goose-down filled parka and black ski pants, eighteen year old Tommy slid his skis back and forth across the icy snow as if checking the wax adhered to their base, but in reality, it was a nervous twitch.

Competing with the wind howling across the cornice,

Tommy yelled, "I don't like it. Let's traverse the ridge and find a different chute."

"Tommy," the boy next to him, dressed in a green parka, shouted, "we've skied this chute before. And we've skied it in worse weather."

The teenager to the other side of Tommy, hugging his red parka close with ski poles dangling from his wrists, yelled, "Let's get off the top. It's freezing up here."

"I'm not skiing this chute," Tommy shouted in defiance.

"What's wrong with it? It looks the same as every other time we've skied it," his friend in the green parka screamed above the wind.

"I don't know. Something doesn't feel right!" Tommy countered.

"We have to stick together. Those are the rules," the red-parka-clad teen yelled, his teeth chattering from the cold. "We're skiing this chute, and you need to follow."

"You need to follow," the teenager with green parka repeated before pushing forward with his long silver ski poles, their brown leather straps stretching against his wrists from the pressure.

The two teens standing on either side of Tommy slipped over the icy edge, arms extended as they dropped from the cornice, momentarily looking like sky divers before their skis impacted the soft snow at the top of the chute. Tommy watched as snow billowed from behind the two as they began making rapid and short traverses across the face of the narrow chute. Hesitatingly, Tommy began to push forward. He then stopped. Something told him to not push off. Something told him not to ski this particular chute.

Looking down at the retreating figures of his friends, he felt a shudder and watched snow begin to crumble beneath the cornice. Quickly pushing himself backward with his ski poles, he felt another tremor and saw cracks begin to form beneath his skis. The ice crusted snow began crumbling. Frantically, he continued to push himself backward.

The cornice gave way and fell into the chute. Tommy was knocked to his backside and his skis dropped over the edge, pulling him forward. With his ski poles uselessly floundering from his wrists, Tommy madly used his black-gloved hands to scoot himself farther backward away from the edge. Looking down, he saw snow and ice cascading down the chute, ripping the spindly evergreen trees from its edge. Tommy watched as the green parka, and then the red, was overtaken by a torrent of snow and ice.

Standing up and traversing the ridgeline, Tommy recklessly skied down the next chute to the elevation he saw his friends taken by the ice and snow. Crossing through the scraggly pine trees that separated the two chutes, to where tons of snow and ice had claimed his friends, Tommy kicked off his skis and began screaming their names and absently digging here and there in a failed attempt to rescue them. Finally realizing that his friends were lost, he put his skis back on and skied down to the nearby Loveland Ski Area. Walking into the ski patrol hut, Tommy told them his story.

After the search parties had finished retrieving the bodies of his friends, Tommy drove back to Boulder alone that evening. Parking in the driveway of his home, he methodically pulled his skis from the rack atop of the car and placed them in the garage before walking into the house. His mother silently watched as he walked past her and stepped out onto the back porch. Pulling a folding aluminum chair with polyester weave seat from the wall, Tommy unfolded it and sat down. The chair's thin tubular frame creaked and groaned under his weight. Looking up at the Flatirons covered with a fresh dusting of snow looming above with its starry background, Tommy silently contemplated the day.

A few moments later, he could hear someone step onto the porch and pull another aluminum chair from the wall, sitting down next to him. His father's Old Spice deodorant wafted over him as he examined the ridgeline above Boulder.

After a few moments, his father softly said, "I heard what happened today."

"Rotten luck for Jimmy and Bill," Tommy's replied in a trembling voice. A single tear broke from his left eye and slowly worked its way down his cheek.

"Why didn't you follow your friends?"

"I don't know. Something told me that I shouldn't," Tommy whispered, trying to keep the quaking from his voice. "I tried to tell them to not ski that chute. They wouldn't listen to me."

"Have you ever had a feeling like that before, something telling you to beware and not understanding?"

"Sometimes," Tommy replied, looking over to his father's ruddy face, deep wrinkles, and blue eyes.

Silently watching his son, Tommy's father patted him on the back before saying, "I call it my little voice."

"You have the same feelings?"

"All the time."

"You call it your little voice?"

"That's right. My little voice talks to me all the time, sometimes keeping me out of trouble. I think everyone has a little voice. In some people it's weak. In some it's strong. Very few people learn to listen to their little voice."

"How does it work?"

"It's hard to say. It might be the subconscious mind seeing the intangibles or linking small details together that our conscious minds don't. Like today, maybe your little voice saw a crack in the cornice or felt a barely discernible trimmer—or both. You'll never know."

"How do you know when to listen? How do you know it will be right?" Tommy asked, wiping the tear from his cheek.

"If your foundation is solid, your little voice will be as well."

"What do you mean if your foundation is solid?"

"If your conscious mind makes good decisions, your little voice will make even better decisions." After a few moments of silence, his father added, "Tommy, always listen to your little voice."

CHAPTER 19

East Falls Church, Arlington, Virginia, April 30, 2016:

Jogging through an old-growth-tree-strewn neighborhood of Colonial and Craftsman styles homes, the streets still sheltered from the late morning rising sun, Tommy reminisced about the day his friends were taken in the avalanche. With bright green patchworks of well-manicured lawns tumbling by in slow cadence with his feet, he jogged down the street, the dog trotting beside him. Running along the city street, Tommy thought of his father's words while they sat on the back porch looking up at the flatirons on that winter evening. Passing under a tall oak, its shade cascading down onto the ground in front of him, he wondered how often his little voice had saved him.

He could count the obvious times, but having become so accustomed to unhesitatingly following the little voice's guidance, he wondered if there were times that he didn't know of? As the street spilled down into a narrow gulch with homes built along its slopes, his mind shifted to his father having the same guiding voice. His father had said that everyone has a little voice, some strong and some weak. Was the little voice something passed from generation to generation? Was there some special genetic link? Would his children's voice be as strong as his? His father had also said that most people ignored their little voice, never learning to listen. Could he teach his children how to use their little voice? Knowing he would likely never have the answers to those questions, Tommy jogged along the North Arlington street, contemplating them anyway.

A late model brownish Chevy Trailblazer following two blocks behind broke him from thoughts about little voices. With two heads bobbing over the dash in the interior, the small dented blazer was in need of a good carwash. Tommy calmly smiled at the predictable sight. A throbbing head as a reminder of his over indulgence of Irish whiskey the night before and aching teeth and fingers as a reminder of yesterday's painful garage exploit, his first thought was that Jacob had sent more thugs to try and discover the computer virus's location. He quickly dismissed the idea, deciding that Jacob would never allow his employees to use such shabby transportation, worrying that it might tarnish his self-proclaimed lofty reputation. Tommy also dismissed the idea that it could be CIA or FBI surveillance that Sid or Agent Scott had undoubtedly arranged, the Trailblazer providing a far-too-recognizable character for use by a government agent. Finally, his thoughts ventured to Steve, the short beady-eyed man he had seen two days before. It certainly would not be beyond Steve to hire several cheap thugs to carry out his criminal intentions. Tommy's calm demeanor wasn't spoiled by the pursuing vehicle, for a pedestrian tunnel cutting under Interstate 66 two blocks farther along his planned route would not allow the Trailblazer to follow.

A convenient break in traffic allowed Tommy and the stray dog to cross busy Washington Boulevard without delay. Just as he jogged across the wide street, a long line of multi-colored high-end cars filled the gap before the

Trailblazer had a chance to follow. Glancing over his shoulder, as he trotted between several three-story apartment buildings with wide green lawns and loud rattling air conditioners poking from every other window, Tommy scrutinized the Trailblazer as it waited for traffic to pass by. Watching his pursuers stopped at the busy boulevard, Tommy decided that he was finished with reacting to the events unfolding around him. As he had decided the day before, it was time to go on the offense. Slowing his pace, Tommy elected to confront the two men following him.

His reduced gait allowed the dirty Trailblazer to cross the boulevard during another break in traffic and catch back up to their quarry. Slowing to a walk, passing a large baseball field on the north side of the Interstate, Tommy began making his way to a small brown brick detached restroom at its far corner. The Trailblazer pulled up and parked along the street adjacent to the baseball field, and two young men with dark hair stepped from the vehicle. One was dressed in a T-shirt advertising the Los Lonely Boys Band and the other wore a blue and red plaid short-sleeved shirt. Both wore oversized blue jeans. The two men were clearly watching Tommy's movements.

The dog dutifully obeying a command to sit at its entrance, Tommy entered the restroom. Hinges in need of oil screeched a high-pitched whine as he pushed the restroom's metal reinforced door open. Met with a strong scent of urine, Tommy saw a small nook containing a double sink, followed by a urinal then a toilet partitioned off with thin tan metal panels.

With a wall obscuring the washbasins from the entrance, Tommy stepped into the nook and noticed that the small space was also equipped with a paper towel dispenser to one side and a soap dispenser mounted between the sinks.

After several attempts, he was able to pull the metal paper towel dispenser from the wall before positioning himself next to the partition separating the sinks from the restroom's entrance. The pain in his fingers, mouth, and head numbed as adrenaline began to pump into his veins in anticipation of the confrontation. As he waited patiently, several minutes later, Tommy heard the restroom's heavy metal door screech open and the shuffling of two pairs of shoes across the tiled floor. As the first of his pursuers stepped around the corner into the nook, Tommy slammed the paper towel dispenser against the side of the young man's head. The thinly designed container crumpled upon impact.

The young man dropped to the floor, and his companion was quick to attack, his fists striking blow after blow to Tommy's face. Reeling back onto the sinks, Tommy began shielding the younger man's blows with what was left of the paper towel dispenser. The dispenser quickly broke into half, and the young man's fists found the gap between the two pieces. Desperate and dazed, Tommy backhanded the man with the edge of the broken dispenser, slicing a deep laceration in his assailant's cheek. The young man stepped back, as blood coursed down his face, and stumbled over his partner's motionless body before falling backward onto his buttocks. Jumping onto the bloodied man and straddling him, Tommy roughly slammed him back to the floor. The man's head struck the tiles with a loud whack.

Pressing the edge of the dispenser down onto the wide eyed man's throat, Tommy growled, "Why are you following me?"

"You don't remember?" the young man whimpered in response, tears forming at the corners of his eyes.

"Remember what?"

"The other night." The tears broke loose and rolled down his cheeks. "We tried to get you to leave Anna alone."

"What?" Tommy asked the young man, releasing some of the pressure from the paper-towel dispenser against his throat.

"Anna, she is his girlfriend," the young man said, gesturing to his motionless partner.

"Oh, for Christ's sake," Tommy bellowed, removing the paper-towel dispenser's edge from the young man's throat, leaving a bright red mark just below his chin. "Are you Jesus?"

"I'm Emanuel, that's Jesus," the bloodied young man said, pointing to his unconscious companion.

After ensuring the two young men would survive their injuries, Tommy and the dog continued their run along the trails of North Arlington. His fingers and teeth began throbbing again as he increased his pace. Passing under Interstate 66, he followed a trail that ran beneath a long line of high tension power lines that led into Falls Church.

Three hours later, Tommy walked along the street leading up to his house. A block away, he began suspiciously examining his small white home as the stray dog trotted alongside. Other than his lawn needing mowing, nothing looked out of place, and no little voice warned him of some unforeseen danger. Looking down,he saw that the dog seemed to be examining the house too, his attentive blue and gray eyes peering at the front door. Based on how Tommy left the two men in the garage, he was pretty sure that it would take several days for Ralf and his companions to recover from their meeting, and he knew the CIA surveillance would simply watch his movements, never becoming aggressive or involved. Steve was the unknown variable, but Tommy was unsure of the beady eyed man's intentions.

Strolling down the middle of the street, a light breeze ruffling his wavy brown hair, he approached the steps leading to his front door. Glancing up at his neighbor's yellow house, an exact replica of his, built in the 1940s to house soldiers returning from the war, Tommy thought of the two men he had verbally accosted along the street a block from the small garage where he had been tortured. He knew they were the same men he had seen entering his neighbor's house, and it made sense that they worked for Sid. His neighbor taking a last minute business trip while Tommy was being investigated for the murder of a CIA agent seemed all too convenient. Tommy wondered if the government wasn't putting his neighbor up at the nearby Key Bridge Marriott or some other high-end hotel until the investigation was complete, and wished their roles could somehow be reversed. Walking past his old white Chevy pickup, he looked down and stopped. The corner of a small black box peeked out from the left wheel well of the truck.

At first, Tommy thought it must be a magnetic box used for spare keys. While he had owned several over the years, he had never placed one on this truck. Glancing up at his neighbor's house to ensure no one was watching, he reached down and grabbed the black box. With his pickup concealing his movements from the yellow house, he examined the little box in his hand. Like a key holder, it had a magnetic backing that held it in place, but this box had no compartment.

This box had a short black wire antenna protruding from one end and a small red light that blinked several times a second on the other. While he had never seen one before, Tommy knew he was holding a tracking device in his hand, specifically designed for automobiles.

Without further delay, Tommy continued walking along the street. Coming abeam the next car in line, a green Ford Fusion, he discretely slipped the tracking device into its rear wheel well, before moving around the vehicle to the sidewalk and walking up the concrete steps leading to his front door.

On the front stoop, Tommy looked down at the stray dog. The dog looked up at Tommy with wide questioning eyes.

"Is anyone there?" Tommy whispered to the dog,

The dog cocked his head to one side and whimpered.

Twisting the handle and cracking the door, Tommy peeked inside. The living room was still a mess—strewn magazines, cushions ripped open, and their fluffy filling thrown across the room. He glanced down the short parquet floored hallway. Hearing a faint rustling sound coming from the rear of the house, Tommy opened the door farther and gestured for to the dog to enter with a nod. The dog obediently stepped across the threshold and trotted down the hallway, disappearing into the kitchen.

After a few minutes, Tommy began wondering what happened to the dog and called out, "Dog! Dog! Where are you?"

"He's in here with me," a soft voice called out.

Stepping into the house, Tommy strolled down the hallway and looked into the kitchen. Dressed in faded blue jeans and a white blouse, Caroline was crouched on the kitchen floor, scratching the dog's neck. The dog's tongue lulled to one side in pleasure. Caroline looked up at Tommy, her bright blue eyes bracketed by short blonde hair, and smiled.

"Great job," Tommy snarled at the dog as he stepped into the kitchen.

"What'd you want him to do?" Caroline giggled.

"Maybe a bark or come back to get me or something other than leaving me waiting on the front stoop. And what are you doing in my house?"

Standing up and walking over to Tommy, she said, "It's a dog, not a person. He's not going to come back and bark in Morse code that all's clear—and you left the front door unlocked."

"I always leave the front door unlocked."

"Maybe that's why you found two men searching your house."

"What are you doing in my house?" Tommy asked again. "You're starting to scare me. Are you sure you're not a stalker?"

Reaching up and putting her arms around his neck, she leaned in close and whispered in his ear, "I told you I'm a professional executive headhunter. I search out individuals with unique skills. You are currently being evaluated."

Stepping back from Caroline, pulling her arms from his neck, Tommy said, "Well, whatever the job is, I don't want it. I just want you out of my life. I've got enough going on without some scary woman showing up and giving me some bizarre evaluation for God knows what."

"Fair enough." She laughed before turning and walking from the kitchen toward the front door.

Hesitating for a moment, Tommy called out, "What's the job?"

"I can't tell you until this whole murder and computer virus issue is cleared up," she called back before stepping out on the front stoop and closing the door.

CHAPTER 20

Georgetown, Washington, DC, April 30, 2016:

Sitting in his study, dressed in navy blue silk pajamas with thin red piping along the seams, Jacob clenched his long stemmed ivory pipe between his teeth, wondering if Ralf had obtained the location of the computer virus yet. Normally, Jacob thought, Ralf was a model of quick efficiency. Bluish smoke from the pipe slipped between his thin lips then meandered across his left shoulder before it was whisked away by a breeze from the home's central air system, blowing out through a vent on the wall above his head. With his neatly combed blond hair slicked back on his head, his light green eyes sparkled as he wondered how much pain Ralf inflicted before the arrogant Tommy Luck had broken down, telling him everything.

Glancing through the long glass-paned windows facing the home's rear garden, examining the rose bush's green tentacle-like vines and delicate leafs, Jacob felt as if he could wait no longer for Ralf to call. He wanted to hear how Tommy Luck had begged for his life. He wanted to hear how Luck admitted that it had been an error to not respect a man of Jacob's stature.

His thoughts turned to his most recent meeting with his government contact. With such a valuable computer virus on the market, Jacob had begun to ask the government man over more often. He had to smile thinking about how the man could not seem to resist the hundred-year-old brandy he served in order to pluck information from his dull-witted mind, no matter how trivial it might seem. While Jacob had cringed at the thought of his neighbors seeing this lowly man entering his home, he knew that the tarnishing of his reputation would be worth it in the end.

Meeting with the government man the night before had once again been fruitful, his lips loosening more with each sip of brandy. Last night the man had told Jacob how several different forces were vying for the computer virus. And while he was unsure who Tommy's client might be, the government man had told him that the final transaction seemed to be stalled due to these dueling forces. Good news, Jacob recalled thinking, giving him more time to coerce the location of merchandise from Tommy. The government man also told Jacob of Tommy's greatest weakness.

"He has an uncommon sense of loyalty that nearly caused his death on several occasions in Thailand last year," the man had said.

"The existences of several ex-wives seem to disprove the notion of loyalty," had been Jacob's rebuttal.

"Sadly," the man had replied, "his uncontrollable philandering seems to be another weakness, but trust me, loyalty is his Achilles heel."

Jacob pondered Tommy Luck's advertised weakness, wondering how he might use that knowledge to his advantage. His thoughts were interrupted when his cell phone began ringing and vibrating on the table next to him.

He hoped it was Ralf with news of Tommy Luck and, seeing the very same name on the caller ID, he felt a wide grin break across his face, nearly causing the pipe to drop from his mouth.

"Hello, Ralf. I had hoped to hear from you yesterday. Did your conversation with Mr. Luck proceed well? Have we learned anything useful?" Jacob tried to keep the excitement from his nasal voice but knew that that would be an impossible task.

"There was a problem, boss," Ralf muttered on the other end of the line.

"Ralf, did you find out where he's keeping the computer virus?" Jacob queried his employee, feeling his heart begin to sink.

"There was a problem, boss."

"So, you did not find out where he's keeping the computer virus." Jacob felt the excitement of the moment quickly fading to despair. "What was the problem? Hopefully, you did not kill Mr. Luck during your interrogation."

"No, he's still alive, but he got away from us," Ralf confessed.

"Did I not warn you that Mr. Luck is clever?" The clear sound of frustration was now building in Jacob's whiny voice. "Did you manage to talk to him at all?"

"We talked for over an hour. I had him strapped to a chair. We used a plastic bag over his head to wear him down and then we went to work on his teeth then his fingers. He's tough. I've never seen a man last as long with what we were doing to him. He busted out while we were working on his fingers. He managed to knock both me and one of my men out."

"Figuratively or literally knock you out?"

"Really. He really knocked us out unconscious," Ralf replied.

Based on his answer Jacob realized that Ralf likely did

not know the difference between the two words, figuratively and literally.

"He managed to escape from three men who presumably had a clear advantage?"

"There were only two of us with him at the time. My other man was outside keeping watch. Normally, there's a lot screaming involved. I didn't want anyone nosing around the garage we were using."

Jacob mockingly said, "So you're telling me that two men were knocked unconscious by a man strapped to a chair."

Ralf spent several minutes explaining to Jacob what had occurred in the garage before saying, "The man with me in the garage has a bad skull fracture. I won't be able to use him for quite a while—if ever again. He's currently in a coma, and they're concerned there might be some brain damage from all the swelling. And I've got a golf ball size welt on my forehead. You were right. This Tommy character is clever, boss."

"Tell me this, Ralf," Jacob asked, with his frustration now replaced with resignation, "during your hour long conversation with Mr. Luck, did he tell you that he has the computer virus? Do you believe he has the computer virus?"

"No doubt about it, boss. No one would have put up with that much pain unless they were hiding something. And he never said a word about not having the virus."

Silent for a moment, Jacob calmly continued, "I'm told that one of Mr. Luck's weaknesses is his loyalty, the kind of loyalty that creates a venue for men to make mistakes."

"I wouldn't know, boss."

After another brief hesitation, Jacob said, "He has children living in Arlington."

"Yeah, that's right, boss. His kids live less than a five minute drive from his house."

"Good, I want you to abduct them."

"You want me to kidnap his kids?" Ralf replied, clearly surprised at Jacob's request. "That's a big step from trying to work information out of this character with the use of a little pain. And the doctor told me to stay off my feet for a couple days to let this head injury heal. I've been real dizzy."

"You heard me, Ralf. Take his children and hide them someplace."

"Boss, this Tommy character is pretty dangerous from what I've seen. The wrath of a man like that is not something I want to be dodging for the rest of my life."

"Abduct his children and put them someplace safe," Jacob repeated his instructions. "You won't have to worry about Mr. Luck extracting revenge. I will make sure once he turns the virus over that his days are limited."

"What about his children? They're bound to see us."

"Just make sure they don't see you, Ralf. Stay in bed or wherever you are until your head heals. I wouldn't want to lose you. I will ensure the men you employ enjoy the same fate as Mr. Luck when it's all over. And I'll make it worth your while, of course."

"When do you want me to kidnap them?" Ralf asked.

"If he injured you yesterday, his guard will be down. He won't think you're capable of arranging anything for a couple of days. I want it done tonight."

After a short hesitation, Ralf said, "All right, boss, I'll arrange it."

Disconnecting the call, Jacob silently sat in his study, once again examining the rose bush wrapped around the edges of the long glass paned windows looking out on his rear garden. The pipe now dormant, he held its long ivory stem in his right hand and lightly taped its extinguished bowl on his silk covered thigh.

Smiling to himself, Jacob quietly said to the otherwise empty room, “You will regret your impertinence, Mr. Luck. You will give me what I want.”

CHAPTER 21

Williamsburg, Arlington, Virginia, April 30, 2016:

A two-story Harris-Teeter grocery store with tall, broad windows and green trim stood to one side of the strip mall, and a long row of one-story businesses, with a similar façade, to the other. After waiting for a break in traffic, Tommy jogged across the busy Harrison Street, passing behind a daisy yellow Volkswagen Beetle. With the stray mutt trotting along beside him, he thought about the call he had received from Anna an hour earlier. He was surprised to hear from her again after Lieutenant Heywood's untimely comment about being implicated in a murder, as the female police officer spirited her from his house. Moving through the strip mall's wide parking lot packed with cars, he wondered why she had called and arranged a meeting. Anna had been cryptic on the phone, not answering any of his questions.

He assumed that the public meeting was because she didn't want to be alone with him due to her concern about his involvement with the murder of the CIA agent. Darting around a brand new slow moving black Ford Escalade with a paper license, he asked himself if she was suddenly afraid of him, why a meeting at all? Having to squeeze between a shiny emerald green Audi and an equally glistening white Nissan mini-van, reminded him why he hadn't driven to the meeting. The parking spots in this strip mall were two small for his old white pickup.

"Hey, get a leash on that animal," an older man wearing a brown corduroy jacket and shiny red Italian shoes angrily called out as Tommy passed him and stepped up on the sidewalk.

"Not my dog," Tommy replied over his shoulder.

Walking down the sidewalk along the strip mall, he was enveloped in the aroma of coffee and baked goods as he passed a Starbucks Coffee shop. Then the smell of wet hair touched his nose as he moved past a Super Cuts hair salon. The odor of dry dog food finally met him as he passed a pet supply store, just before turning into a small and narrow Japanese restaurant. The dog silently and obediently took up a sentry position at its front door.

Stepping into the restaurant, Tommy stood in the small foyer looking over a chest high bamboo and paper partition, with the scent of wasabi and tempura now tickling his nose. Scanning the tables, he spotted Anna, dressed in a tight fitting black skirt and white blouse, at a small table in the back corner. Brushing past a frail oriental waitress setting a sushi boat down between an overweight woman and her plump daughter, he made his way down the narrow aisle between the tables. Looking down into Anna's large brown doe-like eyes as she looked up into his, Tommy silently pulled the chair out from across the table and sat down.

With long black hair spilling over her shoulders, Tommy could not help but recall her lying naked in his bed, its white quilt highlighting her golden skin much like her white blouse did now. Scooting his chair up to the table and placing a white cloth napkin on his lap, Tommy smiled at the Peruvian beauty. Anna remained silent and unemotional, looking back at him.

"So, Anna, what's this all about?" Tommy broke the silence. "Why the puzzling phone call and the meeting?"

"Your house is wired, your phones are tapped, and you are under constant *vigilancia*," Anna replied flatly. "And what I have to say is not something that I want those listening to hear."

"*Vigilancia*? You mean surveillance?"

"Yes, surveillance."

Leaning back in the chair, eyebrows arched in surprise, Tommy said, "Go on."

"You have in your possession something that my employer would like and would be willing to pay a high price for," she said in a very businesslike tone.

"The computer virus." Tommy chuckled in disbelief and picked up a paper pouch of chopsticks, tapping them on the table top. "You want the computer virus."

"*Exacto*," she replied, her eyes sparkling with no trace of emotion.

"Your employer doesn't happen to be Jacob Livingston?"

"Who is Jacob Livingston?"

"Never mind. So our meeting at the Irish pub? Your boyfriend, Jesus? It was all setup so you could meet me."

"Jesus is really my boyfriend. The night we met, I had followed you to the bar. I then called my boyfriend to meet me," Anna began explaining." I was told you're very bright, and if I had been alone at the bar you might have suspected something was wrong. So I called Jesus."

"Jesus obviously had no idea that you were sleeping with me to give yourself cover from the people watching."

"No idea."

"Maybe you should have told him. I beat the crap out of him and his pal Emanuel earlier today."

"I didn't say he was a smart boyfriend," she replied. "He serves a function."

"The same function I was serving no doubt. And your attraction to me was nothing but a sham to get to the computer virus?" Tommy laughed softly. "Not that it's upsetting. I had a great time. It's just surprising and maybe slightly disappointing."

"Look, nothing personal, but you're too old for me."

"Why didn't you ask me about the virus earlier?"

"Like I say, you are under constant *vigilancia.* You are being watched right now, and they think I am nothing more than one of your girlfriends who learned you are implicated in a murder. They believe I am worried to be alone with you."

"Six million dollars," Tommy responded.

"*Que*?" Anna replied with a confused look on her face.

"I want six million dollars for the computer virus. I've already been offered five and a half. If you're employer wants it, it'll cost him six."

"It seems a bit high to me, but I'll relay the message."

The frail-looking oriental waitress, wearing a black skirt and white shirt, stepped up to the table, interrupting their conversation. Tommy told the woman that they weren't ready to order, and she shuffled away.

"If not Jacob Livingston, who do you work for?"

"I'm not at liberty to say," Anna replied, shaking her head.

"Well, tell your employer that I'm not selling to a nameless buyer. Before we strike a deal, I want to know his name," he said while pushing his chair back and standing up from the table. "I want him to personally be at the transaction. And tell him that I've got several interested parties, so he needs to move if he wants the merchandise."

Turning away from Anna, Tommy walked down the

narrow aisle, once again brushing past the oriental waitress, and out into the strip mall parking lot to the waiting blue-and-gray-eyed dog.

CHAPTER 22

East Falls Church, Arlington, Virginia, April 30, 2016:

The light was beginning to fade along Washington Boulevard as Tommy drove his white Chevy pickup into the Westover shopping area with the stray dog in the truck bed peering through the cab's rear window. A dark band of churning clouds approached from the west as the sun had begun to recede below the horizon, turning the sky golden-red. Tall, ornate green lampposts began turning on above the sidewalks in no rational order, illuminating the street with a yellow hue that partnered with that of a smattering of headlights from cars and trucks driving along the Boulevard.

Inspecting the approaching clouds, Tommy pulled into the parking lot next to a Seven-Eleven, the first parking lot he knew to be along the Westover shopping area. A fine mist of rain began falling, moistening the truck's windshield. Before shutting the truck off, Tommy turned the windshield wipers on, whisking away what little moisture had accumulated on the glass, checking to make sure they were working in anticipation of a thunderstorm later that evening.

The truck's driver side door gave off a high-pitched squeal as Tommy swung it open. Closing and slamming the door shut was an equally noisy event that he had to perform twice to get its latch to close. He didn't bother locking the old pickup. Its aged and faded condition was an excellent advertisement to the fact that there was nothing inside worth stealing. Strutting across the parking lot, with the dog padding along beside, he passed an overweight woman dressed in dirty pink tights and an oversized white T-shirt, printed with a blue and red *FORWARD* and a smaller statement calling for four more years of Obama and Biden leadership.

Silently laughing at the implications of a homeless person wearing a campaign message, Tommy jogged across Washington Boulevard between a break in traffic. Maneuvering around people dressed in a variety of pricey and colorful clothes, he wandered down the opposite sidewalk, passing a boutique coffee shop and then a dry cleaner, the dog trotting along on his left side, sniffing at the grass along the edges of the walkway.

"You ever hear of a leash law?" hissed an older woman wearing a long gray jacket that was too heavy for the weather as he walked past, her voice cracking from ancient vocal cords.

"Mind your own business, old lady," Tommy called back. "He's not my dog."

Stepping into a long narrow parking lot, crowded with cars, situated between the boulevard and a short strip mall of green facade businesses, he scanned the customers sitting on a wooden deck in front of a Thai restaurant on the other side. Seeing the beautiful petite brunette sitting under a wide red and white umbrella at a round plastic table on the deck, he walked across the parking lot.

Climbing three steps to the deck, he could not help but grin at the beautiful woman he was to meet. Becky, with a matching smile, dressed in a white blouse, blue windbreaker, and dark green skirt, watched Tommy making his way over to the table. With a nearly empty glass of white wine in her right hand, bright blue eyes peeked out from under her long brunette hair, and Tommy immediately became aroused. He realized that she had such a hold on him that he always began feeling vulnerable in her presence—at least sexually.

"Hello, beautiful," he said in greeting while pulling out a chair from the table, it plastic legs bumping across the wooden planks of the deck.

"You made it. I haven't heard from you since our last meeting, and I was beginning to wonder if you remembered our date or if you had decided to replicate your Thailand disappearing act."

"I thought it was a meeting," Tommy commented with a crooked smile as he sat down and gestured to the waiter standing near the restaurant's entrance. The dog sat down, stretching out behind his chair, licking between his hind legs. "But I like the idea of a date."

She softly giggled and reached out, taking Tommy's hands into hers. "Maybe the idea of a date was wishful thinking."

The waiter showed up at the table, a slender oriental man with a wrinkled white shirt and oversized ears, and Tommy ordered a Jameson on the rocks in Thai.

"I am not Thai," the waiter said in a Chinese-accented English, "and the dog is not allowed on the deck."

"You work in a Thai restaurant," Tommy replied, looking up at the waiter's small round face and wide ears, "and the dog's not mine."

"They hired me because I look Thai." The skinny waiter shrugged his shoulders. "I am Chinese, and you need to get the dog off the deck."

"Jameson on the rocks—two rocks," Tommy reordered his drink in English. "And bring the lady another glass of wine."

Shifting around, Tommy looked down at the blue-and-gray-eyed dog and raised his right eyebrow. The dog whimpered before standing up and moving off the deck, taking a seat at the base of the stairs. Tommy silently looked up at the waiter, who shrugged his shoulders again before turning and shuffling off toward the entrance.

"Why do you always order Jameson?" Becky asked.

"It's good Irish whiskey," Tommy said in such a way that it was difficult to tell whether he was making a statement or asking for validation.

"But it relatively expensive and you never have much money."

"Think of it as my way of holding on to some shred of dignity. I could easily order a cheaper brand. I like brandy, and there's a lot of good cheap brandy out there, and the drunk is the same. But drinking cheaper liquor, it would be tantamount to admitting that I have a problem. It would be as if I had relinquished my last hold on self-respect. So instead, I order a decent brand of whiskey, and the problem is solved."

Pushing several strands of long dark hair off her face, Becky took a sip of wine before asking, "Anything new with the computer virus?"

"I've got two new clients since our last meeting."

"I thought you didn't have the virus."

"Let me rephrase that. I've got two new clients for a computer virus that I don't have."

"Who are your new clients?"

"I will say their sales perks couldn't be any different," Tommy replied, ignoring her question.

"What kind of sales perks would that be?" Becky giggled in anticipation of a burst of dry humor from her table mate.

"While one is trying to lubricate me with the company

of a deliciously exotic woman, the other has been trying to convince me with the trappings of a new twist on a healthcare plan."

Raising her eyebrows, Becky asked, "And what's that?"

"I'll be less likely to need a healthcare plan if I sell it to him."

"You're speaking in riddles."

Looking Becky in the eyes, Tommy asked, "What do you know about a guy named Jacob Livingston?"

"I've never heard the name," Becky replied. "Who is he?"

Immediately noting deception in her reply, Tommy said, "He's the guy who hired the three thugs that picked me up from the Silver Diner parking lot. The men you watched usher me into the black BMW."

"Who is Jacob Livingston?" she repeated.

"Some self-proclaimed nasally weasel who wants the computer virus," Tommy replied, again sensing that Becky knew more than she was claiming. "His thugs took me from the Silver Diner parking lot to a meeting with the jackass at the Kennedy Center. Yesterday they decided to convince me to give the computer virus to them with the use of a hammer and Dremel Tool." Tommy held up his damaged fingers. "I was hoping you could tell me who he was."

She winced as she looked at Tommy's damaged fingers. "Maybe I can have someone look into this guy. Is he one of the interested parties?"

"He is. I'm not sure of the identity of the other client. I've strictly been dealing with his emissary."

"The deliciously exotic emissary?" Becky asked with a hint of jealousy in her voice.

"Yes, the deliciously exotic emissary."

The waiter showed up with their drinks and Tommy

took a long swallow of whiskey, the cool liquid sending a painful spasm through his jaw as it washed across the holes in his teeth before numbing the nerves. Looking over at Becky, he felt as if she wanted to tell him something or ask a difficult question.

"So you've been abducted to meet with this Jacob Livingston, you've been questioned by the CIA and FBI, you've been physically harmed, and you've been charmed by a beautiful woman?"

"And I got in a fist fight in a public restroom with a jealous Hispanic man and his pal," Tommy added to the list, noting that she knew about his interrogation with the law enforcement officials even though he had not mentioned the event.

"All that happened in two days?"

"Those are the highlights. I've also found a tracking device on my truck and, apparently, there are several microphones in my house, and my phones are tapped."

"And you don't have the computer virus?" Becky asked with a suspicious look.

"And I don't have the computer virus. I wish I did have a copy. I've got this Livingston guy offering me five and a half million, and I've offered to sell it to the exotic emissary's employer for six million—and I think he's going to take the offer."

"It's worth that much?" Becky asked, clearly astonished.

"Apparently so. What've you been up to? Have you heard anything in the dark recesses of the NSA about my circumstances?"

"Nothing, I've been working some intelligence from the Middle East. Boring stuff. Talking to you is the most exciting thing that's happened to me in months."

"No word on Sid's suspicions concerning my activities?"

"Nothing." She sighed. "I been thinking about calling him, but if he discovers I've been talking with you, I could get in big trouble."

Tommy took another long swallow of whiskey, the same pain scorching through his jaw. "You know anyone who's looking to own a dog?"

The blue-and-gray-eyed dog whimpered at the bottom of the steps.

CHAPTER 23

Denver, Colorado, August 12, 1991:

Fifty round tables, draped with white clothes and topped with flower bouquet center pieces, stood in the enormous banquet hall. With high wood paneled walls and a matching ceiling, a wide stage and dance floor was carved out on one end of the massive room and three large crystal chandeliers hung overhead. Soft music played over the speakers mounted to each side of the stage, and seventeen-year-old Tommy Luck was bored.

Sitting at a table in the center of the room, Tommy had been invited to the glitzy Farmer's Ball by his father, an annual attendee. It was the first time his father had invited him to attend, and Tommy had happily accepted. Surrounded by a sea of weathered older men and women, he had not talked to anyone all evening. Given the choice of attending the function again would have prompted a swift "no" from the young man.

Sensing someone watching, Tommy glanced over his shoulder to the rear of the room where two long tables stood, topped with heavy crystal bowls full of red punch. Standing next to one of the tables was a familiar looking blonde girl his age. Dressed in a long green gown with a red sash, the young woman had light blue eyes that shone from across the room and a wide smile, revealing bright white teeth. It took several seconds for Tommy to register that she was the very same girl that he had walked into the red barn with three years before. The very same girl whose father had attacked him in the bathroom after her younger sister had told him of his daughter's afternoon interlude. The youthful beauty Tommy remembered had developed into a stunning young woman, and he smiled back.

As casually as he could muster, Tommy stood and maneuvered between the rows of tables, chairs, and an ocean of chattering of adults, toward the beautiful blonde. He could see her light blue eyes following him, watching his every step. He could see her smile widen even further. Walking up to her, he said nothing, just took her hand and smiled back.

"You're as handsome as I remember," she said, breaking their momentary silence.

"Wow," Tommy uttered, nearly speechless.

"I can't remember your name, though," she giggled, "But I can remember the barn."

"Tommy, it's Tommy," he replied, before laughingly saying, "Where's a barn when you need one?"

Looking at the floor and shuffling her feet, she then looked up and glanced to from side to side before softly saying, "Let's find a barn." And the beautiful blonde began to pull Tommy toward a set of double doors to one side of the room.

Passing through the doors, with block printed *EMPLOYEES ONLY* posted overhead, Tommy asked, "Do you have any idea where you're going?"

"None," she sniggered, as they began walking down a narrow hallway with dirty red carpet and white walls, past a suspicious looking waitress carrying a tray full of empty glasses.

Glancing behind each door they came to, she finally

pulled him to a small room stacked with boxes and extra chairs.

After thirty minutes of talking and kissing, Tommy and the beautiful blonde once again stood next to the yellow-cloth-covered table, topped with the punch bowls. Giggling and laughing together over their immediate attraction to one another, and their backroom rendezvous, she stood on her toes and kissed the side of his face. As she was pulling her wet lips from his cheek, Tommy looked up from her and saw the girl's father, the man who had attacked him in the bathroom three years before, strutting toward them. Just in front of her father were two younger men of equal size, one slightly older than the other. The two men were jogging toward the young giggling couple. Their scowling faces told Tommy that he was in trouble.

Gently grabbing the blonde by her arm, twisting her so she could see the approaching men, Tommy asked, "Who are the guys with your father?"

Her face quickly changing from one of joy to terror, the beautiful blonde replied in a quivering voice, "They're my brothers. You better get outta here, Tommy. Pops is still furious about the first time we met."

"I can't just leave without telling my dad," Tommy whispered to her, trying to remain calm.

Without saying a word, the older of the two brothers slowed to a walk and stopped directly in front of Tommy before giving him a powerful shove. The push knocked him backward over the yellow-cloth-covered table. The table toppled onto its side, and the punch bowl fell with a loud crash, spilling its red contents onto the wooden floor. With a hateful grimace, the older brother hopped over the overturned table and jumped on Tommy, pounding away at his face with large calloused fists. The blonde beauty screamed. Tommy wasn't sure what she screamed, and he didn't care. He realized that he was in for the fight of his life. The younger brother then stepped over the table and gave Tommy a vicious kick to his chest, leaving him wheezing for air. With his hands and arms busy trying to block the fists raining down on his face, Tommy bucked the man on his chest, knocking him backward, before looping his left leg around the older brother's neck and pulling him over, pinning him to the floor. With the older brother temporarily restrained under his leg, Tommy grabbed the younger brother's foot as it swung in for another blow, twisting it as hard as he could to the right. Cracking cartilage in the young man's knee was followed by a high-pitched shriek. Tommy continued to twist the foot. The younger of the brothers fell to the floor grasping at his knee, crying in pain.

The older of the brothers twisted out from under Tommy's leg and scrambled to his feet. Tommy shimmied backward, jumping to his. The older brother lunged again, but Tommy scooted to the right, and the man lost his footing on the floor slick with fruit punch, falling to his hands and knees. Tommy jumped on his back and began pounding at her brother's temples from behind. The older brother's knees collapsed then his elbows. With the older brother flat on his stomach, Tommy continued to smash away at his head. Finally, the older brother's face fell to the floor, one of Tommy's blows knocking him unconscious. With blood running freely from his mouth, Tommy looked at his bloody knuckles then down to his blood soaked shirt.

Powerful hands grabbed Tommy from behind and threw him into the overturned table, his back painfully smashing into one its upturned legs. Rolling off the table and looking up, he waited for the big farmer to grab him again.

Tommy's father seemingly appeared out of nowhere, tackling the big farmer and knocking them both to the floor. They rolled across the punch soaked wooden floor, before Tommy's father ended up on top, swinging his fists down hard on the big man's face.

"Tommy, get the hell out of here," his father yelled between blows.

"Your son is a lecherous pig," the big farmer screamed, trying to block the blows striking him in the face as best he could.

"You're as blind as a goat, you big oaf," Tommy's father bellowed as he smashed the man in the face with his fist, again and again. "Your wife's sexual exploits make my son's seem amateurish."

"What?"

Grabbing a heavy crystal pitcher laying on the floor next to the struggling men, Tommy's father hissed, "You should have never threatened my child," just before smashing it across the big farmer's face.

Sprinting from the banquet room, Tommy ran down the hallway and into the hotel lobby, its other occupants gazing at him and his bloodied clothes. He ran from the hotel's entrance, its brass rimmed double doors swinging out freely.

Cars and pickups sped along the busy downtown street in front of him. Looking left then right, Tommy walked over and leaned onto the hotel's brown stone wall. The cool night air calmed him. After several minutes, the blonde girl came out from the hotel's entrance with tear-soaked cheeks.

Stepping up to him, she handed Tommy his father's car keys, saying, "Your father wants you to drive home. He'll find some other way home. He needs to stay and try to help sort things out."

"I should help too," Tommy replied, looking back at the lobby's brass doors.

"No, he said you need to go. He doesn't want my father to see you when he wakes up." she sniffled. "And Tommy you've got to take me with you."

"What about your brothers? What about your father?" Tommy reached out and took the beautiful blonde into his arms.

"He'll beat me bad if he sees me," she said, squeezing up next to him. "I can't go home. Not yet. Not till he has time to calm down," she cried, and her tears flowed down her red cheeks, soaking Tommy's shoulder.

CHAPTER 24

East Falls Church, Arlington, Virginia, April 30, 2016:

Still somewhat lucid after finishing his seventh Jameson on the rocks, Tommy sat on his cushionless couch with the dog at his feet. A thunderstorm raged outside, rain pelting the windows and bright flashes of light illuminated the surrounding neighborhood followed by loud claps of thunder. Absently watching Fox News' Bill O'Reilly's *No Spin Zone*, listening to an endless stream of pundit's opinions on the upcoming presidential election, he was thinking of the young blonde girl at the Farmer's Ball.

They had had an unusual attraction that seemed to get them into trouble each and every time they met. That unusual attraction had eventually led to a marriage and child named Rose. The wedding had been tense with her father refusing to walk her down the aisle and her brothers peering at Tommy from the pews. The reception had been even livelier and included yet another physical altercation with her brothers. But Tommy would always look back fondly on the beautiful blonde girl who became his wife and then the mother of his first child. She had been strong willed and tough as nails, but even she could not endure Tommy Luck's chaotic lifestyle.

Just as Tommy was pushing up from the couch to go

to the kitchen and refill his glass of whiskey, his cell phone began ringing. Swaying slightly from all the alcohol he had consumed, Tommy reached down to pick the cell up from a side table and glanced at the Caller ID. Tommy saw that his daughter Ann was calling from her phone.

"Hey, sweetheart," Tommy answered, hoping she wouldn't hear the slur in his voice.

"Dad," Ann's whispering voice echoed from the cell.

"Hey, sweetheart, what's up?" Tommy repeated, once again trying not to slur.

The stray dog looked up with concerned eyes and whimpered.

"Dad, something is wrong," Ann whispered again.

Immediately feeling a surge of soberness sweep over him, Tommy asked, "What's wrong, Ann? Where's your mom?"

"Mom's on a date. I don't know what's wrong. I just have a feeling that something bad is going to happen—and I'm scared."

"Where are you?"

"Will and I are in my bedroom. We're under the bed."

"Is someone in the house?"

"I don't know. I haven't heard anyone. I just have this bad feeling," Ann softly replied, her voice wavering slightly with what sounded to be fear.

"Okay. It's going to be Okay. Is your bedroom door locked?

"No. Should I lock the door?"

"No. Do you and Will have something to protect yourself?"

"We have Will's baseball bat."

"Okay. Here's what I want you to do," Tommy began explaining to Ann as he moved toward the front door, the stray dog following at his heels. "Get out from under the bed. That's the first place someone will look for you, and you can't swing a bat from under a bed. I want you and Will to get out from under the bed and stand next to your door. Remember, don't lock the door. If someone steps through the door, you tell Will to swing that bat like he's going to hit a homerun. Tell Will to hit whoever comes through the door low. Tell Will to hit him below the knees as hard as he can."

"All right, Dad."

"That's not all," Tommy continued as he swept the trucks keys off a small table while passing through the foyer. "Once Will hits him, I want you guys to slam the door shut with all your might. Put your whole bodies against the door. Then lock it. You got all that?"

"Okay. If someone comes through the door, Will hits the guy in the knees then we both slam the door shut and lock it."

"Good. That's right," he replied as he jerked the front door open. "That should give me time to get there. Now hang up and dial Nine-One-One. Don't talk to the person who answers. If there is someone in the house, I don't want them to hear you talking. Just keep the line open. They'll send the police to check it out. I'll be there in three minutes. Okay?"

"Dad, please hurry," Ann pleaded.

"I will, sweetheart," Tommy tried to reassure his daughter as he stepped out on the home's front stoop. "You just do as I say."

Rain cascaded down as he ran out to his pickup, his heart racing as water soaked his clothes. A flash from a distant bolt of lightning revealed his white pickup parked in front of his house in ominous shades of gray. The squeal from the trucks driver's side door as Tommy pulled it open was drowned out by a thunderous clap. The blue-and-gray-eyed dog jumped over the edge of the truck's bed onto its metal base as Tommy slide onto the cracked blue vinyl seat and inserted the keys in the ignition. The truck's door didn't latch when he slammed it shut, but Tommy didn't care. The truck roared to life with its traditional low rumble, and he threw it into gear while simultaneously stepping down hard on the accelerator. The enormous engine howled as the truck shot forward, the unlatched door rattled, and the dog slid to the rear of the bed on the wet metal base from the sudden acceleration.

With wipers furiously swatting water from the windshield, Tommy ignored a stop sign at the first intersection, before making a sharp left turn, the truck's rear wheels skidding across the wet pavement. Three minutes and two more skidding turns later, he drove his white truck up onto the front lawn of his ex-wife's house at nearly forty miles an hour. Slamming on the brakes, the truck's skidding tires cut two deep furrows into the damp lawn before bumping into a large oak tree with a rope swing hanging from its limbs. The dog slid across the wet bed to the front, bouncing off the cab. As Tommy jumped from the truck, a bright strobe-like flash came from the living room window followed by a loud report of a handgun. Leaping over the hood and racing up to the entryway, Tommy threw the front door open at a full sprint with the stray dog right behind him.

Jumping over a woman's motionless body in the hallway, Tommy saw Scar and a new companion. Both dressed in black. The newest team member was curled up on the floor moaning and clutching his right shin. Scar, with his Colt .45 automatic in hand, had his shoulder against Ann's bedroom door, attempting to force it open.

Tommy surged down the hallway and dove toward the black figure at Ann's door, throwing all his weight into

Scar as he attempted to turn and bring the Colt .45 to bear. The dog simultaneously leaped onto the man holding his shin, with teeth clamping down onto a wrist, and tugging at the man's arm. Tommy's lean body rammed against the bigger man with little effect. Dropping his weapon, Scar stumbled back several feet before grabbing and raising Tommy overhead. Scar then slammed Tommy onto the polished wooden floor, knocking the wind from him.

Immediately dropping to his knees, Scar straddled Tommy and grabbed his neck. With large hands wrapped around Tommy's throat, Scar began squeezing. The hands felt like a vise grip on his throat. Struggling under Scar, his wet back slipping and sliding across the wooden floor, Tommy could hear the blue-and-gray-eyed dog growling and tugging at the other man, who screamed in pain.

Like the experience with the plastic bag placed over his head in the garage two days before, Tommy began to see small black like darts racing across his vision from a depleting supply of oxygen. Knowing he was close to passing out, Tommy reached out to his sides with both hands, searching for the dropped handgun. Finding it with his left hand, he swung the weapon up with such force that it struck and shattered Scar's front teeth. Scar released Tommy's neck, reeling backward as the handgun's muzzle entered his mouth.

Tommy pulled the trigger. A muffled report and Scar's cheeks blew outward, shredding into tatters a fraction of a second before his head jerk backward. A fine mist of blood, brain, and bone sprayed the hallway ceiling and rained down on Tommy, the dog, and Scar's moaning partner.

Scar's new partner, still trying to beat the dog off

while holding his shin, watched in terror as his companion's body crumpled to the floor. Tommy turned his attention toward the moaning man, the dog obediently releasing his wrist and backing off. Crawling over, Tommy struck the man's shin with the handgun's blood-and-saliva-covered muzzle. The man shrieked in pain and Tommy could see his shin bone shift. Realizing that Will broke the man's tibia with the baseball bat, Tommy pushed the weapon into the leg again, producing another howling cry.

"Why are you here?" Tommy growled.

"Mr. Livingston—"

"I know who sent you, dumbass," Tommy interrupted, "I want to know what you were supposed to do."

"We were to take the kids," the man confessed, his voice cracking in pain.

"Where?"

"A house in Anacostia. We were supposed to take them to the house until your business with Mr. Livingston was complete." Sweat glistened on the man's forehead, and tears streamed from his eyes.

"Where's Ralf?"

"I don't know. He couldn't come. We were to call him when we got the kids to the house. You hurt him bad the other day."

"What happened there?" Tommy asked, pointing the bloody muzzle of the handgun toward the woman's motionless body lying in the hallway.

"She surprised us," the man cried as tears continued to flow from his eyes.

Hearing Ann begin to cry out from the other side of her bedroom door, Tommy pressed the Colt into the man's black sweater covered chest, just over his heart, before saying, "You should have never threatened my children."

The man looked up at Tommy with terrified eyes, begging, "Please don't. Please don't."

Looking down with a cold and emotionless expression, Tommy pulled the trigger. A bright flash erupted in the dark hallway and a loud crack the resonated against its walls. The man's body convulsed once, and then he let out a long sigh as the air expelled from his lungs one last time.

Placing the bloody Colt into his waist band, Tommy turned his attention to Ann's bedroom door, calling out to his children, "Hey, it's Dad. Everything is going to be okay. Just stay in there for a few more minutes."

Hearing a pair of muffled "Okays," Tommy moved down the hall to the motionless woman's side and placed his right index finger against her neck. Tommy immediately recognized the woman as one of his ex-wife's neighbors. Feeling a pulse, he examined her body for wounds. Finding a small bullet hole in her lower abdomen, Tommy ripped a piece of fabric from her dress and gently pushed the cloth into the wound. Rolling her on her side, he repeated the procedure on the much larger exit wound. Picking her limp body up, Tommy then moved her to a couch in the living room.

Knowing that the police would be there any minute, Tommy went back to the hallway and dragged the two lifeless bodies into the kitchen. Turning off the living room and kitchen lights, he moved back to Ann's bedroom door and gently knocked.

"It's time to come out, you two," he said softly through the door.

Ann and Will emerged looking around the hallway, before asking in unison, "What were those loud pops?"

"No time for questions now. We're getting out of here, right now. Understand?"

"Why?" Ann asked. "What's that smell, and why's the floor sticky?"

"Why are all the lights out?" Will asked.

"I'll explain later. Now let's get in the truck."

Guiding his children, down the dark hallway with the stray dog following, past the kitchen and then living room, he tenderly pushed his children through the front door and out into the raging storm to the still idling pickup on the front lawn. The dog loyally jumped into the truck's bed, watching Tommy and the children through the cab's rear window. Backing out of the front yard, Tommy could see approaching flashing lights of a police department cruiser. He wondered if the responding officer might be one of those who searched his house several days before, as he put the pickup into gear and drove away.

CHAPTER 25

Rosslyn, Arlington, Virginia, May 1, 2016:

The cell phone sitting on the bedside table began buzzing and vibrating, waking Becky from a deep slumber in her Rosslyn apartment. First rubbing her eyes, guided by its glowing screen, she reached out across darkness and picked up the cell.

"Hello," she answered in a sleepy voice.

Sid's low grumbling voice greeted her, "Becky, we may have a problem."

"What time is it?" Becky asked, rolling over onto her side and looking out the window with the hush of satin sheets rubbing against the silk of her nightgown. It was still dark outside, but the storm that had raged over Washington, DC, earlier had abated. The lights from city mistily twinkled through her bedroom window.

"One o'clock in the morning. We may have a problem."

"What?"

"The police found two dead men in the house of Luck's ex-wife. They had both been shot at close range—very close range. Luck and his children are missing."

"Two dead men? Who are they? What time did this happen?"

"Earlier tonight, around eight o'clock. The two men are a couple of thugs out of DC."

"Why did it take the police this long to contact you? What did our surveillance team report? You think Tommy killed them?"

"The police received a Nine-One-One call at seven-fifty-eight, but no one was talking to the operator. The nine-one-one operator followed standard operating procedures and dispatched a deputy to the scene. The surveillance team reported Luck leaving his house in a hurry just before eight o'clock. They followed protocol and began pursuing him using the tracking device mounted to his pickup. It took about five minutes for them to realize that someone had moved the tracking device and mounted it to the rear of another car parked out on the street in front of his house. They lost him." Sid's normal solemn voice resonated exhaustion and frustration. "The deputy responding to the Nine-One-One call arrived at eight-eleven. The officer found the two bodies in the kitchen and a wounded woman in the living room, in an otherwise empty house. All the victims had been shot with what appears to be a forty-five or nine-millimeter handgun. It took the police department a while to connect the active murder investigation of the CIA agent, Luck, and his ex-wife's house. About the time they connected all that together, the ex-wife showed up at the house, explaining she had asked a neighbor to check on the kids. The police realized that the neighbor was the wounded woman, but they're unsure who shot her. She's currently in surgery and unable to shed any light on what happened. One nine-millimeter Berretta was recovered at the scene. It had not been fired. Whatever weapon was used on the victims was not in the house. Lieutenant Heywood called me ten minutes ago."

"The two men were out of DC?"

"That's correct. The police aren't sure why they were there. While both have rap sheets, neither has ever been implicated in a burglary or a kidnapping. Their rap sheets are filled with mostly assault and battery convictions."

"And our problem is we don't know what they were doing there, whether or why Tommy killed them, and whether this has something to do with the computer virus," Becky said, laying out the issues.

"Luck's daughter called him on her cell just before he departed his house. We can assume she called because someone had broken into the house. There were signs of a break-in on the back door of the house. I'm presuming that Luck received the call from his daughter and raced over to the house. Vehicle tracks across the front lawn indicate someone showed up and stopped in a hurry. Lieutenant Heywood believes the tracks are from Luck's truck. I tend to agree with his conclusion." There was a delay on the line before Sid requested, "I need you to call Luck. Find out where he is and what happened. We need to find out why those men were there and if this was freelance burglary or if those men were working for someone and it concerns the computer virus. If this is not a freelance burglary, which it doesn't appear to be, then it could be Luck's client or some other party interested in the computer virus is trying to gain some leverage."

"What if he doesn't answer?"

"That could mean that there were more than two thugs at the house, and they managed to abduct Luck and his children," Sid grumbled. "Or he's decided to disappear. He did a good job of that in Thailand last year."

Hanging up the phone, Becky immediately tried Tommy's cell. His cell phone had been turned off. She then climbed out of bed and walked into the living room, carrying her cell. Turning on a light next to a long white leather couch, she again peered out onto the Washington, DC, skyline and the solitary red light at the top of the Washington Monument flashing above the city. After a moment, she selected another number on her cell and made a call.

"Howard Macintyre, Inspector General," a woozy voice answered.

"Two men were just found dead at Tommy's ex-wife's house," Becky replied, sitting down on the couch, the cool leather cushion quickly conforming to her body with a faint hiss.

"What two men?" The inspector general's voice immediately perked up, no trace of sleepiness remaining.

"They don't know. A couple criminals out of DC. The think they might have been trying to abduct Tommy's children, and he stopped them. He and his kids have disappeared."

"Why would two men try to abduct his children?"

"I've got a feeling that they might have been Jacob Livingston's men. It would not be beyond that man to try and kidnap Tommy's kids to get the virus," Becky replied with clear concern in her voice. "I think we've gone too far. Jacob's ruthless."

"Seems to me we've had this conversation before. Tommy Luck is more than capable of handling himself."

"We've involved his kids," Becky snapped. "He can handle himself, I'm just not sure he can handle both himself and his family. We started this."

"We didn't involve his children. We may have started the ball rolling with Jacob Livingston, but Tommy Luck is as complicit. He made a copy of the virus."

"He says he doesn't have a copy," Becky argued vehemently. "He says he doesn't have a copy."

"Think about it," the inspector general fired back. "The CIA man who followed Tommy Luck from the post office box is found murdered. Luck's fingerprints are at the scene of the crime. He told you he has two clients, and now two men are found dead in his ex-wife's house. You, yourself, said that you thought he had a copy."

"We need to help him out of this situation. It's the right thing to do."

"We're not doing anything to help him. That train has already left the station. We can give him our apologies when it's over if he's innocent. You are not to tell him anything. Do you understand me, Becky?"

"Yes."

The inspector general disconnected the call upon hearing Becky's reply.

CHAPTER 26

Fairfax, Virginia, May 1, 2016:

The storm had passed, and Tommy and his two children had been waiting in the cab of the old white pickup next to a small faded blue clapboard house in Fairfax nearly four hours. The ancient white pickup was parked under a stand of three bushy trees to the side of the house, somewhat concealed from the road. With Will's head on his shoulder and Ann's on the passenger door, Tommy listened to his children's slumbering mutters while trying to make sense of all that had been going on around him. The stray dog stood at the side of the truck, scanning the neighborhood, as if on lookout duty. With the onset of a headache and nausea from his overindulgence in alcohol several hours earlier, Tommy began considering his situation. From Tommy's point of view, the key to the events surrounding the computer virus seemed to center around the unusual appearance of beady eyed Steve.

Tommy knew Steve to be the associate of John Smith, a disgruntled agent who had been using NSA assets to steal corporate secrets, selling them to the highest bidder. John Smith's scheme had come to an end when his activity had been discovered and, unbeknownst to him, his corporate secrets had been replaced with a computer virus designed to download all the data from the server on which it was loaded, sending the information to the NSA. The computer virus then destroyed all evidence of itself and any data on the source server.

John Smith had been bright and imaginative but lacked any moral foundation, much like Jacob Livingston. John Smith was also not a man one would want to find as an enemy. Tommy had been the deliveryman for John Smith's final transaction in Thailand, passing the computer virus to his Turkish client. Discovering that all John Smith's former deliverymen had disappeared, Tommy took charge of the delivery, transferring the flash drive on which the virus had been loaded under his own terms and conditions. This act of self-preservation had quickly created an adversarial relationship between Tommy and John Smith. Fortunately for Tommy, John Smith had been murdered shortly after the delivery. But, then again, Steve was supposed to have been killed in Thailand last year, as well.

What Tommy knew about Steve was that he lacked the intellect to orchestrate a complex plan. Steve's job during the Thailand operation was to simply keep track of the deliveryman, and he had failed dismally. While Tommy believed that Steve was somehow an important key to his current problems, he knew the beady-eyed man could not be pulling the strings. Steve had to have an accomplice—someone much smarter than the little beady eyed man. Tommy knew that to extract himself from the death of the CIA agent and the problems surrounding the computer virus, he would need to discover the identity of Steve's accomplice. The question was how.

The dog gave off a low muffled bark as a pair of headlights turned into the drive of the blue clapboard house. Tommy gently raised his son's head from his shoulder and stepped out from the old white truck. The dog took up a position next to him.

Gravel crunched under the wheels of a green Ford F-150 truck as it rolled to a stop, halting in the center of the driveway. A young woman climbed out from behind the steering wheel wearing a floral summer dress. Her long legs and flowing blonde hair seemed to glide effortlessly toward the house's entry.

"Hey, Rose," Tommy softly called out. "What's going on, beautiful?" With a smile on his face, he began walking toward the young woman.

Rose, with blonde hair, green eyes, and standing nearly as tall as Tommy, turned to his voice and smiled before beginning to walk toward him. The dog gave off another muffled bark. Tommy reached down mid-stride and stroked his head, silently telling the mutt it was okay.

"Dad! What are you doing here at this time of night?" His oldest daughter asked, embracing Tommy on the front lawn. "It's like two in the morning."

Releasing Rose from his hug and taking a step back, Tommy said, "You're right, it's like two in the morning. Where have you been?"

"A date." Rose chuckled at Tommy, before asking again, "Why are you here?"

"I gotta little problem."

"Dad, you always gotta a little problem." Her long blonde hair fell across her green eyes. "Whose dog is that?"

"It's a stray I can't seem to shake."

"You have a dog? That's amazing."

"It's not my dog," Tommy declared. "And this problem is a little more complex than those of my past."

"What happened to your fingers?" Rose interrupted, looking down at his swollen digits lashed to the blood-stained tongue depressor.

"They're fine. Look, I've some bad people trying to get something from me and tonight they threatened your little brother and sister. They tried to kidnap them. I need you to take care of Ann and Will for a day or two while I figure a way out of this."

"I've got school during the day," Rose replied, placing her hands on her hips but keeping the wide smile on her face. "It's the end of the semester at George Mason. What should I do with them?"

"Frankly, I don't want you to go to school. If they were able to find Ann and Will, it won't long before they find you."

"If they're looking for me, this is the first place they'll look," she said, gesturing toward the house.

"I agree. That's why I want you to take them down to the bay. I want you to take them to Fishing Creek."

"But that's your house. Won't they look for them there too?"

"Sweetheart, everyone knows me as an unemployed drunk, and they all believe that I have no valuable assets whatsoever. No one searching for me would think to look and see if I own anything, much less a house situated on two acres overlooking the Chesapeake Bay. Even if they discover that a Thomas Bacon Luck owns a house on the water, no one will think it's me. They'll think it's a different Thomas Bacon Luck."

"I'm not sure the world could handle more than one Thomas Bacon Luck." She giggled. "When do you want me to leave?"

"Tonight if you can. It's only a three-hour drive," Tommy said while reaching into his back pocket for his wallet and handing Rose two hundred dollars he had withdrawn from an ATM on the way to her house, emptying his bank account. "I'll feel a lot better knowing you guys are safe. When you get there, I want you to get my twelve gauge out of the upstairs closet and load it. I want you to keep it near you at all times. There's a three-fifty seven in the closet as well. But be careful, that handgun carries quite a wallop."

"How long do you want us to stay there?"

"I'll be down in two days. If you don't hear from me in three, I want you to drive to Colorado and go to your mother's. Take your brother and sister with you."

"What will Sarah say about that?"

"I'll call her and explain. Don't worry about their mother."

"Dad, Sarah will never listen to you. She'll call the police."

"You don't need to worry about that, the police are already after me," Tommy admitted to his daughter, smirking and shaking his head.

After loading Will and Ann into the green Ford pickup, Tommy looked down at the blue-and-gray-eyed dog, saying, "I want you to go with the kids," as if he was talking to a person. The dog looked up at Tommy then jumped into the rear of the green pickup, once again sliding across its metal bed.

Helping carry Rose's suitcase from the house, Tommy said to his oldest daughter, "Remember, if you don't hear from me in three days, get off to Colorado."

Looking at her father with a crooked smile, Rose responded, "Three days, aye," in her best sailor imitation.

Hoisting Rose's bag, he swung the luggage into the bed of the pickup next to the dog.

After hugging each of his children goodbye, Tommy watched as they drove down the road in front of the house, the Ford's red taillights fading into the darkness. Standing in the front yard, Tommy shuffled his feet across its wet grass. He knew what he needed to do next, but did not relish the thought of the phone call.

CHAPTER 27

Annandale, Virginia, May 1, 2016:

After driving the twenty minutes to Annandale, Tommy drove along Interstate 50, looking for a place to pull over and make the phone call. Headlights zoomed past in both directions, and the lights from the businesses surrounding the elevated Seven Corners twinkled in the distance. Tommy didn't know much about the CIA capabilities but was sure part of their surveillance included his cell phone activity. He had taken the battery out of his phone before driving to Fairfax, and its two parts currently sat on his truck's dashboard. GPS function aside, he assumed that each time a call was made on his cell, they would be able to pinpoint his location, based on vectors from cell towers, at least that's what he had read in fictional spy novels. Pulling into a darkened strip mall, he sat silently in the truck contemplating the phone call. Finally building the courage, he placed the battery back into his cell and dialed Sarah's number.

"Where are my children?" Sarah screamed in a harsh greeting.

"The kids are fine," Tommy said in as calm a voice as he could muster. "They're safe."

"What have you gotten yourself into?" her voice spat

through the cells tiny speaker, "You're a no-good drunk and a worthless father!"

"Look—"

She hysterically interrupted Tommy, "The police want to talk with you! They think you killed two men in my house! What were two men doing in my house?"

"Look—"

"I want to know where my children are!" she interrupted again. "I want to know what two men were doing in my house! My neighbor is in the hospital! She's been shot!"

"I can't tell you over the phone," Tommy said between her rants. Sweat quickly built up on his brow as he imagined Sarah's pale face turning red, and her wide arms and hips jiggling in rage, as she shouted into the phone.

"Why can't you?" she screamed, "You killed two men in my home!"

"I'll call you in three days, and tell you where the kids are. They're safe," Tommy yelled back before disconnecting the call and disengaging the battery from his cell.

An enormous wave of relief swept over him. Since their divorce, seeing Sarah, or even talking to her on the phone, always made him tense. Trying to explain to her why there were two dead men in her kitchen, a wounded neighbor in her living room, and her children were missing would have been a nerve-wracking experience. Thankfully, he managed to avoid the entire discussion, and simply reassured her that the kids were safe in a short, intermittent conversation.

Driving back to Rose's house, Tommy pulled his old white pickup around to the rear of the house to ensure a random passing police cruiser would not see it. Stepping through the back door into the house, he didn't turn on the lights, rather he found the living room, sat down on the couch, and began waiting. Around five in the morning, a phone in the kitchen began ringing. He answered the phone, and Rose informed him they had arrived at his Chesapeake Bay house. He breathed a sigh of relieve. With the news that his children were safe, he stretched out, hoping to drift off to sleep. Lying on the couch looking at the dark ceiling, Tommy wished he'd stopped off at a liquor store before leaving Arlington.

CHAPTER 28

East Falls Church, Arlington, Virginia, May 1, 2016:

Sitting in a red Toyota Sedan at the end of a street, Steve calmly surveyed the small house Tommy called home. A pair of binoculars and a cell phone sat atop of a green official looking log book on the seat next to him. A resident of the neighborhood was busy trimming a hedge at the side of one home, another sat on his front stoop in a plaid robe reading the newspaper which had been delivered just an hour prior. Steve looked up at the early morning sky, bright blue without a cloud in sight, and silently predicted it would be an unseasonably hot day.

Parked under a tall oak tree, Steve was counting on the car not standing out in the sleepy upper-middle-class neighborhood. After all, he had changed cars nearly every day so as to not attract attention. Hopefully, the neighbors wouldn't recognize the same man sitting in the car, but it ultimately did not matter.

Steve would present his forged Virginia Department of Transportation identification and simply tell the nosy neighbor or policeman that he was conducting a study of traffic patterns in the neighborhood while presenting a log of his notes and numbers. Looking at his watch, he picked up the cell phone and made a call.

"What do you have?" the Midwestern-accented voice asked.

"He disappeared yesterday evening, and no one has heard from him since," Steve replied. "According to the local media, there was a ruckus at his ex-wife's house where two men were killed and some lady wounded. The police want to question Mr. Luck about the incident but have been unable to find him."

"Who were the two men? Who was the woman?"

"The men were strong-arms out of DC. The woman was a neighbor who just happened to be in the house. The ex-wife asked her to check on the kids while she was out on a date."

"Were the two men hired by one of the other parties looking to acquire the virus?" the voice asked.

"It would appear so, but I don't know who."

"Try and find out who the men were hired by. We don't want another client to get in the way of our plans."

"How could they get in the way of our plans? Why would the seller go to another client when we're so close to completing the transaction?"'

"We've already been through this, Steve. Money is a powerful lubricant, and everyone has a price. The threat of violence is an entirely different level of motivation. We don't want the seller to have second thoughts about who the computer virus is to be sold. We need to be prepared for all possibilities. Just find out the identity of the other interested party," the man on the other end of the call calmly requested. "Then check out whoever it is. We need to find out who this other person is that's seeking the computer virus. We need to ensure they don't contact or persuade the seller to sell to them or someone else."

"I'm not sure how to do that. I haven't got a lot of resources here," Steve complained, his beady eyes darting from the man trimming the hedge to the one reading the newspaper.

"You have one resource. Find out what she knows."

"She's not necessarily pleased with everything going on. I don't think she'll be willing to tell us anything," Steve continued complaining. "Don't you think she'll be reluctant to tell us anything?"

"We need to limit the outside interference. Call her and see what she knows. We've got enough dirt on her that it's in her interest to keep us informed. If she seems evasive, then let me know. That will be a good indicator that something's up." The person on the other end of the line hesitated before continuing. "It doesn't matter whether Tommy reappears or not. The important elements of the plan are on track, and his presence is not necessary to wrap up the transaction. Our top priority right now is to find out who else is after the virus. We need to be prepared to change our plan."

Disconnecting the call, Steve selected another number and called. Creedence Clearwater Revival came on the radio, playing "Bad Moon Rising," and he began tapping the toe of his shoe on the black floor mat in rhythm with the song.

"What are you doing calling me?" a woman's voice answered. "You're putting the whole deal at risk by calling."

Listening to her voice, he couldn't help but imagine her naked and fantasize rubbing his hand across her skin. She was such a beautiful and exotic woman that he would regularly daydream about a midnight interlude with her, even though he knew the chances of such an encounter were highly doubtful, if not impossible.

"Who were the men murdered in Mr. Luck's ex-wife's house last night?" Steve asked, reaching down to the seat next to him and picking up the pair of binoculars in his free hand. Bringing them up to his eyes, he looked at Tommy's house, in an attempt to think about something other than the woman's glistening naked body.

There was a pause before the woman sighed and then answered, "I'm not sure, but they could be a couple of henchmen working for a man named Jacob Livingston."

"What's his interest?"

"He wants the computer virus."

"How did he find out about the virus?"

"He's well connected and a smart man," the woman replied. "That's all I know."

"How did you find out about this Jacob Livingston? Has he contacted you?"

"All I know is that he met with Tommy and is now considered a person of interest in the CIA investigation into the sale of the virus," the woman snapped back. "Don't call me again. The next time I want to hear from you is on the fourteenth."

CHAPTER 29

Boulder, Colorado, December 6, 1992:

The brown Datsun 1600 Wagon was speeding down the icy country road with eighteen-year-old Tommy sitting in the passenger seat. His freckled and white-blond-headed friend Kevin was sitting behind the steering wheel driving, as the two teenagers laughed and drank Coors beer from aluminum cans. The old Datsun's engine shrieked a high-pitched whine as its black RPM needle bounced off the red line limit on the gauge. Rolling pastures with cows nibbling at brown prairie grass peeking through drifts of snow bracketed the ice-covered road.

Amidst their playful laughing and drinking, Tommy suddenly felt anxious, a gut feeling telling him that something was amiss. Glancing over at Kevin's smiling face, Tommy tried to shake the odd and uncomfortable sensation. He tried to tell himself that everything was fine. But the sense of concern continued to swell as he looked through the windshield down the narrow icy road.

"Kevin," Tommy stated in a voice as calm as he could muster, "you need to slow down."

"Take a chill pill, man." Kevin laughed, pushing his long hair from his face. "Don't be a pussy. We're having fun."

"You need to slow down," Tommy urged his friend again, examining the road ahead as if trying to discover the source of his anxiety.

"It's a straight road," Kevin explained to Tommy, laughingly. "We can see a mile ahead of us. Nothing is going to happen."

Turning to Kevin, Tommy firmly said, "Slow the fuck down."

Glancing at Tommy with a wide smile, Kevin was about to reply when there was a loud bang, and the car violently swerved to the right, skidding across the pavement toward the edge of the road. As the right tires left the pavement and dug into the gravel shoulder, the Datsun began to roll.

The Datsun flipped onto its side, and Tommy was viciously tossed into the door as both passenger windows shattered. The imploding glass mixed with gravel and sprayed the interior of the car as if it were shrapnel. His body then slammed into the ceiling as the Datsun toppled onto its roof. Ripping through a barbwire fence next to the road, the car began violently rolling out onto the snowy landscape. A flashing scene of arms, legs, seats, and dashboard filled Tommy's vision as he and his friend tumbled and bounced inside the car's interior as it took one roll after another. Another shattering of glass and twisting of metal, and suddenly Tommy felt the rush of cold fresh air as he was tossed from the confines of the car, his body cartwheeling through the air. Hitting an icy snow drift hard, Tommy bounced across the frozen pasture, each impact knocking the wind from his lungs. After one last cruel bounce, his body began skidding across the ground, past a brown and white cow with wide, panicked eyes, before finally coming to a stop.

Tommy lay on the cold ground looking up at the clear blue sky for several minutes, afraid to move for fear he had broken bones. Shifting his hands and feet first, he then moved his arms and legs. While they were sore, he didn't feel as if he had broken anything. Rolling over onto this belly, he raised his head and inspected the ground around him. Directly ahead, a trail plowed through the snow between two bewildered cows marked his exodus from the Datsun.

To his left, another three cows with large quizzical-looking eyes stared at him lying on the ground. To his right, some four hundred feet away, lay the bent and twisted Datsun on its roof with steam rising from its hood. One wheel was still spinning.

As he pulled himself up to his hands and knees, his body ached with tenderness. Standing brought more pain. Shuffling over to the damaged Datsun brought even more painful twinges and throbbing. His heart raced as he hobbled toward the misshapen vehicle. Both passenger doors had been ripped from their mounts, and the windshield was gone.

Beer cans, glass, the doors, and bits of chrome marked the Datsun's brutal passage across the prairie. Approaching the car, Tommy leaned down and peered inside to see the fate of his friend, hoping Kevin would be all right.

Lying in a hospital bed six hours later, Tommy saw his father enter the room and take a seat next to him. Looking up at the blond-haired and blue-eyed man, Tommy reached out and grabbed his hand, asking "Why?"

"Life is not an easy proposition, son," his father softly commented, caressing Tommy's forehead with his free hand.

"But what happened?" Tommy asked, looking pleadingly at his father.

"The front right tire blew out."

"But why?"

"It just blew out, son. There are some things out of our control."

"You say that like it doesn't matter." Tommy quaked as a tear broke from the corner of his right eye and worked its way down his cheek. "A tire blew out, and my friend is dead."

"Life is not easy," his father calmly replied. "Nor is life fair."

"But I survived,"

"You survived, and your friend is dead."

"You talk of about life as if it were a roll of the dice."

"Life is sometimes nothing more than a roll of the dice. You survived. Your friend did not. It is as simple as that."

"You sound heartless," Tommy growled at his father. "My friend is dead, and all you can say is that life isn't fair? Life isn't easy?"

"Life is not easy, and it certainly is not fair. Some people get all the breaks, and others get nothing. The average person can expect an occasional break, but that's about it. You got a break today."

"But why me?" Tommy muttered, turning away from his father and looking out the window. "We were in the car together."

"Tommy, listen to me, life is not fair. You should never look back and worry about your past misfortunes or look forward and hope for a break. You just need to realize that life's not fair and forge ahead, recognizing it's ultimately out of your control."

"So if life is not easy, and it's not fair, then there is no such thing as happiness," Tommy sarcastically remarked, looking back at his father.

"Happiness has nothing to do with the fact that life is inherently unfair. Happiness is based on who we associate with and how we treat the people around us."

"But why did it happen to Kevin and not me? We were in the car together, and I was the only one tossed out. Why couldn't have we both walked away from the accident? Why just me?"

"Life is not fair, and happiness is not a straightforward deal. But I can tell you from experience that happiness is a life where you choose your friends, and are loyal to those friends, supporting each other when things get tough because it will get tough at times." Hesitating for a moment, his father continued, "Happiness is a matter of focusing on the good things that happen, no matter how small they might be, and realizing that you have no control over the bad things that happen to good people."

"It's difficult to support your friend when he's dead," Tommy mockingly responded, locking his blue eyes onto his father's.

"You have a choice right this moment. You can quit feeling sorry for yourself and recognize that you got a break today, or you can choose to live a life wallowing in self-pity. Which will it be, Thomas Bacon Luck?"

CHAPTER 30

Fairfax, Virginia, May 1, 2016:

The sun had been up for several hours, but Tommy continued to lie on the couch, looking up at the ceiling, thinking of the day that the Datsun's front tire had blown-out while he and his friend Kevin had been speeding down the country road. He could still clearly remember the chaotic tumbling inside the car as it rolled across the prairie. He could still recollect the feeling of the fresh cool air as he was ejected from the car. He could still recall how he bounced across the ground, coming to a stop on his back, looking up at the sky. Lying on the couch with his feet dangling over its armrest, Tommy considered the unusual words his father had offered him, '*Life is not easy, nor is it fair.*'

Having spent a lifetime witnessing the misfortune of those around him, Tommy had realized a long time ago that his father's advice about how one could only find happiness by carefully choosing one's friends and remaining loyal to those friends, supporting each other when things got tough, rang so true. Finally, he remembered how his father had given him a choice that day, either spend a life wallowing in self-pity, or focus on the good things that happen, no matter how small they might be. With his jobless lifestyle and incessant drinking, he wondered if he might not have given up and begun wallowing in self-pity.

"Christ, I need a drink," he muttered, sitting up on the couch.

Running his left hand through his hair, he looked out the small living room's window onto a clear morning, a brilliant blue sky unfolding above with no clouds obscuring its beauty. Raising his shaking hands in front of his face, Tommy wondered whether his tremors were due to the throbbing in his fingers or his memories of Kevin's death, finally attributing the shaking to a lack of alcohol the night before. He examined his trembling fingers. They appeared angry and purple mounted onto the tongue depressor. He knew he should see a doctor, but also knew he would have to provide identification if he did so. Not a practical thing to do at this point, with at least three law enforcement agencies hunting for him.

Maneuvering his way to the kitchen, Tommy looked into the cabinets searching for something to clean his fingers. Finding a bottle of rubbing alcohol, gauze, and medical tape, he filled a bowl with the clear liquid. Unwrapping his fingers, releasing them from the tongue depressor, he dipped the purple swollen fingers into the bowl. Pain coursed across his hand and then up his arm. Holding his right hand in his left, he let the pain ebb before wrapping the fingers in the gauze and strapping them back onto the blood-soaked tongue depressor with the medical tape.

With his fingers still throbbing, he looked around the small kitchen for something to eat. He finally settled on a bowl of cereal and one-percent milk. Tommy hated one-percent milk, thinking it tasted more like water than a dairy product. Leaning against a light green counter that looked as if it had yet to be replaced during the house's forty-plus year existence, Tommy began to ponder his situation.

As he took the first bite of the watery tasting cereal, the holes that Ralf had drilled in his teeth shrieked in pain as the cold milk touched the open nerves. As the pain receded, Tommy began counting the groups or individuals that would be looking for him. Lieutenant Heywood with the Arlington County Police Department would certainly want to question him about the deaths of the two men at his ex-wife's house. Mr. Scott with the FBI would still be trying to pin the murder of CIA agent on him. Sid would want to resume surveillance on him in order to find the computer virus and the client. Jacob Livingston wanted to find him in order to obtain the computer virus. And, finally, Steve was watching for a reason Tommy had yet to discover. And, of course, there was Anna's employer.

After another bite of cereal and a burst of pain, he turned his thoughts to how the sequence of events had unfolded. After placing advertisements in the *Washington Post* and *The Economist Journal* announcing the sale of a computer virus he had been associated with the year prior, someone had sent ten thousand dollars to a post office box. Presumably, that same person had then sent him an obscure note and the key to the post office box. The minute Tommy picked up the money, the wheels had been placed in motion, making it appear as if he were selling the computer virus. The alleged name of the orchestrator was John Smith, but he was dead. Asking himself why someone would use the dead man's name for the setup, Tommy took another bite of cereal, and another burning pain tracked across his lower teeth. Standing next to the kitchen counter, he realized that the culprit had obviously used John Smith's name to be certain that the CIA would link the computer virus with the Thailand operation last year, and himself.

If the setup already succeeded in implicating him in the selling the computer virus, Tommy wondered why someone would kill the CIA agent. Why kill the agent that could verify that Tommy had gone to the post office box and picked up the money? Or maybe the person who killed the agent and the person trying to set him up for the computer virus were two different people?

Leaving fingerprints on the shell casing and the newspaper undermined the computer virus setup, as well. By all accounts, with shell casing and newspaper evidence, Tommy should have been immediately placed under arrest by the FBI and Arlington County Police Department. Only Sid and the CIA's larger goal of recovering the computer virus had blocked Agent Scott and Lieutenant Heywood from taking Tommy into custody. What about the shell casing discrepancy? Was leaving a casing from a revolver without the murder weapon an oversight or on purpose? It would certainly be questioned by the investigators and in a court of law. Tommy scooped another bite of cereal into his mouth, holding his tongue over one of the larger holes in his teeth to protect the nerve, as he considered the possibility that two forces were working against one and other. One force wanted Tommy as a fall guy for the murder. The other wanted it to appear as if he was selling the computer virus.

With the last bite of cereal in his mouth, Tommy grimaced in pain, and his thoughts turned to the search conducted by the two men that he had interrupted. The shorter of the two men claimed that they had already accomplished what they were tasked to do but they had taken nothing. Tommy wondered if that had been another act to ensure that the CIA believed he was offering the computer virus for sale.

Finally, as he drank the watery milk residue from the

bowl, trying to let it slide across the side of his mouth where he had no damaged teeth, Tommy began thinking of Jacob Livingston's somewhat late entry into the affair. How had the self-proclaimed rich and powerful Jacob found out about the computer virus? Had he seen the advertisements or had someone told him of the computer virus? More importantly, how had Jacob found Tommy? Unless he was also watching the post office box, someone had to have directed Jacob to him. Was Jacob Livingston behind the murder of the CIA agent? While he seemed capable of the act, how would the death of the CIA agent benefit Jacob Livingston?

Three possibilities occurred to Tommy. The first was that the computer virus had actually been put on the market and someone had set him up to distract the authorities away from the real seller. If that were the case, Tommy had to ask himself why the real seller would not reveal himself to Jacob. After all, Jacob had been willing to pay five and a half million dollars for the software.

The second possibility was that someone was simply trying to extract revenge for one of Tommy's past deeds. If that were the case, Steve would certainly have a good reason for vengeance, but Tommy didn't believe the beady-eyed man was smart enough to put a plan like this together.

The third scenario was someone trying to extract revenge at the same time someone else was trying to set it up to look like he was selling the virus. Because those two possibilities would not work in conjunction with one another, two different forces would have to be at work.

Regardless of the reason, to set this plan in action, the person would need detailed knowledge of the Thailand delivery and the computer virus. And that was a short list of people.

Tommy knew that Steve was the key to figuring out

what was going on, and that he likely had an accomplice. Finding Steve would be tough, and his accomplice exponentially more difficult. Standing at the kitchen counter with the empty cereal bowl in his hand, Tommy decided that he would focus his efforts in three areas: clearing up the nonsensical statement made by the smaller of the men who had searched his home, verifying who had set up the post office box, and finally finding out how Jacob Livingston learned about the computer virus. Tommy knew that finding the answer to any of those three questions would not solve the riddle, but would certainly lead him to the next step.

Using a beige phone mounted on the kitchen wall covered in ancient floral wallpaper, Tommy called an old friend who had joined the postal service and worked his way up in their investigation department. Now running all investigations into postal fraud, Tommy's friend Ben was very influential within the United States Postal Service.

"Benjamin Gifford, Investigation Branch," a sleepy gruff voice answered.

"Hi, Ben, Tommy Luck here. How are you doing?"

"Wow, it's been a long time since I've heard from you." Then after a short hesitation, Ben asked, "You know what time it is in California?"

"Sorry, buddy, I'm focused on a little problem and didn't think of the time difference."

Ben laughed. "When do you not have a little problem?"

"I can find trouble where there's none to be found." Tommy chuckled. "The difference with this problem is that it is one only you can help with."

"What is it?"

"It concerns a post office box at the Westover office in

Arlington, Virginia. I picked a package up there several days ago that's gotten me into somewhat of a jam. I was told that a man named John Smith arranged for the box, but the John Smith everyone believes set it up is dead. I need the name of the person who really set it up or at least a description. The box number was ten-thirteen."

"No problem. I can handle that. Where do I contact you when I get the information?"

Giving Ben his cell phone number, and telling him to leave a message as a call to it would go to his message service because he had removed the battery, Tommy disconnected the call and turned his attention to finding a DC Metro telephone book. Digging through the cabinet below the beige phone, Tommy found the thick book and laid it on the counter. Within five minutes, Tommy had found what he had been looking for, the phone number and address for a Jacob Livingston, the only one in the metropolitan DC area. According to the phone book, Jacob Livingston was a resident of Georgetown, a wealthy neighborhood in Washington, DC. Ripping that page from the phone book, Tommy folded it up and placed it in the back pocket of his faded jeans.

Using the beige phone again, Tommy called Sid. He knew that he would have to immediately leave his daughter's house after the call, as the CIA would undoubtedly trace it.

"Good morning, Sid," Tommy said to the CIA agent.

"Luck, we need to talk," Sid grumbled, sounding slightly surprised.

"That's a fact. However, I'm calling to make a deal."

"I've got a couple of questions first," Sid groaned.

"Fire away."

"What happened at your ex-wife's house?"

"Two men tried to abduct my children, and I killed them," Tommy unhesitatingly admitted.

"Do you know who the men work for?"

"Jacob Livingston. One of the two was among the trio that had their way with me in the garage the other day. I'm sure your surveillance team told you about the incident."

"The woman?"

"Shot by the men before I was able to get there."

"The weapon used?"

"A colt forty-five that is currently in my possession."

"All right, what's your proposed deal?"

"You get me some information and don't interrupt me for two days, and I'll give you the name of the parties interested in the computer virus."

"Not good enough, Luck. I need more. Based on the fluidity of the situation, the computer virus is going to transfer hands soon," Sid grumbled. "We need to meet today, and you need to tell me everything you know."

"So you believe that I don't have the computer virus?"

"I didn't say that."

"Great." Shaking his head in disbelief, Tommy sighed. "You give me what I want, and I'll meet with you in one day at a place of your choosing. I'll tell you everything I know," Tommy countered his offer.

After a short pause, Sid asked, "Why should I trust you?"

"You and I worked together last year, and you know I'm capable of disappearing. You also know I have good instincts, and my good instincts tell me that you have the same. While you won't admit it, I imagine you believe me when I say I don't have the virus, and I didn't kill your CIA agent. And I know you need to wrap this up before the virus is delivered to whoever the client happens to be, and as you just pointed out, whoever has orchestrated this is likely ready to move.

“All right, let’s say I agree to the deal. What do you need from me?”

“As you know, I had two fellows break into my house the other day and tear it up. I caught them in the act and was able to get a few answers out of them. I’ve got a couple more questions, but I don’t know their names or addresses.”

“Why not tell me your questions? Allow me to talk to the two men?”

“Because your persuasive powers are limited by your profession. Mine are not.”

After a long silence, Sid said, “Physical descriptions can only go so far. Do you have a license plate or something else to find them?”

“Something else,” Tommy replied and then went on to describe their injuries. “With their injuries, they had to have been taken to a hospital. Can you do something with that?”

“I can check the local hospitals and doctor’s offices. That might be enough.”

“Sid, it’s important to both of us that you don’t interrupt.”

“I won’t, on one condition,” Sid’s low baritone voice rumbled. “Don’t remove the tracking device from your pickup again, and put the battery back in your cell phone.”

“Agreed.”

CHAPTER 31

East Falls Church, Arlington, Virginia, May 1, 2016:

Driving back into Arlington, Tommy parked on the street behind his house. Moving through a neighbor's driveway whose backyard adjoined his, he hopped a short and sagging chain-link fence separating the two lots. Surrounded by old growth trees, he was sheltered by a late morning shade as a breeze ruffled his hair. Watching the neighbor's yellow house where he believed Sid had his surveillance setup, Tommy slowly walked up to the backdoor of his home and entered.

The house still a wreck from the first search, .Tommy moved to his sage green bedroom, digging into his dresser drawer and retrieving several changes of attire, as well as his running clothes. Filling a small backpack, he swung the bag over his shoulder and stepped into the kitchen. Opening a cabinet, he slipped two bottles of Jameson Irish whiskey into the backpack before departing the house along the same route.

Opening the raucous truck door and sliding onto the old cracked blue vinyl bench seat, Tommy's cell phone began to ring, Sid's number flashing onto the device's small screen.

"You don't give a guy much time," Tommy told the CIA agent. "I was hoping I had time for a run."

"Would you rather I called back later?" Sid taunted.

"Probably best I take care of this as soon as possible. After all, I've got a date with you tomorrow."

"I've got two names and addresses that fit the injuries you described," Sid's low voice growled. "Their names are Alfred and Larry. Alfred came in with a laceration to the left earlobe. Actually, his left earlobe was missing, and blunt trauma to his testicles. Larry came in with the same injury to the left ear and blunt trauma to his head. Larry is still in the hospital with a severe concussion."

"Addresses?" Tommy asked.

Sid rattled off the addresses of the two men before saying, "Larry won't be home. As I said, he's still in the hospital."

"Larry is the little one, the guy with the head injury. Alfred is a big guy, but that's okay. It didn't take too much coercion to get him to start talking last time. He'll work fine."

"One more thing," Sid added. "I talked with the hospital reception about how they arrived. Apparently, they were dropped off at the main entrance. A red sedan just left them on the curb then took off. No one saw the driver. Reception had to call the emergency room to send a couple of gurneys and attendants."

"So they had an accomplice," Tommy commented. "Could they give you the make and model of the car that dropped them off?"

"No, just that it was a red sedan."

"Where and what time tomorrow?"

"The McDonald's in McLean," Sid replied. "Twelve noon."

"I'll be there."

"You'd better be."

CHAPTER 32

Annandale, Virginia, May 1, 2016:

Thirty minutes later, Tommy was standing next to a waist high chain-link fence hidden behind a height-matching green hedge, watching the big white-blond Alfred mowing the lawn along the side of his house. The chain-link fence and hedge ran along a narrow alley, accessing four or five small one car garages behind a row of homes, one of which was Alfred's. Hidden behind what was obviously Alfred's garage, Tommy patiently waited. Dressed in cutoff blue jean shorts, and a red and green plaid short-sleeve shirt, Alfred went about his task with a precision that was uncommon for the typical weekend obligatory chore. If not for a slight wobble in his gait and a bright white bandage on his left ear, Tommy would have never recognized the man as one of the assailants who had searched his house and attacked him several days earlier.

With a muscular ease, only developed from his ritualistic long-distant running, Tommy bounded over the hedge and fence with little effort, stepping up next to the small faded red garage to the rear of the house. With his back to Tommy and the small piston engine loudly sputtering out exhaust, Alfred had no idea that the parameter of his property had just been breached. Peeking into the garage's open door, Tommy could see a pristine black 1964 Ford Thunderbird, its details announcing a day when cars were built with as much chrome on the inside as the out. Tommy stepped into the garage, closing its dirty white door behind him so that only small gap remained, allowing him to keep an eye on Alfred's progress. A small puddle of oil near the door, next to the front grill of the Thunderbird, revealed where the Alfred stored his lawn mower.

Waiting until Alfred had moved his lawn care efforts to the home's front yard, Tommy quietly stepped from the garage and walked to the back door of the small clapboard home, it's weathered red sides clashing with the freshly cut grass and bright green leaves of several tall oaks surrounding the structure. White trim around each window gave the house a barn-like appearance. Its wooden screen door, with drooping wire mesh attesting to its age, faintly squealed as Tommy pulled it open. A second squeal accompanied the closing of the door, once Tommy was inside. Walking down a narrow corridor with a polished wooden floor, Tommy glanced at several pictures hanging on the walls as he made his way to the front foyer, each showing Alfred at various ages standing amongst a family of five equally large siblings.

"Now where would I keep my home protection?" Tommy muttered to himself, looking around the homes front entrance.

Peeking into a closet to one side of the foyer, he smiled while pulling out a wooden baseball bat. He then moved over to and sat down on an overstuffed sectional sofa covered in a red, white, and green flowery fabric and turned on the television. Hearing the lawnmower stop, Tommy calmly turned off the television, stood up, and moved over to the wall next to the screen door he had come through several minutes earlier.

Alfred was whistling the *Addam's Family* theme song as he swung the rear screen door open, it humming the same squeal as Tommy's entry. Tommy silently ratcheted the bat back. Alfred stepped across the threshold and began moving down the short corridor that Tommy had navigated earlier. Once Alfred's back was exposed enough for a successful use of the impromptu weapon, Tommy swung the bat into the back of his knees, the same method the big man had used on him several days before. The bat struck with a vicious precision that buckled Alfred and forced him to his knees. Alfred screamed a low guttural noise. Raising the bat over his head in order to gain adequate momentum, Tommy's next blow was to Alfred's left shoulder, knocking him to his hands and knees, producing another piercing scream that echoed in the hallway. Having heard a distinct crack when the blunt instrument struck, Tommy raised the bat up to examine it, wondering whether the noise had come from his makeshift weapon or Alfred's shoulder. Finding no cracks during his inspection, Tommy then placed his foot on the big man's side, pushing Alfred over onto his back. Alfred cried out in pain, looking up at Tommy with an expression that indicated that he already knew who would be the victor in this match.

"Remember me?" Tommy asked, swinging the bat from side to side, once again mimicking Alfred's attack on him several days earlier.

"What do you want? I didn't come back for you, even though you deserved it," Alfred muttered in a pain-racked, quivering voice.

"I've got a couple of questions I didn't have a chance to ask you the other day. You said John Smith hired you."

"That's right, a guy named John Smith," Alfred replied with clear resignation in his voice.

"What did John Smith look like?"

With a hint of defiance appearing on his face, Alfred's simple reply was, "He was a tall guy."

Tommy chuckled at the man lying at his feet. "Look, buddy, you're lying on the floor with what will probably turn out to be a broken shoulder or collar bone. You've got a guy over you with the baseball bat that inflicted all the damage, and this same guy is more than willing to inflict more. You gotta be a little more descriptive than just 'he was a tall guy.'"

"Tall, skinny guy with red hair. Red curly hair. Pale skin and lots of freckles."

"Age?"

"He looked to be in his mid-forties," Alfred groaned, rubbing his left shoulder with his right hand.

"Accent?"

"He was an American," Alfred replied, adding, "Mid-west or West coast. He didn't sound like he came from the Northeast or the South."

"Anything else?"

"What? Do you want to know what he was wearing too?" Alfred taunted.

"Did he show you identification? How do you know his name?"

"He introduced himself. I figured the guy was an idiot. Most of our clients don't tell us their names. They just give the name of who they want taken care of, an address, and the money."

"How'd he get a hold of you?"

Before answering, Alfred tried to push his back up against the wall. His face erupted with an agonizing expression when his left elbow touched the floor. With sweat now breaking out on his brow, Alfred said, "Larry and I do a lot of muscle jobs together. Larry arranges them. I'm not sure how he found us."

"Your little friend Larry told me that you had accomplished what you came for. What did John Smith task you to do?"

"We were supposed to wait for you to go for your morning run and then throw your house around. Make it look like we were searching for something. He told us that you'd be gone for three to four hours on your run."

"I was still gone for two hours. Why so long to trash my house?"

"John Smith paid us well but told us you picked up a large sum of money from a post office box two nights earlier, and he said that we could keep that too if we found it. That's what kept us there. We were supposed to be gone by the time you returned, but we wanted to find the money."

"Did he tell you why he wanted the house to look like it had been searched?"

"No, and we didn't ask," Alfred moaned, wincing as he shifted his left arm. "We just did as we were told."

Tommy chuckled. "A couple of good little soldiers."

Leaving Alfred on the hallway floor, Tommy walked out the back door, dropped the wooden bat on the freshly mowed lawn, vaulted over the chain link fence, and began striding back to his pickup, two blocks down the street. A block from his truck, he saw a white Chevy Impala parked on the side of the street and squinted in an attempt see who was sitting inside. Spotting the two clean cut men in business suits and sunglasses that had been hanging out in his neighbor's house, and the same men who were down the street from the garage he had been tortured in, Tommy knew they were a couple of Sid's men. Realizing that they were likely reapplying the tracking device to his pickup, Tommy smiled and waved as he passed by.

The two men looked away, ignoring his greeting.

Walking up to the white truck, Tommy inspected the rear of the pickup and saw the little black box, with its flashing red light, remounted in the left wheel well. The pickup's heavy door squealing as he pulled it open, Tommy climbed onto its blue vinyl seat, having to once again slam the door a second time to get it to latch.

As Tommy sat on the truck's cracked vinyl seat, he pondered the information that he had obtained from the man still lying on the hallway floor with a likely broken shoulder. Alfred's description certainly did not fit the John Smith Tommy had known. The John Smith that he knew had been tall and athletically built, not skinny. John Smith had a dark complexion and short dark wavy hair, looking as if he had Persian or Arabic linage. No to mention, John Smith was dead, killed in Thailand over six months ago. The man that Alfred described seemed to be anything but Persian or Arabic. In fact, fair skin and red curly hair didn't describe anyone Tommy had met in the past five years. Maybe he was an agent for someone else? But then why would the tall, fair-skinned man claim to be John Smith? What would he have gained by claiming to be John Smith? Feeling confused and tired, Tommy reached for his cell phone and searched his contacts, selecting one.

"Tommy, what are you doing? You've got every policeman in Arlington County looking for you," Becky's sweet soft voice answered.

"Those men who trashed my house, I had a chat with one of them."

"What did he say?" She asked.

"Claims a guy named John Smith tasked them with making it look like they were searching for something. Only thing is that John Smith's description doesn't fit the John Smith we knew."

"It couldn't be the John Smith we know. He's dead," Becky flatly pointed out. "And why would someone want it to look like your house was searched?"

"I don't know. I can't figure this thing out. There's so much smoke and so many mirrors that it's difficult to see a logical way to find the truth," Tommy frustratingly admitted. "And I can't go home. As you pointed out, every cop in Arlington is looking for me. Every law enforcement agency in North America, probably."

"Don't forget Interpol," Becky giggled. "Where are you?"

"Annandale. Near Backlick Road and the Little River Turnpike."

"Look, I'm at home and not too far from you. Come over here," Becky cooed. "Sounds like you need some rest."

"If I can get a couple hours sleep, that would help."

Chapter 33

Rosslyn, Arlington, Virginia, May 1, 2016:

Becky gave him her address and Tommy drove the twenty minutes to an upscale apartment building in Rosslyn, its tall brown brick walls interrupted at each level by large tinted windows. Pulling up to the gate that led into the building's underground parking, Tommy looked up and thought that the building had to have been designed and built in the seventies, verified by its minimalist blockish lines. Much like the American auto designs of the era, the architecture of the time lacked any thoughtful embellishments. Typing in the security code given to him by Becky on the small display near his open window, the gate, a web of mesh metal, rose in a slow clattering rumble.

With his backpack over his shoulder, Tommy took an elevator from the garage to the ninth floor, found Becky's apartment number, and knocked lightly on the door.

Dressed in a short red silk dress that could have doubled as a nightgown, Becky opened the door. Her long dark hair fell across sparkling blue eyes, and a thin smile appeared on her face. She greeted him with a shake of her head. "Tommy, you look awful."

"Thanks for the vote of confidence. Like I said, I just need a couple hours' sleep."

Leading him down a short hallway with several small watercolor painting of historic Washington, DC, buildings adorning the walls, they stepped into a spacious cream colored living room with a high ceiling. A polished dark gray granite counter to the rear of the room separated the living room from a moderately sized kitchen. The living area had wide floor to ceiling windows looking out toward the Potomac River and then the city of Washington, DC.

Gesturing Tommy to sit down on a long white leather couch, Becky asked, "What happened with the men at your ex's house?"

"They were more employees of Jacob Livingston, the guy I asked you about during our last meeting."

"Did you find out any more about him?" she queried.

"Did you?"

"I'm really worried that Sid is going to find out about our relationship. He called me and asked me to contact you after the police found the dead men in your ex's house. I'm afraid if I start asking questions, he'll suspect we're working together and quit talking to me about you."

"Well, that little shit Jacob Livingston has upped his game. He sent his men over to kidnap my children. Before I killed him, one of the guys said that they were to take my kids to a house in Anacostia until my business with Livingston was finished. If they had successfully taken them, I doubt I would have ever seen my children again."

"I thought he offered you five and a half million for the virus. Why is he now trying to abduct your children?"

"He offered five and a half, but I told him that I wouldn't take anything less than ten million." Tommy soberly chuckled as he sat down on the white leather couch. The couch felt cool and conformed to his body with a faint hiss. Tommy immediately felt his stress begin to fade away as he stared out at the Potomac River, its brown waters slowing moving out toward the Chesapeake Bay. The Kennedy Center stood on the far side of the river, reminding Tommy of his first meeting with Jacob Livingston.

"Is it worth that much?" Becky asked as she stepped into the kitchen behind him, followed by a clattering of opening cabinets and clinking of glassware.

"Probably not. I didn't like the guy, so I ratcheted up the price a bit," Tommy admitted, now looking at the Washington Monument along the National Mall. "He said if I didn't sell it for five and a half then he would take it from me."

"So he sent his men over to kidnap your children?"

"Yeah. He wanted to use them as bargaining chips to get the virus."

Becky suddenly appeared at Tommy's side with a glass containing three ice cubes and shimmering brown whiskey. Reaching into the tumbler, he extracted one ice cube and tossed it into a vase of flowers sitting in the center of a black lacquer coffee table in front of the couch. Swallowing a mouth full, his teeth screamed in agony as it flowed over the open nerves. The whiskey then created a warm burning sensation as the golden liquid ran down his throat.

"What happened at your ex's house?" Becky asked again.

Tommy gave Becky a brief description of what took place and how he and his two children left before the police could get to the house. "My oldest daughter is taking care of them," he added at the end.

"Where will you hide them?"

"I've got a place on the Chesapeake Bay where they

won't think of looking. It'll take the police several days to discover that I actually own something of value."

"You actually own something?" Becky giggled, "Wow, the wonders never cease."

"Apparently, the two guys tasked with trashing my house got a ride to the Arlington County Hospital before you could get there," Tommy said, changing the subject.

"How did you find that out?"

"I made a deal with Sid. He told me that the receptionist at the hospital said a red car dropped them off at the main entrance."

"No other description?" Becky asked with a concerned expression.

"No. Just that it was a red sedan." Tommy laid his head back on to the couch's cushioned backrest and looked up at the ceiling. "I should have asked Alfred about that, but forgot."

"Who is Alfred?"

"One of the two guys who searched my house I told you about on the phone." Tommy sighed.

"What did he say?"

"Like I told you on the phone, he told me that John Smith hired them to toss the place and make it look like a search. But his description of the guy who hired them was not that of John Smith." After a brief hesitation, Tommy added, "This thing is so complicated that I'm not sure I'll be able to find a way out."

"What description did they give you?"

"Tall, skinny, freckles, red hair, pale," Tommy rattled off a condensed version of the description.

"Nothing else?" she queried.

"Nothing else."

"How about that sleep?"

"Please," Tommy replied, as Becky began pulling him

to his feet, her soft hands sending a tingling sensation down his spine.

Leading him into a light blue bedroom with a king size bed and navy blue satin sheets, Becky turned him around at the foot of the bed and began unbuttoning his shirt, then releasing his belt. Tommy absently pushed the right strap of her dress from her shoulder. Becky smiled and kissed Tommy on the lips, before slipping the other strap off her shoulder. The dress fell to the floor, revealing her thin naked body.

"The gander has quit running." Tommy reached out stroked her bare back. Her skin felt soft and warm as it glided under his fingers.

"About time." Becky softly laughed as she pulled his trousers down. "This hen was tired of chasing."

Becky pushed him back on the bed. Climbing on top, she straddled Tommy. He closed his eyes, concentrating on her soft skin brushing across his thighs. It was as if all his stress was soaked up by the mattress under him. He felt his whole body relax.

Leaning down, Becky placed her cheek next to his and nibbled at his ear. With her long brunette hair draped across Tommy's face, she moved her lips to his. Tommy let out a long shuddering snort.

Three hours later, Tommy woke to find Becky, still naked, lying next to him with the satin sheets swathe over her hips. Her blue sparkling eyes were fixed on him.

Blinking several times, Tommy asked, "What happened?"

"You fell asleep."

"Wow, I must have really been tired," Tommy replied.

Shaking her head, Becky said, "I'm beginning to suspect a conspiracy. Whatever happened to your girlfriend Lawan, the Thai woman?"

"Went back home. She didn't much like living here.

No one smiles. I gave her most of the payoff from the Thailand delivery and told her I'd come back and see her in a year or two."

Reaching out and placing her hand on his shoulder, Becky remarked, "You were with her for a long time."

"Years of faithfulness."

"Back to your wayward lifestyle," Becky teased, making it sound more a statement of fact than a question.

"It was inevitable. Genetics has a way of pulling you back to your natural instincts."

"Back to your philandering ways?" Becky asked, pulling her long hair back.

"You've got to be married or in a long-term relationship to be a philanderer. I am currently not bound by either."

After a few minutes of silence, Becky then asked, "What kind of deal did you make with Sid?"

"Just that I would meet with him tomorrow and tell him everything I know."

Raising her eyebrows in misbelieve, Becky said, "You're going to tell him everything?"

"Everything I know, except about my relationship with you, of course." Tommy winked at Becky. "I need someone on the inside in my corner, and while he may not be a very happy man, he proved to have the makings of a worthy ally last year. I'm hoping I can rekindle some of those old feelings and nurture a truce."

"Where are you meeting him?"

"McLean McDonald's tomorrow at noon. I've got one more task to complete before our meeting."

"What's that?"

Climbing from satin sheets, placing his feet on the plush white carpeted floor, Tommy sighed. "I've got to see a man. But before that, I've also got to find another mode of transportation. It's just a matter of time before the cops find my pickup. and it's probably best if I'm not in it when they do."

"Where on earth will you find another car?" Becky queried with a soft giggle. "The minute you hand someone your ID, you're toast."

"I'm not sure, but I won't find one rolling around under the sheets with you."

After a quick shower, he dressed in a pair of faded jeans and a red short-sleeve shirt. Slinging his backpack over his shoulder, Tommy looked back at the beautiful brunette still lying under the blue covers on the bed. She suddenly flipped the sheets back, revealing her naked body, and raised her eyebrows in a silent offer for fun.

Tommy winked and smiled. "Rain check. I've got work to do."

"Is the gander running again?"

"No, this gander is finished running."

"Will I see you tonight?"

"Not likely. You're the enemy."

Becky laughed as he stepped out of the bedroom. "What's that mean?"

Opening the apartment's front door, Tommy called back, "You work for the NSA, and they're probably looking for me too," before stepping out into the corridor and closing the door.

He took the elevator to the lobby. The doors opened to a wide marble walled room covered a dark burgundy carpet and decorated with large terracotta planters filled with bright green foliage. Absently stepping from the lift looking around, Tommy nearly knocked over a petite auburn-haired woman with fair skin.

"Tommy!" Amber cried out, looking up with a wide smile. "What are you doing here?" Her familiar perfume rose and touched his nose. She was dressed in a flowing knee-length cotton summer dress, and he could not help but smile at the beautiful woman looking up at him.

"I've got a friend who lives here. Is this the building where you have a big apartment overlooking the Potomac?"

"This is it," Amber confirmed his suspicion. "Is your friend male or female?"

"A friend." Tommy smiled down at the beautiful woman. Her sparkling green eyes seemed to draw him in.

"Where are you going?" she asked, cornering him against the wall next to the elevator.

"I've gotten into a bit of trouble and need to ditch my car," Tommy said, feeling the cool marble on his back. "I need to find another mode of transportation—or another car."

"I've got two cars. Come up to my place, and I'll let you use my spare."

Pushed into the elevator, Tommy watched as Amber pressed the button for the tenth floor, silently sighing in relief that her apartment wasn't on the ninth. Entering the apartment, he realized that Amber's flat was directly above Becky's. Looking around, he wondered if she and Becky had shared the same interior designer. She led him down a short hallway with several charcoal drawings of local sights displayed in frames along the walls to a long white leather couch atop deep plush white carpet with views of Washington, DC, and the Potomac River through the living room's large floor-to-ceiling windows.

Like a bad feeling of déjà-vu, Tommy sat on the couch, its leather coolly conforming to his body with a faint hiss, as Amber disappeared into the kitchen behind him.

The sound of glassware and cabinets was followed by Amber presenting him with a tumbler full of whiskey on two rocks of ice. Sitting down next to him on the couch, she reached and up pushed several strands of hair that had fallen across her green eyes back.

"What kind of problems?" Amber's soft voice asked as she gently placed her hands on his thigh.

"Some folks think I have something I don't, and the police think I murdered a CIA agent."

Amber laughed quietly in disbelief. "No, really, what's going on?"

"No, that's really what's going on," Tommy said, trying to hold up three fingers, mimicking the Boy Scout pledge, but the splinted fingers forcing him to hold all four up. "But I've got a meeting with another CIA agent named Sid that will likely clear it all up."

"What happened to your fingers?" she cried, seeing the purple swollen digits mounted on the blood-soaked tongue depressor.

"Accidently smashed them with a hammer."

Amber jumped from the couch and retrieved a first aid box from the kitchen, spending the next ten minutes cleaning and re-splinting his fingers.

"You really need to see a doctor about this," she announced while placing a new tongue depressor below the fingers. "The last digit is broken to pieces."

"Thankfully the joint still works. I'll see a doctor when I get out of this mess with the police."

"What time?" she asked wrapping white cloth tape around the finger mounted on a new tongue depressor.

"What time what?" Tommy asked.

"Your meeting with the CIA man."

"Not till tomorrow. Noon at the McDonald's in McLean. While he wasn't very imaginative in his choice of a meeting location, he's a smart guy. If anyone can help, he can."

"Tommy, spend the night here. Stay here until your

meeting with the CIA man," Amber pleaded, her auburn hair again falling across her green eyes.

"I've got to see someone tonight." Tommy suddenly felt aroused as he looked down at her thin legs and small breasts beneath the fabric of the dress. He wondered if Amber could read his mind as she stood and pulled him to his feet.

"I'll meet you in the bedroom," she coyly whispered. "I need to make one phone call."

"Can't it wait?" Tommy teased, pulling at her arm as he began walking toward the bedroom.

"Five minutes," she replied pushing him away.

Stepping into the bedroom, he silently whispered, "At least Becky's interior designer didn't make it to her bedroom," when he saw a queen size bed topped with a thick white quilt and matching cotton sheets.

Hearing Amber talking in a low tone on her cell, Tommy examined the bedroom, another large window overlooking the Potomac River, small round bed stands on each side of the white quilt topped bed, and a large painting of the Washington, DC, skyline hanging over the headboard. Sitting down on the foot of the bed, Tommy thought he heard Amber say his name to whoever was on the phone and then calmly tell the person on the other end of the line not to worry.

Amber stepped into the bedroom, reached out, and pulled Tommy to his feet. Unbuttoning his shirt, she tugged at his belt, releasing it. Tommy pushed one of the straps from her shoulder, as she pulled his shirt off. He pushed the other off her shoulder, and her summer dress fell to the floor, revealing a green bra and panties.

"What is it with you and green?"

Pushing his pants down, Amber replied, "The color works for me."

Reaching around her, Tommy unclasped the green bra. Amber let it fall to the floor and pushed Tommy back on the bed. Slipping out of her panties, Amber hoped onto the bed and straddled Tommy, her soft and warm skin sending a tingling sensation up his spine. He could feel the warmth of her skin under his hands. He could feel the wetness between her legs on his thighs. Amber leaned down and placed her cheek next to his, nibbling at his ear. Tommy once again had that feeling of déjà-vu as she placed her lips on his and pushed her tongue into his mouth. Tommy didn't fall asleep this time.

Two hours later, with the light fading through the bedroom window, Tommy woke to find Amber, tucked deep under the white quilt and her auburn hair coiled across a pillow, sleeping next to him. After rinsing himself off in the shower, he sat down on the edge of the bed and gently woke his sleeping partner, asking her about the spare car. She groggily told him where to find the keys and which parking spot it was located in. As he began to stand, she grabbed his arm and pulled him down, passionately kissing him on the lips.

"Don't be long," her soft voice purred.

"I won't. I'll be back in a couple of hours at the most," Tommy replied, giving her a departing kiss on the forehead.

Finding the keys hanging in the kitchen, Tommy made his way out of the apartment and to the elevator. Just as he pressed the call button his cell phone began to vibrate and ring in his pocket.

Extracting the phone, he answered, "Tommy here."

"Where are you?" Anna's voice greeted Tommy.

"Rosslyn, at a friend's apartment."

"My boss has agreed to your price."

"That's nice to hear."

"We need to meet."

"Why do we need to meet? We can coordinate over the phone."

"We need to meet," Anna persisted. "I am sure there is a tap on your phone. I don't want to advertise our arrangement.

"When and where?"

"Can you meet tonight?"

"No, I'm going to meet someone else."

"How about tomorrow? One o'clock. I will be at Jacky's Bistro on F Street Northwest," she hesitatingly replied. "You know where that is?"

"I know where it is, across the street from the Kennedy Center. But we can't meet at one o'clock. I've got to meet with a CIA guy at the Mclean McDonald's at noon."

"Why are you meeting with the CIA? Who are you meeting?"

"If you recall, I'm under investigation for the murder of a CIA agent. It was either McDonald's or an office within walking distance of a holding cell."

"Who are you meeting with?" she asked again.

"A guy named Sid," Tommy replied as the elevator doors opened. "What is this, a game of twenty questions? Why do you want to know his name?"

"Tommy, I am coordinating an illegal transfer of a computer virus. You are meeting with a CIA agent. I need to make sure you are not setting me up," Anna explained. "Then let's meet at three o'clock. Can you meet at three?"

"Three o'clock, I'll be there," Tommy replied before disconnecting the call.

The elevator swiftly descended, its doors opening to a shadowy concrete garage. Looking for Amber's car, he found the red Mercedes CLS sedan right where she described, spot C-14. As he strolled over to the car, he saw a shadowy silhouette of a person standing near one of the thick concrete pillars that punctuated the garage. Momentarily hesitating, Tommy clicked the button on the key chain that unlocked the car doors, a loud chirp ringing across the otherwise vacant garage.

"Where you headed?" Caroline's voice rang out, echoing off the garage's concrete walls and low ceiling.

"I'm off to see a man." Tommy turned and confronted the shadow of Caroline. "What are you doing here?"

"I wanted to talk," she replied, stepping from the shadows.

"About the job?"

"No, about your safety."

"What about my safety?"

"Tommy, the situation with the computer virus is full of people who are not who they claim, and one of the men you're dealing with is ruthless and capable of anything.

"Jacob Livingston?"

"Yes," she replied, reaching out and taking Tommy's hand.

"Tell me something I don't know. Who are the people deceiving me?"

"I can't tell you. But you need to be careful," she whispered. "Trust no one."

"The last time someone told me to trust no one, that individual turned out to be the most devious of all involved. And why can't you tell me who is deceiving me?"

"I'm not authorized to tell you. You've got to figure this out yourself."

"How about you?"

"What do you mean?"

"Are you who you say? Can I trust you?"

"Trust no one," Caroline announced again.

"Is all this just another element of the evaluation?"

"Look, I work for an organization of very powerful individuals. They have contacts at every level of government, as well as nearly every criminal organization across the globe," she confessed, looking up at Tommy, her light blue eyes full of concern. "They know things that no other organization knows."

"And you're privy to this information?"

"Some of it." She sighed. "They have included me in much of the information surrounding the computer virus."

"So you know I didn't kill the CIA man?"

"Yes."

"I'm meeting with a CIA agent tomorrow and wouldn't it be nice to have something that would convince him to look elsewhere for a suspect," Tommy said sarcastically.

"You're meeting Sid?"

"Yes, did you know about our meeting?"

"No, when and where are you meeting him?"

"Will you at least tell me if I can trust Sid?"

"Yes, you can trust Sid," Caroline admitted. "Where and what time are you meeting him?"

"Why should I tell you?"

"Because I just jeopardized my job by revealing that Sid is a good guy."

"McLean McDonald's at noon. And you can't share some of your information with the CIA or FBI? Can you help me clear my name?"

"No."

"Then leave me alone." Turning and stepping back up the car's door, he added, "If it's up to me to figure this out, then let me be."

CHAPTER 34

Washington, DC, May 1, 2016:

Driving the red Mercedes across the Roosevelt Bridge, Tommy's cell phone began ringing on the passenger seat next to him. Looking down at the caller ID number flashing on its small screen, he sighed.

After a few more rings, he begrudgingly picked the cell up and answered the call.

"Hello, Sarah," he muttered, feeling his blood pressure rapidly rising.

"Where are my children!" a shrill voice shrieked from the cell, causing Tommy to momentarily pull the phone away from his ear.

"The kids are safe."

"I've lodged a kidnapping complaint with the police. There's a warrant out for your arrest. You're going to lose all your visitation rights, and they're going put you away, you bastard!"

"They've got to find me first." Tommy chuckled at the new charge. "Look, I took them to protect them. There's a guy who's trying to make me give him—"

"Where are my children?" Sarah interrupted. "Why are my children suddenly in danger?"

"I'm trying to explain. There's a guy who is trying to

make me give him something. He is a very bad man and will use anything he can to get—"

"Then give him whatever he wants!" she bellowed, forcing Tommy to once again pull the phone from his ear.

"Because I don't have it," he replied, trying to remain calm.

"Then get it!" Sarah screamed, "Get what he wants and give it to him!"

"I don't know where—"

"I want to know where my children are!"

"I can't tell you over the phone." Tommy's voice rose several octaves. "We don't know whose listening, and I don't want anyone to find out."

"I want my children!" she shrieked again.

"Go screw yourself!" Tommy shouted into the cell. "You'll get them back when they're out of danger."

With sweat beginning to form on his brow, he disconnected the call and turned off his cell phone.

CHAPTER 35

Georgetown, Washington, DC, May 1, 2016:

One side of the narrow street was lined with stone and white washed brick detached homes, the other with tall three story brownstone townhouses. Expensive cars of every make, model, and color were parked tightly along both sides of the road, forcing what little traffic there was to move slowly. Tall trees, neatly trimmed hedges, and ornamental green street lamps decorated with colorful flower pots created a showcase image of the upscale Georgetown neighborhood in western Washington, DC.

Sitting in his out-of-place red Toyota rental sedan, Steve peered through a set of black binoculars down the street at the house. The radio was on playing the seventies Abba's hit "Dancing Queen," and he tapped his right foot in rhythm with the tune on the car's black rubber floor mat. With his cell phone sitting atop the green log book, Steve laid the binoculars down and leaned back into the car's seat to stretch his back.

After discovering that a Jacob Livingston was interested in the computer virus, Steve had simply searched a phonebook and found that the only one listed lived along this street. It had taken him nearly an hour to find a parking spot that allowed a view of Jacob Livingston's house.

The whitewashed two-story brick home had tall and narrow black trimmed windows, each bracketed by black decorative shutters, and a small neatly manicured lawn punctuated by a single Japanese Cherry tree to one side. As the sun began to descend below the horizon, one by one, the street lamps began to turn on in no orderly fashion, casting shadows across the neighborhood.

A middle aged woman dressed in a tight fitting black knee length dress, matching high heel shoes, and a small black beaded purse, stepped from the entrance of one of the brownstone townhouses, carefully making her way down its stone steps while holding onto a black wrought iron hand rail. Abeam a dark blue Jaguar parked close to the base of the stairs, she dug in her beaded purse and pulled out a set of keys. Manipulating the small electronic device with long manicured nails painted red, the woman unlocked the car's door before climbing in. Steve could see the sports car shudder as a pale plume of exhaust erupted from its tailpipe. A green Ford Taurus with a damaged front right fender slowly drove passed Steve's car just as a blue Jaguar pulled out and drove down the narrow street. The Taurus slipped into the empty spot.

"Lucky bastard," Steve muttered while shaking his head. "It took me forever to find a parking spot along this street, and that guy stumbles on one the first pass."

A tall redheaded man dressed in a green suit and pink open-collared shirt climbed out of the Taurus. Wondering if he was a salesman, Steve picked up the binoculars and watched as the man stood next to his car, looking down the street in one direction then the other. The tall redheaded man then walked across the street and up the sidewalk until he was in front of Jacob's house. Turning down the walkway, the man walked past Jacob's neatly trimmed lawn and up the steps to the home's entryway.

Several knocks with a heavy loop mounted onto a brass lion's head, and a slim man with neatly combed blonde hair wearing a blue cashmere robe opened the door.

"So there you are Mr. Livingston," Steve whispered to himself.

The phone on the seat next to him began ringing atop the green log book, interrupting Steve's surveillance. Placing the binoculars down, Steve glanced at the caller ID and then answered the cell.

"I thought we weren't to talk until our meeting on the fourteenth?" Steve sarcastically greeted the caller, once again fantasizing about her naked body glistening beneath him.

"Where are you?" a female voice replied, ignoring his comment.

The radio began playing Journey's seventies hit song "Any Way You Want It," and Steve turned down the volume. Looking back over at Jacob's entry, he saw that the door was now closed and the two men were gone. Glancing down the street, he saw the Ford Taurus was still parked in front of the black-dress-clad lady's townhouse.

"I'm in DC," Steve told the woman. "There's no use hanging out at Mr. Luck's house. With what happened at his ex-wife's, I doubt he'll go back home. The police will be sure to pick him up."

"He's been in Rosslyn."

"Why didn't you call and tell me?"

"What do you think you'll learn by watching Tommy?" the female voice asked, ignoring his question. "Each day you hang out in North Arlington watching his house, you risk being seen and cornered by him. The outcome of an encounter between Tommy and you would risk the entire deal."

"What do you want?"

"Tommy's meeting with Sid tomorrow at the McLean

McDonald's. We can't let those two meet, it might blow the lid off the whole deal."

"Why would it blow the lid off the deal?" Steve asked, examining Jacob Livingston's house again.

"Come on, Steve, think about it. What if he convinces Sid that he's not selling the computer virus? What if he tells Sid something that directs his investigation in another direction?"

"Like what?"

"Tommy's not taking all this lying down. He's trying to figure out who's framed him. You saw him in action last year. He has good instincts," the woman's voice had lost its softness, now having an exacerbated edge. "Sid is no dummy either. He proved himself last year, as well. Those two men put their heads together, and they could figure out what's really going on."

"What's Mr. Luck doing now?"

"Tommy told me he was going to see a man. He didn't tell me who, but Tommy's not dumb. He might be on to something."

"So Mr. Luck has gone to see a man. So what? What could he possibly learn that would lead Sid's investigation away from him?"

"What if he talks to Sid about you?" she asked. "What if he convinces Sid that he saw you and you're here?"

"I doubt Sid would believe Mr. Luck with the evidence stacked up against him. I'm supposed to be dead. Sid would just think it was a smoke screen to direct him away from Mr. Luck."

"Don't be an idiot. You must see how devastating a meeting between those two would be at this point."

Visualizing running his fingers across her bare breast, Steve became aroused. "What do you want me to do?"

"You need to stop Tommy and Sid from meeting one

another. Like I said, they're meeting tomorrow at noon. If you let those two meet, then the deal's off," she said with finality in her voice. "You cannot let them meet. It would be disastrous. "

"Let me talk with the boss. If there's a problem, I'll give you a call."

Steve heard a sigh and, with a soft tone returning, she said, "Call me anyway. I want to know what he says." The woman disconnected the call without saying goodbye.

With Kenny Loggins's "Footloose" now playing from the radio, Steve turned the volume back up and continued to watch the house. When his stomach began growling, he pulled a chocolate donut from a Dunkin Donuts' white paper bag that had been sitting on the rear seat, eating the pastry in three bites. When he was finished with the chocolate, he pulled a maple donut from the bag and ate that as well. With the last evidence of the daylight disappearing, white lights twinkled from heavily draped windows and the soft yellowish light from the overhead lamps dimly illuminated the street. All the while, Jacob and his guest remained in the house.

With the neighborhood virtually empty, it was hard for Steve to see the shadowy figure calmly walking down the street, momentarily hesitating at the front of each home. Steve picked up the binoculars, but quickly realized it was too dark to use them. He really didn't need to place them to his eyes anyway. He could spot Tommy's gait a mile away.

"Now what in the world are you doing here, Mr. Luck?" Steve muttered to himself.

Steve watched Tommy hesitate in front of Jacob's home then step behind the lone Japanese cherry tree in the front yard, before slipping into the shadows along the side of the house.

"So this must be the man you were coming to see," Steve mumbled again.

For a moment Steve considered getting out of his car to see where Tommy was meeting Jacob. He quickly dismissed the idea. The woman was right. Tommy catching him could spell disaster. Maybe the two were meeting in the backyard, he thought to himself. It was a pleasant enough night for an outdoor meeting. But why didn't Tommy use the front door and where did the tall red-headed man fit into what was going on?

Instead of following to see if Tommy was meeting with Jacob Livingston, Steve decided to make a phone call.

"What is it, Steve?" the Midwestern-accented voice answered the call.

"Got a couple of things. First, our friend called and said that Mr. Luck was going to meet with Sid tomorrow."

"That's bad. That's very bad."

"That's what she said. She wants me to stop the meeting."

"Absolutely stop them. If you happen to terminate one or the other, that would be acceptable. Those two sharing what they know could jeopardize the whole transaction."

"Secondly, looks like Mr. Luck is currently meeting with someone trying to buy the virus. And there's someone else with them."

"Another interested party. This game is getting crowded. I wonder if Tommy actually has a copy of the virus, after all. If he's meeting with a gentleman interested in obtaining the computer virus, then he just might have a copy," the Midwestern voice replied as if talking to himself. "Let him meet the man. A deal between Tommy and someone else won't hurt our plans."

"What should I do about this third party at the meeting?" Steve inquired.

"Follow him and find out who he is."

After a moment of silence, Steve asked, "What if it's the same copy?"

"What do you mean?"

"What if Tommy plans on selling this other person the same copy we're expecting to buy? What if he knows where it is and plans on using the same copy?"

"That would indicate that our primary source is lying to us, and I doubt she would do such a thing. We have too much on her. She would never risk us exposing her."

Disconnecting the call, Steve began waiting again. Ten minutes later Tommy's shadowy figure re-emerged from the shadows. He watched as Tommy calmly walked across the street and stood behind the redheaded man's car. After several minutes Tommy crossed back across the street and began walking down the sidewalk the way he had come, disappearing into the night. Fifteen minutes later, the tall redheaded men stepped from Jacob's entryway. Turning and shaking his host's hand, the red headed man walked back to the Ford Taurus and climbed inside.

Starting his red Toyota sedan, Steve watched the Taurus pull from the parking spot and noticed that one of the car's taillights had a missing red lens, revealing its bright white light. He hadn't noticed that when the car had passed him earlier. He attributed the oversight to the fact that it was still daylight when the redheaded man parked his Taurus on the street.

"You'll be an easy car to follow," Steve commented to himself, as he pulled from the curb and began following.

CHAPTER 36

Georgetown, Washington, DC, May 1, 2016:

To one side of the street were moderate size white washed brick and gray stone houses, and to the other tall brownstone townhomes. Lights tinkled brightly behind windows shuttered behind heavy drapes. Tall decorative green street lamps cascaded a yellowish-hued luminance that created shadows among the tall trees and wide bushes along the street. The narrow street, lined with high-end cars on both sides, seemed abandoned as Tommy walked along the sidewalk, inspecting the house numbers branded on brass plaques and posted near the front doors. Passing an oddly-out-of-place green Ford Taurus with a dinted front bumper across the street, Tommy finally saw the number he was searching for and slipped behind a tall Japanese cherry tree near the property's sidewalk boundary.

He could only imagine the costly security systems imbedded into the homes of this wealthy neighborhood, knowing that probing too deeply into a house would surely set off an alarm. Silently stepping across a manicured lawn and past another cherry tree, Tommy found himself standing next to a high brick wall covered in vines separating the house from its neighbor. Looking down a long dark corridor between the house and vine covered wall,

Tommy hesitated. To his left, he could see an oblique view of the living room decorated in antique furniture that looked as if it once inhabited a French villa. An enormous landscape painting depicting an eighteenth century English countryside was mounted on the room's back wall.

Stepping into the passageway between the house and brick wall, Tommy was met with the hot, humid aroma, similar to that of a green house, a mixture of both fresh and decaying plants. Vines tugged at his wrist as he ran one hand along the brick wall to steady himself in the darkness. Passing the protruding bulge of a brick chimney, Tommy could see a small garden at the end of the passageway illuminated from windows at the rear of the home. At the back corner of the house, the garden came into full view. The tall brick wall running along the side of the lot extended around the backyard. Three tall trees clustered together, a brick backyard barbeque and a raised flowerbed filled the small space. A narrow gravel pathway wrapped around the garden filled with flowers and shrubbery.

Peeking around the corner of the house, Tommy could see the illuminated windows that were casting light into the backyard, but his view was too angled to see inside. Moving from the darkness, he quickly maneuvered over to the stand of trees at the rear of the garden, stepping behind their trunks into the shadows.

Through two side by side long and narrow glass paned windows wrapped in a rose bush, Tommy could see two shadows moving about in what appeared to be a study with an enormous chandelier hanging from dark wood rafters.

Next to the long windows were double glass paned French doors showing more of the study. A high-backed wooden chair next to a small square table, a small painting and a charcoal drawing, could clearly be seen from his garden hideout.

A tall, red-haired man stepped into view in one of the windows. His hair was curly, and his arms and legs long and gangly. Dressed in a pink open-collared shirt and green suit, the man was speaking on his cell phone with a concerned look on his face. To Tommy, the redheaded man looked like a salesman. Disconnecting the cell, placing it into the pocket of his green jacket, the tall man drew a crystal glass filled with brownish liquid to his mouth, taking a healthy sip. Pursing his lips as he withdrew the glass, a wide smile broke out on the man's face.

Immediately thinking of Alfred's description of the John Smith who hired him and Larry, Tommy muttered to himself, "I wonder if this is the John Smith causing all of my problems?"

Jacob Livingston came into view wearing tan pants under a blue cashmere robe and sat down on the high-backed chair, carrying his own crystal glass filled with the same brownish liquid. The two were deep in conversation, but Tommy couldn't hear what they were talking about. Wanting to know what the conversation was about, he stepped out from the shadows and moved up to the wall adjacent to the windows, placing his ear as close to the paned glass as possible.

"You're sure he has it?" Jacob's whinny voice could be faintly heard through the window.

"According to my contact, there's no doubt about it," the red-headed man replied in a cheery Midwestern-accented voice.

"This story of yours is so interesting. Is there anything more you can tell me about this investigation? I find your agency stories fascinating. Please tell me more."

"Well, for starters, someone tried to kidnap his children. He caught the scoundrels in the act and killed them. He shoved a handgun in the mouth of one of the poor bastards and pulled the trigger. You can't imagine the mess."

Tommy's heart raced, he knew they were talking about him.

In a completely innocent tone, Jacob began asking, "Where has he taken—"

The sound of a door opening from behind the high brick wall at the rear of the garden, followed by a dog barking, momentarily interrupted Tommy. Pulling his head away from the tall window, he stood as still as possible. Once he was sure the dog hadn't sensed his presence, Tommy once again pushed his ear up next to the window.

"And you're sure the FBI is not investigating this computer virus incident?" Jacob's voice asked.

"No, they don't believe there's enough evidence to justify an investigation. I know what's going down, but all we can do is tap his phone and internet. We're getting nothing. He's going to get away with this whole scheme without ever being prosecuted."

The topic moved away from the virus to small talk. Tommy could detect a mixture of boredom and frustration in Jacob's voice as the conversation droned on. Finally, he realized that the risk of being caught outweighed his continued presence, and he moved back to the dark passageway between the house and high brick wall. Maneuvering back to the sidewalk in front of Jacob's house, Tommy causally walked across the street and stood behind the out-of-place green Ford Taurus. Looking down at the car's left rear taillight Tommy pulled the Colt .45 he had confiscated from Scar and began pounding its hand grip against the corner of the Taurus's red plastic lens cover. On the third strike, the plastic lens dropped off and landed on the street with a faint clatter. Tommy brushed it under the car with his foot.

Looking around to ensure no one saw his act of vandalism, he crossed back to the other side of the narrow road and walked down the sidewalk to Amber's red Mercedes parked on the next intersecting street. Sitting in the Mercedes, Tommy patiently waited.

Ten minutes later the green Ford Taurus passed through the intersection in front of him. Starting the Mercedes, Tommy began to follow using the Taurus's bright coverless taillight to keep track of his quarry. Tommy followed the car as it made a right on Wisconsin Avenue and began to head north. He followed the car through Bethesda then onto the Rockville Pike. He followed as the green Taurus turned onto the Washington, DC, Beltway's entry ramp, joining the eastbound traffic. The Taurus then turned north on Interstate 95 toward Baltimore, passing the Laurel and Scaggsville exit some fifteen minutes later. Just as Tommy began to consider turning around and heading back to Rosslyn, worried that he might end up following the car all the way to New York City, or someplace as ridiculously faraway, the green Taurus exited the interstate onto Highway 32, heading eastbound. Tommy continued following until the Taurus turned and stopped to show identification at the Fort Meade security gate. Stunned, Tommy drove past Fort Meade's front gate and back to Amber and Becky's apartment building overlooking the Potomac River.

As he stepped onto the lift in the underground parking and pushed the button for the tenth floor, Tommy hoped he would not run into Becky.

CHAPTER 37

Kimball, Nebraska, August 4, 1992:

Sitting on a purple vinyl easy chair in his small motel room, nineteen-year-old Tommy Luck was dirty and exhausted after a day of working on a local well servicing unit as a roustabout just south of Kimball, Nebraska. Lying back on the easy chair, he tried to find the willpower to get up and into the bathroom for a shower, but couldn't.

Instead, he looked around his room at the Comet Motel, examining its simplicity: a queen size bed sagging at its center covered with a brown bedcover stood against an off-white concrete wall, and a television airing the local news in static ridden muted color stood on a desk opposite. The room seemed to be dark no matter what time of day it was, illuminated by a single overhead light fixture and a one standup lamp, next to the easy chair. The unwavering scent of cleaning supplies wafted the air. It wasn't much, but Tommy didn't need much. He just needed a place to sleep and shower between shifts.

Pulling a filthy light blue T-shirt over his head, he then unlaced and kicked off his work boots without ever moving from the chair. Running his hands through his long wavy brown hair, Tommy sighed and sat up. Peering at the bathroom door, he once again tried to find the resolve to move. Hearing a scuffle outside the rear the motel, he canted his head to one side, trying to discern what was going on.

Hearing a faint, "I hear you Arabs like to get poked in the ass," in what seemed almost a playful voice, Tommy pushed himself off the chair and walked into the bathroom, peering out the window at the small space behind the motel. "I hear rag head men prefer boys to girls," the voice, now sounding sarcastic, continued.

A thick bramble of shrubs lined the rear of the Comet Motel's boundary and separated it from a set of railroad tracks that cut along the center of the town. Looking left then right through the small bathroom window, Tommy spotted three teenagers standing over a smaller boy, dark haired and wide matching eyes. The boy was scooting across the ground on his bottom. Suddenly the smaller boy attempted to scamper left but was met with a swift kick by a teenager with short blonde hair and wearing a white western style shirt. Tommy watched as a boy dressed in a red plaid shirt grabbed the boy by his shoulder and twisted him onto his hands and knees.

Shirtless and bare footed, Tommy turned, ran across his room. Bursting through the door leading to the parking lot, Tommy raced along the walkway lined with the doors leading into the other rooms. Tommy glanced up at the faded sign depicting a pink comet with a yellow tail on a green background standing overhead, advertising the Comet Motel. He heard a scream followed by a "shut up!" as he sprinted around the corner of the building toward the back.

As Tommy rounded the corner into the back lot of the motel, he could see one of the teenagers had a foot on the young dark haired boy's head, holding him to the ground. He could see that the teenagers had pulled the young boy's trousers down to his ankles. He could see the red-plaid-shirted teenager with his pants pulled down begin to kneel over the smaller boy with an erect penis.

The boy cried out again, no words just a high-pitched guttural cry.

Tommy sprinted toward the commotion, his bare feet painfully pounding across gravel and brittle grass. Ahead, Tommy watched as one of the teenagers spread the boy's legs. The boy let out one last scream, as if preparing for the inevitable.

Leaping, the last few yards, Tommy tackled the two teenagers pinning the boy to the ground, knocking them into the thick brambles marking the boundary of the motel.

As the two teenagers bounced off the bushes and fell to the ground, Tommy turned and reached down, grabbing the red-plaid-shirted teenager from atop the small dark-headed boy and throwing him aside.

Bare bottomed, the small boy twisted over and sat up, looking up at Tommy's bare chest and shoeless figure with frightened eyes. The trio of teenagers quickly stood and glared at Tommy.

"What the fuck are you doing?" Tommy yelled at the teenagers.

"Mind your own business, mister," the red-plaid-shirted teenager screamed back, as he pulled his jeans up.

"The little rag head deserved this," the teenager with the short blond hair and white western style shirt added.

"That's right, this rag head deserved this," the red-plaid-shirted teenager repeated his friend's claim as he buckled his belt.

"You fuckers are going to jail. This is a small town, and you can't hide," Tommy declared, standing between the young boy and the teenagers.

Glancing down at the young dark haired boy, Tommy

saw him looking up with wide innocent eyes as he swiped his wiry dark hair from his face.

Looking back at the three teenagers, Tommy roared, "Now get the hell out of here before I kick your asses!"

The three teenagers quickly began maneuvering through a small opening in the hedge. Just before disappearing through the gap in the bushy bramble, the red-plaid-shirted teenager turned and said, "He's no good. You're on the wrong side, mister."

"No one deserves what you were trying to do, jackass. No one," Tommy growled in response.

Turning and reaching down, Tommy held his hand out to the young boy. The boy took his hand, and Tommy pulled him to his feet, before saying in as calm a voice as he could muster, "Now get your clothes on."

Clumsily the boy first pulled up his underwear and then his khaki pants before looking back up at Tommy.

"What's your name?" Tommy asked.

"Omid Sassani," the boy mumbled his name to Tommy in a quiet voice.

"Do you know those boys?"

With tears beginning to fall from his dark eyes and roll down his cheeks, Omid silently nodded.

Dropping to one knee, Tommy took Omid's shoulders into his hands. "What happened to you today was unfair, and it should never happen to anyone. But life is not fair. Life is never fair. Some people get all the breaks, and others get nothing. You should never look back and worry about your past misfortune or look forward and hope for a break. You just need to realize that life's not fair and forge ahead, recognizing it's ultimately out of your control. Happiness is based on who we associate with and how we treat the people around us. You can choose to live a life feeling sorry for yourself, wallowing in self-pity, and looking out for only yourself, or a life where you choose your friends and are loyal to those friends, supporting each other when things get tough."

Omid silently nodded to Tommy again, his dark wet eyes seemingly older and wiser than his chronological age.

"Let me take you home," Tommy calmly said, still holding the boy's shoulders.

Abruptly twisting out of Tommy's grip, Omid sprinted through the opening in the bramble of scrubs. Standing, Tommy watched the frightened young boy run away, wondering why he didn't want his help. Why would a young boy sprint away from a man who had just saved his honor?

CHAPTER 39

Rosslyn, Arlington, Virginia, May 2, 2016:

Waking at around seven o'clock in the morning, Tommy felt as if he needed to vomit. Vaguely remembering consuming a bottle of Jameson from his backpack followed by two bottles from a wine locker he had found in the dining room, he looked over and saw Amber's bare milky white back protruding from under the white quilt and her auburn hair spilling out onto the sheets next to him. Looking out the window, he could see an airliner pass by on approach to Reagan National Airport, the vibration from its engines softly rattling a glass on the table next to him.

Lying on the bed for a moment, he considered the dream he had been having before waking. A memory really, his mind had been replaying his encounter with Omid Sassani in Kimball and saving the young boy from being raped all those years ago. Watching the boy run away after the incident, Tommy once again wondered why the boy rejected his offer to take him home. Had Omid's life been so harsh, even at that young age, that he didn't want help from anyone? Had that one event shaped the boy's life in a harmful or helpful way, steering him down a path that he would have never wandered? Rolling over and placing his feet on the floor, Tommy wondered what had happened to Omid Sassani and where his life had taken him.

Head throbbing, he pulled himself from the bed and stumbled into the bathroom. After several dry heaves into the toilet, Tommy stepped into the shower and turned on the cold water. With icy cold water painfully coursing down his body, his scalp tingled and the small hairs on his arms and legs stood at attention. Hearing a soft padding of bare feet on the bathroom floor, Amber pulled back the shower curtain and reached in, testing the water.

"No way," she yelped before spinning the hot water handle. "I'm a cold water wimp."

Tommy jumped back as searing hot water pummeled his back, crying, "What are you? A blacksmith? Those handles are delicate instruments! I may need a trip to the burn unit at the nearest hospital."

"Don't be a sissy." She giggled, climbing in and drawing up close to him. "How'd the meeting with the man go last night?"

"Good and bad," Tommy groaned forcing his face under the streaming water.

"Good and bad?" Amber inquired as she wrapped her arms around him.

"Well, I got there at a really good time. But I think the man he was talking with might pose a small problem."

"There were two men at the meeting?" she asked looking up at Tommy with a quizzical expression.

"Yeah, two guys. I only expected one, but there were two."

"And the good?"

"The timing was such that it let me know that the man has an ally."

"And the bad?"

"I found out the man has an ally."

"Do you know who the ally is?" she asked.

"No, but I know who he works for an organization with which I share a sad saga filled with cunning and deceit."

"Why do you always speak in riddles?"

"I come by it honestly," Tommy teased. "A genetic legacy of cryptic communications."

Amber pushed him away and said, "You're speaking in riddles about riddles."

"My father always spoke in riddles. Don't you have to go to work or something?"

"I took the day off. I want to help." Amber's bright green eyes sparkled as she looked up at him.

"I just got three things to do today. First I'm going for a run to leach out some of this alcohol you forced on me last night. Secondly, I'm meeting with that CIA agent in McLean and, finally, I'm driving down to the Bay to check on my kids."

"First of all, I didn't force anything on you last night. I was asleep when you got back. Secondly, I want to tag along with you today," Amber said defiantly, with her hands on her slim naked hips, than adding with a giggle, "Except I'll skip the run."

Draping a robe over her shoulders, Amber walked into the living room while Tommy began pulling on a pair of blue shorts. Sitting down the bed, he could hear the faint sound of a cell phone ringing as he slipped his shoes on, lacing and tying them up.

Pulling an olive drab T-shirt over his head, he walked into the living room.

Her back to Tommy and cell phone at her ear, she said "Yes, I said today. I don't know what he's going to say," she said in a frustrated tone. "Look, I can't talk right now. I'll call you later." Disconnecting the call, Amber turned. "Tommy, you dressed quickly."

The look on her face told Tommy that she was surprised to see him standing there.

"Yeah, I'm a regular Mario Andretti when it comes to getting dressed. Who were you talking to?"

"I called to tell my boss that I wouldn't be in today. He wanted me to attend a meeting with some guy inquiring about our services. Then my boss asked me what the guy was going to ask during the meeting." She sniggered. "Like I would know? I told him I had no idea, that's why we're supposed to meet with him. My boss can be a real moron sometimes."

Kissing Amber goodbye, Tommy headed out for his run, again hoping he wouldn't run into Becky in the apartment building's lobby. Jogging up Lee Highway, Tommy found the entrance to the Curtis Trail and crossed a long pedestrian walkway, with a tunnel like chain-link fence barrier, over the top of Interstate 66. With the traffic on the interstate whisking by below, and bicyclers and other joggers speeding by in the opposite direction on the thin ribbon of a trail, Tommy began to sweat out the prior evening's liquid entertainment.

Thirty minutes into his run, with his nausea and throbbing head slowly ebbing, Tommy began to wonder why the NSA would be talking with Jacob, a man that was clearly a criminal. Tommy had dealt with the NSA last year during the Bangkok delivery and found them to be thoroughly deceitful and dangerous. In the end, he had to murder the NSA's Inspector General to protect himself from further danger. Maybe murder was too strong a word, Tommy thought as he jogged along the trail. After all, the inspector general had been trying to kill him. That made it more like self-defense.

Tommy considered Becky for a moment. She worked for the NSA but had been providing him with a lot of information and support during this whole fiasco. She had warned him of the investigation and divulged everything Sid had against him. She had agreed to remove Larry and Alfred when he had left them on his entryway floor, and she had taken him in when he had no place to go. On the other hand, she had been deceptive when he asked her about Jacob Livingston, and she had known that he had been questioned by the police, even though he never told her.

His thoughts then turned to Amber, who had come into his life shortly before the murder of the CIA man. She claimed to be an investment banker working the Washington, DC, area, but he had caught her speaking in riddles of her own on her cell phone several times, one of those times just that morning. Was she who she claimed? The thought of Amber being a part of what was going on around him was not something Tommy wanted to believe. She had been too good for him to even contemplate the thought.

There was Anna, another woman who had recently come into his life. While she had initially presented herself as someone interested in him sexually, she had come clean and told him the truth. She was a middleman for purchasing the computer virus. Was her employer setting him up? If so, the deal between them was nothing but a shame. Why make a deal with someone you know does not have the product you desire? And if her employer did believe that Tommy had the virus and wanted to purchase it, why set him up for murder? That scenario made no sense.

There was also Caroline, a woman cloaked in mystery. She knew a lot about him and what was going on concerning the computer virus and the murder of the CIA agent. She claimed to be an executive headhunter working for a powerful organization, but Tommy had a feeling that she was far more involved with his situation than she let on. She was an unknown variable who was obviously heavily involved in the mystery surrounding the events unfolding around him.

Then there was Steve. Steve had worked for John Smith, the orchestrator of delivery of the computer virus to Thailand last year where Tommy had been the deliveryman. Steve showing up at the same time as Tommy was being framed for both attempting to sell the same computer virus and the murder of a CIA agent was too coincidental.

But who was Steve working with? Was he the buyer or seller? Had he framed Tommy to cover his own tracks? Or was he simply trying to extract some sort of perverted revenge? Tommy knew that Steve was the key to solving the mystery.

Were Caroline and Steve working together? May be his next step should be to find out exactly who Caroline was and who she worked for? If so, she might lead him to Steve and his associate.

Finally, there was Jacob Livingston. Jacob Livingston's part was straightforward. He wanted the computer virus. Jacob Livingston was simply a sideshow when it came to solving Tommy's problems. Jacob Livingston was a distraction. Tommy needed to focus on Steve and Caroline.

Returning from his run two hours later, Tommy once again worried he would run into Becky in the lobby. Without incident, Tommy rode the elevator to the tenth floor and entered the apartment, hearing Amber typing away on her laptop in the bedroom.

"Hey, beautiful, I'm back," Tommy called out.

"I'm just finishing up some work. I'll be out in a few minutes," Amber called from the bedroom.

"Take your time, I'm going to get something to drink

and then hop in the shower," Tommy replied, making his way to the kitchen.

Seeing Amber's cell phone recharging on the gray granite counter, Tommy took a bottle of water from the refrigerator, quickly draining its contents into his mouth. Throwing the empty bottle into the recycle bin, he moved over to her cell and picked it up. Pressing its small keys and examining the call registry, he found that in the last twenty-four hours two calls were made to "Mom," five calls to local numbers with no name attached, and three calls to someone called "JS." One of the calls to "JS" had occurred about the time he was walking out the door to go on his morning run.

"Ah, crap," Tommy quietly mumbled, immediately thinking that the initials "JS" could designate John Smith.

After a shower, Tommy walked out the apartment door, with Amber in tow, for the drive to McLean to meet Sid, when his cell phone began buzzing. Looking at the caller ID on the cell's small screen, Tommy answered the call.

"Sid, I'm just stepping out the door," Tommy told the grumpy CIA agent, as he and Amber walked toward the elevator doors.

"I'm changing the location of our meeting," Sid's low voice grumbled.

"Why the change?" Tommy inquired, pushing the wall mounted call button for a down elevator.

"Call it a gut feeling."

"Okay, where do you want to meet?" Tommy asked as the doors to the elevator opened.

"Directly across the street from the McDonald's, there's a three-story red brick office building. On the third floor, there's a company called Whitlows Security. I've arranged to use their conference room. You'll have to be buzzed in. Just tell them you're meeting me."

Pulling from the underground parking lot in the red Mercedes, Tommy began to feel uneasy but couldn't put his finger on what was bothering him. Several blocks later, he turned left onto Lee Highway, still unable to shake the feeling that something was amiss. As the red Mercedes sped up the hill, leaving Rosslyn behind, Tommy passed by a red Ford truck then a black Nissan sedan. As he came to a stop behind an old tan GMC panel van, waiting for a red light to change, a dark blue Chevy Suburban pulled up next to them, then an old green Ford Fiesta moved up behind. Tommy looked over as the Suburban's passenger window came down, and a grizzly man with a dark beard streaked with gray looked over and smiled. Tommy smiled back just as the grizzly man pushed the muzzle of an Uzi SMG out the window.

Tommy punched the accelerator to the floor as the Uzi SMG spit out a stream of bullets, ripping half a dozen holes into the rear door and trunk of the Mercedes. Amber, with wide, terrified eyes, let out a high-pitched shriek as the Mercedes crashed into the panel van in front of them. Both the driver and passenger's airbags deployed, slamming Tommy and Amber back into their seats. Throwing the Mercedes into reverse, Tommy stepped on the accelerator again. Its tires spinning, screaming, and smoking, the car's engine pumped out the demanded torque.

"Get down," Tommy yelled at Amber, as the grizzly man pulled the trigger again, aiming at the backward moving Mercedes, another half a dozen holes popping across the hood and front fender. Smashing into the Ford Fiesta, Tommy kept his foot on the accelerator and pushed the smaller car back until he had a gap big enough to escape. Turning the wheel as far left as it would go, Tommy threw the Mercedes into drive and stepped down on the accelerator once more. The Mercedes's tires spun and screamed again as the car lunged forward. The driver of the Suburban, anticipating Tommy's maneuver, put the big SUV into reverse and lurched back, slamming into the right rear bumper of the Mercedes, spinning the car so the two vehicles were side by side.

Looking up into the Suburban driver's window, Tommy saw Steve peering down at him. Tommy gave Steve the finger and stepped on the gas. The Mercedes shot forward. Its rear bumper, still tangled with that of the Suburban, ripped from the car's frame. The car sprang through the intersection, running the red light. More bullets began peppering the back of the car, its rear window first spider webbing then shattering into small blocks of glass that flew into the car's interior.

The Mercedes raced to the top of a hill, becoming airborne when the road turned downward. Sparks flew from its undercarriage as the Mercedes landed back on the road, its shock absorbers unable to hold the weight of the car's heavy frame from the paved street. At the bottom of the hill, Tommy ran another red light, several cars crossing the intersection screeching to a halt with their horns blaring. Speeding up another hill, Tommy kept the accelerator on the floor, leaving the Suburban far behind.

"Are you all right?" Tommy asked, trying to speak as calmly as possible.

"Who was that?" Amber's voice was trembling, and her milky white skin was a shade paler than usual.

"An old friend."

"A friend? What kind of friends do you have?" she asked in a perfectly serious tone and with an astonished face.

Tommy sped along Lee Highway, flying past every car they came upon to ensure there was no chance that

Suburban would catch up. At the intersection of Glebe Road, Tommy made a tire-screeching right turn then a left on Old Dominion Road, racing toward McLean.

CHAPTER 39

McLean, Virginia, May 2, 2016:

Just as Sid described, the three-story red brick office building stood directly across the street from McDonald's. Peering over the bullet-ridden hood, Tommy pulled the red Mercedes into a small paved lot out front, having to use two parking spots to fit the large car.

Looking over at Amber, Tommy asked, "You want to wait for me in McDonald's?"

Examining the damaged hood, the color having returned to her face, Amber shook her head. "Actually, I want to go home and hide in my closet."

"Well, for the moment, let's say that's not an option."

"There are two reasons I'm not waiting in McDonald's. First is that we were just shot at by an alleged friend of yours, and I'd rather be in a security company's locked office as opposed to McDonald's where another of your friends could show up. Secondly, do you see me as someone who frequents McDonald's?"

"Just an idea," Tommy said, shrugging his shoulders. "I'm not sure where you can wait, but you're welcome to come along."

Walking through the building's glass enclosed entry, Tommy and Amber had to wait for what seemed an unusually long time for an elevator to make its way to the lobby and the doors to open. Stepping inside the cramped lift with a dirty blue carpeted floor and imitation wood veneer walls, it groaned as the doors closed and shuddered as it slowly rose. The smell of mildew engulfed them creating a slightly suffocating effect. With grimacing faces, they waited for the quivering ride to reach the third floor.

Stepping from the elevator, they found themselves in an empty white hallway with a set of tan steel doors and a simple black and white sign announcing 'Whitlows Security.'

Tommy punched a button and spoke into a small wall mounted speaker, "Thomas Luck to meet with a CIA guy named Sid."

Amber whispered in his ear while standing next to him, "You don't know his last name?"

"Gellman or Gilman or Gilroy. I can't remember."

A tinny voice suddenly blurted from the speaker, "Come on in, sir," as an audible click came from door's handle.

They stepped into a reception area, two chairs and a coffee table topped with a pile of professional security magazines filling a small alcove. Two soft brown eyes and a forehead framed with blonde hair peeked at them from over a chest high counter. Amber looked up at Tommy, shrugging her shoulders, before taking a seat at one of the chairs and picking up one of the magazines.

"I know I'm a little early," Tommy said to the receptionist, "Is Sid here yet?"

"He's waiting for you. The conference room is just down the hall," the receptionist replied, the sound from the speaker at the door obviously not completely at fault for the tinny greeting.

Leaving Amber sitting in the reception area, Tommy

walked down a narrow white hallway, its walls adorned with pictures of local federal government buildings, presumably those which Whitlows Security held the contract. At the end of the hallway stood a single black wooden door with a long and narrow glass floor-to-ceiling window to one side. Peering through the window, Tommy saw an oval wooden table surrounded by black vinyl cushioned chairs, with another wide window along one wall providing light and views of the street below. Sid, with his silver hair and contrasting dark eyebrows, sat in the chair furthest from the door at the end of the oval table. He was peering back at Tommy through the window.

"You removed the tracking device from your truck again," Sid grunted as Tommy stepped into the conference room. "The deal was you keep it on."

"I didn't remove the tracking device," Tommy retorted. "I'm driving a different car. That truck is probably on a nationwide All Points Bulletin along with my name and description. And the warrant count continues to rise. My ex-wife claims I'm now wanted for the kidnapping of my children."

"I called the police department search for you off yesterday evening. All the warrants for your arrest have been dropped. The warrant for kidnapping was stopped before it was ever issued. I sent an agent over to your ex-wife's house yesterday to try and explain the situation."

"It didn't work. I got an earful last night."

"My agent claims that she is not a very reasonable person. 'She is a piece of work' was the descriptive quote my agent used to describe the conversation."

"You now know why she's my *ex*-wife."

"You need to keep that tracker on whichever car you choose to drive," Sid growled. "Put it in your pocket for all I care. I want to know where you are at all times."

"Your gut feeling was right," Tommy said, changing the topic, as he stepped up to the table. "I've got an eighty thousand dollar car outside with two dozen bullet holes decorating its hood and trunk."

The smell of stale cigarettes mixed with that of air freshener, as Tommy choose a black vinyl chair two down from Sid, pulling it from the table. With casters on each of its legs, the chair smoothly slipped from the table, and he sat down. Its heavily padded black vinyl cushion made the chair extremely comfortable as the padding depressed under Tommy's weight.

"Not to mention, the rear window needs replacing. Thankfully, the shooter wasn't very good at hitting a moving target," Tommy added.

"Who shot at you?" Sid's low baritone voice rumbled.

"Our old friend Steve and some guy that resembles Jeremiah Johnson in his later years."

"Steve from Bangkok?" Sid asked raising his dark eyebrows in surprise. "I was told he was dead."

"The very same Steve, and I was told he was dead too."

"What else do you have for me?"

"A man named Jacob Livingston, who resides in Georgetown, is trying to get me to hand over the virus."

"So you do have the virus?"

"Christ, you people are relentless." Tommy laughed sarcastically. "I said he's *trying* to get me to hand it over to him. And, no, I don't have the fucking computer virus."

"I know about Jacob Livingston. Go on, tell me more."

"My pal Jacob had his men use a Dremel Tool and hammer to try to beat the location of the virus out of me," Tommy said, holding up his swollen and purple fingers strapped to the tongue depressor, showing Sid as proof. "He then told his henchmen to kidnap my kids. Those are the guys the police found on my ex's floor. Last night, I went to his house in Georgetown to scope the place out. I saw him meeting with a guy and listened in on part of their conversation."

"What'd they say?"

"Not much, but they were talking about me. The interesting part is that Jacob tells this guy he loves the 'agency' stories he tells about all his 'investigations.'"

"Agency? Investigations?"

"Yeah, that's right, agency and investigations, but it gets better. So I follow this guy and guess where he goes?"

"Tell me."

"Fort Meade, home of the National Security Agency. I followed him to the front gate of Fort Meade. He arrived around ten o'clock last night."

"What'd the guy look like?" Sid asked flatly, without even a hint of surprise in his voice or expression.

"Tall, curly red hair, and pale skinned with freckles on his face. Which is the same description Alfred gave me yesterday when I asked what John Smith looked like."

"What else did Alfred tell you?"

"Alfred said that the guy must be an idiot because he told them his name."

"Maybe he wanted to tell them his name," Sid commented. "Because it wasn't his name."

"My thoughts exactly."

"Tell me about Steve."

"I first saw him a couple of days ago, driving near my house in Arlington. He was also driving the car that took the shots at me and my lady pal outside on the way to this meeting."

"Why do you think he's all of suddenly trying to kill you? If he's been in town for a couple days, why wait till now?"

Suddenly the building was rocked by a nearby explosion, the conference room's windows loudly clattering in their aluminum frames. Standing up, both Sid and Tommy looked out the window to see all the windows of the McDonald's across the street shattered, blown out across the parking lot. Flames curled from each of the broken windows, sending a dark black cloud skyward.

First looking at his watch then up at Sid, Tommy asked, "Guess what time it is?"

"Twelve noon," Sid groaned.

"Steve had a backup plan in the event he missed me driving over here."

With his ruddy complexion and green eyes bracketing a large bulbous red nose with deep pores shimmering in a reflection from the glass, Sid asked, "Why have you all of a sudden become a target? Why don't they need you anymore?"

"They needed me long enough to become the patsy for whatever is going on," Tommy responded. "I'm assuming that they were using me to misdirect an investigation into the computer virus reappearing in the wrong hands. And Steve has been their source of information on the computer virus and me."

"Steve may be their source of information, but he was never in possession of the virus. The computer virus went through a number of hands during the delivery. Any one of those people could have copied the virus' code. Any one of those people could be selling the virus. Any one of those people knew of your exploits in Thailand. Steve never had possession of the computer virus."

"He may have never had the virus, but he knows about Thailand."

"He's not smart enough to set this up," Sid commented.

"And I was one of those people who had possession of the computer virus, which is why they chose me as their fall guy."

"They chose you for more than that. They chose you because you're an unemployed drunk with an empty bank account," Sid replied, looking over at Tommy with an expression that lacked any emotion.

"I'll buy that."

Watching the burning McDonald's, Tommy could see a dozen people running around the outside of the smoldering building, helping survivors. Sirens could be heard in the distance.

"Okay, we know why they needed you, but why target you now?" Sid asked, again. "Why not earlier? Why not later? Why ever target you? Even if we never found enough evidence to charge you, we all would still have believed it was you who sold the virus."

Looking down at his feet, Tommy thought about Sid's question. After a moment he looked up at Sid and announced, "You. You were the reason."

"What do you mean?"

"This meeting. Our being together. Whoever's behind this knew about this meeting and thought that it could spoil their plans if you and I were to share what we know."

"So the question is what bit of information do you have that could help me figure this out?"

"It's not just one bit of information. It's the information we both have. It's the sharing of information. They know if we share what we have, if we become allies, we could figure out who's behind selling the virus."

It was Sid's turn to hesitate, thinking about the implications of Tommy's answer. Sid finally asked, "Who did you tell about the meeting?"

"Becky, a girl named Anna, another named Caroline, and the young lady waiting in the reception foyer outside all knew."

"You either have a lot of secretaries, or you're juggling a lot of girlfriends who like to keep tabs on your activities."

"I didn't think passing along information about a meeting with you would become a life-threatening event. How about you?"

"The four members of my team, the CIA Deputy Director, and NSA Inspector General. I've been keeping him in the loop."

"So, anyone of those could be playing both sides, or they're talking with someone else. And how does the tall, redheaded NSA man fit into this?"

"I think I know who the redhead is," Sid grumbled to Tommy, his low baritone voice echoing off the walls of the conference room.

CHAPTER 40

Fort Meade, Maryland, May 2, 2016:

Wearing his rumpled khaki pants and a brown tweed jacket, Sid stepped out of the elevator on the sixth floor of the NSA building into the small reception area. The same slender young blonde woman from six days ago, now dressed in a dark blue skirt and white blouse, sat behind the reception counter.

"Can I help you, sir?" the woman asked in her high pitched voice with a wide smile, as if Sid was the first person she had greeted that day.

"The inspector general," Sid grunted, feeling as if his dialog with the receptionist was a rerun from his previous visit.

"Just down the hallway," the young receptionist squeaked, smiling again, pointing to one of the three short hallways protruding from the lobby that Sid knew led to the inspector general's office.

Walking down the navy-blue-carpeted corridor, passing the same square mirror with black wooden frame hanging on the beige walls, Sid could see the large wooden door leading into the Inspector General's office at the end. Arriving at Judy's desk, once again verified by her brass name plate, Sid saw the auburn-haired middle-aged secretary was busy typing on her computer. He immediately felt the same attraction to her he had six days earlier.

Looking down at Judy, Sid nodded in the direction of the inspector general's door as the secretary glanced up with large dark brown eyes. "Is the boss in?"

"Yes, Mr. Sid, and it's so nice to see you again. You don't have an appointment, you're lucky he is. The inspector general is a busy man."

The smell of flowery perfume wafted the air around the secretary's desk and once again mixed with the stale cigarette odor emanating from Sid's tweed jacket. Sid looked at the fire extinguisher mounted on the ceiling that doubled as a hidden camera and gave the lens a scowl, hoping the inspector general was watching.

"Sid," he grunted, looking back down to Judy. "It's just Sid. You can leave out the mister."

"Just a moment, Sid," Judy replied, her brown eyes sparkling, before picking up the phone and calling the inspector general. Hanging up the phone, she stood. "You can go right in."

As the secretary began moving for the door, Sid once again beat her and opened it himself, the heavy door easily swinging inward.

The inspector general stood up from his desk as Sid stepped through the door, extending his long gangly hand with a smile. "This is an unexpected pleasure, Sid. Why in person and not a phone call?"

Stepping to the front of the desk, Sid was met with a pungent smell of aftershave. Giving the inspector general a quick hand shake, Sid replied, "Some things need to be discussed in person and without an appointment."

With the two cardboard boxes gone, the wide oak bookcase's shelves were now filled with personal memorabilia. Pictures of a tall blonde woman and two small redheaded children that Sid assumed to be the inspector general's family, a baseball with a signature scribbled on its side, and several books on criminal investigations filled its shelves. Glancing over the inspector general's shoulder, Sid examined the four once-bare nails that now had several personal awards and two framed posters, exuding the value of teamwork, hanging from them.

"What on earth would you need to discuss with me in person? Is there a problem with Becky?" the inspector general queried, his smile vanishing as he sat down behind his desk.

"What do you know about Jacob Livingston?" Sid asked as he sat down on the slick leather chair opposite of the inspector general, firmly planting his feet on the plush blue carpet, shifting his buttocks to the rear of the cushion in order to not slip out.

"Just what I've told you. He deals in stolen corporate databases, and we've been watching him for quite some time. To date, we've not been able to gather enough evidence to pass the case onto the FBI. We discovered he was talking with Thomas Luck, and I passed the information and the transcripts of his calls to you." The inspector general weaved a black Skill Craft government-issued pen through the long pale fingers of his right hand.

"How do you think he discovered that the computer virus was on the market?" Sid asked, looking out the window. Shifting his gaze from the tops of distant oak trees to his reflection, he could see his silver hair contrasting with his dark eyebrows in the glass.

"Maybe he reads the *Washington Post*. He's a very intelligent man."

"Have you ever met him?"

"Why would you ask that?" the inspector general asked, nervously shifting his tall, lanky frame.

Sid's eyes shot back to the inspector general, before

saying, "Seems that a man matching your description met with Jacob last night in his Georgetown residence."

"You had someone watching him? You must be really stretching your small team thin to be keeping an eye on Jacob Livingston," the inspector general announced, raising his red eyebrows.

"Let's just say I came across a description of the meeting and the attendees."

"I imagine there are quite a few people matching my description in the Washington, DC, metro area."

"The man that was seen talking with him also works at the NSA." Sid had to readjust his rump on the slick cushion. It had begun to slide out.

The inspector general began tapping the end of the black pen on his desk top. "Where did you get your information?"

"An interested party was following a lead on Jacob and witnessed the meeting. He then followed the redheaded man to Fort Meade."

"So it could be anyone visiting Fort Meade?"

"How many tall redheaded men with fair skin and freckles work at Fort Meade? And why the late night visit?" Sid grumbled in a sarcastic tone. "He was seen entering the NSA compound at around ten o'clock yesterday evening. It'll be easy enough to review the gate logbooks and view the video surveillance."

The inspector general looked from the bookcase on his left to the window on his right, not answering Sid's question.

"A man of the same description hired two thugs to vandalize Luck's house," Sid added. "He made sure to identify himself as John Smith. Tell me what's going on, Howard." The CIA man ran his stubby fingers through his silver hair, wishing he could light up one of the cigarettes in his jacket pocket.

Continuing to look out the office window with an unusual scowl on his face, the inspector general began nodding his head.

"You need to tell me what is going on," Sid pressed the inspector general. "You need to tell me why you're hiring thugs and meeting with Jacob Livingston."

The inspector general sighed and looked back at Sid. "It is true that Jacob Livingston deals in stolen corporate databases. The information I sent you provides all the circumstantial evidence you need to see that."

"Why did you hire two thugs and then meet with him?"

"All right," the inspector general said with resignation in his voice. "Several months ago the NSA Director instructed me to attend a dinner in his honor. He was unable to go to due to a schedule conflict and asked me to stand in for him. During this dinner, I struck up a conversation with Jacob Livingston, and he saw some value, for personal reasons I imagine, to develop our relationship. He began inviting me to his house and would attempt pry information from me. I enjoyed the monthly meeting, and I was very good at evading his questions. After our third meeting, I told the director of the relationship and how Jacob was constantly hunting for information I might have. The director asked me to meet with a team investigating Jacob. Up until then, I had no idea of his criminal activity. The team and I decided that I should begin to give Jacob bits of information that would nurture our relationship. The information I passed to him seemed important at face value and could be easily verified, but we knew it to be worthless. It worked well, and Jacob began inviting me over every week to chat. But, once again, our relationship wasn't creating the evidence we needed to make a case against Jacob. Then you came to me explaining that Tommy Luck was selling the computer virus, and I immediately knew that Jacob would be interested. I knew his interest would draw him into your investigation. I knew his actions, trying to obtain the computer virus, would likely exceed the law, and you could collect the needed evidence to put this man behind bars."

"Did the team investigating Jacob know of your plan to tell him of the computer virus?"

"No, I only told Becky what I was doing," the inspector general replied looking down at the now still black Skill Craft pen in his hand. "And that was after I had done so."

"Go on, tell me more."

"I told Jacob about Tommy selling the computer virus," the inspector general admitted.

"What about the two thugs?"

"I knew Jacob would attempt to verify the information I gave him concerning the computer virus and the operation in Thailand last year. I knew the file concerning the operation in Thailand was classified at a level it would be difficult for him to acquire. I knew your people watching Tommy Luck would be keeping a very low profile. I was worried that Jacob wouldn't bite, so I hired those two men. I told them to make it look like a search. I told them of the envelope Tommy Luck had picked up from the post office box and said they could keep the money if they found it."

"You told them your name was John Smith," Sid stated, examining the man's pale freckled face across the desk from him, looking for some sign of deceit.

"It only made sense," the inspector general said, raising his palms up to accentuate his answer before falling back in his chair. "The person who arranged for the post office box and advertisements used John Smith's name, so I used the same to hire the thugs."

"Why didn't you tell me what was going on?"

"Are you kidding me?" The inspector general laughed nervously. "You would have never gone along with such a plan. You would have claimed that the focus should only be on Tommy Luck, the client, and the computer virus."

"You're right about that," Sid grumbled. "Don't you think Jacob would have used you as a bargaining chip at the first sign of trouble?"

"I doubt it," the inspector general replied, pushing his chair back and standing up. "I never gave him anything classified, and if he did, I would have cited the plan I made with the NSA team investigating him."

"When Luck caught the men and left them in the entry, who gathered them up and dropped them off at the hospital?"

"It was Becky. I told Becky about hiring the men after the fact, but before they searched the house. She was furious with me, saying it would endanger Luck. Tommy called her after he laid them out, asked if she could send someone over to pick them up." The inspector general walked to the window, looking out over the NSA compound. "We were worried that your surveillance team might step in and question the two thugs. It was a mistake for me to hire them myself. As you pointed out, my physical description is a disadvantage and is certainly nothing like John Smith's. Becky went over to Tommy Luck's house herself to clean it up, dropping them off at the local hospital. Didn't your surveillance team see her pick the men up?"

"Of course not, they were following Luck. They had audio of the encounter. That was enough. We've been working on finding out who hired the men."

"I'm not sure what the problem is. Jacob Livingston is

a criminal, and with the evidence you gathered, you can put both him and Tommy Luck behind bars."

"Your freelance plan has not only muddled up the primary investigation but also endangered Luck's family. Jacob Livingston is proving to be vicious. He seems to be willing to do anything to get his way."

The inspector general turned and faced Sid. "Does it matter? Tommy Luck is complicit in this entire affair, anyway."

"I don't think Luck has the virus. I don't think Luck ever had the virus. I think someone has set him up to make us believe he had a copy to throw off an investigation into the person or persons who are actually trying to sell the virus."

"What are you saying?"

"I believe Luck is innocent," Sid declared, his baritone voice booming off the office walls. "He doesn't have the virus, and he didn't murder my agent. I think Tommy Luck has been setup by someone else."

CHAPTER 41

Washington, DC, May 2, 2016:

Approaching the bistro, Tommy looked out across the outdoor tables, shaded with red and green striped umbrellas, and saw Anna sipping a cappuccino from a tiny yellow porcelain mug. Wearing a red skirt, white blouse, and shiny black high heel shoes, Anna's dark hair fell over her shoulders. Anna looked at him with her large doe like eyes and smiled as Tommy stepped up to the table. Tommy smiled back, once again thinking of their last encounter in his bedroom.

Pulling a heavy white iron chair from the matching round table Tommy sat down on the seat's thick red cushion, wishing the young woman felt the same attraction as he.

A waiter, dressed in black pants and a hunter green shirt, with a red *Jacky's Bistro* sewn above the right pocket placed a menu in front of Tommy and asked if he would like something to drink while he decided on his meal.

"You sell alcohol?" Tommy asked, looking up at the young waiter.

"We have a fully stocked bar."

"Then I'll have a Jameson on the rocks. Just two cubes of ice, please."

As waiter scurried off with the order, Tommy looked across the street, over a small grassy incline, at the base of the imposing entrance to the Kennedy Center. He then examined a security guard, dressed in a white shirt and black pants, leaning against a small building at the vehicle service entrance with five large pole barriers in their raised position, hoping the Deputy Security Supervisor would not spot him during his rounds.

"You look lovely today," Tommy said, looking back to Anna.

"Thank you, Tommy. And thank you for meeting me on such short notice," she replied, her accent barely discernible. "How was your meeting with the CIA agent?"

"Revealing."

"Why revealing?

"Revealing in that we were able to narrow down the possible suspects."

"Suspects of what?"

"The death of a CIA agent."

"Am I a suspect?" Anna asked, giggling.

Tommy smiled at Anna's teasing question. "No, you're uninformed of a past experience of mine."

"But you are still a suspect?"

"I'm still a suspect, but I am no longer the sole suspect. I think the CIA man is now considering other possibilities." Changing the subject, Tommy then said, "So let's get down to business. What's your boss's name?"

Slipping a small white card across the table, Anna said, "He is a New York City businessman."

Looking at the name Archibald Fenwick printed on the card, Tommy asked, "What kind of businessman?"

"People come to him asking for his services in acquiring items. Mostly art, but occasionally something else. From time to time, he will buy a product and then place it on the market himself. This is one of those times," Anna replied in a businesslike manner. "You can look him up on the internet, if you like."

"I might just do that. Although I learned last year that the internet can be deceiving," Tommy said, running the fingers of his right hand through his brown hair. "How did your boss find out that I was selling the computer virus?"

"I do not know," Anna replied. "He simply told me to contact you and ask to buy the merchandise."

"That's convenient, isn't it?"

"What do you mean?"

"It's convenient that you don't know how he knew I was selling the virus. Seems a lot of people have been told that I'm selling something I haven't been advertising."

"I wouldn't know about that."

"The price is six million."

"My boss has agreed to your price," Anna said in a soft voice before taking another sip of her cappuccino.

"But I need a down payment," Tommy added.

"How much of a down payment?"

A loud sputtering red Oldsmobile with a damaged muffler drove past the restaurant, leaving a dense cloud of black exhaust in its wake that drifted over their outdoor table. Anna waved her hand back and forth across her face, attempting to swat the noxious fumes away. The waiter arrived, delivering the Jameson on the rocks, placing it in front of Tommy.

"How much of a down payment," Anna asked again.

"How much money do you have?" Tommy asked, before taking a long swallow of the Jameson.

"What do you mean?"

"How much do you have in your purse?"

Clearly confused, Anna opened her purse and counted

out the money inside. “Why do you need to know how much money I have?”

“How much?” Tommy asked again.

Frustration could be heard building in Anna’s voice, as she said, “Sixty three dollars and twenty seven cents.”

“The down payment is sixty three dollars. I don’t want the change. You can tell your boss to take it out of the final payment.”

“I don’t understand,” Anna replied, pushing the money across the table.

Draining his drink in one long swallow, Tommy stood up, taking the money from the table, and admitted, “My bank account is empty, and I need some cash.”

As he turned and began walking away, Anna asked, “But when will you deliver the merchandise?”

Calling out over his shoulder as he began jogging across the street, Tommy replied, “I’ll give you a call in a day or two to arrange the delivery.”

Once across the street, Tommy walked along the sidewalk bordering the Kennedy Center and leading to the Potomac River. Out of Anna’s sight, he crossed back over the street, circumnavigating the building in which the bistro business front was situated. Crossing over F Street again, Tommy found a position where he had a view of Anna sitting alone at the table.

“Let’s see where you go, sweetheart,” Tommy whispered to himself, as he watched the beautiful Peruvian sitting at the table sipping her cappuccino.

Looking at her watch several minutes later, Anna called the waiter over and handed him a credit card for their drinks. Once she was finished paying the bill, she stood up and began walking toward the Kennedy Center. Staying well behind, Tommy began following.

Walking past the entrance to the Kennedy Center, Anna then walked down to the sidewalk bordering Rock

Creek Parkway. Passing under the Roosevelt Bridge, she made a call on her cell phone. Once past the Roosevelt Bridge, she placed her cell in her purse and waited for a break in traffic, jogging across Rock Creek Parkway. Walking along the edge of the river's slow moving waters, she followed the sidewalk to the Memorial Bridge, passing by the two large sculpted horses at its entrance, on either side of the road, and joined the throngs of tourists crossing the Potomac.

CHAPTER 42

Arlington National Cemetery, Arlington, Virginia, May 2, 2016:

The sixty-foot-wide road that crossed the Potomac atop the Memorial Bridge passed a wide and busy traffic circle and ended at Memorial Gate. At the gate was an enormous semi-circular ornate and marble wall. Anna stepped into to the Arlington National Cemetery with Tommy following. Entering the cemetery, Anna walked past the visitor's center and turned onto Roosevelt Drive leading up the hillside. With coolness radiating from old growth trees hovering overhead and trimmed emerald green grass surrounding the roads, Anna then Tommy walked up the hill amongst an assorted crowd of tourists and mourners. Turning left on Grant Drive, she traversed the hillside, passing by the four monuments marking Chaplains Hill. Mixing in with the tourists and mourners, Tommy was virtually invisible to his Peruvian quarry.

Straight rows of small marble headstones atop neatly manicured grass solemnly surged up and down the slopes on both sides of the road. More old growth trees punctuated the cemetery and marked fictitious boundaries. Larger more elaborate headstones dotted key terrain features on the property, as if an army's general staff watched its white marble headstone troops in battle. Passing a wooden spoke wheeled cannon with a greening muzzle, Anna continued along Grant Drive until she reached the octagonal USS Serpens Monument.

As she stood next to the memorial, surrounded by more tall trees, a slender white-haired man joined her. Slipping behind a wide oak tree on the right side of the drive, Tommy watched. Dressed in a dark suit and white shirt, the white-haired man began speaking with Anna. Between the chattering of passing tourists and distant traffic noises, Tommy was able to catch every third or fourth word. From his hillside vantage point, it sounded to him as if the white-haired man had a French accent. Tommy clearly heard the words "Luck" and "lying" then the words "make sure" before the two began walking down Bradley Drive, leading to the bottom of the hill.

Once again, Tommy followed, mixing into the tourists and mourners. Walking down the hill a hundred feet behind the two, he watched as they continued their conversation. At the intersection of Eisenhower Road, Anna and the white-haired man briefly stopped and then parted ways, Anna turning down Eisenhower Road and the man continuing down the hill toward the Columbarium.

Assuming that they were headed for the main entrance by different routes, Tommy decided to try and beat them both. Looking up, he saw a black round signpost marking the area as section sixty. Having glanced at a cemetery map as he entered, he knew that section sixty stood between him and the main entrance. Stepping into the sea of headstones, Tommy jogged across the manicured grass, amongst their ranks. In perfectly straight lines, the cold white marble headstones stood in stark contrast to the bright green grass surrounding them.

Jogging through the ranks of marble headstones,

Tommy finally arrived at the main entrance. Standing next to a small kiosk selling trinkets, he waited for either the white-haired man or Anna to arrive. He patiently watched the crowds come and go. After ten minutes, Tommy shrugged his shoulders and decided to leave. The two must have left by a different exit.

Tommy walked back through the cemetery entrance, across Memorial Bridge, and to the Kennedy Center. As he climbed into his white pickup, his cell began ringing. Looking down at the caller ID, it displayed 'unknown caller' across its small screen.

"Tommy here," he greeted the unknown caller.

"Tommy, it's Caroline," her soft voice echoed from the cell.

"What do you want? I thought I told you to leave me alone."

"I need to meet with you."

"No chance," Tommy gruffly replied. "I don't want whatever job you have, and I don't want to see you again."

"I have some important information concerning the computer virus."

"Why can't you tell me on the phone?"

"Come on, you know why." Caroline giggled. "Your phone has more taps than a colander has holes."

Hesitating, Tommy asked, "When and where?"

"Four o'clock tomorrow evening in your house."

"My house has bugs and taps too," Tommy informed her.

"Not any more. I removed them the other day."

"I think you just let the cat out of the bag. Won't those people listening now know their taps are gone?"

"Don't worry about that. I'll remove them again before we meet. Just meet me."

Confirming he would meet with Caroline, he disconnected the call and began driving east toward Annapolis and the Bay Bridge.

CHAPTER 43

Hooper's Island, Maryland, May 2, 2016:

Passing through Annapolis along Interstate 50, it had taken Tommy an hour to reach the Chesapeake Bay Bridge, the area's main link with Maryland's eastern shore. Driving up the southernmost enormous bridge to its apex, Tommy looked out over the long shining waters, spotted with sail boats and cargo transports moving up and down the bay. The sun had begun to set, casting a reddish glow across a scene of dark gray blue water bracketed by bright green shores. It was a sight that never ceased to amaze him. He always felt astonished at both the size of the bay and its two side-by-side breaching bridges.

As his old white Chevy pickup descended onto the eastern shore, Interstate 50 continued east, then south. Passing through wide fields of corn and wheat dotted with old white farmhouses, Tommy remembered driving this same route with his oldest daughter several years before. During the trip, Rose had turned to him and proclaimed this as was her favorite drive, the route to Hooper's Island. At the time they were driving across what Tommy considered the most boring part of the trip, but he understood his daughter. The drive from Washington, DC, to their bay front house was a journey and always punctuated with a joyous time on the shores of the Chesapeake Bay.

Forty five minutes later, the sun had disappeared, and the passing terrain became shadows illuminated by lights from homes and businesses, and overhead stars. Over the Choptank River into Cambridge, Tommy left the interstate just past a Walmart store and began driving west and then south along a narrow road that passed through more farms and fields. With an occasional car or house casting light, Tommy's eyes began to adjust to the darkness as the road meandered once again to the west.

Turning south in the small town of Church Creek, the farms began to give way to tall stands of shadowy lodgepole pines. Rounding a corner after passing through a large thicket of the trees, the Blackwater National Wildlife Refuge presented a stunning view of a long expanse of brackish water dotted with small, tree-filled islands and shorelines outlined with tall cattails and reeds, all illuminated by bright stars and a rising full moon. Tommy cracked a window, letting in the musty smell of still water and fresh foliage. Over the years, Tommy had seen the daytime sky above the refuge filled with brown eagles, white geese, and gray osprey.

The road took Tommy back into a forest of dark lodge-pole trees, winding back and forth for miles, passing swampy fields and desolate homes that looked as if they hadn't been inhabited for years. Opening back up to an enormous swamp of brown water and high reeds, he spotted several deer, their large round eyes reflecting the pickup's headlights, running across the road in front of him. The road coiled down a long peninsula, the water on each side hidden behind a forest of tall, spindly trees. Finally, in the distance, Tommy could see the illuminated bridge that arced over Fishing Creek. Passing a small dock with bobbing boats tied to its pylons, Tommy drove up and over the bridge. He could not help but smile at a place he truly loved, Hooper's Island.

Slowing, Tommy drove down the narrow street lined with wide grassy yards and old Victorian-style homes. Lights shone in the houses' windows and, at the end of each yard, more light reflected from the gentle waves on the bay. Passing the barnlike General Store and then Volunteer Fire Department's long brick and steel garage, Tommy spotted his two storey white Victorian style house standing near the road, a single small oak growing in the front yard and a long grassy backyard reaching out to the bay. Pulling into a drive covered in oyster shells, the old truck's tires crunched to a stop. Tommy sat in his pickup looking up at the wide covered porch protruding from the entry and saw no lights shining from within the house.

Stepping from his truck, Tommy stood in the darkness, listening for sounds. Other than a barking dog in the distance and croaking frogs hidden inside tall stands of beach grass bracketing the steps leading up to the wooden porch, there were none. Slowly walking across the front yard, his shoes crunching across the oyster shells and then the short dry grass covering the front lawn, he stepped up onto the wide porch, the wood planking creaking at the added weight.

Suddenly a blinding flash came from the window just off the entry, followed by a thunderous boom that Tommy recognized as that of a shotgun being fired. Throwing himself at the front door while pulling the Colt .45 from his waist, he grabbed and twisted the handle and began swinging it open. Hearing someone pull the pump action handle of the shotgun back, he hesitated. Another flash of light and thunderous clap splintered the entry frame and shattered a long narrow glass pane on the door in his face.

The impact of hundreds of lead pellets slammed the entry shut and his shoulder burned from several that had struck him. He heard the dog growling as if something were between its teeth and man's moan through the shattered window. Another bright flash of light and an even louder clap that Tommy recognized as the sound of a .357 magnum being fired, and he threw the door open again.

"Rose," Tommy called out, trying to keep the panic from his voice. "I'm at the front door."

Without waiting for a response, Tommy burst into the house, running down the narrow and dark hallway, passing a motionless man lying against the wall, clutching his chest.

With a still chest and no blood pumping from his wound, Tommy knew the man was near death or dead. Surging into the living room, Tommy looked to his right and saw Will lying on the polished wooden floor in the corner with a bloody forehead and the .357 clutched in his left hand.

To his left, lying next to a short set of stairs leading up to the house's kitchen, he saw another man moaning and holding his thigh, as blood erupted in torrents through his fingers. Tommy kicked away a handgun near the man. It spun across the wooden floor and came to rest under a long curved green couch. He raced to his son's side.

Will looked up at Tommy with wide eyes. "Did I get him?"

"You got him," Tommy replied, realizing that the powerful recoil of the .357 magnum had smashed the weapon into his son's forehead when he had pulled the trigger. "Where are your sisters?"

"Dad!" Rose called out from the hallway behind him, holding Tommy's pump action shotgun at her side.

"Rose, where's Ann?" he called back, realizing he had

run past Rose as she stood in a door along the dark hallway.

"She's in here with me," Rose called back.

"Ann, are you all right?"

"Yeah, I'm alright," she answered stepping from the doorway. "But, Dad, look." Ann gestured out the open back door to a tall shadowy figure running across the lawn out to the bay.

A smaller shadow was racing after the larger, and Tommy watched as the blue-and-gray-eyed dog bit at the man's ankles, slowing him. Hearing a car come roaring into the driveway, its headlights cutting through the house's windows and illuminating his two daughters standing in the hall, Tommy ran back to the entry and looked out the shattered door. As the shadows of four men stepped from the car, Tommy immediately recognized the squat figure of Sid.

"The CIA's here. Rose, please don't shoot them. Tell them what happened," Tommy called out, running toward the back door and giving chase to the man making his way toward the bay.

Bursting through the backdoor, Tommy sprinted after the fleeing shadow of the man. Sucking in lungs full of air, he could smell the fresh cut grass and the brackish water of the bay on a slight breeze flowing across the long lawn. Consumed with rage, he pumped his arms and legs as hard he could, and the distance between him and his quarry quickly closed. The shadow of the man, then of the dog, pushed through a waist-high stand of beach grass at the end of the yard, and Tommy watched as the two jumped from the lawn onto a thin ribbon of sand that stood four feet below the end of his property and marked the edge of the bay. Feeling an anger welling up that he rarely experienced, Tommy sprinted to the end of the yard, forcing his way through the beach grass, its tall, spindly spines grabbing at his legs and hips. With the dog standing on the sandy shore, barking at the man wading out into the bay, Tommy pushed off the grassy edge, vaulting over the beach onto the tall figure.

It was a perfect tackle, Tommy hitting the tall man at the shoulders and grabbing him with vise-grip-like hands. As the two men tumbled into the shallow brown water, Tommy began smashing at the figure's head with his fists. The brackish water began burning at the pellet holes in Tommy's shoulder then at small lacerations being created on his fists from pummeling the man's face. Ignoring the pain from his damaged fingers, Tommy grabbed the man's collar and pulled his head out of the water. Ralf's hawk nose spewed a mixture of blood and bay water as his large soft eyes looked up in terror. Tommy forced Ralf's head back under the brown water, and the tall man flailed and scratched in a failed attempt to free himself.

Pulling Ralf's head from the water again, Tommy shouted, "You screwed with the wrong guy's family," before forcing him back under, bubbling and thrashing.

When the flailing began to ebb and a gush of bubbles burst from the surface of the water, Tommy pulled Ralf's head from the water again. Coughing out a stream of water, Ralf weakly tried to push away. Tommy wanted him to die and without saying a word, forced his head under one last time.

As more bubbles burst from the surface and Ralf's arms fell limply to the side, Tommy was grabbed from behind and pulled backward. Ralf surfaced, sputtering and coughing. Twisting around, Tommy saw two men pulling him from Ralf, and Sid calmly standing on the shoreline watching the efforts of his two agents.

"Luck, we prefer our witnesses alive," Sid bellowed

from the shore, as the blue-and-gray-eyed dog gave an approving bark.

One of the CIA agents turned and grabbed a gasping and choking Ralf from the water, while the other pushed Tommy back to the shore. Climbing up to the lawn soaking wet, Tommy joined Sid and watched the two CIA agents dragging Ralf from the bay.

"Lost my temper," Tommy mumbled, as the dog sat down at his feet.

"I don't blame you, Luck," Sid grunted. "If three men broke into my house and tried to harm my children, I would have done the same."

"Did my kids tell you what happened?" Tommy asked as the local volunteer fire department siren began echoing across the island.

"Your girl, Ann, got this feeling that something wasn't right. Turning off the lights, the girls took the shotgun into the front bedroom in case someone came through the front door. Your boy took the handgun and hid with the dog behind the couch in the corner of the living room to cover the backdoor. Three men came through the back, your son waited for one to go down the hallway. Your oldest daughter shot him point blank in the chest, and then fired at someone coming through the front door."

"That would be me." Tommy chuckled, touching the pellet wounds on his shoulder.

"The dog leapt on our friend Ralf, and your boy stood up and shot one of the men in the leg." Sid pointed to Ralf as the two CIA agents hustled him toward the house along the dark lawn. "The recoil knocked your boy on his ass, and Ralf, seeing things weren't going his way, raced out the backdoor with the dog on his heels."

"Ann seems to have inherited one of my better traits," Tommy commented.

"What's that, your knack for survival?"

"Something like that. I wonder how they found out about this place."

"I'm not sure about how, but we do know who they work for."

"Livingston," Tommy mumbled.

"Livingston," Sid grunted in confirmation.

"How did you know to come down here?" Tommy asked Sid. "I can understand your agents following me, but you came along. There must have been a reason."

"The NSA has been sending the transcripts of Jacob Livingston's cell phone conversations to me every couple of days. I was reviewing them today, and the last transcript I read was Jacob directing Ralf to come down here and kidnap your children. That was three hours ago. We've also got him ordering Ralf to arrange the abduction of your children from their Arlington home two nights ago." Standing in silence for a moment, Sid added, "To be honest, based on your bank account, we didn't even think to check to see if you owned any property. I'm somewhat surprised you have a home on the Chesapeake Bay."

"Why didn't you call the local police? They could have been here before Ralf and his gang."

"We did, but I didn't want them walking in if Ralf was already here and risking a shootout. These are country cops. They've never dealt with the likes of Ralf. There's only one way onto this island, and we have it blockaded about three miles up the road next to an old wooden church. I told them to be discreet for traffic headed onto the island, but stop all cars moving off, north toward Cambridge. Cambridge County has two police cruisers tucked away behind the building."

After another moment of silence, Tommy muttered, "That man deserves to die."

"A lot of men need to die. Which one are you talking about?"

"Livingston."

"Livingston deserves to spend a long time in a penitentiary, living a life he would consider well beneath his social status," Sid grumbled. "I'm going to leave one of my men here to stay with your children. The other two will be escorting Ralf and his companion to the local hospital. You need to get back to Washington. We need to wrap up this murder investigation and sale of the computer virus. I have several good leads, but your presence seems to be speeding things along."

"What about the dead guy in the hallway?"

"We've asked the local fire department to send an ambulance for the two live ones, and a van for the dead one. I've called Special Agent Scott and the FBI will be sending more folks to help."

Turning, Tommy looked down the long lawn at lights shining from his Victorian house. "Last time I worked for a government agency I got paid."

"Last time you worked for a government agency, it was the NSA, and in the end, the guy paying you tried to kill you. This time you're working for CIA," Sid replied, "and we're cheap bastards."

"Sid," Tommy said, looking at the stout CIA agent, "I'm flat-ass broke. I used the last of my cash to fill up my truck to get down here. And that truck sucks gas down like it has a turbine engine. I don't even have enough money to get back to DC."

Reaching into his hip pocket and taking out his wallet, Sid handed Tommy a hundred dollar bill saying, "The gas is on me."

"I'm risking my life for a hundred dollars?"

"Look on the bright side, we won't try and kill you when it's all over."

"You promise?"

Sid looked at Tommy with a straight face. "No."

"Whatever," Tommy mumbled as he began walking toward the house.

Standing next to the bay watching Tommy walk away, Sid flatly asked, "San Diego, July 12, 1995?"

Without turning, Tommy replied, "It was me. Life's funny, isn't it?"

"What do you mean?"

Stopping and turning, Tommy said, "Aberrant coincidences—it's almost as if parts of life are scripted out well before hand." Scratching his head, Tommy then said, "It was a revealing moment for me."

"What's that?"

"Killing the two men in the Seven-Eleven that day was easy—too easy."

"We both learned something that day," Sid grunted. "You learned the ease with which you can deal out violence. I learned that rules need to be broken at times. Sometimes you can't put a boundary around reality."

Turning and once again walking toward the house, Tommy called over his shoulder, "Please keep that in mind over the next twenty-four hours."

"Why twenty four hours?" Sid called back.

"Because that's how long it's going to take me to figure this out."

CHAPTER 44

Georgetown, Washington, DC, May 3, 2016:

Standing in the shadows next to the sidewalk, Tommy looked down the dimly lit street. The stray dog standing faithfully at his side, Tommy reached down and stroked the animal's head. Tall brownstone homes stood to one side of the street and moderately sized, whitewashed brick and stone houses to the other. Tall, ornate green lamps posts, with small baskets of blooming flowers perched in their iron tentacles, spilled a golden hued luminance, creating shadows among the trees and bushes that lined the street. Lights shone around the edges of heavy drapes hanging behind tall glass paned windows, masking the residences' interiors, and faint ground level spotlights marked the pathways from the sidewalk to each of the houses. Even with high-end cars crowding the curb on both sides of the street, the narrow road seemed as if it were deserted.

After spending some time trying to console his children and a few moments with the ambulance's medical personnel to remove three lead pellets from his shoulder, it had taken Tommy two hours to drive back from Hooper's Island to the wealthy Washington, DC, suburb of Georgetown. Having watched Jacob Livingston's house for nearly an hour, Tommy had begun to wonder if the little twerp was home or not. Other than an overhead light above the entryway, illuminating the home's wide wooden door, only a single light glowed from behind the drapes of the front room. Walking across the street, Tommy duplicated his path from several days earlier, moving past the Japanese cherry tree into the shadows and along the side of the house to the backyard. The dog followed at his heels.

The rooms to the rear of the house were dark, the only light showing through a partially opened door splashed into the study where Tommy had watched Jacob talking with the NSA agent several days earlier. Slipping on a pair of latex gloves, Tommy pulled a small flashlight from his pocket and examined the panes of glass on the French doors leading into the study. The old doors had ancient putty wrapped around the molding inside and thin wooden decorative trim holding the panes in place on the outside. Taking a knife from his pocket, he slowly wedged the blade under a segment of the wood trim and gently pulled it out. Repeating the procedure three more times, the pane of glass easily slipped out into the palm of his hand. Pushing his hand through the opening, he began to feel the top edge of the doors, finding two slim boxes side by side. Tommy knew it to be a fairly common and simple system, tripping the alarm if the magnetic contacts inside the boxes were broken when the doors were opened. Over the years, he had supervised the installation of many similar devices in various buildings across the country. By feel, Tommy took his knife and slowly scraped the plastic coating from a pair of wires protruding from one of the slim boxes, until their coppery core was exposed. Gently he twisted the exposed wires together, circumventing the magnetic switch.

"He's got to have more than that," Tommy muttered to

dog at his feet. "There's got to be a motion detector or something more in there."

Using his flashlight, he scanned the walls in the room through the two side-by-side tall windows, finally discovering a small black box with a rectangular white lens mounted high on the wall above two paintings and a high-backed walnut chair with red velvet cushions. Examining the trajectory of the white lens, Tommy decided that the French doors were out of the motion detector's field of view, as well as the chair directly below the sensor. Upon examining the hinges on the French doors, he realized they swung outward, a common characteristic of many older homes.

Working the knife's blade on four more pieces of trim midway up the French door, Tommy repeated the procedure he conducted on the upper pane of glass before reaching in and grabbing the handles, gently pulling the doors out. Getting on his hands and knees, Tommy began crawling through the room in what he knew was referred to as a pet alley, an area to allow dogs and cats to move freely around a house without setting off motion detectors. The dog cautiously followed. Coming to the wall where the motion detector was mounted, Tommy carefully pushed himself up and sat down on the walnut chair.

Looking around the room with his flashlight, Tommy found more magnetic sensors protecting a painting by Monet and a small charcoal drawing by Georgia O'Keefe.

"He is rich," Tommy whispered to the dog as he shifted his position on the high-backed walnut chair. "Now let's see about powerful." The stray dog took up a position next to his feet, sitting down on the edge of a blue and red Persian rug.

Sometime after midnight, Tommy heard the front door open, followed by the faint beeping sound of someone punching the buttons on a security system control box. He could hear the footsteps, hard soles on polished wood floors, move from one room to another and then the sound of a faucet running and glassware being moved around.

He listened to the hard soles walk toward the study. The sound stopped at its threshold and study door was pushed open. Light from the outer room flooded the dark study.

"Hello, Jacob," Tommy said, calmly greeting the silhouette that appeared in the doorway, the dog giving off a faint growl.

"Mr. Luck?" Jacob's shocked nasally voice blurted out as he flipped the light switch. "What are you doing here?"

The room suddenly illuminated by an overhead light revealed Jacob standing in the doorway dressed in tan corduroy trousers, a tweed jacket, and white polo brand shirt. "And what's a dog doing in my house," he cried out, pointing at the dog at Tommy's feet. "That's an authentic Persian rug he's lying on."

Blinking several times in the sudden bright light, Tommy replied, "We're just admiring your lifestyle. It seems very luxurious."

"You need to leave immediately, or I will call the police," Jacob threatened, placing his hands on his hips.

"That's a great idea. Maybe we can also tell them about the three thugs you sent to my house on Hooper's Island while we're chatting."

"I sent no people to your house."

"That's not what your pal Ralf is telling the FBI," Tommy answered as he stood and walked across the room to the two long windows, bracketed by thorny rose bushes. The dog remained on the rug, watching the two men. “He was very specific about how he ended up on Hooper’s Island, and I’m sure he’s telling the police the very same details in return for a shorter prison sentence. And I believe that your conversation instructing them over your phone will verify Ralf’s testimony. That wasn’t a very smart move.”

“My phones are tapped?”

“You’re an idiot. Of course, they’re tapped. The minute you decided to do business with me, the NSA, CIA, and FBI began focusing on your every move.”

“What do you want? Why are you here?” Jacob whined.

The dog stood up and crossed the room, taking a seat next to the windows as Tommy turned and walked over to Jacob. “Do you remember my story of the pigs and hogs?”

Taking a step back from Tommy, Jacob replied with thick sarcasm, “How could forget such a long-winded description?”

“Good.” Tommy chuckled as he abruptly grabbed Jacob by the tailored tweed lapels of his jacket. “Then you’ll understand why I’m here.”

With the blue-and-gray eyed dog watching in silence, Tommy tossed Jacob across the room, bouncing him off the wall before he became entangled with the high-backed walnut chair and fell to the floor. Lying on the floor looking up, he let out a soft whimper as he wiped his face with a pasty hand. The dog stood up and let out a single bark of approval.

“This is really a piece of garbage,” Tommy commented as he walked over and pulled the Monet from the wall.

“That’s a Monet!”

“Well, someone should have told Monet he needed glasses. There’s not one crisp line in that piece of crap.”

“You don’t even know who Monet is, you imbecile,”

Jacob hissed at Tommy from the floor, spittle spewing from his thin lips.

"Claude Monet, born to Parisian parents, he was their second son. Who's the imbecile now, pal?" Tommy said, tossing the Monet like a Frisbee across the room.

It bounced off a bookcase, knocking a crystal decanter from a shelf, both falling to the floor with a clatter. Tommy then picked up the small tulip and kingwood writing table next to the high backed chair. Looking down at Jacob, Tommy raised it over his head before smashing the table onto the gilded walnut chair, sending broken bits of wood flying across the room, and scratching deep gouges in the elaborately carved ornamental shelves and lambrequin motifs.

"That's a 1760 Van Risenburgh you just destroyed," Jacob cried, looking up with a frightened expression.

"Let's get down to business, Mr. Livingston. You have had me kidnapped and tortured, but your gravest mistake was trying to kidnap my children. Now I could tolerate a scumbag like you hurting me, but not my children."

"As I said at the Kennedy Center, you will give me the computer virus," Jacob replied defiantly. "Or I will take it."

Tommy laughed. "I just don't understand how such a stupid person was able to get as rich as you are. You're lying on your ass with a very angry man above you, and you still think that things are going to go your way. You'll be lucky to survive the next ten minutes, and yet you still think I'm going to give the computer virus to you. You are an unabashed fool. You must have inherited your money."

Jacob slipped his back up against the wall and peered up at Tommy with clear hatred in his eyes. Tommy reached down, grabbed Jacob's neatly combed blond hair, and threw him onto the edge of the Persian rug. Pushing back the blue and red Persian rug with his foot, Tommy straddled Jacob. Tommy then placed each of Jacob's wrists under his knees, pinning his arms. Pulling the handgun from his waist, Tommy laid Jacob's right pinkie onto the bare wooden floor.

"What are you going to do?" Jacob whimpered, half-heartedly struggling.

"Do you play the piano?" Tommy asked as he raised handgun over his head. "That's what your pal Ralf asked me just before he preformed this same procedure."

Swinging the handgun down, Tommy smashed the butt of the weapon onto Jacob's exposed finger. Jacob let out a shrill squeal when the butt struck, blood spurting from under his finger nail, splashing onto the edge of the rolled up Persian carpet. Grabbing the next finger in line, Tommy raised the handgun again.

"Who told you where my children were staying?" Tommy demanded, "Who told you?"

"Someone sent me a note. I don't know who it was," Jacob screamed, his eyes wide with pain and fright. "It was a note. It looked like a woman's handwriting."

Swinging down the butt of the weapon again, Tommy smashed Jacob's ring finger with the same results. Jacob screamed, and the dog whimpered in the background. Tommy then grabbed Jacob's middle finger, stretching it out on the wooden floor.

"That's bullshit. You know who told you," Tommy growled at Jacob. "Who told you where my children were?"

"I don't know. It was a note claiming that your children were staying on an island in the Chesapeake Bay. It had the address of your house on the note. I swear I don't know who it was!" Jacob cried out with tears streaming down his cheeks, his legs uselessly flailing in an attempt to escape Tommy's hold.

Tommy again swung the butt of the weapon down, impacting Jacob's finger with a horrific whack. Jacob screamed again and continued to struggle under Tommy, as blood oozed from his fingers onto the floor. Tommy repeated his question two more times, smashing the index finger and thumb on Jacob's right hand. Jacob continued to scream, claiming he didn't know who had sent him a note with the location of Tommy's children.

"A whinny asshole like you couldn't help but tell me who it was after that workout." Tommy shrugged his shoulders. "You must be telling the truth."

"I really don't know. I really don't know," Jacob whimpered.

Standing up, Tommy released Jacob's arms. Holding his right hand with his left, Jacob rolled onto his side into the fetal position, moaning and mumbling something indiscernible. Slipping the handgun into his waist at the small of his back, Tommy pulled the small knife from his pocket, flipping the shiny silver blade from the grip.

"One last task." Tommy leaned down. "I want you to remember this discussion every time you look into a mirror."

Looking up with frightened eyes, Jacob mumbled a quivering, "What?"

Slipping the knife under Jacob's nose, Tommy said, "I want you to remember this conversation every morning for the rest of your pitiful life." With a flick of his wrist, Tommy sliced off a good portion of Jacob's nose. "It'll help you recall our discussion of pigs and hogs, as well."

Jacob let out a high-pitched scream as the tip of his nose rolled down his cheek and fell to the floor. Tommy stood and kicked Jacob's nose across the room. The nose bounced to a halt at the base of the French doors. Wiping the bloody knife on Jacob's right trouser leg and then leaning down one more time, Tommy pulled Jacob's wallet from his hip pocket. Extracting a large wad of cash from its interior, he threw the wallet at Jacob, striking him on the side of the face.

"That's payment for the time I had to wait for you to get home," Tommy grunted.

"You'll never get away with this," Jacob whimpered, blood flowing through his fingers as he held the stump of his nose with his left hand.

"I was never here," Tommy replied.

"I will tell them you were here."

"Then it's my word against yours, a man who's about to be charged with home invasion and attempted kidnapping."

"They'll find evidence you broke in," he said, shifting his head so he could see Tommy, blood continuing to run from between his fingers.

"I doubt it." Tommy chuckled, holding up his latex covered hands before walking out the backdoor, kicking the tip of Jacob's nose out the door as he passed. Outside Tommy reached down, picked up Jacob's nose, and tossed it over the back wall, mumbling to the blue-and-gray-eyed dog, "That'll make a nice treat for the neighbor's dog. Sorry I didn't give it to you. I was concerned it might be poisonous."

Walking to his truck with the dog at his side, Tommy drove to Amber's apartment building, once again hoping he wouldn't run into Becky as he waited for the elevator in the parking garage.

Entering Amber's apartment, Tommy directed the stray dog onto the white leather couch before he walked around the granite countertop into the kitchen and pulled a bottle of Jameson from the cabinet above the sink.

Shuffling into the kitchen wearing a green satin nightgown, Amber yawned groggily. "I was supposed to go to your bay house with you."

"Sorry, I forgot."

"Where have you been? I've been worried sick about you, and what's the dog doing on my couch?"

"Had to see a man," Tommy replied before taking a long swig straight from the bottle of whiskey, "and the dog's not mine."

"You have blood on your pants," she exclaimed. "Where'd the blood come from?"

"Another thing that's not mine," Tommy informed Amber, taking another long pull of whiskey straight from the bottle, again.

"But where'd it come from?"

"I met with a man that required a lesson in humility."

Shaking her head, Amber shuffled out of the kitchen and into the bedroom. After draining the bottle of Jameson, Tommy stumbled into the bedroom and stripped off his clothes, curling up next to Amber.

CHAPTER 45

Rosslyn, Arlington, Virginia, May 3, 2016:

Waking to the sound of water running in the bathroom, Tommy pushed himself up, placing his shoulders on the headboard and rubbing his temples. With his head throbbing and mouth feeling as if he had eaten a bucket full of sand, he began contemplating yesterday's events. Finding his children defending themselves on Hooper's Island against Jacob's men had scared Tommy—his fright warping into a rage that had pushed him to break into Jacob's house and assault the egotistical man.

Tommy's one concern now was whether he should have eliminated Jacob entirely from his life. It would have been an easy enough task, with the narcissistic man lying on the floor of his study completely helpless. Between the cell phone transcripts and what Ralf had told Sid, Jacob was certainly going to see the inside of a penitentiary, but Tommy's concern was that prison walls were only so high and the arrogant man could continue to wreak havoc in his life from behind bars. Jacob had already proven that children were not off limits when it came to getting his way, and that worried Tommy.

Hearing a glass of water faintly rattle on the bedside table, he looked out the window to see an airliner on approach to Regan-National Airport, it wide white wings glinting in the light of the rising sun as it descended from above the Potomac River. The dog appeared at the bedroom door, looking up at Tommy quizzically with a wagging tail.

The running water came to a stop, and Amber stepped from the bathroom wrapped in a towel. "When was the last time you went to bed sober?"

"The last time I couldn't find something to get drunk on," Tommy groaned coarsely.

"You should try going to bed sober sometime," Amber snapped. "You could actually wake up without a hangover."

"I would never wake up because I would have never gone to sleep. I can't sleep without a couple night caps."

"A bottle of Jameson is a night cap?"

"The more I drink, the better I sleep. I slept like a baby last night."

Looking down at the dog in the doorway, Amber asked, "What's the dog's name?"

Slipping his legs from the bed onto the floor, Tommy grunted, "Not my dog and I don't know his name."

Walking over and sitting on the edge of the bed, Amber asked, "Where did all the blood on your clothes come from?"

"I paid a visit to a guy that's been threatening my children," Tommy admitted. "I took his nose to remember our conversation."

"Jacob Livingston?"

Tommy silently watched for a moment while she dried her hair. "How'd you know his name?" he asked.

With a look of confusion, Amber replied, "You said his name in your sleep last night."

Ignoring the obvious lie, Tommy climbed from the

bed and walked into the bathroom, asking over his shoulder if she was going to go to work today. Amber answered yes to his question, and Tommy began brushing his teeth. Taking a quick cold shower and dressing in his running clothes, he kissed Amber goodbye and began walking down the hall, past the framed charcoal drawings of local sights hanging on the wall, to the apartment's front door, with the stray dog padding along behind him.

Just as he was stepping out the apartment door, Amber called to him, "I forgot to tell you, the garage gave me a temporary replacement while they worked on the Mercedes. It's in the garage if you need to use it." Then giggling, she added, "Try not to get it all shot up if you do."

"That was nice of them," Tommy called back. "What kind of car?"

"Another red Mercedes. My car will cost a bundle to fix, and they'll make more than enough to cover the cost of the temporary replacement. But you wouldn't know anything about that."

Stepping out the door, taking the elevator to the lobby, and walking out onto the streets of Rosslyn, Tommy moved around the corner of the apartment building and leaned against the wall. The stray dog took up a position next to him, sitting at his feet. After a short wait, Amber stepped from the apartment building.

Looking down at the dog, Tommy said, "Stay here, dog. Don't follow me, I'll be back." The dog whimpered and laid its head on its front paws.

Wearing a white blouse and black skirt with a brown leather brief case looped over her shoulder, Amber began walking down the sidewalk toward the Rosslyn Metro Station entrance. Falling in behind her, Tommy followed a block behind, keeping track of her bobbing auburn hair in the crowd. In the Metro Station, Tommy waited out of sight until she had climbed onto the blue line metro train heading into Washington, DC, before he sprinted across the station, weaving through the business-suit-clad crowd, onto the car directly behind hers.

The metro train clattered and wobbled along the underground tracks, passing under the Potomac River, Georgetown, and then Foggy Bottom, the musty damp smell of the metro line mixing with that of its human cargo's aftershave and perfume. The metro's well-dressed passengers, busy reading newspapers or typing on their laptops, all but ignored Tommy in his running clothes. He only generated the occasional odd look or stare. Ignoring the intermittent glances, Tommy hung onto the silver bar above his head to keep from falling over as the train rocked back and forth on the track.

CHAPTER 46

Langley, Virginia, May 3, 2016:

Sitting in his office on its weathered chair behind his gray metal desk looking out the room's long narrow vertical window, Sid turned his attention to the whiteboard on the wall. Pondering the names listed on the board, he tapped his fingers on the worn calendar desk mat. It had to be a team attempting to sell the computer virus and frame Tommy Luck, but who from the list of names was on that team?

The black multi-line phone on his desk began buzzing, breaking him from his thoughts. Reaching out, Sid answered the phone. "Special Operations Department, Sid speaking."

"Sir, this is Devin. I'm calling from Bangkok."

"Go ahead, Devin."

"It's about the woman named Lawan and the computer hacker," Devin replied.

"Go ahead, Devin," Sid grunted again.

"According to Thai immigration, both left the country two weeks ago. The hacker traveled across the Malaysian border on April fifteenth, and the woman crossed the Lao border on the seventeenth."

"Where are they now?"

"No idea, sir. I'm headed to Kuala Lumpur tomorrow

morning to see if the computer hacker is still in the country or if he's moved on. If I can't find him, I'll go looking for the girl in Laos."

"Let me know," Sid muttered. "I'll check with the TSA to see if they've come to the States," he said before hanging up the phone.

Looking back up to the whiteboard, Sid wondered how these two could fit into the mystery of the computer virus and the death of his agent. The Thai computer hacker certainly could have made a copy of the virus but why would Tommy's old girlfriend set him up? And who would they team up with? Sid focused on the name 'Steve' written in red below 'John Smith' at the center of his spectrum on the whiteboard. Tommy claimed Steve was alive. Steve certainly had knowledge of Thailand. He certainly had a motive to set Tommy up. Standing up, Sid walked over to the whiteboard.

Steve was the key to the mystery, and Sid realized that he needed to find him. Drawing a large circle at the bottom of the whiteboard, he wrote Steve's name in the center. Sid then drew five more circles that separately intersected the larger circle with Steve's name. In each of the five circles, he wrote the IG's, Becky's, Lawan, the computer specialist who had developed the virus, and the hacker's names. Standing back from the whiteboard, Sid pondered his work.

"It has to be one of these teams," Sid mumbled to himself. "But which is it?"

Walking back over to his desk, he picked up the receiver of the black phone and made a call.

"NSA Inspector General's Office," Judy answered.

"Hello, Judy. Sid from the CIA here, is the inspector general in?"

"No, I'm sorry he's in a meeting with the director."

"When he returns, can you ask him to send over what he has on the NSA computer specialist who developed the virus that was the focus of 'Operation Black Fly'?"

CHAPTER 47

Washington, DC, May 3, 2016:

Watching Amber step from the train at the Federal Center Metro Station through the dirty windows between the two cars, Tommy followed her up the long escalator onto the streets of Washington, DC. Once again keeping at least a block behind her, he followed as she walked down Pennsylvania Avenue, maneuvering around the crowds of people dressed in business attire carrying briefcases and newspapers sharing the sidewalk. He scrutinized her as she approached and entered a large unspectacular gray concrete building. Standing at an intersection, busy with cars streaming past and people waiting for the crosswalk, Tommy peered at the building, knowing it looked familiar.

"Holy crap," Tommy whispered to himself, as he read the sign inscribed on the side of the building, "the J. Edgar Hoover building. What the hell is she doing meeting with the FBI?"

Gazing at the FBI building for a few moments, Tommy shrugged his shoulders and plugged a set of headphones into his cell. Placing their small buds into his ears, he began to jog in the opposite direction along Pennsylvania Avenue. Running down to the Potomac River and then across the Memorial Bridge, Tommy found the trail along the edge of the river and ran west. Just past Roosevelt Island, he ran up a curving trail and pedestrian bridge over the George Washington Parkway, back into Rosslyn. At the top of the incline, the blue-and-gray-eyed dog mysteriously joined him, and they ran past the Key Bridge Marriott, standing majestically across the busy road. They crossed Key Bridge into Georgetown, turned down a hill toward the Potomac River and ran up the C&O Canal, all the while Tommy pondering Amber's entrance into the FBI building.

Bracketed by the still brown waters of the cannel and tall trees his shoes struck the gravelly path in a slow cadence. Running along the path, Tommy mulled over what he had learned over the last several days. He first considered Steve and his failed attempt at killing him. If Steve had taken the time to set him up, why would he now try to kill him? Was it because he was to meet with Sid? Or was Steve here to simply extract revenge? If it was to stop the meeting, did the sharing information with Sid up the stakes enough to lose their fall guy? Steve's part in his current problems still seemed fuzzy. Why did Steve try to kill him?

Tommy's thoughts moved to Anna. She indicated that her employer was willing to pay six million dollars for the virus before meeting with the white-haired man. She seemed to legitimately want to buy the computer virus and, if that was the case, setting him up would only harm her cause. But how did her employer discover Tommy was trying to sell the virus?

Reflecting on Jacob Livingston, now out of the picture, Tommy knew he had simply wanted the computer virus. Just as with Anna, setting Tommy up would have only complicated the transaction. He certainly was not behind the CIA man's murder. How did Jacob Livingston discover Tommy was trying to sell the virus?

He had followed Amber to the FBI building to a meeting presumably with Agent Scott. Tommy had never tried to hide his relationship with Amber, and the FBI surveillance had more than likely had identified her. It would make sense that they would want to question her. But why had she not told Tommy of the meeting?

Approaching the Chain Bridge, Tommy's cell began ringing in his hand. Pulling the small earphones attached to the phone from his head, Tommy stopped under a stand of large trees on the river's edge and answered the call. The dog looked up, panting an approval to their mid-run break.

"I found the tracking device that was supposed to be attached to your truck at a gas station in Cambridge," Sid gravelly voice rasped from the cell phone.

"I had to attend a meeting that you wouldn't have approved of—remember the agreement we made on Hooper's Island."

"What agreement?"

"You can't put a boundary around reality," Tommy replied.

"That wasn't an agreement. That was a comment."

"I beg to differ."

"I heard about your meeting. Our friend Ralf sang like a bird and confessed everything, implicating Livingston. Along with the transcripts of his phone conversations, he's done for. We arrived at Livingston's house with a warrant for his arrest about the same time as an ambulance. Someone removed his nose."

"I don't know what you're talking about," Tommy lied.

"He claims that you broke into his residence and assaulted him. He claims you crushed his fingers and cut his nose off."

"Is there any evidence against me?"

"There was evidence of a break in, but no, we combed the place and found nothing implicating you—not that we were looking very hard."

"I guess it's my word against his," Tommy replied.

"You'll need an alibi."

"I have an alibi."

"As long as your alibi is not that dog, you're safe," Sid grunted.

Tommy chuckled. "You can't put a boundary around reality?"

"It doesn't work like that," Sid grumbled. "With all the excitement at your bay house, I forgot to tell you that the NSA's Inspector General was the man you saw talking with Livingston."

"I don't seem to have too much luck with the NSA's Inspector Generals, do I?"

"He's the gentleman who directed Livingston your way. Apparently, Livingston deals in stolen data bases, and the NSA has been trying to gather enough evidence to charge him with a crime. The inspector general has been meeting weekly with Livingston after being introduced at a social event. He maintained that relationship as a part of the NSA investigation. The inspector general thought that the news of a virus that is capable of downloading databases and shipping them off to a remote site would attract Livingston's attention. Figured he would go out of his way to get a hold of it."

"That solves the mystery about who sent Livingston my direction," Tommy commented, wondering if the inspector general also informed Anna's boss about the virus. "Guess he was right about Livingston doing anything to get a hold of the virus." Even though Tommy knew the answer, he then asked, "Did Livingston tell you who told him where my children were hiding?"

"Yes and no. He said he received a note describing where your kids were staying. The note directed him to your house on the bay. He didn't know who the note was from but said it looked like a woman's hand writing. Apparently, that was the question his attacker poised to him several times while working his hand over with the butt of a handgun. I imagine the man that assaulted him believed his story, having left him alive on his study floor."

"Without a nose," Tommy added.

"Without a nose."

"Why would some woman send a note to Livingston informing him where my children were hiding?"

"To get you out of the picture?" Sid asked. "You know any women who might want to see you disappear?"

"Counting my two ex-wives, two." Tommy chuckled. "The question is what woman knew where my children were hiding?"

"Maybe he discovered you had a place on the Chesapeake Bay and sent Ralf and the others down there on a hunch."

"Then why tell you an absurd story about a note with a woman's handwriting?" Tommy asked. "Did you see the note?"

"You're right. There's no reason to lie about the note at this point. He claims to have destroyed it."

"That's convenient, claims of a mysterious note of which he has no evidence," Tommy remarked. "What did Ralf say?"

"Ralf just said that Livingston directed him down to your bay house and said that the children would be there," Sid replied.

"So according to Ralf, Livingston was sure that they were there."

"It would appear so. What women knew where you children were?" Sid asked.

"Becky, a friend named Amber, and another woman named Caroline."

"If I were you, I'd quit keeping all your girlfriends in the loop. It seems each time you do something goes wrong."

"Sound advice, but a little late," Tommy muttered. "What about Becky? Maybe Becky wrote the note to Livingston."

"Why would Becky tell Livingston where your children were hiding?"

"I just have a feeling that she's more involved than we suspect."

"She knew about the inspector general involving Livingston, and she was the one who picked up the two gentlemen you left on the floor of your foyer, but my gut instinct tells me that was the extent of her involvement," Sid replied.

"She knew about the inspector general and Livingston?" Tommy asked, sounding slightly astonished at the revelation.

"She must have known about the inspector general's plan to involve Livingston, but it sounded like she wasn't happy. As for all the other stuff, she was just following orders. I believe she is who she professes. I can't believe that she would be that stupid or devious. She's professional enough to put orders from her supervisor over friendship. I think you should look elsewhere for the leak to Livingston. Maybe your pals Amber or Caroline told him."

"Maybe," Tommy replied, silently shaking his head at the news of Becky's involvement.

"What are you going to do next?"

"I got a few things up my sleeve," Tommy answered.

"You don't want to include me?"

"Once again, your professional ethics would just get in the way."

Disconnecting the call, Tommy reinserted the earphones and began running across Chain Bridge with the blue-and-gray-eyed dog at his side.

CHAPTER 48

Rosslyn, Arlington, Virginia, May 3, 2016:

Running another three hours along the trails criss-crossing Arlington, Tommy slowed to a walk as he entered Rosslyn and its towering skyscrapers, passing business men and women on their lunch break. As he approached Amber's apartment building, his thoughts turned to his meeting with Caroline at four o'clock. Caroline was a completely unknown quantity to Tommy. He wasn't sure whose side she was on, but she was certainly involved with the mystery and mayhem surrounding him.

Entering the tall 1970s apartment building, he made his way to Amber's apartment and took a long hot shower. Dressing in faded blue jeans and a red and blue plaid shirt, he moved to the living room and sat down on the white leather couch. The dog sat at his feet. Examining the Washington, DC, skyline across the Potomac River, Tommy sipped on a glass of Jameson and relaxed, forcing the mystery of the computer virus from his thoughts.

A ringing cell suddenly interrupted his peaceful moment, and he answered the phone, "Tommy here."

"Hi, Tommy, it's Becky."

"Hey, what's up?" Tommy wondered if she was standing in her apartment directly below him.

"I just wanted to check to see if you were all right. I hadn't heard from you in a couple of days."

"You want to get together tonight?" Tommy contemplated what Sid had told him about Becky earlier. Maybe she would be willing to tell him of her involvement with a little private prodding.

"We can get together later, but I've got a late meeting at Fort Meade I have to attend first."

"What time's your meeting?"

"Eight o'clock. I should be back by ten."

"Let's make it ten-thirty at your place. Give you a chance to slip into something more comfortable."

"You really need to work on your lines." Becky laughed softly. "You can really sound like a chauvinist pig at times."

"Well, at least I'm a fun chauvinist pig." Tommy chuckled, before disconnecting the call.

Taking another sip of Jameson, Tommy decided to go for a walk around Rosslyn. With nothing to do but wait for his meeting with Caroline at four o'clock, he became concerned that he would spend the remaining afternoon hours pondering his situation over a bottle of Jameson. The last thing he wanted to do was show up drunk for his late afternoon rendezvous with Caroline. Slipping on his flip-flops, Tommy and the dog stepped out Amber's apartment door.

Cars and trucks whizzed by along the Rosslyn streets in a building crescendo to the evening rush hour. Walking along the street with the dog at his side, Tommy stopped at a small deli and purchased a pastrami on rye and quickly gobbled down the sandwich. Continuing along the street, he crossed an overpass above Interstate 50, with traffic speeding by below in both directions. Passing a large apartment building on his right, someone yelled at him from one of its balconies about the Arlington leash law and Tommy gave them the finger. A little further up the street and he and the dog stepped down a wooded embankment onto the grounds of a familiar memorial.

Standing in the parking lot above, Tommy gazed onto the Marine Corps' Iwo Jima Memorial, with its five frozen men permanently straining to raise the flag atop Mt. Surabachi. With the words, 'Uncommon Valor Was A Common Virtue,' etched into its black base, Tommy contemplated the men who had experienced such a hard fought battle. Many of men who had battled over that small island never returned. Many more had and became functioning members of society, never losing sight of their goals and ambitions. Thoughts of those men and their test on Iwo Jima, Tommy wondered what happened to him that he had seemingly given up on life. Why did he find himself happy with a simple daily routine of drinking and running?

With the dog standing at his side, wagging his tail, Tommy glanced over toward the Netherlands Carillon and froze. The white-haired man that had met with Anna the day before and the two men who had trashed his house, Alfred and Larry, were sitting on the low circular divider surrounding the tall structure, talking.

Glancing down at the dog, Tommy muttered, "Time for a little uncommon valor."

Striding toward the three, Tommy walked from the parking lot down a second embankment filled with trees and then through the viewing standings, and out onto the trimmed grass surrounding the Iwo Jima Memorial. With the dog keeping pace next to him, Tommy glanced out across the Washington, DC, skyline, seeing the Iwo Jima and Lincoln Memorial, separated by the Potomac, followed by the Reflecting Pool, and the World War Two and Washington Monument, all pointing to the Nation's

Capitol. It was a magnificently patriotic sight, but Tommy turned his focus back to the three men. Those three men were involved in the events consuming his life. Feeling anger slowly building, he and the stray dog began jogging.

The white-haired man saw Tommy first, quickly ending the discussion with Larry and Alfred, and began briskly walking up the hill toward the Fort Myer Army base. Alfred, with his left arm in a sling, and Larry, with his ponytail sticking out from under a white bandage, turned to face Tommy. Their faces turned red, indicating a building rage of their own. Tommy began to sprint, pumping his arms with tight fists to help buildup speed. He could see Larry's rage falter, his pallor whitening and clenched jaw slackening. A low growl erupted from Tommy just before he pushed off his feet and dove at Alfred.

Standing atop thick thighs, Alfred reached out with his muscular right arm and pushed Tommy's diving body aside. Tommy grabbed Alfred's neck as he flew past, swinging them both over the low divider onto the concrete surface surrounding the Netherlands Carillon. Spinning and sliding across the concrete, Tommy clinched down on Alfred's neck harder, pulling the big man closer. As they came to a stop, Tommy leaped on top of Alfred and began pummeling his face with tightly closed fists. Out of the corner of his eye, he saw Larry running toward a faded red Chevy Nova frantically fumbling in his pockets for keys as he ran, his ponytail bobbing with each step. The dog nipped and bit at his shins, slowing Larry down.

Alfred let out a loud grunt, grabbing Tommy with both his thick arms and throwing him off. Tommy bounced and skidded across the concrete. Jumping to his feet, Alfred began running toward Larry, now standing beside the red Nova, still groping in his pockets for the car keys while the dog bit at his wrists. Tommy leaped to his feet and began chasing Alfred, tackling him from behind as they reached the Nova. With Tommy on his back, Alfred slid across the side of the car, falling into Larry. Alfred's sling became entangled in the car's side mirror, ripping it from its mount, before they all fell to the ground in a heap. The dog stepped back and began barking at the struggling men.

Tommy reached up, grabbed the side mirror dangling from its adjustment cable, and tore it from the car. As Alfred twisted onto his back, Tommy smashed the mirror into his forehead. The side mirror struck with a loud whack and blood burst from a laceration on Alfred's head.

Wedged between the front tire of the Nova and Alfred's now motionless body, Larry was squirming to free himself. With the dog still barking in the background, Tommy pushed Alfred aside and leaped atop Larry. Grabbing the little man by the throat, Tommy raised the side mirror high above his head. The blue-and-gray-eyed dog quit barking and sat down on the grass next to the curb, watching Tommy with Larry under him.

Looking down into Larry's frightened eyes, Tommy growled, "Unless you tell me what you were doing with the white-haired man I'm going to put you back in the hospital with another concussion."

Struggling under Tommy, Larry squealed, "He wanted to know who hired us to search your place. He wanted a description. He wanted to know why."

Alfred, lying next to them muttered, "He was going to pay us. He just wanted to find out who else is interested in you."

"What'd you tell him?"

"Everything," Alfred muttered again, "We told him everything I told you the other day."

"What'd he say his name was?" Tommy growled again.

"Archibald," Larry squeaked in an irritatingly high pitch, "He didn't give us a last name."

Pushing himself up to his feet, Tommy threw the side mirror onto the pavement next to the Nova, its mirror shattering into shards and spilling across the street.

Looking down at Alfred and Larry, Tommy calmly said, "You clowns stay away from me. I've got enough problems without two idiots like you muddling around."

Turning, Tommy and the dog walked past the Netherlands Carillon, across the grass surrounding the Iwo Jima Memorial, up the embankments filled with viewing stands and trees onto the Rosslyn street. Passing back over the overpass above Interstate 50, a middle aged woman dressed in a green skirt, walking in the opposite direction, curtly informed Tommy that he was in violation of the Arlington County leash law.

"Go fuck yourself, lady," Tommy spat, as the woman stalked by.

Before returning to Amber's apartment, Tommy stepped into a small cell phone shop along the street. He bought a prepaid cell and slipped it into his pocket.

At three thirty in the afternoon, before Amber returned to the apartment, Tommy found the keys to her loaner red Mercedes and made his way to the underground garage. Climbing into the car, with the stray dog hopping into the passenger seat, he started the car and began the drive to his Arlington house and his meeting with Caroline.

Hopefully, whatever information she claimed to have would shed some light on what was going on and allow

Tommy to extract himself from the mystery surrounding the murdered CIA agent and the computer virus.

CHAPTER 49

East Falls Church, Arlington, Virginia, May 3, 2016:

Pulling up in front of his North Arlington home, Tommy and the dog peered up at the house. The beautiful silhouette of Caroline, wearing blue jeans and a red T-shirt, was looking down at them through the house's front window.

Stepping from the Mercedes, Tommy and the dog made their way up to the front stoop, where Caroline opened the door.

"Something is wrong with this reversal of roles," Tommy muttered as he stepped across the threshold, past Caroline. "I feel like my house has turned into some warped version of a community property."

Pulling several strands of short blonde hair from the corner of her mouth, she smiled a crooked grin. "I like this house, but you do need to hire a maid. This place is a mess."

"Maids cost money. Not something I seem to have much of lately," Tommy grunted. "You know about the Hooper's Island episode?"

Caroline took Tommy's hand. "Yes."

"Did you know he was sending his men to abduct my children?"

"No, of course not. Jacob Livingston is an evil,

greedy, short-sighted man. I tried to warn you that he was capable of anything."

Pulling away from her, Tommy walked down the short hallway into the kitchen. Taking a tumbler from one of the cabinets, he extracted an ice tray from the freezer, twisted the top off a fresh bottle a Jameson from counter next to the refrigerator, and looked over to Caroline, who had followed him into the kitchen.

"You want a drink?" Tommy asked.

"Yeah, that would be nice."

Filling the tumbler with two ice cubes from the tray and whiskey from the bottle of Jameson, Tommy handed the drink to Caroline before repeating the process with a second glass from the cabinet. Taking a long swallow from his glass, he looked over at Caroline, who was sipping from her tumbler, and shrugged his shoulders.

"I know this whole computer virus mystery seems a bit out of hand," Caroline said.

"A bit out of hand? It's far beyond that. My oldest daughter killed a man last night. My youngest child injured another with a three-fifty-seven magnum. I've got men trying to abduct my kids, I've been tortured and shot at, and the FBI has me under investigation for the murder of a CIA agent." Tommy laughed. "The CIA is using me for bait to figure out what going on with the virus, for Christ sake."

"I told you not to trust anyone the other day. There are people involved with this mystery who are not who they claim."

"So you said," Tommy grunted, taking another long drink of whiskey. "Is it Amber—who had a meeting at the J. Edgar Hoover building today? Is it the freaking NSA Inspector General—who is paling around with a known criminal? Is it Anna—the emissary for some white-haired freak trying to buy the computer virus? If it's not one of them, then who is it? How about a name."

"They were all it. You are slowly figuring this thing out. There's light at the end of the tunnel."

"Is there someone else posing as someone they're not?"

"I could get fired if I gave you any names."

"Then what am I doing here? What was so important you couldn't tell me over the phone?"

Caroline giggled, taking his hand again. "Maybe I just wanted to see you and give you a pep talk."

Turning and looking at Caroline, Tommy realized just how beautiful she was. Her short, straight blonde hair, bright blue eyes, and soft white skin excited him. Reaching up, he caressed her face. She pushed her head into his hand.

"So what's the job offer? And if I take the job, will your powerful employers extract me from my current problems?"

"I can't tell you, and no."

"Then what good are you?"

"Let me show you," she replied, pulling him toward the bedroom.

Standing his ground, Tommy looked up at the ceiling and muttered, "What's going on?"

Giggling, Caroline asked, "What?"

"A month ago I couldn't get a bedroom date to save my life. Ever since I've been implicated in the death of the CIA agent and the sale of the computer virus, I seem to be the luckiest guy in all of North America."

Caroline giggled again. "The girls just can't say no?"

"It has been a juggling act."

"Well, if I were in your shoes, I'd enjoy your current sex life," Caroline commented, pulling him toward the bedroom again. "Because if you can't extract yourself from the murder rap and computer virus problem, the only intimate time you'll have to look forward to is shower time in prison."

Nodding his head, Tommy replied, "Good point."

An hour later, Tommy looked across the sage green bedroom at the procession of strewn clothes: his plaid shirt, her bright red T-shirt, a white bra, his jeans and then hers. Caroline reached out from under the white quilt and pulled him back to her side.

"You need to get going," she whispered.

"I'm not meeting someone until ten-thirty."

"You're not meeting Becky till ten-thirty. But you need to follow her first."

"Follow her to Fort Meade? Why would I follow her to Fort Meade?"

"Tommy for such a smart guy with good instincts, you're pretty dumb." Caroline snickered. "Not everyone is who they say they are."

Climbing from the bed, Caroline reached out and took his hand, kissing it. Tommy leaned down and passionately kissed her on the lips.

Thirty minutes later, Tommy waited patiently in the red Mercedes, watching the elevator in the parking garage under Becky and Amber's apartment building. At six-twenty, the elevator opened, and Becky walked through the doors, making her way to her red Volvo. Tommy started the Mercedes as she pulled from the parking spot and followed her out of the garage onto the streets of Rosslyn.

CHAPTER 50

Northwest Washington, DC, May 3, 2016:

As Tommy followed the red Volvo onto the Roosevelt Bridge and over the Potomac River, the square white structure of the Kennedy Center, with its enormous windows pouring light across its wide terraces, loomed ahead. Keeping an eye on the taillights of the red Volvo so as not to lose her, Tommy began to ponder his mistrust of Becky.

He could never put his finger on why he suspected Becky of being more involved than she let on, but Caroline's guidance had prodded him to find out. Becky had provided Tommy with a lot of information over the last few days. She had warned him about the CIA and FBI investigations, and she had given him a safe haven when he was eluding the police department. But with Sid's earlier revelation about her involvement with the inspector general, Caroline's assistance, and his gut instinct telling him to not trust her, it was now clear that Becky didn't have a meeting at Fort Meade.

Passing the imposing Kennedy Center, the dog panting in the seat next to him, Tommy was happy the meeting wouldn't occur there, where he might have a run in with the deputy security supervisor he'd teased several days before. He followed the red Volvo as it made a right onto

New Hampshire Boulevard. The dog's attention was captivated by the all the illuminated action, the bright lights of passing cars mixing with that of overhead lamps and businesses, while Tommy struggled to keep track of Becky's car in traffic as they approached DuPont Circle.

After waiting several minutes for a red light, the Volvo then began driving around the circle, busy with both car and pedestrian traffic circling the tall black statue of Samuel DuPont in the center of the round grassy park. Turning north on Connecticut Avenue, the red Volvo joined the traffic pouring in and out of Washington, DC, along the congested street. Tommy followed. Slowing near Twentieth Street, Becky's red Volvo turned into an adjacent neighborhood.

"So, Caroline was right," Tommy muttered to the dog, "Becky's meeting wasn't at Fort Meade."

Following Becky down a narrow street with three-story apartment buildings to one side and brownstone townhouses to the other, he watched her pull up to the curb and park. Tommy stopped behind a car pulling out from a space and slipped the Mercedes into the empty spot, next to the row of brownstone houses.

A shadowy Becky, now on foot, began walking back along the sidewalk on the other side of the narrow street toward Connecticut Avenue. Tommy hunched over in the driver's seat, waiting for her to pass. The stray dog hopped down onto the car's floor boards with a faint whimper.

Giving her adequate time to pass by, Tommy sat back up and saw her through the rearview mirror twenty yards down the street. Climbing from the car, he and the dog watched her turn the corner of a building onto the Connecticut Avenue sidewalk, and they followed.

Turning onto Connecticut Avenue, he caught a glimpse of Becky as she stepped into a restaurant a block up the street. As Tommy approached the restaurant, an older man dressed in a black suit brusquely commented, "Washington, DC, has a leash law."

"Go complain to the dog's owner, old man," Tommy grunted. "It's not my dog."

Looking through the restaurant's tall street front windows, Tommy watched Becky talking with the hostess. He then watched her walk to the rear of the room and begin climbing a set of stairs leading to the second floor.

Looking down at the dog, Tommy said, "Wait here, Dog," before stepping through the restaurant's entrance. The blue-and-gray-eyed dog dutifully sat down and began watching the traffic moving along the avenue.

In the restaurant, Tommy was met with the smell of grilled steak, beer, and an assortment of spices. With a long wooden bar to one side, the restaurant's tan walls were covered in memorabilia and chalkboards, advertising drink and food specials. Small square tables with burgundy cushioned chairs packed a room that was covered with short hunter green carpet. The chatter of patrons, occasionally interrupted by the chef barking out a ready order, overwhelmed soft music being piped into the room. Tommy saw Becky climbing a set of stairs that hugged the wall near the back of the restaurant and led up to an upper dining area. Watching her reach the top of the stairs, step beyond the landing, and disappear, Tommy worked his way through the crowd and took a seat along the bar. Ordering a Jameson on ice, he patiently watched the landing to the upper dining room.

A young, slightly plump, woman with shoulder-length blonde hair and bright green eyes dressed in a black skirt and white blouse, looking as if she just left work, pulled up the stool next to Tommy. Looking over, Tommy winked and smiled at the young woman, before going back to sipping his drink and watching the upper landing.

"Just a wink and smile, and no follow-on game?" the blonde cooed in a sweet voice.

"No follow-on game. You look a bit too young to me."

"Maybe I should be the judge of that. I'm twenty three, divorced, and lonely."

Laughing at the woman's boldness, Tommy replied, "Well then, I guess I've got a chance—you being lonely and all."

The two began chatting with one and other as Tommy kept an eye on the stairs leading to the upper dining room. Several minutes later Tommy watched Steve's short and beady-eyed figure, dressed in a dark blue suit, enter the restaurant and begin talking with the hostess. The hostess gestured toward the stairs, and Steve followed Becky's earlier path to the upper dining room.

"Would you do me a favor," Tommy interrupted the woman sitting next to him talking about her ex-husband.

Her bright green eyes smiled at his request. "It depends on the favor."

Tommy pointed toward Steve. "See the short guy climbing the stairs?"

Swiveling her stool around, she replied, "Yeah, I see him."

"That guy knows me, and I think he's meeting with someone else who knows me, a woman. Can you take a look to see who he's meeting with?"

Her green eyes narrowed, and the tone of her voice became suspicious. "Are you a jealous husband or something?"

"No, actually I'm working with the CIA on a matter of national security," Tommy responded, hoping she would not ask for credentials. "That man is a known criminal, and I can't let him know I'm here." Tommy realized his honesty would be unbelievable to the green-eyed woman.

"So you really are a jealous husband wanting to catch your wife cheating."

Tommy looked down at his drink and smiled. Then looking back to the young woman, he said, "You're right. I'm here to catch my wife cheating on me, but how about we just pretend he's a criminal, and it's a matter of national security?"

The woman's face lit up. "Wow, spy stuff. Yeah, I'll help you out."

Slipping from her stool, she made her way through the crowd to the base of the stairs. Looking back, she smiled at Tommy before climbing the stairs and disappearing into the dining room. Ten minutes later the green eyed woman, still smiling, walked down the stairs, made her way back to the bar and climbed onto her stool.

"He's meeting with a petite brunette with blue eyes," she announced with a laugh. "He's not a very attractive man, and she's beautiful. You must be really lousy in bed or something."

"That's what I was afraid of."

"Afraid I would think you're lousy in bed or that he was ugly?" She laughed again. "Or that I thought she was beautiful. And don't worry, I'm not a lesbian."

"Yeah, right, the lonely divorcee lesbian coming on to an older man."

The young woman took a sip of her drink. "First, she tells him she has the merchandise, but she wasn't sure she wanted to go through with the deal. He told her that everything has been set up for it to work perfectly. She then tells him that he should not have tried to kill some guy named Tommy and that was not a part of the deal. He said that it wasn't his idea. Then he told her that, tentatively, the meeting to transfer the merchandise would be in three days at the Washington Monument—at three o'clock in the afternoon. Those were the important parts anyway. You weren't lying, this is about national security or something."

"How in the world did you get all that?" Tommy asked, clearly astonished.

"I took a table next to them and listened to their conversation while I was reading the menu. Then I told the waiter that nothing looked good to me, and I left. I really like this spy stuff."

"You're good at it," Tommy announced, as he slipped off his stool and began digging in the pockets of his jeans.

"Hey, where you going?"

"Someplace quiet to think about all you just told me," Tommy replied, tossing a twenty dollar bill on the counter.

"I don't even know your name," the green-eyed woman declared, clearly disappointed.

"Tommy. My name is Tommy," he answered, turning from the bar and walking out of the restaurant. The dog fell in behind him as he walked down the sidewalk toward the red Mercedes.

CHAPTER 51

East Falls Church, Arlington, Virginia, May 3, 2016:

Leaning back in the driver's seat of Amber's red Mercedes parked in front of his house, Tommy sighed, wondering whether he should still keep his appointment with Becky. If he were to meet with Becky, he didn't want to go back to Amber's apartment. With no place else to go, he had driven back to his Arlington residence. After all, Sid had told him that the police were no longer searching for him, Jacob Livingston's surveillance had abruptly ended yesterday evening on Hooper's Island, and Caroline claimed to have removed all the electronic surveillance equipment from his house. That left the FBI and CIA, two agencies that weren't out to hurt him, and Steve, who was currently meeting with Becky.

Walking up the steps to his front door, he twisted the front door handle and looked down at the stray dog to see if it sensed anything wrong. The dog looked up and gave a short bark, telling Tommy it was all clear. Stepping into the dark house, he made his way to the kitchen, turned on the light, and found the half empty bottle of Jameson on the counter. Filling a glass with two ice cubes from the freezer and three fingers of Jameson, Tommy walked into the still-cluttered living room and sat down on the cushionless couch, turning the television on with the remote control. The dog sat at his feet.

With Fox News' Hannity on the television, Tommy pulled his cell from his pocket and began thumbing through his contacts. Selecting Anna, he wrote down the number. He then pulled the prepaid cell from his pocket and punched Anna's number, before hitting the call button.

"Hello," Anna's slightly accented voice hummed from the cell.

"Hello, beautiful, what are you up to?"

"Ah, Tommy, Jesus and I are just watching television. What about you?"

"Same, catching up on current events," Tommy replied. "How is my friend Jesus?"

Anna giggled. "Other than an angry looking cut on the side of his head, he is good."

"If your boss is still interested, let's meet on the Constellation in Baltimore harbor in two days."

"Your phone is tapped," Anna said angrily. "I do not want anyone to know of our meeting."

"This is not my cell. It's a prepaid one I purchased just today with cash—they're incredibly cheap."

"What is the Constellation?"

"The USS Constellation is a big wooden sailing boat. Your boss should know what I'm talking about," Tommy answered. "Let's meet on the stern."

"What is a stern?"

"The back of the ship," Tommy responded patiently. "I'll walk up to the quarterdeck at twelve noon."

"What is a quarterdeck?"

"The place where you step onto the ship from the gangplank."

"What's a gangplank?"

"The walkway to the quarterdeck." Tommy softly

laughed at his inability to communicate with the Peruvian beauty. "I want cash. One hundred dollar bills, please."

"What time do you wish to meet?" Anna asked, her tone very businesslike.

"Twelve noon," Tommy repeated his earlier instruction, avoiding using any more nautical terms.

"In two days at noon on the stern of the USS Constellation in the Baltimore Harbor," Anna repeated his instructions. "You want the cash in one hundred dollar bills."

"Exacto," Tommy confirmed before disconnecting.

CHAPTER 52

Rosslyn, Arlington, Virginia, May 3, 2016:

At ten-thirty in the evening, Tommy gently knocked on Becky's ninth-floor apartment door. Becky, wearing a sheer knee-length nightgown, her brown nipples showing through its thin fabric, answered the door, smiling. Taking the beautiful petite brunette into his arms, he gave her a long passionate kiss in the doorway. Silently, she took his hand and pulled him into the apartment, closing the door behind them.

"Wait a minute," Tommy whispered, opening the door back up and letting the dog inside.

"Your dog?"

"A stray dog," Tommy corrected her. "I don't own a dog."

Guiding Tommy down the cream-colored hallway with its small framed watercolor paintings of Washington, DC, historic buildings and into the large living room overlooking the Potomac River, she gently pushed him down on the white leather couch. The blue-and-gray-eyed dog lay down on the floor at his feet. Without saying a word, Becky walked into the kitchen, past its dark marbled countertops, and pulled a bottle of Chardonnay from the refrigerator. With the bottle and a corkscrew in one hand and two crystal wine glasses in the other, she returned to the living room and sat down next to Tommy, the compression of the cushion pushing her shoulder into his.

"I've missed you," she softly whispered, cutting the thin aluminum covering before twisting the corkscrew into the bottle's top.

"It's been a very revealing couple of days." Tommy chuckled, picking up one of the crystal glasses, examining it above his head in the light from the city shinning through the window.

Pulling the cork from the bottle with a faint pop, Becky asked, "How so?"

"Let's have a drink," Tommy replied as he considered the best way to extract the truth from Becky.

Pouring light golden liquid from the bottle, Becky queried, "So what have you learned about the computer virus?"

"As best I can figure, someone is trying to shift suspicion onto me in order to sell the virus. Based on how many people actually were in possession of the virus last year, that is a finite list," Tommy explained before taking a sip from his crystal glass. "Which is exactly why they're trying to shift suspicion."

"Who do you think is responsible?"

"Steve is at the top of the list," Tommy answered, watching for Becky's reaction.

"That makes sense," her soft voice purred in response. "There's probably no love lost there after what you did to him in Thailand last year. Anyone else?"

"What do you know about Howard Macintyre, the NSA Inspector General?"

"He's the guy I delivered the computer virus to when I returned from Thailand, but he's very committed to the NSA. I doubt he would ever betray the agency."

"Did you know he has been talking with Jacob Livingston?"

Dropping her chin to her chest, Becky hesitatingly replied, "Yes."

"And?"

"I thought it was a mistake for him to do so, but he's the one who involved Jacob in this whole affair in the first place," Becky confessed. "They meet each week for drinks, and it slipped out after Sid came and told the inspector general that you were trying to sell the computer virus. He had no idea that Jacob Livingston would stoop to any means to acquire the virus."

Tommy raised his eyebrows in disbelief. "Slipped out?" Already knowing the answer, Tommy then asked, "Why would the NSA's Inspector General meet weekly with a known criminal?"

Becky shrugged her shoulders. "They met at a party and Jacob befriended him."

"And the inspector general accidently let the news of a classified computer virus that he knew Livingston would be interested in slip out? That's not what Sid told me."

"That's what the inspector general told me."

"Come on Becky, what's the real story?"

Looking into Tommy's eyes, Becky sighed. "The NSA has been after Jacob Livingston for a long time for dealing with stolen databases but couldn't gather enough evidence against him to pass to the FBI. After Sid told the inspector general about the possibility that you were trying to sell a copy of the virus, he decided that it would be a good way to gather that evidence. So Howard told Jacob about the virus, knowing he would want to get a copy of it. The inspector general then told Sid about Jacob, hoping he would catch him trying to obtain the computer virus. We knew Jacob would try to verify all the information the inspector general had given him, and he did.

While we were monitoring Jacob's calls, we found that one of his employees had a contact in the CIA. That contact had been passing him information for several years. That man no longer works at the CIA thanks to the inspector general's action."

"Who were the two men I caught searching my house?"

"I found out after the fact that the inspector general hired those two thugs hoping that Jacob's man would be watching. The inspector general knew that the FBI and CIA would be keeping out of sight, and he wanted to give Jacob assurance that you did have the virus and were trying to sell it. And indeed, Jacob's man Ralf saw the search by the inspector general's hired thugs, setting into motion Jacob entering the picture."

"And you picked them up after I left them on the entryway floor. You took them to the hospital."

"Yes. The inspector general instructed me to pick them up."

"And a violent criminal became one of the players in the Thomas Luck versus the fantasy virus mystery," Tommy muttered.

Shifting on the couch, he looked out onto the Potomac River and watched a large yacht gliding down its waters. Staring at the brightly lit yacht, he wondered if this beautiful woman, who just told him about the inspector general, would also tell him about her relationship with Steve? Taking another long swallow of wine, Tommy looked down at a woman he wanted to believe. A woman he was willing to ignore his inner voice for.

Laying her head on his shoulder, Becky whispered, "Tommy, I'm more involved with this investigation than you know."

"Tell me."

Looking up at Tommy, with sadness in her blue eyes, Becky said, "I've been working with Sid. I was assigned to his department at his request after you picked up the envelope at the Westover Post Office. He asked me to reestablish our relationship, so I could find out whether you had the virus and whether you killed his agent."

"And what of Steve?"

"Steve contacted me after he saw us together," Becky quickly admitted. "He wanted a copy of the computer virus that everyone thinks you have. He wants to buy it, and the inspector general had me playing along. I told him that I had acquired a copy. I know he tried to kill you two days ago. I am sorry. I had nothing to do with that."

"If Steve came to you after the murder of the CIA agent, looking for a copy of the virus then there is someone else out there trying to sell a copy," Tommy mumbled to himself.

"I don't know, but I really got the feeling that I was a second source. It was almost like I was the backup plan."

"Did Sid know you were playing along with Steve?"

"No, the inspector general told me not to tell him."

"Why not? Sid is running the investigation into the computer virus."

"Watching how things have transpired, I think the inspector general saw a chance to steal the lime light. He wants to solve the case before Sid and take all the glory," Becky replied. "He's like every other ranking bureaucratic public servant in Washington, DC. He'll do anything to get ahead."

Tommy raised his eyes in disbelief for a second time. "And you didn't tell Sid?"

"I'm on loan to Sid, but the inspector general has made it clear that I work for him. If I cross the inspector general, my career is shot."

"When did you tell Steve that you had obtained a copy

of the virus?" Tommy asked, running his fingers through his hair.

"I told him that I could probably do it three days before he tried to kill you. The inspector general instructed me to tell him that I did not have a copy but could get my hands on one," Becky whispered. "I had no idea he was going to try and kill you."

"So, Steve must be the one responsible for setting me up for the CIA man's murder."

"I don't know. Like I said, I think I was playing second fiddle. I think I was the backup plan because the meeting to transfer the computer virus was tentative. What doesn't make sense is the complexity of the transaction," Becky added. "We both know that Steve is not a terribly bright person, and he couldn't possibly be the one who planned the details of the sale."

"Why did Steve wait three days to attempt to kill me? My meeting with Sid had to have prompted that. But that would mean that he was worried we could figure out what was going on. But what is going on? Who is his main source for the virus?"

"I have no idea," Becky admitted.

"Did Sid tell you why he changed the location of our meeting?"

"No, he just said he had a feeling."

"Did Steve tell you why he wanted to stop the meeting?"

"Yes, and you were right, he was worried about you and Sid teaming up."

"He told you that?"

"Yes, after the fact. When I found out what he did, I told him our deal would be off if he tried to kill you again."

Tommy scratched his head. “How did he know I was going to meet with Sid?”

“Tommy, you’ve got more people watching and listening to you than anyone can count. I have no idea how he found out, but I’m not surprised.”

“And your meeting with Steve tonight?”

“You followed me?”

“Someone gave me advice to follow you.”

“Who?”

“Can’t say,” Tommy flatly replied.

“The meeting was to confirm the transaction date and place,” Becky explained. “But Steve backed down and claimed it was still tentative.”

A smile crept across Tommy’s face. The woman next to him had admitted her part to the affair that had complicated his life. He pulled her face to his and kissed her moist lips, before asking, “And the meeting with him at the Washington Monument was to do what?”

“We want the meeting to go down because it’s a set up to take him into custody,” Becky whispered. “He’s still wanted for misappropriation of NSA assets, but the additional charges of trying to acquire a classified program would have sent him away for a long time. The Inspector General has arranged for his arrest at the meeting. “

Standing up, Tommy reached down and took Becky’s right hand, pulling her up next to him. As she began unbuttoning his shirt, he slipped the straps of her nightgown from her shoulders. The gown fell from her body. As she unbuckled his belt, he ran his hands across her bare hips, before leading the beautiful brunette into the bedroom. Tommy gently pushed her back on the light blue satin sheets.

CHAPTER 53

Trinidad, Oklahoma, December 8, 2013:

A light flurry of snow floated down outside pub's single window that looked out onto a parking lot filled with four pickup trucks of various make and model. Beyond the parking lot were several gas stations, and finally Interstate 40 with sixteen wheelers and a spattering of cars whisking past, their tires spinning across the pavement sending an audible high pitched hum coursing through the small town.

The pub, a renovated double wide trailer with a long bar to one side and six round dark wooden tables in the center, was a popular watering hole for the locals of Trinidad, Oklahoma. Raising a glass filled with two ice cubes and Jameson Irish whiskey to his mouth, Tommy looked across the table at his aging father. His father, blue eyes sparkling with intelligence under a head of short gray hair, looked back, carefully scrutinizing his son.

"You've seen a lot more than the average person," Tommy's father commented before taking a sip from a brown bottle of Coors beer. "A lot more than any of your bothers."

"Is that good or bad?"

"That depends on how you look at your experiences," Tommy's father replied. "How you look at yourself."

"I am a drunken construction site manager-product of your teachings." Tommy softly laughed, teasing his father.

"I taught you nothing," Tommy's father replied in a serious tone. "It's all about genetics."

Looking at his father quizzically, Tommy asked, "What do you mean?"

"I use to think that a father was obligated to teach his children to be the best they could and survive an unfair world. But what I have learned is that fathers don't teach their children anything," the old gray haired man responded.

"What do you mean?"

"I attempted to teach you, but it really didn't matter in the end. They were simply sea stories or family adventures. While I had hoped that the passing of my experiences and knowledge would help you avoid the same pitfalls I encountered, they meant nothing. You would still be the person you are now whether I had been there or not. Whether I had told you of my experiences or not," Tommy's father explained, shaking his head. "You are a product of your mother and me but only in terms of your genetic makeup, not our teachings."

"That sounds pretty deep. You don't think I took any of your advice or stories?"

"What I'm saying is that it didn't matter whether you did or not. There is something bigger than all the teachings a father or mother can do. The code written into your genetic makeup trumps anything I could have done to make you who you are."

"Why do you say that?"

"Remember when I did a tour in Vietnam?"

"Yeah," Tommy recalled. "You were gone for nearly a year. Not that I was old enough to remember."

"I was an F-Four squadron commander and had a

bunch of men working for me—mechanics, avionics and hydraulic specialists, and pilots to name a few."

"Yeah."

"Being the squadron commander, I was everyone's boss and couldn't really befriend any of them except for my Executive Officer, Jack Jevers. He was a tall, dark-headed man with bright green eyes. He had a low voice, but his laugh was more like a high-pitched screech. Before he sat down on a chair, he would always hike up his pant legs," Tommy's father reminisced. "We would sit in my stateroom each night and drink. He drank scotch, and I drank bourbon. And he would always start a conversation off with 'the way I see it.' He was an incredible man."

"He was killed in Vietnam," Tommy added, remembering the day his father called home and informed his mother of Jack's death.

"He was shot down just south of Hanoi and never bailed out of the jet. His wingman watched him go down."

"What's this have to do with genetics?"

"Jack had a brand new baby boy when we left for Vietnam. The kid wasn't more than two months old," Tommy's father continued. "I met Jack's son last year. Now a man, he's shorter than Jack and doesn't have his dark head of hair but has he does have same bright green eyes."

"So genetics passed on his eye color."

"Far more than his eyes," Tommy's father explained. "I met him at a restaurant in San Diego, and before he sat down, he hiked up his pant legs and then he ordered a glass of scotch. I told him about his father and how much I admired the man. Then Jack's son looked at me and said, ‘The way I see it,’ before talking about his life without his father.”

“Maybe he watched a bunch of home videos of his father?”

“Maybe he didn’t.” His father shook his head, his blue eyes silently scolding Tommy. “I made a small joke about his father, and he laughed with a high-pitched screech. We are who we are, not because of what a father or mother teaches their children but because of the genetic code that we pass on to our children.”

Not convinced of his father’s theory, Tommy said, “I don’t know that I buy it.”

“What about twins separated at birth? When they are reunited, they wear the same fashions and typically have the same hair styles.”

“Are you saying that I would have become a structural engineer with or without your influence? I would have the same personality?”

“Yes,” his father replied. “You would be the same person on the same course in life.”

“So, what about Edward Whymper and selecting the easy or hard route in life?” Tommy asked, “What about looking at each step and every decision as a reflection of our last?”

“We have choices in life, but the courses of action we select are already built into us,” Tommy’s father continued. “Apprehension and boldness mark the boundaries of a personality. Your personality falls closer to the bold side than your brothers’.”

“I’m not sure about that,” Tommy remarked. “They both are incredibly successful entrepreneurs.”

“I didn’t say that they’re not bold, I simply said you’re a bit closer to the boundary, and it’s far more complex that simply two boundaries.”

"So what you're saying is that our path is predetermined. Our path is set before we are born. "

"To a large extent, yes. We always have a choice but our decisions are based on who we are, and the path we will choose has already been selected by our genetic makeup."

CHAPTER 54

Rosslyn, Arlington, Virginia, May 4, 2016:

Lying on the bed, looking at shadows that criss-crossed the ceiling, Tommy was thinking about his father's words that cold day in Oklahoma. Was his father right? Would he be sitting on that bed in the midst of all this turmoil with or without his father's guidance? Or were his father's words simply the old man trying to find an excuse for all the pebbles in his pockets—his bad decisions throughout his life?

Tommy's thoughts then shifted to his parents' relationship, and how it had hardened his mother, slowly eradicating any softness. His father had never been able to control his philandering, yet for some reason, his wife, Tommy's mother, never stopped loving him. Tommy had never understood his mother. She had been a beautiful woman who attracted nearly every man she met. Yet she chose to stay with the one man she could never wholly have. Tommy had no doubt that his own warped sense of loyalty and stubbornness was a product of both his parents. His father bequeathed Tommy a wandering eye. His mother passed him a sense of loyalty and resoluteness that eclipsed everything but that wandering eye.

Interrupted by his cell ringing at the base of the bed, Tommy glanced at a clock on the bed stand and saw an illuminated *12:17 AM* glowing in the darkness. Slipping to the edge of the bed, he reached down and pulled the cell from the pocket of his faded jeans and answered the phone.

Answering, he listened to the caller for several minutes before grunting and disconnecting the call. Lying back on the bed, its satin sheets feeling cool against his skin, Tommy crossed his arms behind the back of his head and considered what the caller had just told him.

"Who was that?" Becky asked sleepily, with the sound of shifting satin as she moved across the sheets, wrapping her arms around his waist. "And do they know what time it was?"

"It came from California. It was just past eight o'clock his time."

"Who was it? What did they want?"

"It was from a friend of mine who works in the investigation branch of the US Postal Service."

Perking up, Becky pulled herself up on one elbow, looking at Tommy, asking, "What did he say?"

"I asked him to find out who set the post office box up. Apparently, it wasn't John Smith after all. It was a woman who seduced the postmaster, several times, to get what she wanted. The postmaster has been lying the entire time about who rented the box."

"If John Smith is dead, it couldn't have been him," Becky commented before asking, "Who was it? Did he have a name?"

"No, but he did have a pretty good description."

"Who was it? Did you recognize the description?" Becky asked again anxiously, "Do you know who set up the post office box?"

"I know who it was," Tommy muttered as he climbed from the bed.

Dressing, he left Becky as she looked questioningly at him from the bed. Silently leaving the bedroom, Tommy walked to the elevator, the stray dog at his side, rode the lift to the tenth floor, and knocked on Amber's door. Kissing Amber when she answered the door, Tommy made his way to the kitchen, around the gray granite countertop, and poured himself a glass of Irish whiskey. After his second glass, he decided that he was too tired to drink anymore and made his way into the bedroom, curling up next to Amber on the bed.

CHAPTER 55

Boulder, Colorado, January 23, 2014:

A chilling breeze blew across the sidewalk, as Tommy looked up at the gray stone building, its two spirals and a bell tower pointing to a sky with a churning background of dark clouds. Tall leafless trees mixing with evergreens seemed to highlight the bleakness. With a long camel overcoat, covering a dark suit protecting him from the weather he had become unaccustomed to, Tommy climbed the gray stone stairs, bracketed by thick black iron banisters, leading up to the church's wide wooden doors. Having flown into Denver that morning from Bangkok, Tommy was back in his hometown to say farewell to his father, a day he had hoped would never come. With a ten-hour time difference from the island he had been living on in the Gulf of Thailand and a twenty-four-hour journey under his belt, he was exhausted. If it were not for the ceremony, he would be sound asleep at a local hotel.

Pulling one of the wide wooden doors open, he was met with a hot gust of air smelling of incense. His mother, standing next to his two brothers near the front, looked small and frail. Dressed in black, Tommy could see her arthritis-gnarled hands, white hair beneath a black lace scarf, and loose gray skin as he strode down the blue carpeted aisle between long rows of wooden pews. He saw Sarah, his second ex-wife, with Will and Ann on the right. To his left, he saw Betsy, his first ex-wife, and her two brothers next to his daughter Rose. He took his position next to his brothers and mother as the service began.

The service was short. The family walked down the aisle and out the wide wooden doors to say farewell the departing attendees. Standing to the left and behind his mother, Tommy could sense the rage in his middle brother, his brown eyes seething hatred and arms shaking. Tommy knew that the rage was about to be directed at him.

"Nice of you to make it," his brother whispered to Tommy in a hushed hiss.

"You know I wouldn't have missed sending Dad off."

"Of course not, you two couldn't have been more alike. I'm sure it was like sending a brother-in-arms off," his sibling quietly spat with thick sarcasm. "You heard how he died?"

"I heard," Tommy replied.

"A man killed Dad for sleeping with his wife."

"I heard," Tommy said again, hoping to defuse the confrontation by not engaging with his brother.

"Leave your brother be," their mother interrupted with a faint cracking voice.

"Dad was a philanderer, and he was killed because he was sleeping with another married woman," Tommy's brother said slightly louder, ignoring their mother.

Having enough of the sarcasm, Tommy looked his brother in the eye. "A fitting death then."

"Yes, a very fitting death. And you're probably proud of him," his brother raised his voice, poking his fingers into Tommy's chest.

"To be murdered at the age of eighty-one by a jealous husband?" Tommy chuckled. "I not so much proud of him as amazed. I hope I still have the wherewithal to get it up at that age."

Ann and Will, followed by Rose, stepped out of the church, stopping next to Tommy. His ex-wives stalked past the children and down the steps to the sidewalk in front of the church.

His brother watched them pass. "A sad procession of your failings."

"Leave my family out of your rants," Tommy firmly responded, with Will, Ann, and Rose all scowling at their uncle.

"You are nothing but a drunken untrustworthy fool," his brother said, poking Tommy's chest with his index finger again. "You're a failure as a father."

Tommy's oldest brother turned to face them. "Not here. Take your opinions and problems away from Mom."

Taking Will and Ann by the hands, Tommy led them down the steps, followed by Rose, across the street to a small park, the cold frigid brown grass crunching under their feet. His brother followed, grabbing Tommy by the collar in the park and spinning him around. Tommy let go of Will and Ann's hands as he spun and punched his brother in the face. His brother stumbled back several steps before falling onto the brown dry grass that carpeted the park.

"If you ever talk that way in front of my children again—" Tommy firmly began scolding his brother.

Before he could finish his sentence, Tommy was hit in the side of the head by another fist. As he turned to face his assailant, another fist struck him in the jaw, then the stomach. Tommy began to block the blows as Betsy's brothers attacked. Stumbling backward, Tommy glanced over to see his children watching the assault with frightened faces. He felt his middle brother begin to strike him from behind, and Tommy swung his elbow back, smashing his neck. He looked up at the church's entry to see his mother and oldest brother standing stoically watching the assault in silence. He blocked one of Betsy's brothers from striking him in the forehead. Tommy struck the other brother with a jab to his face, knocking him back. Out of the corner of his eye, he saw his two ex-wives watching from the sidewalk with their lips twisted into approving smirks. Tommy reached back and grabbed his brother standing behind him, throwing him back to the ground in front of Betsy's brothers. Looking back over to his children, Tommy saw terror on their faces. He dropped his hands to his sides and let the blows rain down.

CHAPTER 56

Rosslyn, Arlington, Virginia, May 4, 2016:

Sitting on the edge of Amber's bed that morning, Tommy was looking out the window onto the Potomac River thinking about his father's funeral and the fight that ensued. Vividly recalling the look on his children's faces, Tommy had known at the beginning of the scuffle that he could have fought them off. His three assailants had never been in a life-and-death situation, and they had no idea what a man was capable of when it came to survival. It was a skill that he honed over the years, a level of harnessed cold violence that he could unleash when his life was threatened.

On that cold day in the park, fending off his attackers, the last thing Tommy had wanted was to have his children observe that level of aggression from their father. He knew that releasing the anger that accompanied that skill, he would not be able to stop until his three assailants lay bloody and beaten on the ground. To spare his children from witnessing his unrestrained rage, he had dropped his arms and let his aggressors have their way. They knocked him to his knees and then to his belly. They had finished their assault with several rib-cracking kicks. In the end, only his children had come to his side. Every one of the other witnesses had turned and walked away.

Hearing the soft ruffling of sheets as Amber moved on the bed behind him, Tommy's mind shifted to the phone call he had received the night before from his friend Ben at the postal service. Shifting to the side of the bed, Tommy reached into his pants pocket and fiddled with a small pen like device.

He then turned over and began gently shaking Amber's shoulder until she sleepily rolled over and looked up at him.

"Amber, what do you do for a living?" Tommy asked the beautiful fair-skinned woman lying next to him.

Stretching her arms and yawning, she replied, "You know what I do. I'm an investment banker." The comforter fell from her shoulders, revealing a slink aqua colored silk nightgown, as she reached across the bed and wrapped her arms around his waist. "I told you what I do for a living," she groggily answered.

"Let me rephrase the question," Tommy continued, carefully watching Amber's reaction. "What were you doing at the FBI headquarters yesterday?"

"Tommy, I can explain." She pulled her arms from Tommy's waist. The grogginess had disappeared from her voice.

Running his hand through her thick auburn hair, Tommy said, "Let me rephrase the question again. Look, I know you work for the CIA, or FBI, or NSA."

"Tommy, what are you talking about?"

Turning away from Amber and looking back out the window onto the early morning Washington, DC, skyline, Tommy said, "I know you work for one of the agencies, or the police department? Do you work for the police department?"

"Tommy—"

Interrupting Amber, Tommy turned and faced her, gently placing his finger over her mouth. The stray dog appeared in the doorway, sitting down and watching the scene unfold in the bedroom.

"I followed you yesterday and watched you enter the J. Edgar Hoover building."

"Tommy—"

Interrupting Amber again, Tommy placed his hands on her shoulders. "Look, I'm tired because I didn't sleep last night. When I'm tired, I get angry real easy. I don't have my traditional full-on hangover in motion to numb my senses either, and that makes me even worse. Now, I know you've probably read my file and know that I'm capable of some pretty outrageous violence. What I really need is the NSA Inspector General's private number."

"I don't know the inspector general's private number," Amber exclaimed, now fully awake.

"Maybe you're not listening. I know you work for one of the agencies. So get me the number to the inspector general before I get angry."

Amber silently moved off the bed, walking from the bedroom, around the dog in the doorway, into the living room. Tommy could hear her talking on the phone, but couldn't make out of the words. A few moments later, she returned to the bedroom with a slip of paper in her hand. The paper had a phone number printed in a shaking script.

"Thank you, sweetheart," Tommy said, smiling at the beautiful auburn-headed woman. "I figured you could get the number."

With Amber standing at the edge of the bed, Tommy typed the number onto his cell phone, before hitting the call button.

A clear Midwestern-accented voice answer the phone, "Howard McIntyre, Inspector General."

"Good morning, Mr. McIntyre," Tommy said.

"Who might this be, this is an unlisted number. How'd you get my personal number?"

"This is Tommy Luck, a name I'm sure you're familiar with. I'd like to schedule a meeting with you."

"Why should I agree to a meeting with you?"

"Because if you don't, I'll schedule one with your boss, the NSA Director," Tommy said calmly into the cell as Amber crawled back onto the bed and pulled the covers up to her shoulders, eyeing him suspiciously.

"You actually think the director would meet with an unemployed drunk who has been the focus of an investigation concerning a stolen computer virus and the murder of a CIA Agent?"

"As a matter of fact, yes I do. I think he'd be interested in hearing about a stolen computer virus. One that was sold by several disenfranchised NSA agents last year in Thailand and one that is currently being offered for sale. He'd also love to hear how you informed a known criminal of its existence. I'm sure he'd rather I talk with him than the *Washington Post.*"

Tommy heard paper being shuffled in the back ground before the inspector general responded, "I'm free tomorrow, eleven o'clock."

"No, I think we'll meet today at three o'clock, on the National Mall near the Reflecting Pool."

"Mr. Luck, I am a very busy man." The inspector general's voice was clearly frustrated. "My entire day is scheduled with meetings."

"Fine, can you transfer me to the director?"

"Are you trying to blackmail me?"

"I couldn't blackmail you unless you have done something wrong. Have you done something wrong?"

After a long delay, the inspector general replied, "Three o'clock near the Reflecting Pool. Is there some reason you chose the Reflecting Pool?"

"It's a nice place to reflect on the crap you've put me through over the last week," Tommy answered, before disconnecting the call.

Turning to Amber, Tommy asked, "So who is it? FBI, CIA, NSA, or the police department?"

"I currently work for Jason Scott. I'm an FBI agent. But I normally work in their IT department on various internal software packages. When it was discovered that I had a relationship with you, I was tasked with gathering evidence that either implicated or cleared you of the CIA agent's death."

"Weren't you the model of efficiency, we met on the twenty-first," Tommy commented. "Obviously the FBI knew about the computer virus before the CIA Agent's death."

"Our meeting was purely accidental. The FBI wasn't involved until the CIA agent was murdered. We met and then CIA surveillance team saw me with you. Jason Scott tasked me when the surveillance team informed him of our relationship."

"Ah, that explains the 'JS' on your speed dial. I was concerned it might be the number to John Smith, whoever that might be. Rather, it stood for Jason Scott. I could get used to all these duty-bound sexual encounters." Tommy chuckled. "It's a hell of a lot easier than trying to pick a woman up. Why didn't you tell me you worked for the FBI on the first night if you hadn't been tasked with watching me yet?"

"Some men get scared when they find out a woman is an FBI agent. It was a harmless lie."

"To be honest, I don't care. I'm tired of all the deceit. I just want to clear my name and go back to my dull drunken life."

"No one forced me, I love your company. I went to

Agent Scott yesterday to tell him I wanted out. I told him how I felt. I just want to have a normal relationship with you. No more lies."

"That's a great story, but I think there's a bit more to it than that. I received a phone call last night from an old buddy. He currently runs the investigations department for the US Postal Service. As a favor to me, he checked into the rental of a post office box in Westover."

"Tommy." Amber's voice trembled.

"This guy has a lot of influence in the postal service. Every employ knows when he shows up on your doorstep that there could be a serious problem. He questioned the Westover Postmaster about the box in question. The same box where a large sum of money was sent, implicating me in the sale of a computer virus and the murder of a CIA agent."

"Tommy, I can explain."

"Apparently, the person who rented this box was a petite auburn haired woman with green eyes and fair skin," Tommy continued. "She romanced the postmaster and convinced him to rent her the postal box under the name of John Smith. That sort of blows your claim that you weren't involved until Agent Scott came to you after his surveillance team saw you hanging out with me."

Amber's eyes welled with tears. "Tommy, I can explain."

"Who are you, Amber?"

"I'm a software engineer and a former NSA agent," she mumbled, looking frightened. "I left the NSA four months ago to take a job with the FBI."

"You're the one who developed a computer virus at the bequest of the former NSA Inspector General that has been the bane of my life for over a year," Tommy retorted, as he realized who Amber was. Swinging one leg over Amber, he sat up and straddled her.

"I wasn't the specialist that developed the virus, I was his assistant. Look, Tommy, it wasn't supposed to happen this way. I made a copy of the computer virus when I was with the NSA. Then Steve showed up last month and offered me two million dollars if I can make him a copy of the virus, he didn't know I already had one."

"You should have called Jacob Livingston," Tommy remarked, looking down at Amber. "He offered me five and a half. And I got a guy named Archibald offering me six."

"It all seemed so simple," Amber continued in a trembling voice. "The only complication was that if the virus were to show up on some corporate data base, the investigation would eventually come to a halt for lack of suspects. They would have to dig deeper and inevitably they would have found their way to me. I needed to divert attention away from myself. I decided to plant evidence so that whoever investigated would have a prime suspect—someone they could focus all their attention on. Even when the investigation came to a halt, they would still believe it was this person. After Steve contacted me and told me what happened in Thailand, I knew you were the perfect person to distract them. I planned on planting just enough evidence that they would think it was you but could never prove it. I bought the advertisements and the post office box in John Smith's name, and I sent you the key and the envelope with the money to the box. Had the plan gone the way I wanted, you would have only been affected for a short period of time."

"And you established a relationship with me to ensure your plan was working?"

"Yes, I did," Amber confessed in a whimper. "The plan was to set it up so they wouldn't be able to gather enough evidence to charge you. Your life wouldn't have changed, and the momentary inconvenience of the police checking you out would have been inconsequential."

"Don't you think that bedding down with the prime suspect would not have caused them to scrutinize you, as well?"

"My involvement with the development of the virus was minor and not recorded," Amber explained. "They would have discovered my part only if they interrogated the virus's programmer as a prime suspect. We had an affair during the development of the virus, and he was married. He doesn't want anyone to know I assisted him for fear of the affair being discovered. If Sid believed it was you from the start, they would have never focused on anyone else."

"You seem to have had a few affairs relating to the virus."

"Like I said, if things had gone as planned, it would have been nothing more an inconsequential inconvenience for you."

"Involving me was inconsequential? You knew I was strapped for cash and used that weakness to draw me in and set me up," Tommy said, looking down at Amber. "And your definition of just enough evidence included killing a CIA agent and leaving my fingerprints at the murder scene? Those fingerprints alone could put me away for a long time." Over his shoulder, Tommy could hear the blue-and-gray-eyed dog panting in the doorway.

"Steve was just supposed to follow to make sure the CIA man could identify you. I didn't know he was going to kill the man or leave your fingerprints. He has a grudge against you about what happened in Thailand. He must have gotten a hold of a shell casing you used during the delivery. He wants you to pay for what you did to John Smith and him in Thailand."

"How do you know that?"

"He asked for my help to set you up for a long prison sentence, and I refused."

"Is Steve working alone?"

"He's working for someone else. He simply represents a client." She began crying. "I was surprised that he had the brains to put your fingerprints at the murder scene. He's not a smart man."

"Who's he working for? The client must have some deep pockets to come up with two million dollars for the computer virus."

"I've asked, but he won't say."

"Why'd you have him try to kill me the other day?"

"I didn't tell him to kill you. I told him to stop the meeting, and you know why. You have good instincts, and if you were to team up with the CIA man Sid, you might have figured out what was going on. I couldn't risk the two of you getting together." Tears freely rolled down Amber's cheeks. "I just told him to stop you, not to kill you."

"Why would he try to kill me when you were in the same car? Wasn't he worried about killing you?"

"When things started getting out of hand, I tried to stop the deal. I told them that I wasn't going to go through with the transaction." Amber's voice quaked. "Steve told me that it didn't matter. They had another source if I backed out. It didn't matter if I was killed or not."

"Ah, the Becky connection," Tommy muttered to himself. "She claimed she felt like she was playing second fiddle, and she was right. She was Steve's back up source, in the event you pulled out. What did you know about Jacob Livingston?"

"I knew everything about Jacob Livingston," Amber confessed looking up with red rimmed eyes. "Sid told

Agent Scott that the NSA had been following the movements of a man who deals in stolen corporate secrets for nearly a year. But they've been unsuccessful at putting enough evidence together to—"

"You sent a note to Jacob Livingston," Tommy interrupted. "You told him where my children were hiding. You were the woman who sent him the note."

"Things were getting so out of control. Steve tried to kill you and nearly killed me. You met with Sid. Everything seemed like it was falling apart. I didn't know what to do. I panicked. Yes, I sent a note to Jacob Livingston and told him where your children were. I am so sorry."

"So let me get this straight, you set me up in order to draw attention away from your deal with Steve. You were then assigned to work with Agent Scott to find out if I had killed the CIA agent, retrieve a computer virus that you knew I didn't have, and find out the name of my non-existent client. You also linked up with a known criminal and told him where my children were hiding to distract me. You couldn't make this shit up. You're like a triple agent, or something."

"It really got out of control. I wasn't thinking straight. I never meant to draw you in this far, and I didn't mean to harm your children. I just needed to sidetrack you. I was just juggling more things than I could handle."

"You told a known criminal where I was hiding my children," Tommy said again, leaning forward and clinching the pillow behind Amber's head. The dog began whimpering behind him.

"I didn't think he would harm them," she sniffled, pushing her hands against Tommy's chest.

"Jacob Livingston is a known violent criminal," Tommy replied, glaring at Amber as she began to squirm under his weight. "You knew there was a good chance that he would harm them. You knew that I would focus all my attention on that nasally twerp to protect them."

"Yes." She began sobbing, "I knew."

"Where and when are you to exchanging the virus with Steve?"

"At the Korean War Memorial at three o'clock today. Steve will be waiting with the money."

"That's convenient timing." Tommy sniggered. "I'm meeting the inspector general at three o'clock not far from the memorial. Where are you hiding the computer virus?"

"It's in the trunk of my car, under the spare tire."

"Which car?"

"The Porsche."

Looking down at Amber, Tommy pondered what he should do to the woman who had caused so much trouble for him and his children. Finding himself in an unforgiving mood, he felt a hot rage welling up inside.

Jerking the pillow from behind her head, Tommy stared coldly down at her. "You're about to become a pebble."

"What do you mean? I don't know what that means," Amber's voice trembled. "What do you mean? I don't understand."

"Much too long of a story to explain. You should have never involved my children. That was your biggest mistake. I could have forgiven you for involving me, but the minute you put my children into danger you became nothing more than a pebble to me," Tommy said, looking down at the beautiful green eyed woman beneath him.

As he pushed the pillow over her face, she began thrashing and kicking, trying to free herself from his grip. Tommy pushed the pillow harder into her face, and Amber scratched and kicked to no avail. Slowly her thrashing began to subside, not striking anything but the mattress.

Her hands came up to Tommy's shoulders one last time and lightly squeezed, before falling to the mattress. Tommy felt the dog jump up onto the bed before it licked him across the cheek. Turning and seeing the dog's big blue-and-gray eyes looking back, Tommy removed the pillow. Amber gasped for air, her eyes red with burst blood vessels. With a look of terror on her face, she began sobbing hysterically.

"If I ever see you again, I'll finish the job," Tommy said emotionlessly, looking down at her.

Climbing from the bed, he took a quick cold shower, dressed in his running clothes, threw his small backpack over his shoulder, and left Amber sobbing in the bedroom. As he walked to the elevator, he realized he had wanted to kill Amber. It had been easily within his grasp but the blue-and-gray-eyed dog he refused to call his own had stopped him with an innocent lick to the cheek. The simple instinctive actions of a dog changed the outcome. The act of the small beast forcing its way into his life had saved a life.

CHAPTER 57

East Falls Church, Virginia, May 4, 2016:

Running through Rosslyn, following Lee Highway west, up a steep hill, and then catching the Curtis trail, paralleling Interstate 66, Tommy jogged in an attempt to ease a growing anger over his situation. Why had he once again found himself mixed up with the likes of the NSA's Inspector General, Becky, Amber, and Steve? What was it about him that attracted these people? Was it his lifestyle? Was being an unemployed drunk an invitation to be a fall guy for every screwed up government operation? Sweating profusely, he had free-running rivers of perspiration coursing down his body, and his wavy brown hair quickly became soaked as the dog padded along beside.

Overhead, limbs created mosaic shadows along the narrow pathway as a soft, warm breeze allowed for a small level of evaporative cooling. As was his normal fashion, Tommy would consider the day before him on his runs, thinking about the issues and silently arranging a schedule in his head. Today was different, with his mind swirling around a seemly boring and routine life drawing him to trouble. He knew what he needed to accomplish that afternoon, and he had already resolved the issues. Today he was running to work out the ire that was consuming him and to ponder why his routine life attracted trouble like the delivery in Thailand last year and now the sale of the computer virus in Washington, DC, this year.

Reaching his North Arlington neighborhood after a forty-five minute hard run, he slowed to a walk a block from his house. One week ago he had been told that he was the primary suspect in a murder of a CIA agent and in the illegal sale of a classified computer virus, and now Tommy knew the end of his problems were at hand. Over the course of the week, he had determined who was behind the mystery of the computer virus and who had murdered the CIA agent. It was just a matter of tying up loose ends. Today he would meet with the inspector general and beady-eyed Steve, settling his score with both parties. Tomorrow he would complete the transaction with Anna and Archibald Fenwick, putting the entire sordid affair behind him.

Striding up the concrete steps to his home, the stray dog walking along behind him, Tommy began to finally feel at peace. As he opened his front door and stepped into the small foyer, he smelled a familiar scent and walked down the short parquet floored hallway, peeking into the sage green bedroom.

"Hello, beautiful," Tommy said, greeting Caroline who was lying on the bed.

Dressed in a loose floral patterned summer dress, Caroline rolled onto her side, short straight blonde hair falling across her face. "How was your evening?"

"No one is who they claim, and my emotions are in full swing. I forgave Becky for her involvement and then, several hours later, just about killed Amber for her involvement. But on the bright side, I think I've got all the answers I need to wrap this up."

Caroline yawned. "Not all the answers."

"What do you mean?" Tommy asked, walking over

and sitting on the bed next to her. The edge of the mattress depressed with his weight and rolled Caroline up next to him.

"I'm not sure where to begin," Caroline whispered, pushing several strands of short blonde hair from across her eyes.

"I'd tell you to start from the beginning, but I'm not sure where the beginning is. Maybe you should just start with your employer."

After a short hesitation, Caroline began, "My employer, normally referred to as the Society, is a very powerful organization of business and political leaders from across the globe. Called *institúti de aperta commercium*, roughly translated as The Society for Free Trade, it is an organization that was established in the late fourteenth century. The Society was initially founded for nothing more than acting as a council between Monte dei Paschi di La Siena headquartered in Siena, Italy and the Berenberg of Hamburg, the two largest banks at the time. The Society's purpose was to ensure trade between the two countries would flourish without constraints created by financial institutions or governments. Powerful European business leaders, politicians, and scientists were invited to join the Society, eventually expanding across all of Europe, Asia, and the Middle East as the influence of the Society grew. In the early fifteenth century, the Society made a decision to become a secret organization in the wake of a Catholic Church takeover attempt.

"As the Society developed, scientists were dropped from the rolls and the ranks filled with only prominent businessman and politicians. Later powerful criminal leaders were included, due to a flourishing black market. Today it remains a secret society of powerful individuals whose single goal is to ensure that world commerce flows as freely as possible. They have had influence in the creation of the North American Free Trade Agreement and the European Union, to name a few recent achievements. They are an organization of men with the sole purpose of shepherding the world's economy forward. They work in concert with the world's governments in an attempt to keep commerce open and profits flowing. While their primary focus is business, they delve into politics when necessary, as the two worlds are closely intertwined."

"Is Jacob Livingston a member?"

Caroline sighed. "Of course not, Jacob Livingston is a small man who lacks the moral basis to be a member."

Teasingly, Tommy commented, "But their ranks do include criminal elements with moral standards."

Ignoring Tommy's remark, Caroline explained, "The Society for whom I work has very sensitive and important odd jobs periodically that require someone with unique talents. The man who normally handles those jobs had an unfortunate accident."

"Was he killed?"

"Yes," Caroline answered.

"Was it a job-related accident?"

"Yes." Caroline looked at Tommy with scolding eyes. "Shortly after his accident, the Society tasked me with finding an individual for the job opening."

"Do you always do their hiring?"

Ignoring Tommy again, Caroline continued, "The list of requirements for this position is fairly lengthy, and I searched high and low for someone fitting those qualifications. Then I caught wind of the story about your exploits with the computer virus in Thailand."

"You've got to be kidding me." Tommy softly laughed, lying back on the bed next to Caroline. "Was one of those requirements an eerie ability to stay alive against all odds?"

"Unbeknownst to me, several months ago, my employers discovered that a copy had been made of the computer virus you delivered in Thailand. Realizing that this virus could wreak havoc in corporations across the globe, they began devising a way to obtain that copy to ensure it was never used."

"Interesting timing, don't you think? Your Society's handyman gets killed, you find me, and the virus comes onto the market."

"Let me finish, please," Caroline demanded. "I asked my employers to obtain the CIA file on the Thailand operation. At that time, I had no idea that my employers were also putting a plan together to obtain the copied computer virus, but they immediately made the connection and asked me why I wanted the file. I told them I thought you might meet the qualifications for the job. It was then they told me of the computer virus and their need to obtain it. After I read the file on the Thailand delivery, I confirmed that you fit the lengthy list of qualifications and informed my employers—"

Tommy interrupted again. "That file had to be top secret. You had access to a top secret CIA file?"

"I was given a copy when I asked for it. My employers have contacts in every law enforcement agency. Obtaining that file was not difficult. When I informed my employers that you fit the qualifications, they did what they do best. They revised their plan to retrieve the computer virus in a way that would test your skills."

"So you hired Steve," Tommy said flatly.

"No, not Steve. He's an idiot. I can't tell you who I hired until it's all over."

"Why not?" Tommy rolled onto his side and slipped his hand under Caroline's dress onto her hip. "I've got most of the answers already."

"Just let me tell you what I've been authorized to say."

"Go ahead."

"My employers directed me to hire a specific man to acquire the copied computer virus. We then gave him the name of an individual who had the copy and general instructions concerning how the transaction was to go down—"

"Amber, the assistant to the person who wrote the virus code," Tommy announced, nodding his head. "You gave the man Amber's name."

"Yes." Frustration was beginning to build in Caroline's voice.

"How did they know Amber had a copy?"

"Will you please let me finish and quit interrupting?"

"Go ahead."

"Stop interrupting," Caroline firmly demanded, again. After a few moments of silence, she began explaining, "As I said, my employers knew that the virus in the wrong hands could wreak havoc on the corporate world and have a devastating effect on the global economy. So they put a plan in motion to buy Amber's copy of the virus and ensure it would not be sold on the open market."

"Why didn't they simply tell the authorities that she had a copy?"

"Because of their secondary goal. They always have a secondary goal. Nothing is one dimensional in their world."

"What was their secondary goal?"

"You're not listening to me. They revised their plan in order to test you," Caroline replied. "They instructed me to hire a man that they knew had issues with you."

"Steve. It's got to be Steve."

"They instructed this man to set you up," Caroline continued, ignoring Tommy's conclusion. "They wanted to see your problem solving skills."

"Let me get this straight. They selected, and you hired, and they instructed? Or they selected, you hired, and you instructed?"

"I passed some instructions on but not all."

"What about the death of the CIA agent? Did they orchestrate his murder as well?"

"I'm not sure. Like I said, while I acted as the as a middleperson, there were certain instructions I was not privy to. However, I wouldn't put it past them. They rarely let things get out of control."

"From my perspective, it's been way out of control from the start." Tommy slapped his hands together. "So this has been nothing more than a job interview?"

"As I said, my employers never tackle a problem one dimensionally. They have a position within the organization that is extremely important and requires someone who is capable of handling a lot of variables. They saw an opportunity to test your skills while retrieving the computer virus. I told you several days ago that this was nothing more than a job evaluation."

"I'm not looking for a job. Especially one that might put me in danger."

"You haven't seen the compensation package. I can tell you from experience that they pay very well. They would like to set a meeting up with you to discuss the opportunity."

"So I passed their test."

"You've almost passed the test."

"What's left?"

"You need to attend your two meetings today—and, of course, your meeting tomorrow with Anna and Archibald."

"You are well informed," Tommy muttered.

"I work for the Society," Caroline said in a business-like tone. "Of course I'm well informed."

CHAPTER 58

Washington, DC, May 4, 2016:

Howard Macintyre, the National Security Agency's Inspector General, was sitting on the park bench next to the Reflecting Pool on the National Mall, coolness radiating from its soft brown waters. Lincoln sitting on his marble throne under its heavy roof supported by thick marble columns could be clearly seen from the bench to one side and the tall white spirals of the World War Two Memorial, then Washington Monument to the other. The elm trees provided shade and masked his presence from traffic both on Constitution and Independence Avenues.

Under normal circumstances, the inspector general would have found the scene surrounding him soothing, but his usual grin was gone, replaced with a concerned scowl. On this day, knowing what Tommy Luck was capable of, the inspector general was anything but calm. He was frightened.

The inspector general saw Tommy approaching from the Lincoln Memorial, walking along the edge of the Reflecting Pool with a dog at his side. He knew it was Tommy because he had watched him leave for Thailand at Dulles International Airport the year before. Howard could not help but chuckle at Tommy's attire, maybe as a way of venting his stress. A colorful Hawaiian shirt depicting orchids or some other tropical flower, faded blue jeans, and flip flops—not what he expected from an unemployed drunk capable of extracting himself from complex situations. Tommy had obviously looked him up on the NSA website, as he was walking directly toward the Howard with the clear look of recognition.

"You must have looked me up on the NSA website," Howard told Tommy as he stepped up to the bench. "You knew who I was."

"I didn't need to look you up. I saw you meet with Jacob Livingston a couple of nights ago," Tommy replied, sitting down next to the tall, redheaded man, the bench moaning at the added weight.

The dog walked behind the bench, lay on the brown dry grass, and began licking his hind leg.

"I never met with Jacob Livingston," the inspector general claimed, crossing his arms over his chest. "Is that your dog?"

"It is," Tommy replied, ignoring the inspector general's lie.

"You know there's a leash law in this city."

"So I've been told. I didn't know that the NSA's authority covered city ordinances," Tommy replied before saying, "My father was a drunken philanderer who would never give advice on a single question but rather talked of grains of sand and pebbles, choosing a path, and taking time to look at each decision. He also taught me to rely on my inner voice. What he told me is that if your foundation is sound, then your inner voice is, as well."

"My father was a devoted Baptist minister who would give advice on any little problem that arose," Howard professed in a trembling voice.

"No wonder you make such bad decisions, you never had a chance to refine your skills as a young man."

"Excuse me?" Howard responded, clearly offended at Tommy's allegation.

"Have you ever heard of a man named Edward Whymper?" Tommy asked, looking across the Reflecting Pool at a couple, a skinny man and fat woman who were obviously tourists, dressed in matching khaki shorts and bright red T-shirts, wandering down the sidewalk. A light breeze blew across the two men, carrying with it the mixed smell of exhaust fumes and the musty water of the Potomac River.

"Yes, he's was first to ascend the Matterhorn from a southerly route. He was among a party of seven and only three returned from the climb. Four fell into a crevasse, and there were allegations that the rope had been cut."

"That's right. Imagine looking down at four of your companions, your friends, attached to you by a rope dangling over a steep crevasse. You watch their arms and legs flailing in midair and looking up at you with pleading eyes. A climbing axe wedged into the ice, or simply the soles of your boots struggling in the ice crusted snow are the only thing keeping you from following them over the edge. You feel yourself slipping closer to the edge when crusted snow begins to crumble at your feet. You're panicked. The rope at your waist is pulling you down. The two men above you are panicked, crying out and yelling, not knowing what to do, but seeing the same sight as you. You see the only inevitable outcome is that they will drag you over the edge, killing everyone. Then an idea comes to mind to cut them loose, all the while your friends below are begging you to pull them up. In the midst of all this chaos, you must make a decision. In the midst of all this turmoil, you cut the rope, sending your friends to their death."

"No proof could be found that the rope was cut."

"Maybe not, but imagine if that was the truth, and Edward Whymper had cut the rope. On the other hand, there is a loyalty so great that a man would die trying to do the impossible. I've seen it happen. The bigger question is why and to what end? If Edward Whymper had died that day, what would the history books have read? In his case, he would have become famous for the eight failed attempts, not the first ascent from the south and not the words he wrote some years later."

"So what's your point?" The park bench creaked as Howard nervously shifted.

"My point is that I'm feeling a lot like Edward Whymper looking over the edge at a long line of people dangling in a crevasse, and I'm ready to cut the rope. I feel no loyalty to you or any government agency."

"What on earth do you mean?"

"Edward Whymper's most famous quote that goes like this, 'Climb if you will, but remember that courage and strength are naught without prudence, and that a momentary negligence may destroy the happiness of a lifetime. Do nothing in haste, look well to each step, and from the beginning think what may be the end.'"

"I don't understand what you're trying to say," Howard said, shifting on the bench again.

"Like the most inexperienced climber among Edward Whymper's party making a decision that cast four of them into a crevasse, you have been making decisions in haste and not looking well to each step, specifically where it concerns my children. You, your agency, and, by fiat, my government are pulling me over the edge, and I'm ready to cut the rope."

"I did what needed to be done."

"And I will do what I need to do," Tommy replied in a cool tone. Looking left and then right at the line of park benches situated along the Reflecting Pool, Tommy commented, "You do realize that I killed your predecessor on this very bench?"

"I knew you killed him on one of these benches, I didn't know which."

"It was this very bench." Looking down at his shirt, Tommy said, "And I was wearing this very same shirt when I did so."

"There was trace DNA in his pocket and around his hand matching yours. If he was going to inject himself with a muscle relaxant to commit suicide, I doubt he would have done it through his jacket pocket and the waist band of his pants."

"He could have been trying to hide his worldly exit from all the tourists." Tommy laughed softly. "After all, this is a nice place to end it all, with the Lincoln Memorial to one side and the World War Two Memorial to the other."

"Are you planning on killing me?"

"I'm sure you're aware that I have extracted revenge on every person who placed my children in danger during this affair. Each and every person but one," Tommy said looking up into the inspector general's eyes. "And you are the last name on that list…well, actually, there is one more name."

"You didn't kill Jacob Livingston."

"No, I didn't. But I doubt the penitentiary he's sent to will provide the standard of living he's become accustomed to, and with that nose job I gave him, a day won't go by that he doesn't regret his actions. It gives him a piggish look, which is somewhat fitting, considering the story about pigs and hogs I told him the first time we met."

"You'd didn't kill Amber."

"No, I didn't. I'm sure you heard what I did, though. I

have never been very good at doling out violence to women. However, I'm sure she won't forget our last encounter and will do everything in her power to avoid one in the future."

"She quit, you know. She quit the FBI and has disappeared."

"I'm sure she realized she was headed for a little penitentiary time herself."

"Why do you say that?"

"She was the one selling the computer virus," Tommy announced calmly.

"I don't believe you," the inspector general declared.

"You told Jacob Livingston, a clearly ruthless man, that I was trying to sell the computer virus," Tommy said, ignoring the inspector general's declaration. "You have no idea what that man did to me. That man threatened my children, tried to have his men kidnap them. That alone is worth taking your life. You placed your career over any concern about the health of three innocent children. You are a pitiful man."

"You won't get away with it," Howard said in sudden burst defiance. "The former inspector general was different. He was trying to kill you."

"What do you think your superiors would do if they found out that, unbeknownst to the investigating officer, you told Jacob about the computer virus for personal gain? I think you'd find yourself out of a job." Then smiling at the frightened man, Tommy said, "Don't worry, I'm not going to kill you. I'm tired of knocking off scumbags like you. I would rather you wake up each morning and think about what you did. I'm actually here to give you a warning."

"What?"

Looking at the Inspector General with an emotionless expression, Tommy said in a flat tone, "If you ever involve me or my family in another of your government-funded sordid affairs, I will cut the rope, and you will feel a level of pain and remorse that you thought impossible. It will be a revenge on you that is worse than death. And I learned a couple of good tricks over the last week."

With no hesitation, the inspector general replied, "You have my word." He was clearly shaken.

"Good," Tommy said as he stood from the bench, its wooden slates groaning a sigh of relief. "I'm glad we have an understanding."

"You won't tell anyone that I involved Jacob Livingston?" Harold asked weakly, looking up.

Tommy laughed at the inspector general. "You are piece of work. With no remorse for what you did to me and my family, you simply want to know if I'm going to destroy your future with the NSA." Shaking his head, Tommy began to walk away, the stray dog leaping to his feet and following. Stopping and turning, Tommy said, "Actually, Livingston is already telling everyone who will listen that you involved him. Something about entrapment. You'll probably be out of a job within a week."

"No one will believe him. He's a criminal."

Shaking his head and laughing, Tommy repeated his earlier assessment. "You are a piece of work. Do you think the CIA and FBI will stay quiet about what you did? Your time with the NSA is limited," he said before turning and walking away.

Leaving the inspector general, Tommy walked around the end of the Reflecting Pool, passing a small building selling war trinkets at the entrance to the Vietnam War Memorial and the steps leading up to the road encircling the Lincoln Memorial. Following a gray concrete sidewalk that cut across a field of foot-trodden browning grass toward the Korean Memorial, Tommy could see the greenish frozen patrol with an etched black granite background on his right and the tip of Washington Monument, sitting on its hilltop site to his left. At the end of the sidewalk on a wide circular concrete pad was a tall pole with an American flag swinging in the breeze, surrounded by black stone benches and more elms.

Stepping onto the enormous concrete circular pad with the dog trotting behind him, Tommy saw Steve's unimposing frame, dressed in khaki pants and a blue jacket, leaning against one of the trees, watching his approach with small dark beady eyes. Behind Steve, an older-looking man wearing a tweed cap and dark business suit, sat hunched on one of the black benches, two silver aluminum canes resting against his left thigh. A black canvas bag sat at the end of the bench. Tommy walked past Steve, the small man silently watching his passage, up to the stooped figure. The stray dog sat down, taking up watch on Steve.

"Tommy, what a pleasant surprise," the older-looking man greeted him with a clear Midwestern accent as Tommy sat down on the stone bench, next to him. "Although, I was expecting Amber."

"She couldn't make your meeting," Tommy coolly replied. Examining the man—his light brown skin, short curly dark hair with graying edges peeking from beneath the tweed cap, and thick bushy eye brows, Tommy quietly shook his head. "Looks like you've had an injury since we last met, John Smith."

"An unfortunate accident in Thailand last year." John Smith painfully shifted his head to see Tommy better. "One that I thoroughly blame on you."

"Considering you're supposed to be dead, I would count my lucky stars."

A breeze blew across the Korean War Memorial, bringing more of the musty aroma of the Potomac River's brown waters. Shifting again, John Smith took one of his silver canes in his right hand.

"And I would have been dead, had my associate not quickly come to my aid," John Smith said gesturing toward Steve with the cane. "Seems the former inspector general sent a man to dispose of me, but his work was less than efficient. Sadly, he did manage to nick my spinal cord."

"I met up with the same gentleman," Tommy replied. "He won't be poking people in the back anymore."

"That's welcome news," John Smith commented, stiffly moving his body on the stone bench. "Looks like you have an added beauty mark since our last meeting."

Running his right index finger along the thin scar that rose from his jaw to the corner of his mouth, Tommy responded, "This is my reminder of our Thailand adventure. One of Jainukul's employees was thankfully a little off on his marksmanship. It has a twin brother on my back."

"Your dog?" John Smith asked pointing to the dog with his cane.

"Yeah, my dog."

"I've always disliked dogs. Too demanding for affection. I wouldn't have thought you the type to have a dog. Does he have a name?"

"Dog," Tommy answered.

"That's imaginative," John Smith replied.

"It seems to fit."

"Are you here to deliver the computer virus, or gloat at ruining another one of my plans?"

"Gloat. I've another client."

John Smith sighed. "That is not good news for either of us."

"Apparently, we both have been playing the pawn role

for some global society of businessmen and politicians. They used you to set up me up for a reemergence of the computer virus. They used me to retrieve the virus and get it off the market."

"What on earth do you mean?"

"This has been nothing more than a job interview. You were hired by a chick named Caroline. You were hired to buy the computer virus from Amber and set me up because of your distinct dislike for me. They set us both up as a way to test me."

"That's ridiculous," John Smith grunted.

"You weren't hired by Caroline?"

"Yes, I was hired by Caroline. It is ridiculous to think that my employment was simply based on my hatred for you or that this was a test for you."

"Were you hired to buy the computer virus from Amber?"

"Yes," John Smith muttered with a quizzical look.

"Did they tell you to kill the CIA man and place a shell casing at the scene?"

"Caroline tasked me to set you up while retrieving the virus. She told me to make it as hard as possible for you to wiggle out from under the allegation. While I had some guidance from Caroline, it was up to me to figure out how to make it all come together. So I thought to myself, 'How about planting evidence against him for two crimes, bringing in the FBI and local authorities.' I obtained the shell casing with your fingerprints from your exploits in Thailand last year. It was my idea to murder the CIA agent and place the shell at the scene. Of course, my faithful friend over there carried out all the manual labor." John Smith once again pointed a trembling cane in Steve's direction. "I did thoroughly enjoy it, though. Watching you squirm under the pressure. It was very pleasant. I do wonder how your fingerprints ended up on the newspaper. Imagine, fingerprints on a paper published that very day found at the scene. I was elated at the news."

"I doubt a man's life was worth testing my skills at solving problems. An organization that hires a scoundrel like you is no place for me. I'd rather return to my drunken unemployed lifestyle than rub shoulders with the likes of you."

"It's been a perfect fit for me." John Smith let out a raspy cluck that Tommy knew to be his chuckle.

"I don't doubt it. Hopefully, they paid you well."

"I received a very generous down payment. The final payment was to come after I obtained the computer virus." Then after a momentary hesitation, John Smith added, "Go ahead, I'm sure there's some warning you want to give me along with this ridiculous story about a job interview. Maybe a warning that I should leave you alone or you'll do terrible things to me."

"Of course there's a warning. I wouldn't want to disappoint you, John Smith," Tommy replied. "Rather than leave me alone, it's leave my children alone. You can do as you wish to try and extract your perverted revenge on me, but if anything happens to my children, you will see a level of rage you thought impossible. I won't kill you, but if you think your life sucks now, hobbling around with an injured back, wait till you try life as a quadriplegic."

John Smith let out another dry, raspy cluck. "That would be too easy a revenge." Then looking at Tommy, his dark brown eyes peering from under his cap, John Smith said, "But I will exact revenge on you, and I won't kill you either. I want you to live a long life regretting what you've done to me. I want you to wish to die but find yourself unable."

"Fair enough, John Smith. See you next time you come out of your hole."

Standing, Tommy looked down at the stooped man on the bench. Last time Tommy had seen John Smith he had been full of confidence and drive. Now the man below him appeared as nothing but beaten and hateful.

"It's too bad, John Smith," Tommy commented.

Gathering his canes, with clenched teeth and sweat breaking across his brow, John Smith painfully stood up. "What's too bad?"

Shaking his head at the once imposing figure of John Smith, Tommy answered, "Had I known you were going to be here, I would have called our mutual friend Sid. I'm sure he would love to put you up in a luxurious four-by-eight concrete room—indefinitely."

"You knew Steve would be here, why didn't you invite the CIA man to take him into custody?" John Smith asked, wavering on his two canes.

"Just being Steve, the beady-eyed punk, is punishment enough. A long prison sentence, where he'd have a bed, three meals a day, and some sexual play in the showers at night would actually be an improvement to his miserable life."

"I will so enjoy our next encounter," John Smith growled.

Turning, Tommy began walking away. Striding past Steve, still leaning against the elm tree, Tommy reached out and punched the short man in the nose. Stumbling backward, Steve tripped on the edge of one of the tree's roots and fell onto the concrete. The dog raced up and bit the Steve on the ankle, before falling in behind Tommy.

Walking away, Tommy looked back, saying over his shoulder, "Next time you try to kill me, little man, find a better driver. You can't drive for shit."

CHAPTER 59

Baltimore, Maryland, May 5, 2016:

Stepping from the old white Chevy pickup, Tommy looped the cord attached to the flash drive containing the computer virus over his head and around his neck, tucking the thin device under the collar of his shirt. The parking lot was thick with cars, and colorfully dressed families were herding their children to and fro. With the blue-and-gray-eyed dog trailing behind, Tommy found his way to the pedestrian crosswalk and patiently waited for the green walking figure to appear overhead before crossing the street.

A man with two children at his side waiting next to Tommy muttered, "You ever heard of a leash law?"

The dog whimpered, and Tommy turned. "Mind your own business, or I'll have the dog bite you, jackass."

The man glared at Tommy while his two children looked up with frightened faces. When the bright green walking figure presented itself overhead, the man briskly pulled his children across the street, ahead of Tommy and the dog.

Tommy crossed the street and passed by a large glass-enclosed tourist information center. Baltimore Harbor came into view, surrounded by tall downtown skyscrapers. Making his way out to the dock with wood and concrete piers, Tommy saw his destination, its black and white sides with gold trim and tall masts unmistakable. Maneuvering through the crowd of tourists, passing the various restaurants lining the harbor, he and the dog made their way to the USS Constellation.

Stepping up to the gangplank, Tommy looked down at the dog. “Stay here, Dog.” The dog obediently sat down at the ship’s entrance, watching Tommy continue up the wooden gangplank.

At the top of the gangplank, Tommy examined the ship’s black and white wooden sides with gold trim. Loving this old wooden tall ship, he had brought his children here many times, showing them a craftsmanship that exalted days gone by. He imagined that he could smell the salt soaked into its timbers from the hundred years of roaming the sea. Stepping onto its worn wooden prow, Tommy looked aft, searching for Anna and her employer. Not seeing the beautiful Peruvian, he walked over to the ladder leading to the first deck, climbing down into the vessel.

Wearing a tight-fitting red dress that showed her voluptuous round hips, Anna sat on a bench near the crew quarters at the rear of the ship, next to the same white-haired man she had met with at the National Cemetery. It was the same white-haired man Tommy had seen meeting with Larry and Alfred. A large green canvas bag sat on the deck at their feet. Amber and the white-haired man watched Tommy as he approached, stooping so not to hit his head on the low wooden overhead beams crisscrossing the space.

“Hello, Anna,” Tommy said as he stepped up to their bench, his voice echoing off the low timber ceiling.

The white-haired man stood, extending his hand, saying with a French accent, “Hello, Mr. Luck. My name is Archibald Fenwick.”

"We briefly met two days ago, although we didn't get a chance to exchange names," Tommy replied, shaking Archibald's hand. "Archibald Fenwick is the last name I would associate with a French accent."

"My father was English, my mother, French. I grew up in Paris. Yes, I met with the two gentlemen at the Netherlands Carillon in order to verify that there were no other participants vying for the merchandise. We needed to ensure there was no one else interested in the computer virus."

"Well, it's a pleasure to meet you, anyway," Tommy replied, smiling at the white-haired man.

"Do you have the computer virus?" Archibald asked.

"I do," Tommy responded, pulling the flash drive from under the collar of his shirt, letting it swing across his chest, as he scanned the crowds to his left and right. "And it looks as if you have the money."

"Yes, I do," Archibald answered, gesturing to the canvas bag at his feet.

Several tourists dressed in khaki shorts and brightly colored floral shirts walked by, eyeing the trio suspiciously. Tommy glanced over his left shoulder and then right.

"Are you looking for someone?" Anna asked, standing from the bench.

"Just looking at my selection for a rendezvous. In retrospect, I think I should have selected something a little more discreet," Tommy said, as a family of four chattered with each other about the history of the Constellation on the other side of the deck, their voices reverberating on the ancient wooden bulkheads.

"Shall we?" Archibald asked, reaching out for the flash drive.

Pulling the device from his neck, Tommy handed the

flash drive over to Archibald. As he reached down and picked the canvas bag up, Tommy heard someone walking up from behind, hard soles shuffling across the wooden deck. With the heavy bag straining his shoulder as he lifted it, Tommy watched as Sid stepped past with the usual grimace on his ruddy face.

Dropping the green canvas bag, Tommy sighed. "I was wondering if you were going to show up."

Sid nudged his chin in the direction of the canvas bag containing the money. Archibald and Anna stepped forward, each taking a hold of one handle of the bag. Straining against the weight, they lifted the bag and placed it in front of Sid. Tommy shook his head, realizing he had missed an opportunity to sell the flash drive and resolving his financial problems once and for all.

"Better late than never," Sid groaned, glancing down at the canvas bag. Looking up at Tommy, Sid then asked, "Is that your dog sitting next to the gangway?"

"Yeah, that's my dog. I hope he's behaving himself."

"Baltimore has a leash law, you know," Sid grumbled.

"So I'm told. Is part of the CIA's authority is to enforce local canine statues?"

"What's his name," Sid asked.

"Dog."

"That must have taken you quite some time to come up with that name," Sid commented in a perfectly serious voice.

Once again looking to his right then left, Tommy asked, "Where's your team? This can't be a one man show."

"Actually, Anna and Archibald are my team. They work for me," Sid replied, slipping his right hand into his tweed jacket.

"Well then, this was a wasted trip," Tommy mumbled, beginning to wonder where Sid fit into all the chaos surrounding the computer virus. "You know how much gas that truck of mine truck uses? I spent a bundle to get here, all for another government setup. You guys are relentless."

"I'm sure you can come up with the money for gas," Sid grunted, as he pulled a pack of cigarettes from his jacket. Plucking a single cigarette from the pack, he placed it in the corner of his mouth. "Maybe you can use some of the sixty three dollars you took from Anna or the money you took from Jacob Livingston. He claims you stole nearly a thousand dollars from his wallet."

"It's not like the CIA was paying me for risking my life. I needed the money."

Putting the pack of cigarettes back into his tweed jacket, Sid took the flash drive from Archibald, examining the device. "Is the computer virus on here?"

"Yeah, I retrieved the flash drive from the trunk of Amber's car," Tommy replied. "Is this another one of those private operations that government employees seem to prefer to pad their pockets? Considering what I've witnessed between the Thailand delivery and this debacle, it wouldn't surprise me."

"No, this is all in the name of Uncle Sam. Call Anna and Archibald an insurance policy," Sid grunted. "I needed to ensure you weren't actually trying to sell a copy of the virus. Anna's freelance and had no idea the CIA was paying the bills."

"I've been working for the CIA?" Anna blurted out, clearly surprised as to her employer's identity.

"Yes, and you did quite well," Sid responded. "And the recordings?"

Reaching into his pocket, Tommy withdrew a small black pen-like recording device. "As I said last night on the phone, the recordings cover my discussions with Amber and John Smith."

"That should be enough to clear you of all the charges," Sid replied as he took the recording device from Tommy and slipped it into the outside pocket of his tweed jacket.

Eyeing Sid, Tommy said, "You could have told me these two have been working for you when I called last night. It would have saved me a trip."

With an emotionless expression, Sid said, "I figured Baltimore was as good a place as any to retrieve the computer virus."

About the Author

Growing up in the Rocky Mountains and graduating from the University of Colorado, Patrick Ashtre chose a career in the military as opposed to one slugging it out in the office cubicles of corporate America. After serving twenty-six years in the Marine Corps as both an infantryman and aviator, he took a fancy to a horizon of water over that of mountains. Spending his final tour in Japan, Ashtre retired from the marines and moved to the small tropical island of Phangan, located in the Gulf of Thailand, where he owned and operated a popular beachfront pub. After eight years of living, working, and traveling throughout Southeast Asia, he is now in the process of moving back to the Colorado Rockies. With a misspent youth and experiences from around the globe as a canvas, Ashtre will likely fill the pages of many more books before he closes his laptop for the last time.